FIRE & FLIGHT

BOOK I : HEIRS OF TENEBRIS TRILOGY

Julia,

Welcome to tenebris!

Brianna R. Shaffery

BY BRIANNA R. SHAFFERY

Cover and map design by Marcella Thaler.

Publishing Services provided by Paper Raven Books LLC

Printed in the United States of America

First Printing, 2022

Hardcover ISBN: 979-8-9861732-0-7

Paperback ISBN: 979-8-9861732-1-4

I'd like to dedicate this novel to my family for all their support and enthusiasm, not just through this adventure, but in all of them.

Y'all are the best.

TABLE OF CONTENTS

MAP OF TENEBRIS

Eurland

Sea of Harmony

Corvus

Shelton
Bay

Gossamer

Hart

Woodlane Manor

Covington

Glendale

Caselle

Huntington

Godberd Woods

Mageffery

Union River

Shadow Forest

Barrier Plains

Halberry

Amber Dunelands

Union River

Eurland

Corvus

Capital

Fortune Falls

City

Towns

Charity

"Go on then, kill me!"

The challenge echoed in Cedric's mind as he battled against the nightmare's hold. Blankets bound his limbs together, twisting around him like the strongest rope. The last thing he saw was a blinding flash of scarlet energy and silver hair splayed across the courtyard's pavers. Her lips were speckled with crimson.

Blood.

Cedric's eyes burst open. His whole body jerked awake. He'd lived through that nightmare—had since relived it a thousand times over. He could recall every word, every emotion that coursed through his veins in those few long minutes, but most importantly, he could name every regret that had surfaced in his heart because of those eternal moments.

To this day, Cedric wanted to hear an honest answer to the question he had asked then. But she'd never blessed him with the truth, and when she had, it was only in the twisted versions of his subconscious's imaginings. Maybe if things had been different, if he had been a different person, he would know the truth. Maybe she would've been willing to offer an answer instead of trying to provoke him.

And maybe, just maybe, if he was someone else, things would be different now.

His eyes flicked to the crystal ball on his workbench. Cedric doubted things would be. But one question begged his attention, the one he always asked himself after one of these nightmares: What did she stand to gain by taunting him in such a way?

She always had a purpose or reason for her actions, and that's what made her a force to be reckoned with. Cedric shook his head. There was no point in shooting arrows in the dark. He'd just have to continue living with the fact that he would never know what her intentions were for certain, only their outcome.

The sentiment weighed heavily upon him, and Cedric forced himself to sit up in bed. He ran his fingers through his hair. Dim sunlight filtered in through the gaps between the curtains and windowsills, illuminating the barren space of the simple, one-room cottage around him. This place, this monotony and empty semblance of comfort, was all he had left in his life now. The cottage hadn't changed in all the centuries since he'd built it for sanctuary, aside from needing to replace worn fixtures as time dragged on.

It was a monumental effort to swing his legs over the edge of the bed and drag himself to his feet, something that proved harder with each day that passed. His bare feet padded over the plush carpet toward his workbench on the opposite side of the room.

The aged wood groaned in protest when Cedric leaned his weight on it. He eased his stance. The glass orb flicked to life, and Cedric focused on the staticky haze within its image until it cleared. A faint scarlet aura pulsated from the glass sphere. The image Cedric conjured took shape within the crystal ball.

The girl was still asleep, her face twisted in a grimace. Cedric knew she was more than likely trapped in a nightmare of her own. It was such a pity too, though Cedric wasn't sure if it was because he knew exactly what stalked her nightmares or the fact that he was sometimes visited by the same flames.

With a heavy sigh, Cedric placed his hands on either side of the crystal ball. The coolness of the glass radiated off of it and greeted his hovering hands. His brows furrowed in concentration as his eyes fell shut. Heavy *thuds* echoed from the scene Cedric conjured within the glass ball and rattled the orb on its stand.

Cedric's red eyes opened and focused on the picture before him. The girl curled tighter into herself. Another *thud*, more rattling. Lilac-colored eyes burst open, apparently blind to the world around them as whatever nightmare held tight to her struggling consciousness.

He could see the wild desperation in her frightened features.

And maybe, somewhere in a tremendously deep pit inside him that he didn't stray to all that often, Cedric felt guilty.

1. THE GIRL WITH SILVER HAIR

Nyla woke up cold and alone. Haunting silhouettes writhed overhead. Heavy footsteps rattled the ground as the impact echoed through the air, the same blossoming thunder that had woken her. Her heart thudded erratically against her chest. Nyla swallowed. Her eyes flitted everywhere. She screwed them shut briefly in an attempt to calm herself—only to have them burst open when she heard it again. Panicked gasps were ripped from her trembling body. A ray of golden sunlight glinted off of her matted silver hair. Small prey shook the underbrush and the sapphire leaves overhead, occasionally breaking twigs or letting out their own anxious chirps and whines, in response to the threat that neared. And, as if she were struck by lightning, Nyla remembered that she was now prey as well.

Something *big* was coming.

Nyla scrambled up. Her frantic mind stirred with a flurry of things to remember, like where she was and what she had with her. All the while, the ever-present quaking of the earth reminded her that speed was her ally.

She shoved aside a chunk of hair that had fallen in front of her eyes while her hands blindly worked to roll up her sleeping bag. Giants were supposed to be extinct, but the thought provided little comfort as something *boomed* over the ashy, rust-colored landscape. Blankets were hastily shoved into her bag, even as man-eating giants terrorized her mind. The earthquake beneath Nyla's feet intensified with each booming footstep. She barely took the time to slip on her shoes before she hoisted the bag onto her shoulders. Without another glance, Nyla took off in a sprint.

Darting between the trunks of the trees, not particularly concerned with the path she took, Nyla only cared that her feet took her away from whatever monster drew closer with each thundering crash.

She swatted and slapped at the twigs and feeble branches in her way as she ran. A voice inside her head nagged at her and gnawed at the fear brimming in her blood. It told her she'd forgotten something important. Nyla forced herself to recall what she'd definitely packed in her haphazard escape. Her brows knitted together at the effort to remember what she'd managed to grab this morning. Already lightheaded from her desperate sprint toward uncertain safety, Nyla picked through the images of her flight. Nyla knew that she hadn't taken out any of her clothes or anything crucial to her survival that she could've forgotten, so why did that voice eat away at her?

Nyla's feet faltered and stuttered into an abrupt stop. She doubled over to catch her breath, a hand weakly planted on the rough bark of a dark gray tree to hold her steady. The tree looked as though it had been charred in a recent fire, but she knew it was healthy. All the trees in the Shadow Forest had the coloring of charred embers and rough bark.

Her eyes sparked with revelation.

She'd left behind a shirt but, more importantly, the thing that it was carefully wrapped around, the only item that actually meant something to her. She could see the portrait in her mind's eye. It was worn and creased, and in places, the paper was burnt, but it still showed the smiling faces of her family.

With a wide-eyed glance over her shoulder, Nyla's lips quivered at how wild the plant life was. Their leaves danced and wobbled, as if the plants themselves could tremble in fear. And who knew? Maybe they could. After all, the Shadow Forest was alive in more ways than one, a fact that sometimes haunted Nyla's nightmares. The shadows provided a place for her to hide but also for other things, dangerous things, to lurk. And as if to show how meek and powerless she was, her own legs trembled, from fear, from desperation, from the tremors that rumbled over the earth and toyed with her balance.

Wood snapped in the distance. The echo reverberated inside her skull like a cannon blast. Her head whipped up expectantly. The forest's thick brush prevented her from seeing more than a few feet in front of her, but Nyla didn't need to see all that far ahead to know with a crippling certainty that whatever stalked closer had the ability to snap trees in half.

If she stayed put any longer, the beast would be upon her.

Her eyes drank in her dim surroundings, all too focused on the trees around her. Their trunks ranged in size. Some were slim, no wider than the width of Nyla's hips. Other trunks were much bigger, as wide around as she was tall. The echoes of the splintering trees breaking and falling with a *thud* made her already jittery nerves frenzied. Her fingers brushed the hilt of the knife at her hip. She knew it would be useless. Her heart beat wildly. She closed her eyes for a second to steel herself against the itch pleading with her to keep moving forward. But she had to find it—Nyla *needed* that portrait.

With that determination, she turned and sprinted back toward her campsite. It was difficult to keep her path, but Nyla managed. Rocks as dark as coal jutted up from the soft earth. Fallen trees, their trunks twisted and fractured, lay in her path and forced Nyla to scramble or launch herself over them. Some trees were freshly fallen and oftentimes too big to lunge over, and Nyla knew that it would be a miracle if she found her campsite again in spite of all the course changes she'd had to make.

She kept her eyes on the forest ahead of her, but her ears were tuned into the sharp, resounding *cracks* and splintering of nearby wood. The thought of being crushed to death under a tree briefly flashed through her mind, but the thumping footsteps ahead overpowered any other noise, even her own thoughts.

Blinded to anything but her goal, Nyla stumbled and spread her arms in a panic. Luck was on her side, and she recovered with only a slight falter in her steps. She fought to ignore the pictures that flickered through her mind with each pound of the beast's footsteps. Each image showed a horrible death at the hands of whatever hideous monster was coming. Nyla swallowed the lump in her throat, knowing that the gruesome scenarios only fanned the flames of her fear.

Nyla swatted another cluster of blue leaves out of her way. The thin branch snapped. Her lungs burned with each breath.

She crashed through a sickly bramble bush and saw the portrait, half covered by the folded shirt. It lay exactly where she'd left it the night before, now bathing in a puddle of sunlight. The canopy overhead rustled violently with the intensity of the unsettled ground. Nyla fought to keep her footing as she swung her bag off of her shoulders and stooped to pick up the portrait. Her movements slowed. She arranged the shirt more protectively around the portrait and laid them gently in her bag. Her mind flooded with relief. Once the pack was resettled on her shoulders, she clutched at what was left of her rationale.

Her eyes glanced all around. Her surroundings melded together just like the tangle of broken thoughts that raced through her head. Nyla vaguely knew where each direction would take her, trying to follow their path in her mind's eye, focusing on the dense forest before her.

Each *thump* brought the beast closer. She'd never outpace it now. There was only one place Nyla prayed could hide her, her only option. Mentally, she saw the river and the glistening rocks that often grouped together. They formed dark clusters, staining the fine amber sand of the riverbank.

Nyla knew that small creatures burrowed in the earth beneath them, sheltered from the world by clumps of jagged rock. Even if she couldn't find a crevice big enough for herself, there might be a cavern along the shoreline.

On one rainy morning she had done just that, hunkered down in a shallow niche in the granite wall, the world outside finally forgotten.

And that was exactly what she intended to do now.

Nyla gathered up the last of her courage and energy, sprinting off toward the river. A trail of jagged onyx rocks sprung up in her path, and Nyla followed them. They would lead her to the river. The rocks and trees she passed blurred together in her hurry. The monster's footsteps still rained down upon the ground, one rattling *thud* at a time. Nyla tried to ignore the tremble of her hands and the way she had to force herself to stay upright, her sprint more of a stumble than anything else now.

The closer she got to the river, the more rock points jutted up from the ground. Nyla swerved around these as best as she could to avoid getting cut. Even with the danger right behind her, a laugh—albeit bitter and rueful—bubbled up in her chest.

Everything in the Shadow Forest could kill her, especially if she wasn't careful. It wasn't even a matter of if it would, but more so *when* and *how*. And yet this was where Nyla chose to find relief for now.

Exhaustion and relief flooded her veins when the foliage parted and her booted feet landed on the pebbly sand of the riverbank. Even then, Nyla didn't actually stop until she came to the river itself. There, she crumpled to her knees and thrust her cupped hands into the water.

She took gasping breaths and brought the cool water to her dry lips. Once her parched throat was satisfied, Nyla stood and rubbed at the stitch in her side. She shielded her eyes from the dazzling sunlight and scanned her surroundings.

There was a tight grouping of rocks a short distance from where she stood. They glistened in the exposed sunlight. Nyla hurried to them and concealed herself between the narrow gap in the cluster. She sank low to the ground and brought her knees close to her heaving chest. It wasn't comfortable, but at least she was somewhat safe now. Or that's what she tried to tell herself as she waited for the rumbling of the giant's footsteps to fade.

The rocks vibrated, and pebbles shifted through the cracks with each step the unseen beast took. Nyla squeezed her eyes shut and wrapped her arms around her knees. The booming came closer and closer, the echo deafening. She buried her head in her knees and began to recall the legends that shrouded the Shadow Forest in fearsome mystery. They served as a distraction, something to focus on and ground her when she needed comforting the most.

Her eyebrows furrowed, and Nyla pressed her lips into a thin line as she tried to block out the rumble of the beast's footfalls. She delved into the stories she'd overheard in her travels. Nyla had come to realize that these were bits and pieces, different versions, of the same mystery. She'd begun to piece them together, lying awake at night with nothing but the Shadow Forest's symphony to keep her company.

Every so often, when Nyla was forced to pass through a town, she would sometimes catch a group of people gathered around, listening to someone spin tales of the "haunted forest." They always started with the shadows and how some believed that they were wisps of smoke from a fire that had scorched the land centuries ago and that they captured lost travelers—or were the reason so many got lost to begin with.

Nyla would linger, whatever errand she'd needed to run temporarily forgotten as the storyteller wove their tale. She always stayed longer than she intended to, captivated by the words she overheard as she stood in the shadows of the small crowds gathered around the storyteller.

The story started some six or seven, maybe even eight, centuries ago—no one truly knew when anymore. A great fire was said to have ravished the Shadow Forest. They said it was so hot that the heat of the flames was felt for miles in every direction. By the time it was weakened enough for people and rain alike to extinguish it, the flames had destroyed everything in their path. The fire left only ash and a charred tangle of remains.

Some believed that the most remote parts of the Shadow Forest still burned to this day, which would explain the ghost trails of smoke that wove their way through the trees as some travelers claim to have seen.

Nyla didn't know whether or not this was true, but the woman who had told the legend seemed to believe it, and the statement had been met with gasps from the children and muttering from the adults. It left Nyla wondering what would happen if the fires were to spread to other parts of the Shadow Forest and why they hadn't already.

In a different village nestled along the riverbank, Nyla had heard another storyteller claim that the fire left sandy soil rather than ash.

But no matter who was telling the story, or where she was, they all said that the fire was set during a terrible battle of a war long since forgotten. No one seemed to know what the war was about or how it began or how it ended, but there was a war. One man said that it seemed as though history had been erased to hide some disgrace. He shrugged and drank from a bottle before he finished the tale, as if he hadn't said anything of consequence. Nyla remained skeptical of this and thought he only said it to scare the little ones and leave his audience mystified. And in a way, she was. She remembered leaving the crowd shortly after, questioning how much of the world she really knew.

To this day, the storyteller's words echoed in the shadows of her memory.

Nyla had even heard some claim that the fire wasn't set. That story weaver had claimed that the fire was inadvertently unleashed. This version of the legend began at a dire time during the war, when both sides had faced heavy losses and neither could gain the upper hand. A powerful sorceress stole the land's magic. Some speculated that her armies were losing the forgotten battle, and out of desperation, she cast a wicked spell that amassed power, draining it from the land and from those who stood on the field. They say she even drained the life from her own soldiers in an effort to grow stronger.

In doing so, the magic scorched the land with the force of a thousand lightning bolts. No one could ever wield that much power. By greedily stealing that much magic and forcing the fate of the war into her control, she destroyed herself. The army that had been at her side, as well as the forces they warred against, were destroyed along with her.

The destruction didn't stop there. Many theorized it was because of this that so much of the war and that time were seemingly erased from history, leaving only a mysterious smoke and an eerie forest. People claimed that not even the royal historians knew what had happened. They would never admit to it, so what little records there were remained locked up, the key forgotten.

And now, the shadows that lurked in the Shadow Forest, and the unnatural dimness, were the spirits of those killed in the sorceress's quest for power and control, doomed to haunt the Shadow Forest until the injustice that had befallen them was set right.

No one knew what could possibly forgive such an act, but many had tried to free the shadows with this belief. But with so many different ways the story had been told, no one knew for certain what happened all those centuries ago. Nyla certainly didn't. And they were probably just that, legends. But they would explain why the Shadow Forest was painted like a living fire.

Nyla shivered. Not for the first time, she'd wondered what had really happened all those centuries ago.

The sharp *caw* of a bird made her jump out of her skin and the safety of her mind. More anxious chatter of birds and small animals beginning to return filled the air. There wasn't even the distant clap of thunderous footsteps. She exhaled a long breath and leaned her head back against the cool rock behind her.

Danger had passed her by or changed its course. A few long minutes passed before Nyla crawled out of her hiding place and pushed herself to her feet. There was a sort of stillness that wrapped around her then, almost like a rare blanket of peacefulness as she began to walk along the river's edge, balancing on the dark rocks of the shoreline.

She'd almost lost it, the thing she held so close to her heart. Gripped by worry, the portrait weighed heavily on her heart and mind. It captured a family, all in good health and gifted with the company of each other. Soon, the fire clouded her thoughts, and the memory consumed her. She could still smell the smoke and see the fire that had singed her then-dark hair. The sick prickle of heat had rolled over her as she bent over, working in the field. When Nyla had whirled around, she was met with the terrible sight of her home nearly destroyed by flames. The shriek of the fire still echoed in her ears. She ran toward it and wove a path through the deteriorating home.

Nyla shoved aside the memories before they could ensnare her and crouched by the winding body of water she had used as her guide for the last few weeks. The water bubbled and *blubbed* as she filled her canteen—something she had bartered for at some point in her journey—and barely took the time to wash the dirt from her hands before she continued along the water's edge.

She didn't know how long the body of water stretched. For three weeks now, she'd hiked near the quaint babble of its rippling waters. The quiet trickling soothed her.

Her fascination with her surroundings had dulled after a while. There wasn't much to see anymore, all of it now familiar to her—with a few exceptions. She often considered going back home, but the idea left her crestfallen, bitter, and hopeless. By all means, there wasn't anywhere she needed to be or venture toward, only an uncertain sense of safety she might never feel again.

Misery and fear both terrorized and guided her. She'd seen the carcasses of prey gnawed and stripped of their meat by the animals that roamed the woods. Each time she encountered them, Nyla was reminded that those remains could be hers if she wasn't careful. At times like this, Nyla wished for some sort of comfort to quell her active nerves, even if that comfort came in the form of a friend or travel companion.

A twig snapped, sharp and crisp, close by. Nyla stopped dead in her tracks. A quiver of fear ran through her body. Her stomach knotted tight as she picked her head up and whipped around to stare in the direction the noise had come from. A bush rustled, and a little creature hopped out. Its black eyes widened upon seeing her. Its chest heaved with rapid breaths. Nyla was certain that she could see the poor creature's heart beating out of its small chest.

Nyla stared at the pollipes in relief. Pollies were small, sleek-bodied creatures with jet-black eyes in the shape of almonds and a curling, bushy tail. But her favorite thing about them was the myriad of colors their coats could be. She'd seen some with topaz fur and amethyst or iridescent white. She wouldn't be surprised if pollies came in every color known to man.

This pollipes became a flash of emerald fur as it sped away, absolutely harmless. With a sigh of relief, Nyla continued on her path to a destination not yet known to her, knowing that she had traveled south to get where she was now.

As she took short, brisk steps, Nyla glanced around nervously. Usually, silence was a comfort to her, but for some reason her innards twisted in hesitation. Most of the animals were still long gone, like she should've been. Most, if not all of them, had fled and kept moving forward when the danger was present. Some, like her, had hidden away in burrows or other niches. Curiously, whatever had passed through with booming footsteps had all but disappeared, not even to be heard in the far-off distance. Nyla brushed the thought away and hoped it had settled down for a centuries-long slumber.

The crystal waters of what she thought to be the Union River trickled along on her left. She stopped in her tracks, almost laughing at herself. She hadn't the slightest idea where in the Forest she could find Fortune Falls, but there were some people who believed the Union River could lead you there if you only followed it. Through all of her wanderings and steadfast belief in myths and legends, Fortune Falls had never crossed her mind as a feasible destination. Nyla entertained the idea of seeking out the mystical waterfall while she tried to check her excitement. The Falls were the main reason people willingly traveled deep into the Shadow Forest, though most never found it.

Her parents had told her and her siblings stories about Fortune Falls, how the waters could grant your deepest desire. Though there were limitations to the Falls' magic, it was still the most powerful entity known to man. Some said it could even peer into the heart and soul of those who drank from it. And maybe that's why some had never returned home.

As Nyla mulled over what she knew of the Falls and its legends, the pain in her joints and feet faded into nothingness. A plan bloomed within her. It required her to somehow acquire a map and compass. She knew that small towns and port cities lined the river, though she usually avoided those at all costs. But now, that's exactly where she needed to venture. Fortune Falls couldn't bring back her family—she knew that—but its waters might finally grant her peace and maybe even certain security.

After seasons of wandering, Nyla finally had a destination in mind. Renewed hope surged in her heart. Without pausing to allow apprehension to spoil her hope, Nyla walked along the river until she came to a well-beaten path of the Forest. She followed it, with the telltale markers of humanity sprinkled along the way.

A few miles from the river, Nyla was closer to civilization than she had been for weeks. Nature's silence filled her ears as she came to a clearing. She looked up and saw smoke curling around sunbeams in the open sky. She realized she was traveling southwest. Blue leaves rustled as the wind grabbed at her hair. She was close to a town. Her breath died in her lungs for a moment. Nyla's body went completely still. A single word tickled her mind: *people*.

2. HALBERRY

Nyla stood, half hidden by an ashen tree, hesitant to leave the sanctuary of the Shadow Forest. Her purple eyes skimmed over the town's main street and followed the row of log buildings while she tried to pick out the inn. There were a few taller buildings, two or three floors she guessed, but most of them were simple. They blended in with the cobblestone street, all untouched by time, unlike the cities she'd seen from a distance. Most of the buildings had flat faces, but one or two had a little porch and detailing around the doors and windows. Very few were painted. The natural wood tones were dark with weather and age.

The people she could see milling around the dusty street were nearly pristine, proper. They had clean faces and tamed hair—or at least they had taken the time to make themselves presentable. Nyla glanced down at her own clothes. They were discolored and loose. The hem of her pants was shredded, most likely at the hands of the underbrush, and faded from walking on the too-long pant legs. Her shirt was equally faded, though plagued by holes. Both had begun to unravel in places that left thin tears in their wake. Some people carried baskets, while others had burlap sacks. Like hers, some of those bags had been patched, but at least a similar material had been used. Nyla's was more of a patchwork scrap pile than a backpack.

She didn't dare try to imagine what her face might look like. The people in the town were clean, and she was not. A wave of bitterness and envy blossomed in her heart. The least Nyla could do was run her fingers through her hair and brace herself.

As she did so, Nyla surveyed the town square with wary interest. Her fingers worked through the wild tangles in her hair, watching the scene before her with a heart-wrenching longing. Captivated, her eyes settled on a man and woman. They swung a small child between them with ease. The little girl had an infectious grin on her face. A laugh bubbled past the girl's lips, carried away by the breeze to echo in Nyla's ears. Nyla smiled warmly, even though a part of her wished the girl could've been her little sister.

The family turned down another street and out of her view. Nyla's smile faded, lost in the remnants of another life. She blinked, shuttering her mind against the influx of memories. Her eyes fixated on a building near the center of the row. This was more than likely the town's inn and tavern, as it was the largest building in the row. That's where she had to go.

Lingering just a little longer, Nyla took a step forward, and in a few more paces, her feet glided across the cobblestone, her head down. Each step took her farther away from the safety of the Shadow Forest's wild paths for the first time in several weeks. Hidden beneath the sapphire leaves and shadowed by the forest's dim light, the open market road left her exposed. She fought the urge to wrap her arms around herself, knowing they could offer her no protection from her discomfort. She passed each building, glimpsing their signs out of the corner of her eye, but Nyla focused mainly on her feet.

The closer she came to the center of the town square, a low ripple of whispers surrounded her. The hustle and bustle came to a grinding halt before it jolted back to life. Nyla swallowed thickly. Her breaths sputtered.

Some people cast scathing glances in her direction. Others pretended not to see her at all, going about their business as if she didn't exist.

As people began to huddle together, hurriedly whispering and hushing each other, Nyla looked at the road beneath her feet. With her shoulders hunched, she spared sidelong glances at the stores she passed by. One was called "Halberry Herbary," as told by a weathered sign hung by the door.

With each step she took, goosebumps formed on her skin. An inkling of trouble boiled in her blood. Despair settled like a lead weight in the pit of her stomach. Nyla's hands trembled again. She shook them out at her sides, willing them to stop as she approached the tavern. The brightly glowing sun disappeared behind the stone structure, bringing relief to her eyes and instantly cooling the air around her as she hesitated in the shadows near the doorway.

From where she stood, Nyla could hear the din of the crowd inside. Part of it sounded rowdy, with wild laughter and booming voices, but another part was softer, a quiet hum of conversations flowing between people eating dinner. With a deep breath, she pushed open the door and crossed the threshold. Off to her right, there was a small wooden desk crammed in the foyer area, but the room was dominated by the rustic tavern on her left. A cramped hallway divided the two. A narrow staircase along one wall led up to the rooms above. Nyla tuned out the ruckus of the tavern's patrons and finally met the eyes of the fragile woman who stood behind the desk as she approached. The woman had soft eyes and delicate hands that trembled as she took up a pen and placed her glasses on the bridge of her nose.

"Can I help you, dear?" Her voice was dry and weathered, barely audible over the tumultuous laughter spilling from the long room across the hall. The woman shot a cool look of annoyance over Nyla's shoulder.

"I was wondering if you knew of anyone who would be willing to barter for a map or compass?" Nyla leaned closer to the woman, her voice evening out the longer she spoke as she got a handle on her nerves. The woman frowned. Pity flashed in her kind eyes.

"I'm sorry, but I honestly wouldn't know. That's more of a question for Cal, the tavern's keep," she said. "Good luck to you, dear."

Nyla smiled at the woman and turned toward the tavern. Her feet refused to cross the wood planking of the hallway into the tavern, which only seemed to grow louder. Forcing her hands to still, Nyla straightened herself and squared her shoulders. Her joints cracked as she did so, not used to standing so tall. The floor creaked under her boots.

A hush followed Nyla as she made her way toward the bar. She paid it no mind, and soon, the conversations that had stopped mid-sentence started up again. Candlelight from the chandeliers overhead cast pulsing shadows and flickering light over the tavern. The wall behind the bar was made of stone, as it was the exterior wall, but the rest were made of horizontal wood beams. She caught the eye of the portly man behind the bar, who she could only assume was Cal. He put down the glass he had been drying and approached her. Nyla swallowed thickly. Cal's eyes were hardened by years of stopping brawls and interacting with rowdy persons, but the longer she held his gaze, the more skepticism filled them.

"What can I do you for?" Cal asked, his voice gruff, nearly hoarse.

"I'd like to barter for a map and compass. Know anyone?" Her voice was smooth and almost detached. Cal eyed her, lingering on the worn pack with its multiple patches and her well-worn clothes.

"Who sets off on an adventure with no map?" He let out a clipped laugh that sounded more like a bark than anything else.

"Who said I've never had a map? I lost it." That was true—Nyla had, at one point, had a map. That was until a severe wind storm ripped it from her hands one day. That was forever ago, and she'd found that, until now at least, she hadn't needed a map after all.

Out of the corner of her eye, she saw the man seated beside her drain his cup and slam it down on the bar top, making her flinch. For a minute there, she had completely forgotten the full room around her. Cal pursed his lips and excused himself, but before he could say a word to the dark-haired customer, he slapped some libacs on the wood surface and left, nearly tipping over the stool he'd sat on. Nyla held back a bemused smirk as she turned her attention back to Cal, who had resumed an air of disinterest.

"Well, no one has come in to say they want to trade a map or compass for anything. Looks like you're out of luck." Nyla's hope deflated. Her shoulders sagged in disappointment. Nyla's lips pressed into a thin line as she tried to hold back the bitter frustration that rose up in her throat. Cal studied her again, stopping the circular motions he used to wipe the bar down and added, "I'm sorry, Miss. Maybe try the next town. It's busier than here, more travelers than locals there, and a proper general store."

"Well…thanks anyway." Nyla pushed her way back to the door, not meeting the eyes of anyone who glanced her way.

"Any luck, dear?" the woman called after her from the desk. Nyla stopped in her tracks, one hand on the doorknob. She turned, looking up from her feet to meet the woman's sparkling eyes and wrinkled smile.

"No, not today." She forced the words out of her mouth with a thin smile. The only thing she wanted to do was leave. The woman ducked behind the desk and came up, producing a small parcel wrapped in burlap and tied off with twine.

"You're forgetting something. I want you to have this." The woman came around and handed Nyla the package. Her sweet smile broadened.

"I can't take this."

"You're not taking it, dear. I'm *giving* it to you, and I insist that you accept it." The woman huffed and shoved the lumpy package into Nyla's hands. The comforting scent of warm bread wafted from the bag, caressing Nyla's nose. Nyla nodded, thanking her once again before she headed out the door.

The early evening air enveloped her, and she stopped under the inn's awning, leaning against the rough stone exterior, gathering her thoughts as she hid in shadow. Nyla reconsidered the usefulness of a map. Fortune Falls was meant to be difficult to find, and the Shadow Forest was unforgiving. While a map would help her realize her whereabouts in the outskirts of the Forest, the interior of its wooded paths remained uncivilized. The map's only purpose would be to keep her from getting lost now, not finding Fortune Falls, a place anyone seldom found.

Was it something only a select few could find, like Avalon?

No immediate answer came to her mind. Forcing herself to push off of the pitted rock wall poking and prodding her back, as if it too wanted her to leave, Nyla stepped out onto the waning sunlit path of Halberry's town center. She could only pray no one saw her as she made her way toward the grassy field beyond the marketplace. Drifting through the tall grasses, goosebumps prickled her skin. Dread tightened the muscles in the pit of her stomach. Her lips twisted into a grim line as she pushed her way through the dry field, refusing to take even the smallest glances back at the town over her shoulder. There was nothing there for her, just as there was nothing there in the field, only grass.

3. THE MAN WITH THE MAP

Xander tensed at the young woman's question. Who didn't have a map or even a compass? He glanced at her out of the corner of his eye. His eyes widened as he nearly tipped over on his stool.

Silver hair?

Whoever this was could handle themselves just fine without a map or compass. Xander was certain of it. If he'd learned anything growing up, it was that Casters with rare-colored hair or eyes usually possessed powerful magic and certainly didn't need his help. Besides, even if he did help this woman, it would leave him without a map or some of his hard-earned money, and his map was too precious to give up. Any other day, he'd consider giving her a bit of money to buy her own map, but not today. Today, he needed to be selfish and stay out of other people's business.

Numbly, Xander brought his cup up to his lips and drained the last of it. He flinched at the hollow sound of it slamming down on the wooden bar top, slapping some libacs on the counter beside it, and all but fled from the tavern. Warm Hugony air greeted him as he tried to settle his mind while standing under the eaves of Halberry's small inn and tavern. Bright and dazzling, the late noontime sunbeams only danced before his unfocused eyes. All thoughts were consumed by the woman with no map. His mind urged him to offer her his, but he couldn't. He shouldn't. Just this once, he shouldn't. Still, his mind pestered him.

Who didn't have a map? Who didn't at least have a compass? Why was he still thinking about this—about her?

Because it was a distraction.

Xander knew it was better to fixate on the world around him and the peculiar problems of a silver-haired stranger than it was to nitpick at his own insecurities. And after today, they would be all he could think about until he made it to Fortune Falls.

That was *if* he made it to Fortune Falls, the waters of legend, of myths he wasn't certain he believed in.

How could water possess magic powerful enough to grant any desire held dearest to those who drank from it? How could the Falls pass judgment on those who would drink from them?

Xander forced the line of thought from his mind. If he kept wondering about Fortune Falls, then his mind would obsess over the question he didn't want to ask himself. His attempts didn't wholly stop the voice in the shadowy reaches of his consciousness from asking how the Falls would judge him and all that he had done in his young life. It wasn't much, he supposed, but it was enough that the mystical waterfall might deem him unworthy of their grace.

He let out a huff. The light breeze carried it away, and he wondered just how far it might travel, if it might find the far reaches of the place he used to call home. The wind would definitely see Pemberly before he ever did—if he ever returned at all. Xander shook his head. If he kept thinking about home and the Falls, he might never leave this small town. He might never leave the next one or the one after that for the rest of his life.

Stuffing his hands in his pockets, Xander pushed himself out into the street. Swaying a little in his steps, his brows furrowed as he tried to keep himself steady. The whispers and hushed conversations of those around him in the little market square reached his ears. He didn't listen. There was no point in eavesdropping on their petty gossip. It was always the same.

He realized that assumption might not hold true for today. Xander's ears pricked as he neared a group of four women huddled off to the side of the bakery.

"Did you see her?" one of the women asked under her breath. It was the baker's wife, addressing her cohort. "That girl?"

Xander slowed his pace, casually deciding if he were interested in the cart of baked goods mere feet away from the group of chatting women. It was the usual group of gossip spinners, the women who were guaranteed to know everything that happened here in town. The tailor's timid apprentice, the baker's attentive wife, the stern postmistress, and the mayor's ambitious daughter. He didn't understand how they knew so much about what happened in Halberry, but it seemed like they knew before it even happened. If he didn't know any better, he'd say these women were Casters themselves, but he'd never seen them use even the slightest bit of magic. By all accounts, it seemed like Halberry had eradicated every last bit of magic from its borders.

In all his time here, Xander hadn't met a single Caster, not even a Healer. The storefront of Halberry Herbary had remained empty for the first few weeks he'd made the inn his home. Since then, an herbalist had taken up shop there, but not one with magic, just a regular, non-Caster herbalist. He didn't quite understand it, but he'd always thought Halberry had welcomed Casters, but something had changed since he'd last passed through the magic-filled town.

"I did," the postmistress said. "I was on my way to the inn to deliver Miss Betsy's letters, but then I saw her approaching the tavern from the other way. I thought maybe my errands could wait."

The mayor's daughter clicked her tongue. "I don't see why she matters. We've all known so many Casters, like Vidia—"

"Yes, but remember what happened?" the postmistress said bitterly.

"That wasn't Vidia, and it certainly wasn't that girl either," the mayor's daughter replied, rolling her eyes. "Since we pushed all of the Casters out of Halberry, our own neighbors, the town has suffered. My own mother has suffered without Vidia's healing magic. Besides, the field is growing back now."

"But at least we're safe." The postmistress nodded firmly, glaring at the other woman.

So something had happened that made the people of Halberry wary of magic? But why would they turn on the people they presumably knew and had lived in harmony with for however long? It didn't make any sense at all.

"Are we, though?" the tailor's assistant—Amelia, he remembered—asked quietly, her voice barely above a whisper. Xander liked her, even though he hardly knew her. She was always so softspoken and shy whenever he popped into the tailor's to have something mended. Even now, she wouldn't meet the eyes of her friends, though he wasn't certain if it was from shame or her nature. "Are we really safer?"

The three other women seemed to freeze. The postmistress reeled back, her nostrils flaring before she seemed to compose herself. The baker's wife cast her eyes about, as if someone might overhear them. Her inspective eyes landed on Xander, burning into him as if he'd intruded on something sacred.

"Need some help, stable boy?" Her eyes narrowed as she made a gesture of excuse to her friends and took a step closer to the cart Xander had chosen to use as his cover for dawdling so close to the group.

Xander fought the frown of his lip and instead offered a polite nod. "No, thank you, Mrs. Focaccia."

"Then you'd best be on your way back to the inn's stables." The snide dismissal made Xander's blood boil. Not only was she rude to him nearly every time they'd met, but he was finally on the verge of finding out the cause of Halberry's mistrust toward Casters.

Flashing a tight smile to the others, Xander grabbed a loaf of bread and left some coins in its spot, forcing Mrs. Focaccia to pick them up herself. As he walked away, Xander tore off a piece of the crusty bread. Chewing slowly, he considered what the mayor's daughter had said about the field. There were certainly many fields in Halberry, but those were mainly on the outskirts of town and used as pastures for large livestock. Raising livestock was the chosen source of income here in Halberry, but Xander doubted the future politician was referring to those fields. Absently tearing off another piece of bread, Xander turned the exchange over in his mind. There was only one field she could have meant, and that was the vacant lot right at the edge of the town square.

As the tall grasses came to mind, he glanced passed the aged buildings of the rustic town. The faint melody of the chirpets and niphonies, nearly invisible insects that liked to hide away in the brush, reached his ears. Xander noticed for the first time how the air promised the change of season into Harvum, its spicy scent almost hidden amongst the freshness of Hugony. That small comfort was hardly given any space in his mind as his eyes drifted over the marketplace. Sunlight glinted off of a flash of silver hair. Xander swallowed. Had she found her map?

He stared after the woman's retreating back far longer than he should have, taking in the slope of her shoulders as she tried to make herself smaller, the quick steps that took her farther and farther away until she all but melted into the ashen trees of the Shadow Forest beyond the grassy field of Halberry's town center.

Xander's mind returned to the map he had, the only one he could've offered and the one he desperately needed if he hoped to make it to Fortune Falls. Cursing himself and his curious heart, Xander forced himself to take step after step until he reached the front door of the inn and yanked it open.

His furrowed brows and stark frown didn't stop Betsy, the old lady who looked after the inn, from greeting him pleasantly and asking after his day. Taking a breath, Xander forced his mind to quiet so he could at least repay the woman's kindness with his full attention and small talk.

"So you'll be leaving tomorrow, then?" Betsy asked, staring at him over the tops of her glasses. She'd been looking through the inn's record book when he'd come in and hadn't taken them off yet.

"Yeah," Xander replied quietly. He rubbed the back of his neck, glancing away from the woman's intense gaze. Everything about Betsy was fragile. The slight tremble of her hands, the weathering of her voice, but Betsy's mind, and more importantly her focus, was as sharp as a hunter's knife. "That is, unless your nephew's ankle is still healing?"

Betsy scoffed. "Amelia tells me he's been all over town, helping her with the tailor's deliveries. If he can spend these last few weeks galivanting all over Halberry and beyond, then he can surely come around and help his dearest aunt." Betsy took off her glasses and gently placed them on the counter beside the record book as she closed its cover and set it aside. Shifting her eyes back to him, Xander felt pinned by the remorse there. "Although you've been more than helpful here, and I know Cal will be sorry to see you go. Are you sure you can't stay, even just a little while longer?"

"I would love to," Xander said, offering her the tiniest of genuine smiles, "but I'm afraid I can't."

Betsy nodded solemnly. "Then at least come down and join us for breakfast before you leave. Oh, I hope it doesn't rain on you. What an awful way to start a journey."

Xander laughed, gesturing to the window at the front of the entry. "There's not a cloud in the sky, Betsy."

"Maybe not now, but I can feel a storm coming. My joints always know when a storm's coming." She fanned out her hands, staring down at her wrinkled fingers with a slight frown. "They're always so sore," she said, half closing her hands, and Xander wondered if she could even make a proper fist. "And stiff when there's a storm coming."

"I'll be fine, Betsy. I promise."

"Of course you will be." She smiled, taking one of his hands and grasping it between her own. "You're a good young man, Xander, and

I'm glad to have had you here these past few weeks. You've been good company and help."

"I can assure you that you have been more help to me than I have to you and Cal." An idea sparked in his mind. "Betsy, if your joints are bothering you that much, why don't I take over the desk for you?"

Betsy quirked her head. "Are you sure?"

"As certain as the sun sets in the west."

"Well..." She eyed him curiously. "If you're certain. Thank you, Xander."

Xander assured her it wasn't any problem, offering many more assurances as Betsy hesitated every few steps before she finally retreated up the inn stairs, presumably off to her room. Now, all Xander needed was a flood of people seeking accommodation for his distraction to be complete. Otherwise, he'd just trapped himself behind the desk with only his own mind to keep himself company. Subconsciously, his hand floated toward his collarbone, barely brushing his fingers against the warm object there before he caught himself and dropped his hand.

This was going to be a long evening, Xander realized with a sigh.

4. THROUGH THE SHADOW FOREST

The Shadow Forest came to life. Somewhere in the distance, the sharp cawing of a shadowjay, a bird notorious for its ability to hunt and restore magic to the land, reached Nyla's ears. Branches bounced with the pollies jumping from tree to tree, chasing after each other and seeking food.

It had been a long morning. Her sleep the night before was filled with strange dreams of an oppressive smoke and writhing spirits that called out for her to save them. Between those nightmares and the grumbling of her stomach in the early, pre-dawn hours, Nyla had set off for Fortune Falls before the sun even crested the hills surrounding Halberry, armed with only the knowledge of the myths and legends she'd heard since childhood. Breakfast was hours ago and consisted of nothing more than some of the bread and cheese the innkeeper had given her. Nyla tucked the rest safely away in her bag. She decided to supplement the woman's generosity with the Shadow Forest's abundant wild berries later in the morning. It was the height of their ripening season, and as she'd picked some before setting out for the day, her mouth couldn't help but water at the promise of the berries' sweetness. A few sunbeams had managed to pierce through the thick canopy of leaves in the hours since then. Her feet were already sore. But it didn't matter. Her early start would pay off when she reached Fortune Falls. Nyla could rest after she got the answers she was hoping for.

But the anticipation of what to expect sent shivers down her spine. A long time had passed since Nyla had crossed through the depths of the Shadow Forest on her way to the southern region of Tenebris. It impressed an eeriness that never fully went away.

She knew the ashen bark would gradually melt into rough, peeling bark dark as coal. The bright sapphire leaves would slowly fade, the energy sapped right out of their color, muted by shadow. Occasionally, she'd caught a glimpse of bright yellow, orange, or red, only a fleeting spark, against the crackled bark of the coal trees. Bits of bark flaked off like ash from a cinder in the wind.

The grim settings of her memories reminded Nyla of the nightmares she'd had the night before. She only remembered brief flashes, but they were enough to haunt her. They were dark and distorted fragments but enough to make guilt weave its way through her body. Her "family" had called to her, blamed her.

Nyla drew her arms around herself and hugged her body tight, but kept moving forward as the broken nightmare flooded her mind.

It was only her subconscious.

But still, her waking mind persisted, what if it wasn't? What if her family really did blame her for the fire, for being unable to save them both in life and in her dreams? What if that was the only truth Fortune Falls granted her? Nyla didn't know what answers she wanted most about the fire and what had happened to her afterwards, but learning it was because of her wasn't at all what she wanted, even if it were the truth. She already blamed herself. She didn't need the Falls to confirm that condemnation, but rather explain to her why.

Her eyes darted around the twisting branches and thorny bushes surrounding her. A dark shadow draped itself over the Forest like a blanket, one that Nyla knew wasn't there when she'd started out this morning.

When had it gotten darker out?

A shiver ran down her spine. Her skin broke out in goosebumps from the static on the wind. It took all of Nyla's willpower to push the nightmare away and force herself into the here and now.

Electricity lingered in the air.

The first clap of thunder echoed through the air in a warped *thwack-ack*. Nyla clenched her teeth, jumping nearly a foot out of her own skin. Rain followed instantly. It came down in a steady, pelting sheet of water that pummeled the leaves overhead with each *slap* and *pruf* until each drop burst, shattering with a *plop* against the ground. In seconds, her clothes were soaked through. She staggered against the force of the wind that howled and punched her body. Rumbles of thunder *boomed* overhead. Flashes of lightning occasionally poked through the gaps in the tightly woven canopy of the trees. The empty taste of static became the only other indication of the lightning's occurrence.

Nyla didn't know how much longer she could fight against the turbulent weather. Keeping her head down, she looked up through her lashes, desperately searching for anything that could be used as shelter. The farther she battled the elements without finding any cover, the more her hope dwindled.

Up ahead, the storm's grayness and flashes of lightning danced where the tree line had stopped in a rare break. Nyla's eyes caught sight of a cliff face beyond the edge of the trees. Hope swelled in her chest as she ran toward it, desperately wanting to reach the granite wall. Squinting against the assault of rain and wind, she stalked near the base of the cliff to examine it for a crevice big enough for her to take shelter in.

A single flash of lightning exposed what she hoped would be a little cave or niche, a dark hole on the granite surface. Higher up than even the tops of the tallest trees, it was likely her only option. Tilting her head back, Nyla plotted a course that looked safe enough to ascend. She lightly dragged a hand over the granite surface.

The rock was sharp and slippery, but it was the only way. Nyla didn't know how much farther she would have to go to find some other sort of shelter. If she stayed in the biting wind and pelting rain, there was no telling what would happen to her.

With her lips set in a grim line, Nyla began to scale the wall.

As she climbed higher and higher, Nyla reminded herself to take her time. The only thing she needed to do was focus on where she was going, what footholds to take, which crevices looked safe to use. Nearly halfway to the shadowed indentation she'd seen in the cliff face, she moved one foot onto a narrow shelf, her eyes already in search of another grip for her hand.

The foothold crumbled beneath her weight. Her whole body slid, though she fought to stay put, before she came to a grinding halt that jarred her rigid muscles. The knuckles on her hands turned ghostly white with the fierce grip she had on the ridges under her hand. Her foot scrambled to find a hold, toeing at the wall with her boot. She managed to find a crevice barely big enough to rest the toe of her boot on.

Spared, Nyla pressed her body against the granite wall. She exhaled a ragged puff of air. The rough edges of the cool stone scraped her cheek. She welcomed the cold relief from the wild pounding in her veins as the rain and coolness of the wall seeped through her clothes. Nyla caught her breath as she clung to the wet surface.

The rough wall and harsh rain were better than death's grip. If the sting and tenderness in the tips of her fingers were any indication, she hadn't made it entirely unscathed.

Her scattered mind spun, turned upside down from her near accident. The rapid *pitter-pattering* of the rain assaulting the leafy canopy of the forest soothed her. Droplets dripped down her forehead into her eyes. Her lips trembled as she fought the weakness threatening her muscles and the numb chill in her bones. For the first time, she glanced below her and quickly shut her eyes. A fall from this dizzying height would surely mean death. With a quick glance upward, Nyla realized there was only a few more feet before she reached the cave. A voice in her head convinced her that it was too late to turn back now. The storm was much too dangerous. Nyla gathered up her resolve amidst the fatigue in her muscles and continued her ascent with only the rhythm of the rain smacking the leaves below her to soothe her.

When Nyla finally reached the opening of the crevice she had seen from the ground, she slapped one hand on the ledge. The ledge was gritty and wet as she hoisted herself up, placing her knee on the edge. Nyla crawled over the opening until she could sprawl out on her back. Her legs dangled over the edge, attacked by the undeterred onslaught of rain. In a strange way, the pounding droplets alleviated the ache in her muscles. She rested her hands on her stomach, the bleeding temporarily forgotten as she gulped down air.

Slowly, Nyla sat up. Her muscles groaned in protest, all but wailing as she worked the backpack off of her aching shoulders. A small whimper escaped her lips. Her soaked-through clothes clung to her body and irritated her skin. Getting up, Nyla studied her surroundings as she shook the numbness and burning from her body. The niche she expected to find herself in was more of a shallow cave. The hazy light of the daytime storm vaguely illuminated the entire space. It was no more than a few yards wide and just as deep, though it narrowed toward the opening, like a bottle.

She stretched as much of the stiffness away as she could and shook out her aching hands. Blood ran like tears down her left hand.

Nyla started toward the granite wall at the back of the cave and sat down to take care of her hand. A shudder wracked through her body as she leaned against the damp wall. With a sigh, she ignored the goosebumps still lingering on her skin and dug around her overloaded bag with her uninjured hand until she found the bundle of clean scraps she used as bandages. Nyla gingerly poured water from her canteen over her hand, washing the blood away. There wasn't anything more she could do, despite her instincts. She wrapped it with a grimace.

With the last of her energy, Nyla pushed herself up and fumbled to change out of her wet clothing. Settled down once more, she resigned herself to watch the storm. It was the only thing she could do at this rate. Any head start her early morning had given her, as well as any sense of purpose, slowly dissipated. She'd lost a whole day of travel.

Nyla's eyes shut briefly. Low rumbles of thunder growled outside, followed by stark flashes of lightning. Her eyes wavered and fluttered shut as a blanket of exhaustion hit her. She tried to fight it off and keep her head up and eyes open. All too soon, Nyla found herself defeated, lulled to sleep by the constant drone of the rain. She only woke again what could've been five minutes or two hours later, when a deafening crash of thunder startled her into full consciousness.

She smacked her dry tongue against the roof of her mouth and reached for her canteen. The stretch burned her shoulders, but the ache was a good one, something to remind Nyla she was in the midst of an accomplishment. Her stomach grumbled. She opted to finish off the rest of what the innkeeper had given her.

The storm outside raged on. The rain became a stubborn hum, only interrupted by the persistent thunder. Nyla wrapped a blanket around herself and let her mind wander. Her eyes stared, unseeing at times, at the cave entrance.

Soon, her eyes saw the glow of a fire long since extinguished. The air turned hot and thick with molten heat. Nyla remembered how her hand had slipped over the rough stones of her home's fireplace, the only place that wasn't ravaged by flames. Her vision had begun to blur when someone yanked her out. A neighbor, she realized shortly thereafter, come to help.

But her family was already gone.

Nyla shook her head, a feeble attempt to clear away the smoke of a day long since passed, but the fire that had stolen her family persisted in her memory.

Once the fire was extinguished, each of her neighbors had attempted to coax her away to their home, to keep her away from the remnants of her life and the emptiness it would bring her. They had all failed.

Nyla had found herself standing in the middle of the destruction, right in front of the scorched stone fireplace.

What happened next, the recovery of the bodies and the burial and everything else, was a whirlwind she still couldn't decipher. All Nyla knew was that she had stayed among the ashes as long as she could bear it. The sun had dipped low and tranquility had painted the sky, mocking her. But in the dusk, she'd seen a sparkle of something reflecting the light in the rubble.

The portrait.

Nyla let the memories consume her, too exhausted to fend them off, even as bitter tears stung her eyes.

The neighbor who had run into the fire after her coaxed her into staying with him and his wife. It was a chance to grieve and to heal, to hold fast to some semblance of a happy life. And Nyla would've stayed, would've let them guide her back from the dark hollows of her soul.

But already the rumors and talk of curses swept over the once-peaceful valley.

Adding to her anxiety, Nyla believed the fire was set. She had no proof of her theory, as it was mostly an inkling that twisted in her gut, but it was based in the belief that she had seen someone out of the corner of her eye near the edge of her family's yard.

It was this fleeting glimpse in a careening chain of events that haunted Nyla the most. Maybe she only thought she'd seen the cloaked man. Maybe she really had. Either way, that fraction of time bothered her. It kept her up at night as creatures howled and chirped. She couldn't accept that Fate had taken her family and left her a witness to their destruction.

The neighbors' rumors only grew worse once Nyla's hair began to turn into the silver it was now. So, she'd fled. She wasn't able to tamp down the anxiety and paranoia that had slipped into her soul. And what could've only been a few weeks later, very little of her dark hair remained until it had all turned.

Some days later, when Nyla next knelt by the clear water of a spring she had followed, her eyes resembled a mixture of oil and water. There were barely blended hues of purple and the rich chestnut of her eyes. The next time she saw her reflection, her eyes had completely turned, resembling the color of purple lilacs.

Forced to relive the memories, Nyla found herself wishing she'd taken more things to barter with. Or at least more clothes. Or that she'd stayed and tried to make sense of the alleged curse they whispered had befallen her and her family.

Staying certainly would've been easier. Nyla still didn't know what she was doing or where she was going, only that she had to *run*. A constant paranoia guided her footsteps. It stemmed from the crushing grief that squeezed her heart and the odd sensation that someone was watching her. Her only solution was to keep moving.

Now, nearly two years later and having crisscrossed much of the country, Nyla had only the feeling of being stalked. It was an inkling cemented by a firm conviction. A part of her believed that it wasn't a manifestation of paranoia or fear, but pure intuition.

In her heart, though, Nyla wanted nothing more than to find a place to settle down and hide away, both from herself and what she thought others might say. And that's what part of her hoped Fortune Falls could grant her. Security. Safety. A home.

The memories faded. Nyla sat and watched the rain and stark flashes of lightning, her body long since numb from the damp chill and unforgivable cave floor. Just as she'd been lulled back into a sense of security, a hand appeared and clawed at the entry. Nyla's heart thudded in her ears. She rushed forward and grabbed the man's wrist, leaning over to get a hold on his backpack, and helped pull him up. Once he was up, he lay in the opening, just as she had done, catching his breath, eyes closed.

Nyla gripped the knife at her hip and sat back on her heels, ready to jump to her feet. Silence thudded in her ears like a drumbeat, despite the storm raging on outside. Panic and irritation settled in her bones. Her face scrunched up before relaxing again.

"Thanks for helping me up." The young man opened his eyes and stood, finally glancing at her. "Oh, hey, map girl."

"Map girl?" she repeated distractedly, her mind whirling with a thousand suspicions.

He slicked back his dark, dripping-wet hair and looked around. Nyla studied him. The man was taller than she was, though that wasn't a surprise as many men were. Broad-shouldered, Nyla figured he was a lithe sort of strong because if he were bulkier, climbing up here probably wouldn't have been possible for him. He didn't seem much older than she was. Maybe two or three years older, making him nineteen at the most. But what did "map girl" mean? Did he know her from somewhere? Nyla doubted that as she took in his face, his build, and couldn't recall having ever seen him before in her life. Unless—maybe he'd overheard her conversation at the tavern yesterday in Halberry? She wasn't able to consider the hypothesis fully as the stranger turned toward her once more.

"Right, sorry," the man started, glancing at his feet, "I came from Halberry. I guess it was rude of me to just assume that you were the girl who came to town yesterday looking for a map?"

Nyla hesitated as he slowly met her eyes again. "No...I—I was in Halberry. Yesterday. But I didn't find a map."

He only nodded. "I don't mean to intrude on your camp, but that storm's only getting worse." He rubbed the back of his neck. He pulled the sleeve of his soaked jacket down. Nyla suspected that the damp material was starting to irritate him as it had her.

Nyla considered that for a moment as she lingered just inside the cave entrance. Her hands twitched with nervous energy. She nodded slowly and said, "You're right. It's too dangerous to climb back down and nearly impossible to find shelter in this part of the Forest."

"I'm Xander, by the way." He extended his hand toward her with a soft smile.

Nyla turned to him, the hint of a smile on her face, and shook his hand. Old habits of society eased back into her mind for the first time in a long while. "Nyla."

She bit the inside of her cheek. Vulnerability and helplessness set in as Nyla watched him shrug off his neat backpack and walk over to the back wall. "You should, uh, you should probably change into dry clothes…"

Nyla ignored the burning of her ears and eyed the wall beside her with the keen interest of not meeting the stranger's eyes.

He shed his jacket and let it drop to the cave floor. "I suppose you're right…uh, I'll be quick. Promise."

He shot her a grin that Nyla nearly missed with the eager turn of her back. She welcomed the closeness of the fresh air hovering by the cave entrance, no matter how charged it was by the storm. Her ears strained to tune into the sheets of rain before her, and Nyla would be lying if she said the consideration to grab her stuff and climb down wasn't there.

"Okay, I'm done."

Nyla glanced up at the cave ceiling with a fierce plea in her eyes and let a passive mask fall into place again as she turned. She strode cautiously toward him and her spot along the back wall, moving her things over.

A tense silence overcame them. Nyla's heartbeat pounded in her ears, unrelenting. What was she supposed to do? Throw him back out into the storm? She knew she would never be able to forgive herself if she later found him dead, but there was some part of her that wanted nothing more than to tell him to leave.

But she wasn't that sort of person. How could she do that to someone who probably had a family—a family who would search the ends of the earth for him, forced to mourn him? And while Nyla was slightly irked by his presence, she'd make the best of it. It might even be nice, to not be alone. She'd always hated stormy nights. Dreary nights only twisted the loneliness like a knife. And for once, it seemed like there wasn't a monster lurking in the shadows, only a storm and a companionship she wasn't decided about yet. Her lips pursed as the word "companionship" turned over in her mind. It was only because of the storm; that was it. His presence was temporary.

Not another word was said in the minutes that stretched by. The storm began to fizzle out, becoming sporadic. The grumbling crashes of thunder came fewer and farther between, growing ever more distant. When lightning flashed, it wasn't as bright, and the air was no longer charged with electricity or made the hair on the back of Nyla's neck stand up.

She wondered if there was still more to come. Water dripped from the ceiling of the cave's entrance, plopping down into a small puddle that flowed over the edge of the rock wall. The candle Xander had lit earlier sent flickering light over the cave.

Her limbs began to relax. Nyla stretched her legs out and subconsciously fingered the wrapping over her hand. Just as she suspected, the rain picked up again.

"So, how long have you been traveling?" Xander asked out of the blue, looking over at her.

Nyla didn't answer. She shifted away to avoid his gaze completely. A curtain of hair fell over part of her face, but she made no move to brush it back over her shoulder, using it to shield herself from him. A mixture of grief and pain washed over her hidden face. Her only response was to draw her blanket tighter around her shoulders, even as she imagined Xander's expectant gaze on her. She could never keep a conversation, not even as a child. To be fair, though, she'd never sat in one place long enough to. And now, she simply didn't want to—or at least, she didn't want to entertain this conversation.

"Right," he drawled.

Nyla supposed that he sat, his lips pursed, and offended that she hadn't answered. But what could she say? One question led to more, and she didn't want to answer those. Politeness be damned. She needed to save her own heart.

The rustle of a bag shifting and something *clunking* together, like a bunch of wooden utensils, greeted her ears. Nyla couldn't place what the sound might be.

Several heartbeats passed between the silence of the storm outside and whatever Xander was doing to cause the wooden *clunks*. Nyla let go of the breath she'd been holding. Maybe that was the end of it. Maybe Xander had gotten the hint and wouldn't try to converse with her anymore. Maybe whatever that rustle was was something to occupy himself with. Now she only needed to find something for herself to focus on. Something that wasn't the person so close within reach and yet so far away.

She tucked her hair behind her ear and brought her knees to her chest. Nyla stared out at the rain, just as she had done countless times before. The rain droned on, drowning out the nightlife that was sure to be stirring and calming the anxious heartbeat in her throat.

5. FATE, TRUST, AND RAGING WINDS

Xander took up his quiver of arrows in the hopes of a distraction. Nyla's business was hers, and if she didn't want to talk, that was fine. The only problem was he couldn't stand the silence when there was another person right there, mere feet away from him. But for the sake of keeping the peace, Xander supposed he could learn to live with the sound vacuum. He relished the quiet clatter his arrows made and resigned himself to checking them over for the billionth time.

As the afternoon wore on and eventually dragged to a close, Xander strained to be content with the hollow symphony of the storm, but the longer the silence between himself and Nyla dragged on, the more he wanted to ask about her. His fingers tapped his outstretched leg as he tried to find something to distract himself with again. He'd already counted the cracks that he could see in the cave's ceiling and thought about the journey to Fortune Falls, so there wasn't much left to occupy himself with. Any other daydream had already exhausted itself. He'd even given up on pacing. Now, the only thing he could do was sit and stare and try his hardest to swallow the questions and small talk.

Each second dragged on like a century.

Night finally fell, and as the torrential rain returned with a vengeance, Xander sank into a state of semi-consciousness in which his mind wandered and his eyes forgot to see. It was the legend of the two quarreling brothers that stole him away. One of the few stories he knew about Fortune Falls, his father had sometimes told the tale to his sister and himself before bed.

But Xander didn't want to remember that. He only cared about the facts, the meat of the legend.

The tale centered around a man, one of two brothers, who sought control of his family's merchant business. Their father had passed, and the company was placed under the authority of the man's brother. Embittered by the loss of his father and insulted by his apparent exclusion from the company, he became unstable. He would lash out at anyone who dared to approach him and drank himself into a deep stupor. Having tried various ways to gain control of the business, he became desperate.

Mysterious misfortunes plagued the brother and the company's ships, allegedly costing the company tens of thousands of libacs. After a final failed attempt involving the destruction of most of the business's fleet, he fled to Fortune Falls. His brother pursued him through the treacherous Shadow Forest with a small contingent of Royal Guards.

The story went that his pursuers found him on the rocky bank of the waterfall's basin. Upon inspection, the brother exclaimed that the water had been the cause of the man's death, as evident by his blackened lips. When the pursuers returned to the city and spoke of the man's fate, the little lake at the base of Fortune Falls became known as Lake Prienamord, for the man who had wanted what he thought was rightfully his.

Countless other tales had been told of people traveling to the Falls, only to never be seen again. Some said they mistakenly drank from Lake Prienamord. Others believed that they had received what they were searching for and were living in great contentment. But there were some who believed that drinking from the Lake would strip the drinker of everything they held dear and they would never obtain their desire, living the rest of their lives with nothing but a dull, aching emptiness.

When he was a kid, Xander would be mystified, and a little horrorstruck, at the discovery of Lake Prienamord…and the dead brother with blackened lips. But now?

Now, Xander wasn't sure what he believed. In some vague way, he knew that this was the first in a long string of cases in the world that were all too familiar. He recalled the uproar his mother's siblings and cousins had made when his grandfather had handed down the family business to his parents.

And then—Xander shook his head. He didn't need to cleave the wound from his disagreeable departure open again. Not now, not ever. He steadied his hand, a feeble attempt to stop the itch in his fingers. The echoed fervor of a fight and careless words tossed in a volley between himself and his grandfather threatened to flood his heart with remorse.

Lake Prienamord. Fortune Falls. Magic that could read into your very soul.

Maybe this was a mistake. The inconvenience of the storm gave Xander the time he needed to figure out exactly why he was doing this, a sort of trepidation he wasn't sure was worth it.

But who's to say?

After all, no one really understood how Fortune Falls worked or the principles of the magic that fueled it. All anyone knew was that you had to drink from the Falls, not the lake below. How it worked, though? Now that was the real mystery. It was simply a property of the land.

Magic, it's said, tended to shift, much like control.

One moment, you were blessed with power, and the next, you had absolutely nothing, no influence over anything. Magic—and control—were strange things, always shifting and flowing.

There was only one guarantee, though its helpfulness remained to be seen if the legends about the Shadow Forest changing its landscape proved to be true. His map, the one passed through his family for generations, might have been the only map in all of Tenebris to indicate the general location of Fortune Falls. Aside from being his family's map, it was the reason why Xander couldn't give it up. Glancing over at his reluctant companion, Xander wondered if letting Nyla take a look at it would be helpful, or if it would only lead to a stolen map.

Before he could stop himself, Xander heard himself ask Nyla if she knew where she was going. While her answer was vague, Xander realized more than he had before. Nyla had been traveling longer than anyone around their age ought to. And she wasn't all that old either, actually younger than he was anyway.

How old was she anyway? Seventeen? Eighteen? He tamped down the urge to study her anew and instead grasped tightly at the conversation she seemed to entertain.

"If it would help, you could take a look at my map, though I'm afraid I still need it."

Nyla shook her head. "I don't think there's a map in this world that could help me get to where I'm going."

Xander quirked his head. Either she was a hopeless soul aimlessly wondering, or...

"I'm going to Fortune Falls," he blurted. His mind cursed him, but still his tongue did not yield. Nyla turned her head to face him, studying him with narrowed eyes. "Yeah, so...mmm..."

"Me too," Nyla offered, gracefully ending his thoughtless attempt at conversation.

Xander breathed a silent sigh of relief. Now all he had to do was pray she'd entertain a conversation about the Falls—and that he wouldn't have to divulge the extent of his map or its origins to her.

"What do you think it'll look like? The Falls?" Xander already had a picture in his mind, formed by the splash of silver amongst the dark navy of the Shadow Forest's heart marked on his map.

"I don't really know. I haven't thought about it much, just getting there." Nyla started hesitantly. "I guess just a waterfall. A really big, glistening waterfall with magic that you can *feel* in your soul. It holds

46

your heart's greatest desire, so it *has* to be something magnificent," Nyla finished desperately, hopeful.

Nyla said she hoped Fortune Falls was like a sort of Avalon, with magic twinkling in the air like lightning bugs, but Xander expected that it would be more or less like the rest of the Shadow Forest. He even went on to describe the flora he thought could grow that far into the heart's interior. His musing left him wondering whether the Falls would be just as dreary and haunting as the rest of the region or worse. When he'd asked Nyla, she'd only frowned and said that she didn't know.

Xander knew there were people who believed that Fortune Falls was the source of the dark hauntings and others who claimed that the Shadow Forest was only its protector. He wasn't certain which he believed in, supposing only time would tell. He was just about to ask Nyla which she believed but stopped himself. It was an innocent enough question, but he didn't want to irritate her or make her feel like she had to converse with him.

Beside him, Nyla yawned. Xander snuck a glance at her and saw that her eyes kept flicking shut, only she kept fighting off sleep, blinking them open repeatedly. How she'd survived so long on her own was beyond him. Even with nowhere to go, pinned in place by a raging storm and now nightfall, she was still pushing herself. Xander wondered if she'd ever had anyone to remind her to take care of herself. Rather, how long she'd been without a friend, a parent, *someone*, like that?

"I'll take first watch," Xander offered, his mind firmly made up. He gathered up his backpack and started for the cave entrance.

"Sorry?" Nyla stifled back another yawn. She looked at him for the first time in what easily could've been a millennium and made to stand, ready to hold her ground. Even with the sleepiness in her voice, she'd managed to throw enough sharpness in her tone that it made Xander reconsider.

Xander toed the cave floor, hesitant to meet Nyla's skeptical gaze. He ran a hand through his hair, steeling himself. He needed to find the right words to put Nyla at ease and push sleep off for himself just a little longer.

When Xander finally spoke, it was with a calm and even tone. "I just thought that this deep into the Shadow Forest, it might be a good idea to take turns sleeping, now that there's two of us. Just in case, you know?"

"All right, fine." Nyla nodded her head slowly. "We'll take turns sleeping. Wake me up when you want to switch." Nyla languidly pushed herself onto her knees and hauled her bag closer to herself.

As she rolled out a ratty old sleeping bag, Xander wondered how she'd managed to survive out here. It was pretty obvious to him that she'd been traveling for a long time, to the point where most wouldn't consider it 'traveling' anymore but more like 'surviving.' Did she ever have a map or compass? How often did she resupply? What about money? Food, water, friends, a home, protection; what about—

And before he knew it, the words he'd tried to keep down all afternoon tumbled from his lips, and Nyla stared at him with an unnerving gaze that didn't waver. "Haven't you heard what happens to unprepared travelers out here? 'Cause I'm guessing that you've been out here for a while and only have that knife and no map or compass, and...*How have you survived like this?*"

Nyla huffed and glanced up at the ceiling. But it wasn't purely agitation that he saw in her eyes when she looked back at him again.

Xander blinked his eyes shut and fought the urge to turn away from her. He could kick himself right now.

"Yeah," she started almost apathetically, and much to Xander's gratitude, Nyla had turned away from him, "I've seen what happens to people out here."

"And that doesn't scare you?"

Again, Nyla stopped her sleep preparations. Her lilac eyes snapped to him, a sort of fire in them he couldn't name. Xander swallowed nervously. Why couldn't he keep his mouth shut? None of this would

matter anyway when they went their separate ways after the storm...
or maybe after Fortune Falls.

"Of course it does," she said quietly. Her eyes dropped to stare
intently at her hands and the death grip she had on the bundle of
fabric she was holding. Xander shifted on his feet. He just couldn't let
it go. He just *had* to keep asking questions. After a second, Nyla met
his eyes again. "Is that all, or did you want to know more?"

"I'm sorry. I just—"

Nyla cut him off with a sigh, as if forcing herself off of the defensive.
"It's all right. I don't like the quiet all that much either. I'm just used
to it."

Xander blinked, stunned. More questions surfaced, but he bit his
tongue and turned his attention back to his own bag.

Without another word, Xander settled close to the cave's mouth,
where the rain hadn't been blown in by the wind. The wind rustled the
leaves on the nearest trees, much gentler now than it was before. His
eyes focused on the inky void before him. He couldn't make anything
out, but he looked out over the Shadow Forest anyway. The ominous
sounds of the Forest's nightlife floated up to him. Every hoot, every
howl, every rustle of the leaves left Xander to ponder over the possibility
of something climbing up the wall, but he dismissed it. Most creatures
liked easy prey.

But the Shadow Forest was home to many dangerous creatures, the
likes of which didn't exist anywhere else in Tenebris.

Exhaustion was a long way away.

The dim light of the candle flickered beside him. There was never
enough light.

Nyla shifted in her sleep, the material of her sleeping bag crinkling
over the sputtering candle flame and rainstorm. He looked up at that,
half expecting her to be awake. Instead, she curled up on her other
side. Xander spared a glance out toward the abyss before picking up
his knife and a twig he'd found in the bottom of his bag earlier.

After some time, a pile of wood shavings had collected in Xander's lap. All he had to show for his whittling was a toothpick. Xander flicked it away and cleared the shavings from his lap. As the cry of an unnamable creature reached his ears, he glanced over at Nyla again. She was so still. The severe tension and alertness had faded from her features, softened by sleep. Her knife lay by her makeshift pillow. He worried if she were even breathing. Once Xander was satisfied that Nyla was, in fact breathing, he found something else to focus on and pulled a book from his bag as quietly as he could.

Not sure how long he could stay awake, Xander made himself as comfortable as possible. The cave floor was rough, and the wall behind him was too rigid to acquire any semblance of comfort. Still attempting to assess what he knew of Nyla, he listened for signs of danger.

There wasn't much to go on. Not particularly chatty or personable, the only real thing he could gather about her came from her appearance. He knew she had been traveling for a while or didn't have the money to replace her bag and faded clothes. Maybe she'd lost her parents or run away. Those were the only reasonable explanations for someone as young as they were to be off on their own, in a perilous forest, with no companion.

But what about other family, friends?

Xander clenched his jaw. It wasn't uncommon for families to be… difficult. That might be something he and Nyla had in common.

He shook his head and returned to his book. It wasn't his business, his subconscious seemed to repeat *ad nauseam*. The light from the candle wasn't nearly enough to actually read by, but Xander knew what the book said. At this point, the book was something to hold onto, to push sleep away.

Only a few chapters later, Xander found his eyes drooping closed. Yawns escaped his lips. He pressed on. Another page was met with another yawn. There wasn't any way Xander could keep himself awake now. He resigned himself to waking Nyla up. Standing, he stretched his stiff muscles from all the sitting and the frigid dampness of the cave.

"Nyla," Xander whispered. "Hey."

Xander inched closer and again called out to her, but Nyla didn't respond. He hesitantly reached out and gently touched Nyla's shoulder to wake her.

***

Nyla was used to sleepless nights when every whisper of wind through the ash-crackled trees startled her awake. She was all too accustomed to the haunting night symphony of the Shadow Forest— more so than anyone in all of Tenebris probably.

She searched through her bag for something she could scrunch up into a bundle for a pillow and probably her heaviest sweater, which barely kept her warm anymore, but with another blanket, she'd be fine. Hopefully.

She studied Xander out of the corner of her eye as she dragged out her nighttime routine, beginning to wonder what would happen when the sun came up in the morning.

At least Xander was focused on getting himself ready for his self-assigned watch duty.

Nyla bit the inside of her cheek. Even as she entertained the idea that Fate had put them together, forced them into the same cave by the same storm, for some reason or another, was it possible to travel together? They *were* sharing the same shelter. But the theory that Fate had put them in each other's path was farfetched at best.

What if...what if Fate *had*, though? Her eyes bounced with her thoughts, as if they could follow each strand of the process. Maybe, Nyla began to think as her eyes trailed to the bundled-up sweater clenched in her wringing hands. She licked her lips. A quick dart of her eyes assured her that yes, Xander was still there, and yes, he was real.

Nyla allowed her thoughts to entertain the absurd notion that Fate had put them together for whatever reason unbeknownst to either of them. They were both headed to Fortune Falls…It couldn't hurt—could it?

She shook her head. Resigned to another night of restless sleep, pondering over the whims of Fate wouldn't help her get to Fortune Falls in one piece, let alone survive until tomorrow. As she settled into her thinning sleeping bag, Nyla stole a glance at Xander. Outlined in the shadows of the cave's mouth by the candle he'd taken with him, a tiny voice in Nyla's mind asked if she trusted him. At her answer, she screwed her eyes shut and turned her back to him.

They were strangers. She shouldn't trust him as steadfastly as she apparently did. It was with this debate that Nyla's mind exhausted itself, and she plunged into a deep sleep, the likes of which she'd forgotten. Pleasant sunshine and amber fields of grain filled her mind, like those she'd passed in the Barrier Plains. Lying amongst the soft grasses, she watched the clouds float by, completely at ease. Time seemed endless. It was like the world had stopped and, with it, Nyla's anxious mind. As the clouds drifted by, a voice reached out to her from somewhere too far behind to actually hear it, just a vague sound from a world away. She didn't dare turn to look, not when the sunset was so breathtaking and the flowers so vibrant and the meadow so peaceful. She smiled and closed her eyes to warm her face in the sun's light.

The voice attacked her. The dream faded as Nyla jerked away from the light touch. She sprang up with a gasp. Her mind raced. Swinging her fist, Nyla blindly grabbed the unsheathed knife by her side. The blade flashed in the dying candlelight.

The voice jumped back.

Prepared to strike, Nyla's muscles froze and came to a grinding halt.

She hadn't been alone when she'd gone to sleep.

What happened to Xander?

Heat crept along Nyla's cheeks. The shadowy figure that recoiled away from her with their hands raised wasn't a threat. It was someone she should know. An ally. Nyla's hands dropped to her lap.

"Oh, Helpet, I'm so sorry! I…I'm not used to…" Nyla sputtered as she scrambled to her feet, wide awake now. Nyla found that the words stuck in her throat. For some reason or another, she wasn't willing to admit that company and people were commodities of her past. Maybe the goddess of perseverance and wisdom that Nyla found herself praying to could help her. Or perhaps Nyla's efforts were a lost cause, yet another thing destroyed by the fire.

Xander nodded and let his hands drop. "Happens to the best of us."

Even if his smile was meant to reassure her, it only made her stomach roil. "Sorry."

Rolling out his sleeping bag, Xander glanced over his shoulder at her. "I'm okay, really. You weren't *that* close to hitting me."

Nyla bobbed her head and apologized once more, turning away to take up her position at the opening without another word. She wrapped a blanket around her shoulders and savored the last remnants of the blissful dream she'd had until it faded away to join her memories.

***

When the shadowy morning finally came, the pair packed their respective things and avoided any conversation. It wasn't that they didn't have anything to say to each other, but, rather, neither wanted to start the conversation. In the end, it was Xander who had cleared his throat and turned to face Nyla.

"So, I was thinking last night, and it just doesn't make sense for us—" he started, looking at her rather sheepishly.

"To separate? We *are* going to the same place, so…" she interjected, staring over the edge of the opening to overlook the misty Shadow Forest. A mudslide had poured over the side of the cliff in the night and splattered the surface's ridges and creases—and the entrance to their cave.

"Yeah. Besides, two people are better than one in this part of the Forest anyway," Xander said decidedly.

The pair barely spoke another word as they packed up, and Xander started down the rock wall. Nyla shook like a leaf. Her mind relived the almost-fatal slip from the previous day. She fought to keep her breath even as she descended the wall, feeling around the rough surface with her hands and feet as she searched for new footholds. Going up was much easier, she decided. She nibbled the inside of her lip. Hopefully, Xander hadn't noticed her troubles.

At least he hadn't mentioned it.

The longer it took for her to climb down, the more her legs shook. Nyla was nothing short of flabbergasted that the violent quake of her body didn't cause her to slip again.

If Xander was afraid, he didn't show it.

Nyla sent a tentative glance toward the ground. It didn't look like she had a long way to go. She'd jumped from greater heights before, back when jumping was fun and climbing was a game.

Swallowing around the lump in her throat, Nyla closed her eyes and took a deep breath to coax herself into jumping down. As her fear ebbed away, Nyla twisted herself around and took one foot off of the hold it had on the wall, allowing it to almost dangle. Not giving herself the time to rethink her decision, she pushed off the wall and leapt, turning around fully as she fell through the air.

Upon landing, Nyla stumbled forward before her feet registered the solid ground beneath her. Thankfully, Xander caught her arm and helped her regain her balance. Nyla's legs visibly shook, but at least she'd made it down in one piece and saved herself from the exertion of climbing down the remainder of the wall.

"Good?" Xander asked.

"Yeah," she huffed with relief, her insides still rattled.

Without another word, they wove a path through the dim Shadow Forest. The farther into the heart of the Forest they went, the more the blackened roots of the trees gnarled and twisted together. It was almost as if they were trying to weave themselves together to prohibit people from going any farther.

The pair climbed over everything in their path, including the ancient, knotted roots and fallen trees from yesterday's storm. Some roots were tangled so tightly that they often had to scale them, at times pulling the other up and over. It was slow going, but the only way to Fortune Falls. And with each challenge, each obstacle, Nyla's resolve to make it to Fortune Falls was bolstered.

6. WHITE LIGHTNING

Nyla and Xander continued to hike until after sunset, only stopping because it became too dark to see. Xander had a hunch that if it were up to Nyla, she'd keep going, and maybe he would've too, if he were her. The inclination to light some torches crossed his mind, but he was too afraid it would only encourage her. If she was as desperate to reach Fortune Falls as he suspected, Xander couldn't say for certain what lines she wouldn't cross to get there, including self-exhaustion. Most people would have given up and turned back in the face of yesterday's storm or at the first sight of the nightmarish trees and perpetual darkness. But Xander supposed that said something about himself too, as neither of them had been deterred by nature's fury or the Forest's heart.

They made camp in an area between a grove of knotted vines and roots. This was the only clear ground they could find, but it would have to do. Uneven and littered with tree roots, the thick brush offered protection from almost every direction, but the dark night—if it were truly nighttime—made certain that they couldn't see anything coming toward them.

Again, he offered to take first watch, only to insist on it when Nyla began to protest. As if Nyla knew he couldn't be swayed, she pursed her lips, and Xander fought off a pre-victory grin. In the end,

Nyla reluctantly accepted and promptly turned away from him. Xander set about his own camp preparations as Nyla stalked toward her bag. He couldn't help but suspect that last night in the cave was the best night's sleep Nyla had gotten in a long time. Sure, she was unbearably silent now, but she'd entertained *some* conversation earlier and seemed at ease while they'd maneuvered through the Shadow Forest.

Xander settled in a crook made by the woven tree roots to keep watch and spared a glance over at Nyla. She'd set her sleeping bag almost right up against their back defense on the other side of the rough, open square of their camp. A decent no-man's-land stretched between herself and his crackling campfire. Xander considered the strange habit, having noticed how she seemed uneasy about the candle in the cave and her reluctance to help gather firewood just now. His heart wrenched. Something tragic had happened to her, to both of them. And he'd bet her "something tragic" had to do with fire.

If it weren't for the night that closed in on them, he might've given in to the most ridiculous urge that had ever overcome him. But pouring your heart out to a complete stranger, no matter the road that lay ahead of you, wasn't something Xander actually wanted to do, especially unprompted. He couldn't just pipe up and go, "My parents died in an accident, and then my sister was killed too. So, what's your story?"

No, it just wasn't done.

Xander's ears pricked. Some near-distant movement rustled the leaves and snapped a few twigs. The cool breeze that haunted the heart of the Shadow Forest kissed his face. Xander sniffed and forced himself to relax. Plenty of things could rustle the leaves and break twigs.

Still, his hand drifted to his bow and quiver.

He hesitantly sniffed again, but this time, he was certain. Maybe this wasn't the best campsite. He wondered if Nyla smelt it too, the something rotten that the breeze carried with it. It was possible that they'd unknowingly made camp near a predator's old kill site, but the rustling made him assume otherwise. His gaze cut to Nyla. There wasn't any way she was deep enough into her slumber yet that she couldn't hear the branches and underbrush yielding to *something* in their path.

The more the noise steadily grew in volume, drawing nearer, the more Xander's heart sank. He stood, nocking an arrow. His footsteps were silent as he crept toward a tense Nyla. He called out to her under his breath, not wanting to alert whatever was coming of their presence.

Nothing.

How she managed to ignore the situation at hand was beyond him, but the moment she opened her eyes, he knew it was hopeful denial that made her try.

***

As irked as Nyla had seemed, she was actually grateful—and relieved—when Xander had offered to take first watch. But she hadn't wanted him to think that she was a pushover or that she was taking advantage of his consideration. Her face twisted into a grimace as she tried to find a comfortable position to place her sleeping bag so she could curl up and go to sleep. Her body ached, certain to be worse in the morning. The fact only made her long for a featherbed and clean sheets and a proper bath. Not for the first time, and most definitely not the last, the fading memories of homey comfort caused a veil of bitterness to eclipse her heart.

Nyla forced herself to accept her circumstances and resolved to chase after another night of better sleep than she was used to. The night breeze carried the rustle of the sapphire leaves overhead, soothing her soul. She frowned. Her ears strained, her brows furrowing in annoyance. A deeper, more resounding noise was hidden by the gentle laughter of wind and leaves. At first, Nyla assumed it was only Xander or the crackle of the fire he'd built and settled farther into her sleeping bag.

The rustling came nearer and nearer as twigs cracked. The air soured. Nyla gagged and turned away from it onto her side. She refused to open her eyes, praying that she was deep in an uneasy sleep inspired by her dark surroundings. Instead, she found her hand had instinctively reached for her knife as the unseen monster lumbered closer to her consciousness. Nyla refused to accept it. This couldn't be happening again. Not so soon after the giant.

Her pleas went unanswered.

Nyla gripped her knife tighter. The smooth metal of the handle was firm and unyielding beneath her tight fingers. It was all too solid, but still she prayed for this all to be a nightmare. Dread settled in the pit of her stomach. She became even more unwilling to open her eyes as the putrid stench overwhelmed the once-pure air. The ground vibrated underneath her. Visions of titans and giants flooded her mind. The pounding of a large pair of feet—thankfully not as large-sounding as the other morning, though the assumption gave little relief to Nyla's terror—drew closer.

A nightmare, it was only a nightmare.

"Nyla," Xander whispered.

Any hope that this was a nightmare deflated with the sound of Xander's voice. Nyla was up in an instant, her knife ready. Fight or panic—she couldn't tell which—coursed through her veins. Xander, who kept his back to her, and subsequently blocked any easy path of escape she could've taken, was ready with his bow. Given his stance, Nyla knew Xander was willing to put up a fight.

Nyla didn't know what outcome Xander sought, but the only thing her quivering legs could think of doing was going backwards. Ice flooded Nyla's buzzing veins. The coal-like bark of the tree behind Nyla scratched her calf. Her heart fluttered in her throat. Fear overcame her. Nyla wanted to scream, but couldn't. Her skin buzzed with a strange sort of mixture that might've been fear spiked with adrenaline. Every ounce of energy drained from her body. In an attempt to steady herself, Nyla reached out and gripped Xander's shoulder.

Escape.

It was all she wanted, more than anything else at the present moment. She only hoped her nervous energy hadn't affected Xander.

Her heart pounded in her throat. The brush before their camp shook and parted. She closed her eyes as the creature barged into their campsite, unwilling to face the nightmare before her. Beneath her fingers, Xander's muscles coiled even tighter and loosened the slightest bit with a long exhale of breath she felt all the way up her own arm.

***

Xander tensed and steadied his breath. Nyla's harsh grip on his shoulder grounded him to reality as memories and the nightmare before them threatened to overtake his constitution.

A beast taller than the average man, with a protruding stomach, stepped into their campsite. It reeked of body odor and stale death. The horrific odor that had gnawed at the open air was finally explained. Blisters covered the thing's exposed torso, its long limbs, its face. Xander stiffened.

"That's…" Xander gaped, his mouth going dry as he trailed off.

"It's an ogre," Nyla uttered in disbelief at the same time as his own words failed.

At the tremble of fear in his companion's voice, Xander loosed his arrow. The hideous beast let out an enraged roar, but the arrow didn't penetrate the ogre's skin. It merely glanced off of the space over its heart before falling weakly to the ground. The ogre's gray eyes narrowed, focused solely on Xander.

Despite its oafish appearance, the ogre closed in on them with a wicked slyness. The arrow snapped, a *crack* like thunder or breaking bones, under its gruesome foot. Nyla's nails dug into his shoulder at the sharp noise. She'd flinched so hard his hand nearly slipped from the grip of his bow. He set his jaw, ready with another arrow. With every intention of making what he now knew to be a fruitless effort at survival, Xander took a deep breath to combat the past horrors waging war in the background of his mind.

Steady. He needed to be steady.

Nyla's hand slipped from his shoulder.

He barely turned his head to look back at her, his attention mainly on the danger bearing down on them. It was only a glance, but in that single second, Xander swore.

Nyla's eyes flashed.

He'd seen it, had realized with awestruck terror that he had no idea what the white flash across her irises meant, only that it couldn't be anything good. Besides, what he saw couldn't be real…right?

Xander turned to face the ogre, ready to mount one last stand. He'd check in on Nyla as soon as—

Static filled the air. Pure white light flashed and filled every inch of reality like lightning. Xander's eyes shut against the assault of light. The *popping* embers of their campfire fizzled out with the crackle of light and the *whoosh* of a steady gust of wind that died as abruptly as it had come. The ogre let out a ferocious roar.

Then the world behind his closed eyes was still and deathly silent and dark. Static filled Xander's ears like cotton. Begrudgingly, he cracked open his eyes. Uneasy confusion brewed in his gut.

A pile of ash now resided where the monster had stood. He turned to study Nyla. A new layer of fear mixed in her lilac-colored eyes, a stronger sense of absolute horror and sickness. Xander watched her, uncertain and still reeling from the bewilderment of it all. Nyla's eyes concentrated on something far away, on another plane maybe. She was pale, gray even, completely ashen as if the life had drained right out of her. Her unfocused eyes fluttered shut.

Xander blinked away his own confusion and the blood-speckled memories of what could've become their fate as well. He ran a hand through his hair and forced that cold Serenmae day from his mind, forced the angry exchange away too. When his eyes focused on Nyla again, Xander gasped in alarm. Nyla swayed on her feet. She didn't even seem to realize her own faintness, her breathing heavy and obviously unaware of her surroundings. He had to break her out of that daze, for her own sake.

"Nyla?" Xander reached out to her.

She parted her lips as if to say something, though not even a whimper escaped. Her knees buckled. Xander dropped his bow as he scrambled to catch her. "Nyla!"

***

Something flicked over Nyla's eyes like a film. The haze blinded her for a second, no longer than the blink of an eye. The faintness that had settled in her bones only grew stronger. Her body grew ever more fatigued by the effort of even breathing. Nyla wished the ogre would just disappear, leave them alone, anything but exist right there in front of them.

In that moment, Nyla completely forgot where she was, who she was with, and if she were even alive. Her body shuddered with the force of the shock that started in her core. Heat boiled beneath her skin. Raw energy consumed her and fled as quickly as it had amassed like a bolt of light striking in the dark. Nyla opened her eyes. She blinked.

Where was the ogre?

The weight of Xander's gaze sat on her lungs. She peered past him to where the ogre had stood, unaware of her surroundings despite herself. Her body sagged with exhaustion and lost every ounce of tension.

Nyla could hear nothing over her own blood thrumming in her veins and heart pounding between her ears. Her hand floated to the roots behind her as she leaned back against them for support. Something was wrong. Darkness crept along the outer field of her vision. Nyla didn't need a mirror to see how terrible she looked—she could *feel* it. Her limbs were hollow and unbearably heavy at the same time. Her eyes refused to stay open or focus on the physical world around her for any period of time. She didn't know what in Fate's name was happening—*had* happened, only that something had happened, something crucial that she needed to understand.

She wished the roots behind her would swallow her whole and shifted toward them like a beggar. There was a bitter taste in her mouth, as though she had just drunk a canteen full of salt water. The stifling heat of her blood suffocated her. The expelled energy left an oppressive void that curled within her chest. Her arm hung awkwardly at her side, her other hand planted as firmly as she could manage on the knot of roots behind her. Her breath tore in and out of her. Her chest rose and fell with her struggle to stop death's grip on her body. Nyla blinked three, four times, in an attempt to make the black watercolor dots obscuring her vision go away. Instead, the translucent bubbles of oil bonded to the blackness that stalked closer from the edges of her vision.

Alarm coursed through every nerve in her body and screamed at her to grab onto *something*. Her body yelled at her to do anything, but she couldn't listen. Nyla was too consumed by the effort of keeping her eyes open. She succumbed to the flood of numbness and exhaustion inside her. As her eyes flitted shut, she became suspended in darkness. Someone faintly called her name again. A warmth engulfed her as something steady wrapped around her waist, effectively stopping her body's freefall.

It was like floating on a cloud or flying, just as she'd always imagined doing. Suspended in air, her limbs were like fluid as she bobbed. Content for a time, Nyla didn't know where she was for certain, only that the darkness surrounding her hugged her skin like a blanket. All she knew was that she was utterly unafraid. For once, not a single monster or fear lurked in the shadows beyond her vision. In fact, there weren't any shadows at all, only a moonless sky unmarred by even the stars.

All too soon, the weight of her limbs was recognized. Something soft fluttered under her blinking eyes.

Eyelashes.

Yes, her eyes were blinking open, though the world above her remained a haze of vague shapes in a misty shadow.

"Nyla? Hey…Are you all right?" Xander's blurred face floated in front of her.

She tried to sit up. The blankets on top of her shifted, allowing the cool night air to kiss her bare arms. Xander gently pushed her back until she was lying down again.

"Not so fast. Take it easy for a bit. What happened, after the flash?" he asked.

"I-I'm not sure." She paused. Her voice shook, barely above a whisper, like she was still terrified, "I mean, I remember, but it's weird. The ogre was just there, and then it wasn't. And the light…"

Again, she struggled to sit up, and this time Xander let her. He put his arm around her shoulders, and Nyla welcomed not only the stability it gave her, but also the additional warmth.

Xander offered her some water. She took the bottle graciously and drank as if it were ambrosia. Awareness returned to her body, allowing her to remember the world around her and how her own limbs worked. Overwhelmed by the smoky scent of burning wood, Nyla squeezed her eyes shut to stop the tears that threatened to spill over. Her breathing quickened again. Images flashed before her eyes. All of them replayed the same flickering fire that had stopped burning seasons upon seasons ago. Her eyes blinked open, and she glanced away. It was then that she noticed the pile of ash where the ogre had stood was gone and frowned. Xander soothingly rubbed her arm.

"I can put it out, if you want," he offered.

"No, it's fine." The lie hung heavily between them. Nyla choked back tears and nearly failed. She let Xander pull her closer and tried to focus on anything else, anything but the fire, her family, the ogre, the missing ash pile of the ogre's remains, or even Fortune Falls.

"I know that look. It's the kind that people wear when they've lost someone, or everyone," Xander whispered. His jaw clenched. He took a breath before continuing, "Three years ago, my sister and I lost both our parents. They said there was an accident, but I don't know if I really believe that. They just didn't come home that time."

Nyla angled herself to get a better look at Xander, but he stared straight into the fire's core. She studied his profile and saw the same hollowness she felt in his drawn features, even after all this time. He only shook his head like he was trying to clear the memories away.

Xander slowly exhaled. "Then I lost my sister."

"I'm sorry." Nyla swallowed the rocks sitting in her throat. "The fire…it happened a couple years ago. I was…I was the only survivor. Since then, I've just been wandering."

Neither one said another word, allowing their confessions to fill the silence between them and share in their burdens. As the minutes dragged on, Nyla watched the fire lick at the cool night air with Xander still close beside her.

7. THE RIVER CROSSING

Neither said a word as they packed up their blankets and rubbed the exhaustion from their eyes in what easily could've been the predawn hours. Before they'd set off, Xander had spent some time hunched over his map. Nyla had joined him at some point, quietly observing. She'd wanted to ask what it was that he was doing, but was too afraid of breaking his concentration. If the crease between his furrowed brows and the slight downward twist of his lip were any indication, whatever Xander was doing required his absolute attention. So instead, Nyla had looked over the map's markings and waited until he'd sat back on his heels, the only sign that he'd finished his task.

The dark sapphire leaves and coal-like trees absorbed any sunlight that could've poked its way through the thickly woven canopy above. The heart of the Shadow Forest thrived in this perpetual night, where predators never slept and prey always ran. Every rustle, every whisper of the wind, every howl sent goosebumps down her arms.

The depths of the Shadow Forest had few landmarks and was only a deep sapphire patch on Xander's map with a silver mark where Fortune Falls allegedly resided in the center of the forest. When she'd asked about it, he'd only shrugged and told her it was a guess, but Nyla knew better. The map was too richly made to be dependent on speculation. Wherever Xander had gotten it, she only hoped it wouldn't cause problems for her later on and leaned into the hope in her heart that it would lead them true.

As they hiked, she'd finally asked him what he was doing with the map this morning. Xander explained that he was counting their steps and trying to keep track of the miles they'd traveled. According to the calculations he'd made based on their progress this morning, Xander guessed that they had another week, maybe two, ahead of them before they reached Fortune Falls. Nyla was speechless. It couldn't be that far, could it? Their conversation ebbed, and in its absence, Nyla's mind wandered to places it shouldn't.

A lead weight had settled in the pit of her stomach. Since the night before, an unspoken understanding between the pair remained with them as they hiked. She knew it was best to forget the events of the night before and move on. It didn't help her nerves that Xander's hand passed over the quiver of arrows at his hip almost as often as her own hand skirted the hilt of her knife with each distant howl, panicked *squawk* or *squeak*, and the constant chitters of animals hidden by the flora. Every light rustle of the leaves forced each of them to make sure that they were ready for the thing they thought would pounce, but never did.

The only comfort was that they were on the move, and they had managed to put some distance between themselves and where the ogre had attacked their camp. After all, a moving target was harder to hit.

Nyla shivered involuntarily. That small comfort was short-lived when she remembered that danger knew no bounds in the Shadow Forest, let alone its heart. Something told her that the forest became even more unforgiving and ruthless as one got closer to its heart.

Nyla pulled the sleeves of her jacket down over her fingers and balled her hands. The thin material wrapped tightly around her numb fingers. She clenched her jaw to keep her teeth from chattering. Nyla wasn't sure if it was her frayed nerves or the chill in the air that made her tremble as goosebumps erupted along her arms.

Xander insisted they stop to light torches. While Nyla couldn't agree more that the darkness was suffocating, there was a part of her that didn't want to stop or stand in one place longer than necessary.

"It'll only take a second."

"Promise?" she asked skeptically. She didn't know why she made him reaffirm his trivial promise, only that it put her mind at ease. Their travel came to a grinding halt as Xander broke off two lengths of branches from the nearest tree and pulled scraps of cloth from his bag.

"I promise." He glanced up, still bent over his backpack. "You know how to use a bow?"

Nyla shook her head. "I've seen people use one before."

"Just draw the string back and shoot in its general direction," Xander said as if something *was* waiting to attack. He handed her the bow and a single arrow. Nyla turned her back to him, her ears strained with alertness. She spun in a slow circle as her eyes swept over everything and anything, fully prepared to fire if necessary.

Once again, Nyla turned slowly on her heel to take in their surroundings. Static charged the atmosphere. The air cooled, stilling for a moment. She turned again to watch the forest beyond Xander as he knelt, dousing the cloth he had wrapped around one end of each stick with an amber liquid Nyla couldn't quite place. It wasn't long before he handed her a lit torch and kept the other for himself. Nyla gave the bow back and sucked in a breath.

The torches gave off a bouncing light that cast writhing shadows over the twisted and gnarled roots of the coal-dark trees. Nyla and Xander hiked in silence. It wasn't the sort of rigid silence that had enveloped them when they met, but the sort of silence that came with desperation, tragedy, or overthinking.

Nyla still found herself wondering about the ogre. She was especially curious about how it had been reduced to a pile of ash.

There was the possibility of lightning, but she dismissed it as quickly as it had occurred to her. The chances of lightning striking exactly at that moment, when there wasn't even a storm to begin with, at the precise spot where the ogre stood, was just too much of a coincidence. She eyed Xander carefully before her gaze returned to the forest floor. It was almost absurd to think that he had magic, but then again, Nyla couldn't think of another reasonable explanation for what had happened the night before.

No. Nyla knew she didn't have magic, despite the strange things that had happened to her over the past two years. So Xander must've... Nyla dismissed the idea before it even had the chance to marinate. He wasn't a showman, and archery certainly wasn't a fleeting hobby. He would've killed the ogre had the arrow pierced the thing's skin.

Unless...was he using his magic to make himself a better archer?

Could magic do that? Improve someone's talents or skills?

***

Handing over his bow and quiver to a stranger left Xander hollow, especially since he'd seen it in Nyla's lilac eyes that she didn't believe the explanation he'd given her about his map. There was nothing stopping her from taking it and leaving him here to die.

But she wouldn't.

Xander didn't know how his mind could assert that so infallibly, but it did. Even now, just watching out of the corners of his eyes as he wrapped a scrap of cloth around the end of a branch and doused it with some brandy, Nyla was too intent on the Shadow Forest surrounding them to be a threat to him. He quickly prepared the second torch and lit them both.

"Ready?" He traded a torch for his bow and arrow in Nyla's hand.

She nodded wordlessly, still looking past him at the forest beyond.

Her attention to the world around them almost made him wonder if she could see things he couldn't. But so far, there wasn't any sign of danger that he could see. And there certainly hadn't been any obvious use of magic. She was a puzzle, and Xander wasn't certain how many pieces there were or if he'd ever be granted the ability to realize them.

Pushing all thoughts of his companion aside, Xander took her cue and studied the darkness all around them. He focused his efforts on counting their steps, the only gauge he had that could help them use his map. If he lost track, there wasn't much he could do then. There weren't any roads or signs or any other device this far out into the wilds that could help them determine where in the Shadow Forest they were. They would be lost forever, just like so many before them if they weren't smart. Every step took them closer to either Fortune Falls or their deaths.

A long howl sounded in the distance. Xander forced his fist to unclench. His jaw twitched, but he said nothing. Instead, he focused on his own footing and ignored the grumble of his stomach. He had no idea what time of day it was. For all he knew, it could be an entirely new day, and they had walked for a full twenty-four hours without ever knowing. Nyla probably wouldn't mind if they did or had.

She was going to be the death of him. He didn't know how or why he was so certain of the fact, only that he was. His bones *knew* it in a way he had never known anything else.

***

In the few days that followed the ogre incident, the ashy amber dirt beneath their feet gradually morphed into sheets of black stone like the rock points Nyla had used to navigate to the banks of the Union River the other morning. The rock face was smooth, but at the same time, it had a jagged face that looked like frozen ripples on the surface of a river.

The pair's pace slowed. Nyla took small breaths as she focused on her footing. She wondered if this was what ice skating was like. The worn soles of her boots provided little grip on the slick, onyx-colored stone. Even with the torch in her hand, she found it hard to see anything at all. Everywhere she looked, it was pitch black. The trees and their roots twisted in the dark, darker than even coal. They had been swallowed by a bottle of ink, or so her mind insisted. Her whole body quivered. But she had come too far to give up now.

"Hey, Xander?" Nyla piped up shyly.

"Yeah?" He glanced at her over his shoulder.

"Never mind." She bit her lip. Her feet stopped, and she cast a glance in either direction. After a moment's hesitation, she asked, "How long do you think we've been walking?"

Xander stopped dead in his tracks. From the disturbed uncertainty in his eyes, Nyla knew Xander had contemplated the same thing and hadn't come up with an answer either. He shook his hands out, shifting the torch between them as he did so, and swept his eyes over the dark landscape.

Subconsciously, they gravitated toward each other. The absence of their footsteps created an echo-chamber in which the Shadow Forest flourished. Nyla's bright eyes wandered over the gnarled roots and endless rock ahead of them. Her body ached at the idea of all the navigating they would have to do to get over the roots in their path. The uncertainty of how much farther they had to go twisted painfully in her empty stomach. Their torches crackled, filling the still silence.

"Maybe we should eat something," Xander suggested. Nyla's empty stomach clenched at the mere mention of food.

The quiet pounded between Nyla's ears like a heartbeat. Xander swung his bag off his shoulders and started to dig around inside. She watched as he pulled two packs of jerky from his bag and offered one to her, which she took in exchange for some of the berries she had picked the day before, when fruit-bearing plants still graced the Shadow Forest.

Xander quickly built a small fire between them. They sat on the icy stone, listening to their surroundings intently. While nothing snuck up on them, haunting calls and mournful wails echoed in the distance.

It wasn't long before they were up and hiking again, and Nyla couldn't be more grateful for it. The farther they hiked, the closer together the trees grew until their massive roots were gnarled together in tightly woven knots.

They helped each other up and over each massive tree root. Nyla's muscles groaned with each movement. She wanted nothing more than to turn in for the day, so when they emerged into a bright clearing with streaming sunlight, an awed gasp escaped her lips. She turned to Xander, whose brow furrowed in confusion.

Nyla's eyes sparkled. "Where are we?" She started to smile. Excitement brewed in her blood. "Are we almost there?"

Xander shrugged and took off his backpack. He dug around inside it before pulling the map free and knelt on the ground to spread it out between them. Nyla sat on her haunches beside him and waited as patiently as she could for an answer. Xander's furrowed brows deepened.

"I have no idea. I'm guessing we're close, but this isn't on the map," Xander said defeatedly. He ran a hand through his hair and stiffly folded the map back up.

"So…we're lost?" Nyla breathed slowly.

She knew it wasn't Xander's fault. In fact, she didn't blame him at all. The road to Fortune Falls was a tricky one. For all anybody knew, it was different and changed each time someone traveled there. With so much she didn't know and couldn't be certain of, Nyla grasped at what remained of her fragile faith. This was the first and only indication Xander had ever given her that he wasn't certain. They were both fools for believing in a piece of paper or, in her case especially, for believing in their instincts to guide them to such a mythical place. Her eyes studied the sapphire-slowly-shifting-to-indigo foliage around them, so different from the forest they'd just trekked through. The leaves above their heads rustled in the gentle breeze. When her eyes fell back to the grass below, a trail of gray smoke caught her eye on the opposite side of the glade.

Nyla pointed excitedly. "Do you see that?"

A thin tendril of smoke seemed to beckon them forward. Nyla scrambled up. She started toward it, curious as to how a trail of smoke could act so human, when Xander grabbed her arm and pulled her back. Dark shadows crossed his screwed-up face.

"We should go."

"Go? No, I think we should follow it." She pushed his hand away and started forward again. Xander hastily put the map back in his bag, muttering a curse or two under his breath as he trailed after her.

"Are you insane? Haven't you heard the stories about what these things do to travelers, how it leads them to their death? We don't even know where we are, and this *thing* could get us in an even worse situation." He spoke quickly and with a slight tremble of fear in the undercurrent of his voice.

Nyla nodded, but continued anyway. She couldn't explain it, but this was right. The smoke would lead them to Fortune Falls. She knew it with every fiber of her being.

"If it starts to look bad, we turn around. We're already kind of lost, so why not see where the smoke leads us? I have nowhere to be," she said as they reached the edge of the clearing. She paused here, one foot half in the underbrush of the Shadow Forest, the other still safely in the glade. Xander looked between her and the smoke. He sighed and threw his hands up in defeat.

Plunged back into darkness, the smoke led them through the depths of the Shadow Forest. It was nearly impossible to see anything. Their torches created smoke of their own that mixed with the fine tendril of the ghost trail they followed after.

Nyla leapt over a small brook, Xander close behind her. The terrain became more intense, but the smoke led them in such a way that it made their trek almost easy, even as sharp points of the onyx-colored stone jutted up toward the sky. Nyla and Xander wove around these, but the smoke caressed each and every point of stone, almost as if it were saying hello. The farther Nyla and Xander followed the trail of smoke, the more points crept up from the onyx ground until they could barely maneuver around them.

When the soothing trickle of flowing water reached her ears, Nyla perked up. This had to be it. The body of water they were nearing *had* to be Fortune Falls.

Nyla parted the bushes in front of her and pushed a low-hanging branch out of her way. It was just a river. Deflated, she glanced up and down its banks, but there wasn't a bridge or dry point in sight. There was no telling how long the river was, only that it would delay them for too long.

"So, what now, Nyla?" Xander's voice held a hint of strained irritation. He pinched the bridge of his nose.

"We cross it?" She tilted her head, considering the river before them. The smoke trail bobbed in front of them, hovering over the crystal-clear water. It seemed to Nyla as though it were nodding, urging them on.

Dim sunlight danced on the river's surface. It was barely a glimmer, but it was there all the same. Somehow, those thin beams from the sun had found their way through the thick canopy of now fully indigo leaves. Nyla inhaled deeply and exhaled slowly. There was only one way across, and that was to climb and walk on the rocks and boulders dotted throughout the river.

She scanned the water in front of her. Her plan was possible, though the farther from the shore she looked, the distance between the rocks increased. Nyla started out anyway. The smoke led the way, even as it continued to tenderly caress each onyx-colored obelisk as they went.

The rough, gray rocks of the river were a stark contrast to the world around them. Nyla wondered if the slabs were porous, but they were strong and mostly dry as they stuck out just above the water's surface. She glanced behind her and motioned to Xander, who still stood on the bank of the stream. He was only a few yards behind her, his lips drawn into a thin line.

"Well, are you coming or what?" she called out to him.

"I guess so," he answered, his words clipped by exasperation. She waited for him to catch up with her, tapping her foot on the rock, before they pressed on.

They came to a huge slab of rock that had grooves and dips in it. Some of the grooves must've flooded during the last high tide because Nyla could just make out the slender fish-humanoid bodies of the taddlings, the offspring of fully grown taddles, which could out-leap any predator but one, swimming in the shallow pools of the granite's divots. A few feet past the sloped bowl of the rock slab, the stone created natural—if uneven—steps down to the smaller portion of the rock. It formed a hook that the water lapped at, not quite high enough to stay above the surface.

Their footsteps were soft, barely heard over the smooth trickle of water and the chirping of the little black-and-white speckled niphonies, who would probably sing the whole night long. Nyla was grateful for their chatter. The silence between her and Xander had grown uncomfortable again and filled her ears with static.

As they walked, the smoke wavered in front of them and led them across the river. Even as the stones started to become farther apart, the smoke waited for them before it dashed up the path only it could see.

When the pair finally made it across, Nyla turned to Xander, her brows raised. He just nodded. The smoke led the way, and hope crested in Nyla's chest the farther along it led them through the day.

The smoke brought them to a narrow path in the woods lined with the same ashen trees and sapphire leaves that grew in the rest of the Shadow Forest. The dirt beneath their feet was fine, gritty sand. The onyx-colored sheet beneath them just stopped, so unlike the gradual transition they had witnessed when they started off for Fortune Falls. The pair stopped at the clean edge of the onyx ground from the Shadow Forest's heart. The smoke bobbed in front of them as if it was urging them forward or to assure them that this was the way.

Nyla glanced at the trees along the path, an admittedly welcomed sight compared to the coal-dark trees with gnarled roots and bark that bit worse than thorns. Beyond the tree-lined path on either side of them, Nyla could only just make out the darkness of the Shadow Forest's heart. She let out a long breath.

As soon as her foot landed on the sandy path, the trail of smoke darted ahead to the fork in the road and pointed down the route to the left. And just as quickly as it had appeared at the edge of the unmarked grove this afternoon, it dissipated. The smoke had vanished into thin air without so much as a wave goodbye or prayer for good luck and safe travels.

Nyla broke off into a sprint toward the spot when Xander called after her. It was no use, and they both knew it. When he caught up to her, they looked at each other before looking down the path. With a glance down the right, it was clear that the smoke had gifted them with one final direction, and they followed it without a word.

***

Waning sunlight filtered through the canopy of sapphire leaves overhead. The Forest was still fairly dim, but enough light pierced through it to keep a small glimmer of hope, even as exhaustion ground Xander's determination down to a speck of dust, but he carried on. Not that Nyla or the all-too-personified cloud of smoke she'd insisted on following gave him much of a choice.

The longer they walked down the winding and curved trail, the more time Xander had to mull over nearly every life decision he'd ever made. On top of that, the events of the last year, though more specifically the last *week*, wore heavily on his mind.

Nyla was going to be the death of him. He knew that with a certainty that could not be shaken. It made him consider why he couldn't find it in himself to leave. They barely knew each other, had no obligation to each other, so why wasn't he compelled to leave? The sentiment clouded his mind, something he was actually grateful for, all things considering. But the realization came with a plethora of questions and blank gaps to fill in, none of which he could satisfy with an answer.

What exactly had happened to the ogre that night?

Xander, while he was certain he didn't have magic, reanalyzed everything he knew about it for about the millionth time. He knew that magic itself wasn't lethal; it was the Caster's art of wielding it that made it dangerous, much like bows and arrows were useless without an archer.

But how much did he really know about Nyla?

All through the perpetual night of the Shadow Forest's heart, and even the storm of several days ago, Xander hadn't been able to learn much about her. Well, other than what they'd shared over the fire the night of the ogre attack, and who knew for certain how many days had passed since then? You'd never know if you walked for twenty-four hours straight, and it sure gave a guy more than enough time to think. Xander cringed internally.

More like all the time in the world to *over*think.

Xander eyed the path on either side of them. From the ogre attack to the tricks of the dark Shadow Forest and now the wisp of smoke, Xander was beginning to regret the decision to come all the way out here, and for what?

He honestly wasn't so certain anymore.

Why *had* he decided to come all this way? Xander shook his head and focused on the path in front of him, and consequently Nyla, who strode a few paces before him.

Was this normal for her? Following signs or specters or whatever it was that the smoke actually was? How could she trust it, things she couldn't explain? Xander shook his head. Maybe she was just that determined—or desperate—to take a sip from Fortune Falls.

Whatever reason Nyla had for making the trek out here, she hadn't shared it, and now Xander was too afraid to ask. The ogre. The light. The pile of ash. The—

Xander's ears pricked. He tapped Nyla on the shoulder, and she startled, meeting his eyes distractedly.

"Do you hear that?" he asked excitedly.

Nyla shook her head and paused for a second. Her eyes lit up, and a smile tugged at her tired lips. Without so much as a word, they darted off in a sprint toward the direction of flowing water. Xander crashed through the underbrush at the end of the path and came to an abrupt stop at the edge of an open field, breathless, not from the run but from the simple beauty before him. He started to move forward but found that he couldn't, a little too dazed to believe that this was it.

Fortune Falls.

This was it. They'd made it.

A weight settled in Xander's chest that he couldn't explain.

And they'd made it earlier than he'd expected. They'd probably made it earlier than anyone had ever done before. They'd know for certain once they got back to civilization…if they left together or at least traveled through the heart of the Shadow Forest together again.

Maybe Nyla and her mysterious friend of smoke weren't going to be the death of him after all…

***

Bathed in moonlight, the waters of Fortune Falls sparkled with an iridescent sheen. An instant sense of peace enveloped Nyla. The blanket of security put her once-quaking nerves at ease. She grinned lazily, stuck in her place at the edge of the tree line. Xander shifted on his feet beside her. Was he just as awestruck too? Knocked dumb by immobility and relief that they'd actually survived their trek and could now reap the rewards of their journey?

Yes, that was it. They were both in too much exalted disbelief to do anything but stare, wide eyed and transfixed at the prize of their journey. Eventually, Xander seemed to snap himself out of his daze and strolled toward the body of water that fed the cascading water and the mouth of Fortune Falls.

Nyla stood at the edge of the trees for a minute longer, still too caught up in the fact that they'd made it to actually move. When she finally did come to stand next to Xander, she couldn't help herself.

"Is it too soon to say I told you so?" Nyla whispered, not wanting to disturb the tranquility.

Xander only chuckled under his breath, still gazing out over Lake Prienamord.

In the peaceful quiet of Fortune Falls, she realized how her joints were sharp and achy and how her whole body was about ready to collapse. A yawn escaped her lips. Nyla blinked, her eyes watery.

"What now?" Xander asked quietly.

"I don't know. We're finally here, and I'm actually content with just that right now," Nyla answered.

Xander exhaled, humming a little. "I'm going to sleep. See you in the morning."

"Yeah. Goodnight, Xander." She stood at the edge, soothed by the waterfall flowing into the basin of Lake Prienamord. She smiled softly again before she joined Xander at their campsite in the glade.

Tucked into her sleeping bag a few feet from where a lightly snoring Xander lay on his side, Nyla struggled to keep her eyes focused on the twinkling night sky. Everything was so peaceful, and she couldn't help but keep her eyes open, picking out all her favorite constellations. She made new ones too, but she knew she wouldn't remember them in the morning.

8. WATER FROM THE FALLS

Bright, unfiltered sunshine blinded Nyla as her eyes fluttered open. She wet her slightly parted lips, wanting nothing more than to roll over and get some more sleep. Her entire body ached, from her bones, which were almost knobby from how badly they hurt, right down to her tightly coiled muscles. She couldn't move without groaning and for a second considered not moving at all. Then her mind registered the glare of pleasant sunshine in her eyes and stopped. She stared up at the sky, well aware that there were always aches and pains, so that was nothing new.

Clouds floated peacefully along the azure sky, completely undisturbed.

Nyla bolted upright. Her heart beat faster in her chest. The memory of where she was and who she was with slammed into her like a stampede of wild things. It was with that triumphant recollection that Nyla struggled to scramble out of her sleeping bag. The extra blanket she'd used the night before was twisted around her legs, and no matter which way she tugged and unwound her blanket, she couldn't quite free herself. The rustle of the blanket and sleeping bag was like a clap of thunder in the tranquil morning. Her hands stopped. She glanced around, half expecting Xander to be glaring at her, but he was already gone, his things neatly packed away where he'd slept.

Finally free from her confines, Nyla spun in a slow circle.

In the crowning light of day, she saw the sparkling pool of water before her. It was only a small pool of water, the exact opposite of what she'd expected. It must've been deeper than it looked because its depths were enough to feed Fortune Falls. The lake was perfectly round, much to Nyla's disturbed surprise.

That couldn't be natural, but then again, there was nothing natural about this place. Yet, at the same time, there was. Even though it was supposedly formed by magic, it was still a part of nature, and therefore, she reasoned, the lakes—and Fortune Falls—had to be natural.

Nyla turned away from the upper basin and studied her other surroundings. Her whole body felt stuffed with buzzing bees. She always imagined the Falls to be grander. Whenever she thought of Fortune Falls as a kid, she thought of a fairy glade or something similar, with a huge waterfall and a grand, shimmering lake. It was supposed to be serene and unlike anything she had ever seen before. In reality, she had seen something like this before. Waterfalls like this were everywhere. The shimmering lights and mystique disappeared from her mind's eye.

There was still something about it, though, beyond the peacefulness and beauty that made it seem as though the waters possessed a wisdom unbeknownst to humanity.

How could something so underwhelming be so powerful?

The clearing was lined by hopple trees, an almost round fruit sweeter than honey and crisp like a perfect Harvum day, as if the Forest wanted to provide the Falls' visitors with everything they needed to survive. Nyla approached one and plucked the fruit off its branch.

As she ate, Nyla walked over to the edge of upper pool, intent on examining Fortune Falls from above. The slope was steep on the side she stood, but the other side was a gentle incline that had been worn smooth. She crossed over the fallen log that rested over the flowing water to the other side of the Falls. There, she found Xander sitting on a rock shelf close to the waterfall. He didn't notice her, and for that, Nyla was grateful.

She stared at the sparkling water, not quite sure what to do. She thought it would be simple: wake up, drink from the Falls, and be on her way. That was her plan, anyway. But now?

Hypothetical scenarios flashed through her mind. Each one twisted the nerves that sat in her stomach more than the last. What if drinking from Fortune Falls only led to more questions than answers?

What if they deemed her unworthy of their blessing?

What if this wasn't what she really wanted and only led to more anguish?

What if the Falls were just another run-of-the-mill waterfall?

With each uncertainty, her absent gaze shifted away from the waterfall.

"Hey," Xander called up.

Heat crept along Nyla's cheeks as she blinked away her inner demons and faraway stare. She'd only just realized that her stare appeared to be focused on Xander and barely managed to keep herself from cringing.

Nyla offered what she hoped wasn't a sheepish smile and called back to him, "Morning."

She slid down the incline and edged her way to the ledge where Xander sat. The rock shelf was sturdy and smooth beneath her bare feet. Nyla bit back a laugh. In her haste, shoes hadn't even crossed her mind. She sat down next to him and wanted to ask if he'd drank from the Falls, but stopped herself. This sort of thing was too precious, too personal, too *sensitive* to share with others.

Protected by the granite wall's shadow and gently caressed by the mist produced from the gushing water in front of them, their shelf was bathed in coolness compared to the blazing sun of the clearing beyond. Tuning out the rest of the world once again, Nyla stared at the crystal waters, at *answers*. Xander shifted next to her, breaking Nyla away from her thoughts.

"I can't do it," Xander whispered softly.

"What do you mean?" Nyla blinked, her own unspoken concerns passing by unnoticed.

"Since we got here, I've been thinking: is it worth it?" His voice shook as he continued, "What if it isn't what I hoped it would be? What if I'm better off without it?"

Nyla chuckled under her breath. "I've been wondering the same things. I think that that's normal. My father used to wonder if the Falls gave you what you *needed* instead of what you wanted." She paused, lost in the memories of bedtime stories from a lifetime ago. She shook them away and continued, "That's terrifying, especially when what you 'need' just might be…" She trailed off.

Sometimes what you needed wasn't something you were ready to face.

Or worse, sometimes what you needed was your undoing.

For a while longer, the pair sat there and let their legs dangle, completely out of reach from the rest of the world, trapped by their own thoughts.

***

Xander understood exactly what Nyla had left unsaid. It was a fear that had taunted him all morning.

So many people before them had sought these mystical waters. The presumed few who made it had probably drunk and gone on their way, happy and sated with the achievement of their greatest desire, but now that he was here…

He couldn't do it.

Faced with the flowing waterfall, Xander found that these waters could grant him nothing. He hadn't come for riches or love or any other trivial thing and certainly nothing tangible. So what exactly could these waters grant his weary heart?

There wasn't anything.

When there were people involved, these waters couldn't grant him any kind of assurance about how things might play out. Drinking from the

Falls might only give him false hope, and that wasn't something Xander thought he could survive. Not after so much loss and grief, anyway.

Then there was that small part of him that was terrified. He wasn't an awful person, he knew that, but it didn't stop the insecurities from clouding his mind. He might not have lived a life of bad deeds and disgrace, but he certainly hadn't been the best he could have been. Xander didn't want the Falls to judge him for that, for the things he'd said when he'd left home.

By all means, he didn't deserve to drink from these waters. And he probably would've never made it had it not been for the undeterred and unconventional woman beside him. He hadn't made it to Fortune Falls because the Shadow Forest blessed him. He'd only made it because they'd blessed her.

Whatever brought Nyla here, it was something the Falls deemed her worthy of.

The realization stunned him. Questions bombarded his mind, but he forced his lips to remain shut. He couldn't ask them. Nyla deserved her privacy, and he shouldn't go prying into things that were most definitely none of his concern. It probably wouldn't end well anyway, especially since they were still technically strangers even if they had managed to traverse the Shadow Forest together and miraculously survive an ogre attack.

As the scene replayed in his mind for the umpteenth time, Xander reconsidered everything he'd been able to glean about Nyla and what he knew of magic.

***

Time didn't seem to pass as they sat and watched the Falls flow into the basin of Lake Prienamord. Birds swooped low over the lake, sometimes to catch fish, but more often than not, they kept flying. He wondered about the birds who caught their fish from Lake Prienamord. Did they die? Were they affected by the waters like humans who drank from the lake? He didn't have an answer and instead stared absently into the waters below them.

The pair didn't move again until both their stomachs were grumbling, and by that time, Xander was forced to squint his eyes against the light. With the sun smiling high overhead, they dragged themselves up the slope of pebbles and mud and crossed over the waterfall's makeshift bridge to their campsite from the night before. The small fire between their two sleeping bags was reduced to nothing but cooled embers. Xander grabbed his bow and sheath of arrows. He offered to find something more than hopples to eat, knowing full well Nyla could seize this chance to drink from the Falls and maybe even leave.

***

Nyla waved him off, hoping he'd take all the time in the world. She stayed and watched his retreating back until he finally disappeared into the woods. Nyla waited a few more moments, taking the time to shake out her blankets and sleeping bag, packing them away, and tried to decide what she'd do after she drank from the Falls. She no longer needed a map and compass; she could leave as soon as she wanted, without even saying goodbye, let alone thank you.

Nyla shrugged her shoulders.

Later, she promised.

Those were all problems Nyla could face and mull over *after* she drank from the Falls. Right now, she wanted to take full advantage of her privacy and Fortune Falls.

Nyla clamored back down the slope to the shelf they had sat on moments earlier. She stood, admiring the shimmering waterfall once more, and fought her mounting anxiety. She *needed* to do this.

Again, Nyla sought out the legends that had been a comfort to her for so long. The legends her parents had used as bedtime stories.

The legends that promised those who drank from the Falls obtained their greatest desire.

She took a slow step forward. Her legs were like jelly, and so she took a deep breath to steady herself. Her body—her hands especially—quivered, humming with nervous energy. The spray from the waterfall kissed her face, a gentle comfort that soothed her nerves and *shushed* her fears.

Standing close to the shelf's edge, Nyla could just reach out her cupped hands and collect some water from the Falls. Bringing her cupped hands back, Nyla took a step closer to the rock wall behind her. She studied her reflection in the water, her purple eyes staring curiously back at her. Dirt had settled like freckles on her face, making her cringe internally. Conscious of the fact that water had begun to slip through her fingers, she brought her hands to her lips and drank.

Nyla's head spun, and she found herself staggering backwards. Her back crashed into the granite wall behind her. She flushed, heat blossoming outwards from her heart before it settled in every fiber of her being, from the tips of her fingers straight through to her toes. Just as quickly as the heat had come, a cool energy swept through her, lapping at her soul like waves on the sand. Consumed by breathlessness, Nyla gasped for air. Her vision clouded over, but when it cleared again, Nyla saw the flames that had devoured her home. Even now, that eternal flame ate away at the thatched roof and wooden rafters.

As Nyla watched, a flaming timber, charred from the licking of the orange flames, snapped away from its supports and crashed to the ground below. But what was worse was the thick, black smoke that curled in the air and choked her lungs once more. She stumbled back, her knees buckling. For a single, fleeting moment, she thought the Falls had brought her back in time, but she didn't think it was possible to do so.

It didn't matter what she thought, only that she was reliving this grief and desperate helplessness all over again.

Nyla watched in desperation as her younger self watched the blaze destroy her home, held back by the neighbor who had just pulled her from the flames. As her younger self wailed and fought against the grip that struggled to pull her away, more neighbors arrived on scene to extinguish the flames.

Nyla couldn't bring herself to look any longer, even though she knew what happened next. When she was finally able to bring herself to her feet again, Nyla turned her back on the fire. Her face was soaked and flushed with tears as she wiped them away and took a long, shuddering breath. When she glanced up, her eyes were met with the sight of the smoke-obscured tree line.

Through the smoke, she saw a figure standing, nearly hidden by the brush, at the edge of her family's property. Nyla ran toward it and called out, almost tripping when she came to an abrupt stop. The man's face was hidden by shadow, but Nyla could see that his eyes glowed with a hatred she couldn't understand, his gaze firmly fixated on the flames behind her. His gaze shifted from the house to something else. Nyla turned to see what made him frown and saw her past-self collapse, and it was at that point that her neighbors had stopped trying to coax her away from the rubble, to safety, to mercy. Distraught, they'd stopped trying to salvage what was left of her childhood by whisking her away from the destruction of everything she'd known, had held dear.

Her head snapped back to look at the cloaked man again. The figure's scarlet-colored eyes sparkled, but with what, Nyla couldn't tell. Everything about him was severe, cold, *hollow*. Her blood froze in her veins. Worse yet, she didn't know him, had never seen him before in her life. So why was he here, at this moment?

Did he…*had he set the fire?*

Nyla couldn't help but take one more glance over her shoulder, but when she turned back around to face the man, he'd vanished.

The scene faded from her mind, and another took its place.

Unlike before, Nyla's body was swept away, pulled by an invisible current. She tried desperately to claw her way back to the scarring memory, wanting to get a better look at the man with scarlet eyes, but the current dragged her farther and farther away. Her vision went white.

A calm swept over her before the waves crashed over her again. She didn't notice when her vision cleared again. It was too hazy to see anything. A high-pitched whine rang in her ears, and then there was a rush of white static.

Chaos erupted.

Thick, gray smoke choked her lungs and obscured her vision. The ground radiated a sickly, scorching heat. Her body instantly flushed. She wondered if she'd been dropped near the site of a volcanic eruption. A harsh, moaning wind dragged the smoke across the land. Explosions like thunder clapped eerily close, while others sounded as though they were farther off. Metal clashing against metal clanked in her ears. Gruff voices came from all around her. Some shouted, some grunted, and others howled.

It was then that she realized the smoke had the odor of burnt sulfur, a smell that wasn't unlike rotten eggs but was much more bitter and acidic. It only got worse as the near and far explosions kept booming.

Her skin prickled. Nyla turned on her heel, trying to find some clarity, when the dreadful silence returned. Through the haze, she saw a glowing, lilac-colored dome. A shield. She staggered toward it.

Salvation was too far away. Before Nyla could take more than ten steps toward it, people started to wail in what could only be horrible agony. Heavy thuds sounded from all around her. Wood cracked in the distance, falling with reverberating crashes. The smoke was sucked to a central point that she couldn't see, the soft dirt beneath her feet stirring. Streaks of a vibrant crimson shot passed her, blurring her vision. In the distance, where the smoke from the field met, the scarlet morphed into a pulsing black ray. But the glowing red kept coming, washing over her until she was finally forced to shield her eyes from the blinding light.

Darkness eclipsed the world around her. In the distance, she could just make out that little dome of purple. It pulsed weakly, but it still survived. She stumbled toward it. Her feet tripped over and bumped into unseen things in her path. Tree roots, she prayed. Her breath came in shallow pants.

A gust of wind slammed into her. The air was knocked from her lungs, and she fell to her knees as though someone had tackled her with all their weight. The world burst with a searing light. Nyla barely noticed the bleak ground she knelt on, finding it strange that the dirt had changed color.

The wave of color didn't stop.

Yellows, blues, reds, and every color in between swept over the land, but the power behind it was too much. It stole the oxygen from the air, creating a vacuum.

A harsh wind stirred the ashen sand beneath her, blowing it into her face. Nyla threw her hands up and squeezed her eyes shut. Her hair whipped around her as the wind continued its unforgiving assault.

The howling subsided. When the air finally returned and stood still, Nyla brought her arms down. She shyly peeked out with one eye at the world around her.

Shock flooded her veins at the scene that had been unveiled. She found herself standing as she turned on her heel, taking it all in. Trees with crackled bark the color of coal stood where none previously had. Thick and plentiful, the trees she recognized as those that only grew in the heart of the Shadow Forest cut off her view of anything else. Nyla whirled around and around, trying to regain a sense of self and grounding.

Coal-dark trees. Ground of onyx-colored rock. Indigo leaves. The Shadow Forest.

But *how?*

Nyla's hands flew to her temples and pushed the hair back from her face. She gripped the strands absently, forgetting to let go as shock overwhelmed her.

None of this—the trees, the ground of rock, the leaves—was here before…before the—what *was* that?

A two-tone whistle echoed through the trees. Nyla's hands dropped.

Her head snapped in its direction. Another two-tone whistle followed it, its caller repeating the signal for anyone to hear.

Twigs snapped in response, the call coming closer with each heartbeat.

A voice, a woman's voice, cut through the trees next. "There aren't any survivors! *She killed everyone!* Now do you understand what we're up against?"

"What would you have me do?" a gruff voice answered. "Call off the search?"

Nyla edged through the trees toward the sound of the pair of voices. Her eyes darted everywhere. Every sound, every rustle of the wind through the dimly illuminated trees, set her on edge. It was like she'd never left the Shadow Forest, had never made it to Fortune Falls, but she knew better. She'd made it, had drunk from its waters, and now whatever these visions were meant to show her, they were all the proof she needed to ground herself in reality. Now if only she knew what they were meant to show her…

"We need to return to the manor. Our last defense is there, whether we like it or not," the woman hissed.

Nyla stepped through the trees and entered a grove. An empty grove with an unnaturally round lake and a little waterfall. People—battle-weary knights—stood scattered around the grove, dazed and barely interested in the quarrel between the man and woman. Nyla's breath caught in her throat.

Fortune Falls? *This* was Fortune Falls?

But—*how?*

None of this was here before!

"And lead them right back to our citadel!" the man shouted through gritted teeth.

Nyla's breath hitched. The woman, the one who had just offended a military commander of sorts, could've passed for her double. The world was full of things Nyla found she couldn't comprehend today. First, the appearance of the Shadow Forest and Fortune Falls where it previously hadn't been and now a woman in her late twenties with silver hair and a lithe body.

"Did I stutter, General?" the silver-haired woman spat. She spread her arms, gesturing to the newly formed world around them. "Look at what has happened here today. She will stop at *nothing*. There are *no* boundaries she won't cross to exact her revenge on Tenebris. We have one last resort, and I think it's time we take it."

The general staggered back, rubbing the spot between his brows. He glanced sharply at her. "You don't mean—"

"Yes."

The man spat and swore in a manner that made Nyla's mouth gape open. Once his shock had worn off, the general stood to his full height and let out a long whistle that echoed through the trees. He barely looked at the woman again before he turned and strode away to the loosely assembled knights under his command.

The woman hesitated. Nyla watched as she glanced around the grove as if she was expecting something. A few knights stiffly walked through the trees on the opposite side of the grove, returning from their fruitless search for survivors at the haste of the long whistle. But the woman paid them no mind. No, her eyes landed on Nyla. Nyla sucked in a breath and held it.

Could she see her? Did the woman…did the woman know she was here?

Nyla stared back at the reflection of her lilac-colored eyes and subconsciously stepped forward.

But the ground washed away beneath her. The Falls' magic pulled her away from the scene, from the woman Nyla wasn't sure belonged to her future or the long-ago past. Nyla tried to claw her way back to that grove, to that woman and those chainmail-clad soldiers, but the pull of Fortune Falls' magic proved to be too strong for her desperation. Nyla's jaw dropped. But just as quickly as before, another image washed over her vision.

This time she found herself in a dimly lit chamber, a one-room cottage, she soon realized as her surroundings sharpened. Shelves lined one wall with a fireplace positioned at their center. A strong, wooden door stood proudly against her back. A workbench covered in scrolls and dust resided along the far wall, an equally burdened chair cast aside. The thumping of footsteps across a plush carpet made her head snap in the direction it came from.

A man stalked over to the workspace from a disheveled bed in the other corner of the room, and hunched over the workbench, immediately occupying himself with something Nyla couldn't see. Curiously, Nyla took the opportunity to glance around the room, taking in the dingy lighting and once-elegant lounger in front of the crackling fireplace. A cramped kitchen—if she could call it a kitchen—occupied the corner closest to her, while the opposite corner by the door must've been the washroom, as it was screened off from view by a curtain.

Maybe something would be able to give her a clue as to where she was or whose cottage she was in, but there was nothing. Whoever occupied the cottage didn't seem to *live* here or consider it their home.

As quietly as Nyla could, she tiptoed closer to the man, inching over the transition between the bare floor of the entry and soft carpet laid over the rest of the cottage. Cautiously, Nyla tried to peer over his shoulder. A scroll fell to the carpet with a hollow bounce as she positioned herself next to him. The man quickly turned his gaze on it, pausing. Nyla froze, her breath caught in her lungs.

Could he see her?

Nyla's eyes flitted up and found that he was staring at the scroll. He made no move to pick it up, and so she took this opportunity to study him.

The prickling icicles of rigid fear instantly replaced her relief as her eyes saw those of the man standing across from her. They were scarlet, exactly like the man's eyes from the first vision.

Nyla panicked as the pull of transitioning between reality and the vision produced by the Falls engulfed her. Before the current swept her away for good, she groggily glanced at the object on the workbench that seemed to transfix the man.

It was a crystal ball.

An image played on it, and in it, she recognized her sprinting form from just the other morning. With the startling realization that he had been watching her, acid rose in her throat.

Nyla was thrust back into her true surroundings, the spray of the waterfall dotting her face. Some other time, it would've revived her. There wasn't any comfort in it this time. She sank to her knees. Frustration and pain flared up and battled for dominance. In the end, tears won. Sobs shook her body. Nausea overwhelmed her, and for a moment Nyla thought she would be physically sick.

The man's face still floated behind her closed eyes. She let herself give in to the emotions raging war on her rationale and remained on her knees for some time. Another sob choked her. She swallowed thickly and attempted to steady her breathing. With the back of her hand, Nyla wiped the tears from her face and got up. Something wild was brewing inside of her. She wanted to run again. A plan started to form in her head, but it was rash and based solely on one fragment of thought: she had to leave. There wasn't a particular place Nyla wanted to go, but that didn't matter so long as she fled as quickly as possible.

Her hands shook against the granite wall. Numbness weighed her limbs down, but Nyla dragged herself up the slope and to her things anyway. Her bag was just as she had left it, her things mostly packed. Instead of finishing her task, Nyla found herself pulling out the almost-pristine shirt that was now too small for her and knelt on the ground. When it was unfolded, it revealed the portrait. She studied it again, tracing the lines of her family's faces, their smiles. She looked up at the sky as she knelt in front of her backpack. Puffy gray clouds covered the heavens. Her heart deflated. The fragile painting shifted in her loose hold.

***

"Hey!" Xander glanced up and smiled, calling out to Nyla so he wouldn't startle her. She was kneeling before her bag where they'd made camp that night, intent on something he couldn't see. His smile faded almost as instantly as it had formed. Even if he hadn't known her for long, he knew something was wrong. Very wrong. Xander picked up his pace to meet her in the center of the Falls' meadow. "Are you okay?"

At the sound of his voice, Nyla flinched and hid whatever it was she was looking at between the folds of a shirt that she gingerly replaced in her bag. She didn't move to look at him and stared blankly at the bag in front of her.

"I don't know." Her voice was weak and small. She sniffled and wiped the wetness from her tear-stained cheeks.

Xander drew closer and crouched in front of her. Nyla didn't move.

"I didn't think you'd be back so soon," she said. A coolness slipped into her voice, despite its hoarse cracking.

"Packing up?" Xander asked, his voice a little strained. Nyla nodded. "It's past noon. At least wait until morning to start out again."

"Why do you care?" she spat, jumping to her feet. Xander followed her cue, shifting from foot to foot. "We're perfect strangers, and while I'm grateful for your help, I need to leave. Now."

The sun ducked behind a cloud. A muscle twitched in Xander's jaw.

"It's late," Xander pointed out. "And there's some rain coming."

"So? I can manage, thank you very much," Nyla replied, her fists clenched at her sides.

Xander, instead of seeing the purple-eyed, silver-haired girl before him, saw a proud-eyed girl with raven hair. That girl stood with squared shoulders and a stubborn gleam in her angry eyes.

Xander was swept away to a bitter Serenmae day, when the sky was gray and the occasional snow flurry floated down from the depressed clouds above.

95

His teeth chattered, but he kept running. The blistering wind slapped his face until he was raw, even more so than from the fight that still echoed in his ears. His nose was as numb as his hands. None of this stopped him though. He had to get to her. They'd both said things they'd regret, and as the older sibling, it was his job to apologize, to stop her from doing something stupid. Xander focused what was left of his energy and caught up to his sister. She stopped when his hand grasped her shoulder, effectively stopping her from taking another step.

"Where are you going?" he panted.

She turned to him, anger and tears in her eyes. He wasn't sure if the tears were from the wind or remorse. But when she opened her mouth, Xander decided it didn't really matter what put them there.

"Like you care!" she shouted.

"I do! I'll always care about you, Issie," he hissed back.

Issie shook her head. Her lip wobbled, but anger raged in her eyes.

"You always say that, but you never show me. You and Grandfather are exactly the same. All you care about is control and what's best for you! And the rest of us? What's best for us?" Issie shook her head, her lips twisted bitterly. "Neither of you care what's best for us so long as you're taken care of and you're getting what's best for you."

She didn't give Xander a chance to respond. Issie turned on her heel, her hair nearly whipping Xander across the face like a final slap. Xander watched her leave, knowing there was nothing he could do to stop her. Her mind was made up, and maybe getting out from under their thumbs was what was best for her.

So Xander watched her go. He watched her go without so much as a goodbye or a reminder that he did *love her. He just didn't know what to do or what was best for either of them. He was her brother, not her parent. And their grandfather? Xander grimaced and shoved the thought away. He watched, shivering, as Issie reached the bend in the road.*

She barely took a step around the curve. Something big leapt from the thick bushes of the woods beside the road. Issie shrieked. Xander stood, rooted to the spot before he jolted into action, wishing for all the world that he'd pushed harder to bring her home, to delay her in some way.

"Issie!" Xander sprinted forward, reaching them in no time at all as if Balmae had granted him wings, and tackled the beast, a wolf-like demon that reeked of death. Xander blindly stabbed the hellhound with his hunting knife over and over again. It whimpered, throwing him off of itself. Xander rolled, his muscles coiled and ready to spring at the beast again. But the beast had barely taken a couple steps toward the wood before it collapsed.

Xander knelt next to Issie. Dried blood marred her skin, her throat torn. Fearful, glassy eyes stared up at him as he cradled her body, uncertain of what to do, like always. It was too late. He *was too late.*

Always too late.

As Issie had gone, so did the memory. Xander remained in that fog for a moment longer. He always took a few seconds to adjust, to shove the knot of frustration and helplessness—of blame—from his conscious mind. Instead, those emotions only grew stronger, and suddenly, he had someone to direct them at.

But it wasn't Nyla's fault.

It wasn't really anybody's fault; some part of him knew that. That didn't stop him from accusing himself of Issie's murder.

"Xander…" Nyla began softly.

Xander blinked. With a tight shake of his head, he stiffly walked away from her, recognizing the distinguished threat of an emotional collapse looming on the horizon and wanting nothing more than to be far, far away when it happened.

***

In that moment, Nyla watched as Xander's eyes unfocused, withdrawn or whisked away to someplace she couldn't reach but knew so well.

Whatever it was that had stolen him away, it replayed before Xander's eyes, and Nyla watched the clenching and unclenching of his fists. Concern spread through her like wildfire as his muscles tensed before her eyes, and she could do nothing to bring him back from whatever caused the haunted expression to etch itself upon his face.

Nyla watched Xander's retreating back until he disappeared once more into the Shadow Forest. She huffed and glanced up at the darkening sky. A fat drop of rain landed on her forehead and rolled down between her eyes. She frowned and abandoned her pack where she stood. With her knife now in hand, Nyla began to cut branches for a lean-to big enough for herself and Xander—if he ever returned.

By the time she was done and had pulled all their things under the cover of the shabby lean-to, it had begun to pour. Luckily, the branches she crouched under held, and the storm brought only rain. For the first time, Nyla felt secure. She even built a small fire under the cover of the trees and cooked the temporarily forgotten small animal Xander had hunted. There was enough left over for Xander to eat, though it wasn't much.

The longer the time stretched by with no sign of Xander and only her thoughts to occupy herself with, Nyla grew worried. She resigned herself to waiting. Her eyes drooped, and she brought her knees to her chest, grabbing a blanket from the pile of their stuff, and was eventually lulled to sleep by the rain against the branches. Her dreams contemplated the visions from the Falls, so much so that all she could see was the scarlet of the mysterious man's eyes.

Nyla barely registered when Xander returned, completely drenched. She didn't hear his footsteps or the low muttering when he couldn't find what he was looking for in his bag.

Instead, Nyla heard the roar of a fire, a two-tone whistle, and the pounding of her heart in her ears.

She vowed to confront the red-eyed man.

Temperance

A chill ran down Cedric's spine. He knew it was common for people to, on occasion, get a whiff of a familiar scent for no apparent reason, but sensing a magic signature that shouldn't exist anymore? That was impossible.

Could it be her spirit? Or would her spirit have moved on into the afterlife? Bitter hope swelled in his chest. He sent a tentative glance over at Dia. The raverin, a large bird native to Tenebris with the body of a raven, but about the size of an eagle, and just as regal, was sound asleep on his perch above the fireplace. Whatever this presence was, his keen-sensed companion hadn't been disturbed by it. That fact begged the question about whether the presence was truly there. The chill writhing down his spine would not cease. There was something there. There just had to be.

Cedric stiffened and, without moving, reached out with his own magic to find the source of this old, familiar essence like a hound might scent its prey. The crystal ball before him was long gone, forgotten in his search for the thing that made him question his sanity.

There it was.

A scroll rolled off of the workbench and fell to the floor beside him. It landed precisely beside where the old magic lingered, and Cedric grasped at the chance to stare the trace down.

He turned toward them both. Empty air and a dusty scroll greeted him. Cedric hesitated. There was nothing there. It was only a fallen scroll. Perplexed, Cedric turned his attention back to the crystal ball.

Whatever presence he thought was there left. It fled just as quickly as it had come, and Cedric wondered if it *was* possible to feel long-gone signatures like it was to smell smoke when there was no fire or the scent of a childhood home when you hadn't stepped foot in it in ages.

He shook his head. The crystal ball dimmed and sputtered out like a flame. Cedric stared at it for a moment longer. His reflection was distorted, though it was the same as it had been for forever. The wrinkles and gray hairs that should've been there weren't. Where a skeleton should be was a living, breathing man with decent health and warm flesh.

Cedric frowned and turned away. It didn't do any good to dwell on the past or how he'd frozen his future.

He bent and picked up the scroll. With a swipe of his thumb, Cedric cleared away the thick layer of dust. He couldn't even guess what the scroll was, and curiosity got the better of him before he could set it back on the table.

Carefully, Cedric untied the delicate string that kept the scroll from unrolling. The paper was dry and brittle beneath his fingers. Gingerly, he opened it.

His blood boiled. He had half a mind to burn the scroll now that he knew what it was and, with it, the taunting portrait he'd sketched all those years ago. His fingers slipped from the bottom edge as he flinched.

It snapped shut. Behind him, Dia squawked, evidently woken up by the paper *slapping* shut. Cedric turned simmering eyes on the bird, who ruffled his feathers and returned a well-matched glare of disapproval.

"I envy you," Cedric said quietly. The gleam in Dia's eyes softened, becoming curious. "You could fly away, never to be bothered by manifestations of your own guilt or nightmares or years of—of doing nothing."

Dia said nothing in response. Not even a solemn *cawing* to acknowledge the hollow truths Cedric hadn't dared to share with anyone else before the hulking bird. He didn't know what he expected. Dia could offer no sympathy, only a companionship bound by duty.

Even so, Cedric wished he would fly off and never return. He couldn't explain why the fork-tongued creature kept coming back. If their positions were reversed, Cedric wouldn't come back. He'd never so much as spare a glance back at this wretched cottage and its haunting magical essences from centuries long since passed.

Cedric's eyes darted back to the rolled-up scroll, to the portrait. A relic. Only one of many, but the only one he'd kept after all these years. And for what? To feed his anger? To taunt his guilt?

Clenching his jaw, Cedric turned on his heel. Dia *cawed* at him reproachfully from his disrupted sleep. As if sensing his agitation, Dia flapped his wings. In one short swoop, the bird was right behind him. Cedric threw the cottage door open as Dia burst ahead of him into the dazzling sunlight. He let the door slam shut with a grimace. Watching the raverin swoop and circle above him, Cedric battled the tidal wave overwhelming his bloodstream.

9. THE CURSED GIFT

The morning hours went by in a daze. Time passed slowly at first, with Nyla waking up under the lean-to, completely alone, and then the hours were gone within a blink as she tried in vain to keep herself occupied.

Upon waking, her brows knitted with the frown of her lips. The disturbance of Xander's mysterious absence was quickly diminished by the sight of his things piled neatly next to her own in between their sleeping bags.

Armed with fresh clothes and some semblance of wakefulness, Nyla stumbled out of her hasty lean-to and along the sloping ground around the body of water. The ground roughly leveled itself out to make the pebbled shoreline of Lake Prienamord below. After a thorough glance around, Nyla quickly shed her clothes at the base of Fortune Falls and moved behind the cascading water. The granite wall behind the waterfall was rounded out, forming a calm grotto, hidden away from the rest of the world.

The water was cool but comfortable as Nyla slowly lowered herself into the water. Submerged from the waist down, her body was wracked with an involuntary shiver. She reached for the washcloth she'd placed on the narrow ridge carved deep into the face of the granite and began to scrub at the dirt on her skin. The square cloth was scratchy, and its original deep maroon was far beyond recognition, now nothing more than blotches of petal pink and sun-bleached white.

She even tried to wash away the worries growing inside of her, but to no avail. The images or hallucinations—or whatever they were—from the Falls played over and over in her mind. The more she tried not to think of them, the more they haunted her. Every time she sought distraction, her thoughts came back to, and lingered on, the scarlet-eyed man. He was so different, yet so much *like her*.

Nyla couldn't help but wonder what cruel twist of Fate had done this, had intertwined their lives, as she dragged herself out of the water and perched precariously on the granite ridge along the back wall of the grotto. Xander could be back any second. The intruding fears could return from the edges of her mind any second. Whatever peace she'd felt upon entering this glade was only temporary, an illusion from Fortune Falls' magic.

Consumed by the Falls and the red-eyed man, the same questions turned over in Nyla's mind once more. Who was he? What did he want from her? Why was he watching her?

Was he watching her now?

Nyla stood on shaky legs, on edge thanks to her traveling thoughts. With the weathered blanket she reserved for this purpose only, she quickly dried herself off. The makeshift towel was nothing more than bare threads in some places. She bent over and wrapped the towel around her head and brought the ends toward the crown of her head to twist her hair in to dry. Nyla dressed quickly in an attempt to chase away the goosebumps.

She edged her way along the slippery rock-shelf of the grotto back toward the lake's shore. Before she made her way up the slope to the upper lake, Nyla undid the towel twist from atop her head and shook out the long, tangled strands of her hair. She ran her fingers through the drying mass and began to work through the bird's nest it had become. As she crested the slope again, Nyla's mind turned to the other worry tickling the edges of her mind. Where was Xander? Nyla bit her lip. Maybe he was sitting by the Falls again or…

Nyla spied the lean-to. She took a quick peek on the other side of the log bridge to see if Xander might be there before she continued on her way. The smooth waters of the upper basin lapped at the smooth pebbles on its banks. Her chest fell. Xander was still nowhere to be seen.

Had he already come and gone?

Nyla pressed onward with a frown as she struggled to keep the towel and her dirty clothes bundled under one arm. Her fingers absently worked through her hair. It was a relief when she could reach out and part the curtain of leaves to duck and enter the rough shelter. Xander hadn't snuck in, evident by the fact that his things were still next to hers. Nyla clicked her tongue, but remained silent as she dropped the bundle of clothes on her sleeping bag.

Squatting next to her backpack, her fingers wrapped around the smooth wood of her comb. She freed it from the depths of the bag's jumbled contents and started on her hair. Not to waste the beautiful morning, Nyla left the shelter and settled on a boulder by the shore of the perfectly round pool.

The position afforded her the best view of Fortune Falls, and the lean-to as well, in case Xander came back. Her stomach grumbled and squeezed at the emptiness inside her. In a moment, Nyla promised herself. She'd deal with her appetite in a moment, once her hair was under better control.

Her perch on the rock was soon abandoned as she sauntered toward the tree line. She carefully slipped the comb into her back pocket. Berry bushes grew a few feet into the forest, and for that, Nyla was grateful. Though she doubted that someone would miraculously turn up at Fortune Falls, she was hesitant to leave their things unattended for too long.

The shadow berries, a mauve-colored fruit that tasted as bright as a Hugony day and only grew in the Shadow Forest, were perfectly ripe and juicy. Every so often, Nyla plopped one into her mouth to quiet her stomach, wholly convinced that this was what warm sunlight after a rainstorm tasted like.

As the minutes wore on, Nyla began to hum absently. It wasn't anything in particular, but the song tugged at the edges of her memory. The melody was light and soft, but broken as the rest of the song was lost to her. She let the curiosity of it go, knowing she would never fully remember her mother's foreign songs.

When the pouch at her hip was chock full of berries, she returned to the quiet shores of the upper basin to wait for Xander, if he hadn't come back and left already. With her face turned up to the sun, Nyla assumed the picture of serenity. Everything about being at Fortune Falls radiated security. It was like all her worries had been denied entry—with the exception of the anxiety produced by what the Falls had shown her. But she didn't want to think about that now.

Still, the image of red eyes flitted across her mind. The goosebumps returned. Nyla turned her face toward the sun with closed eyes again, hoping the light would wash away the dark anxiety creeping its way inside her core.

The violent rustling of bushes made Nyla's eyes pop open. She snapped her head in the direction of breaking twigs and the clamor of something crashing through the underbrush. Her hand flew to where her knife sat on her hip, only to stumble over its absence.

Panic swelled and rose like bile in her throat. The quick *thump, thump, thump* of her heart pounded in her ears. Adrenaline slowed her surroundings down. Her mind moved too fast, rapidly trying to find something to defend herself with. As the bushes just yards away started to part in the wake of what was coming, Nyla brought her arm up as if she could push the threat away.

Nyla wasn't sure if she was trying to shield her eyes from what she dreaded was coming or getting ready to hit it, but she was sure of one thing: a streak of lightning sprang from her fingertips, effectively striking a grouping of leaves.

Xander emerged a second later, looking over his shoulder in the direction the lightning had soared. He paused to study the singed hole in the leaves of a low-hanging branch that was eerily too close to where he stood. When he turned and looked at her, it was plain bewilderment that was etched across his face. Nyla watched, mortified, as he sucked in a breath, hesitating at the tree line.

Nyla flushed as their eyes met. Everything was hot, sweltering even. She was almost certain that steam was coming out of her ears. No matter how much she willed her legs to move, Nyla was stuck to the ground she stood on. Xander cleared his throat and vaguely gestured to the singed leaves.

"Did you just try to *shoot* me?" he asked, stunned rather than angry or even afraid.

All Nyla could do was stand there and stare at her fingertips, her mouth agape, eyes wide with horror. Her hand still hung in the air. She was terrified of moving even a muscle.

Her eyes snapped up at the movement of Xander's approach. She backed away from him until the backs of her legs hit the bushes behind her. They seemed to wrap themselves around her, folding her into their leaves. Instead of shock or amazement at the potential of what she could do with her newfound ability, Nyla was absolutely terrified by the idea of possessing magic. When she finally found her voice again, she thought it was her duty to warn Xander.

"Don't, Xander. Just don't come any closer." Her lips trembled. Tears began to blur her vision. "I can't control it." She wanted to put her hand up to emphasize her point, but instead she clutched her hands to her chest, too afraid of the lightning that seemingly lurked inside her.

"It's all right, okay? I'm okay, really." Xander approached her like someone would a startled animal.

"You missed me by a long shot!" he added jokingly, an obvious attempt to soothe her and the growing tension in the air.

She jerked her shoulder away as Xander reached out to her, probably to coax her away from the bushes. Nyla couldn't even look at him. She expected to find fear—a mirror of her own thoughts—in his eyes, but no matter how she felt about herself and her newfound magic, Nyla couldn't bear to see it in someone else's eyes.

"I should go," she whispered, but made no move to do so.

"C'mon out of the bush and just take a second to think. Don't rush off again."

Nyla glanced up, a little dazed. She let Xander pull her away from the bushes and took comfort in the hand on her arm. She tried to fight the tears in her eyes. They fell silently down her cheeks until she wiped at them with a shaky finger. Exhaustion coursed through her veins, but she ignored it. A question tugged at her attention as Xander led her across the clearing.

***

Almost getting killed wasn't on the agenda today, and Xander had most certainly not expected his would-be murderer to actually *be* Nyla.

But he wasn't afraid or even wary. All it had taken was one look, and he knew she didn't know she could do that. His erratic heartbeat fizzled out as he led Nyla to the lean-to. A million questions piled up inside him, but he left them unsaid. It was obvious by her shock and panic that Nyla had no idea she had magic. Xander almost laughed.

How could someone *not* know they could wield magic?

"What did you mean by 'again?'" Nyla questioned as they walked back to the lean-to. He only hummed next to her, still digesting what had just happened.

He hadn't meant anything by what he'd said and didn't even mean to say it like that. He just assumed that, like himself, or even Issie,

Nyla was trying to outrun something. Unlike in his case, though, it might've just caught up to Nyla.

Xander parted the curtain of leaves for her and followed Nyla into the shelter. She tossed something in the direction of her bag as she sat, avoiding his gaze like the plague as he sat across from her. Neither one of them said anything. There wasn't anything Xander could think of saying, and instead, his mound of questions simmered inside of him.

He could only imagine the tidal wave of emotions hitting Nyla and kept his own questions to himself. He silently acknowledged that he was a little apprehensive of the answers he might get. He eyed Nyla with uncertainty, and when she finally looked up at him, it was a mixture of worry and shyness that shone in her lilac eyes.

"Do you think this is what happened the other night? With the ogre?" Nyla asked softly, her voice barely loud enough for Xander to hear over the light breeze outside.

"I don't know. Maybe?" He shrugged before voicing the curiosity burning inside him. "So…you really didn't know you had magic?"

Nyla shook her head weakly, distracted by her inner demons once again. Xander hoped she didn't see the doubtful gleam in his eyes.

"I know, I know. How could I *not* know, what with my hair and the color of my eyes? But they weren't *always* like this." She paused. Nyla bit her lip and slowly dragged her eyes away from her lap. She started and stopped again, as if the words wouldn't come. Finally, Nyla managed to force herself to speak. "I thought I was cursed, and it turns out that I *am*."

Of all the things Xander expected her to say, claiming to be cursed wasn't one of them. He couldn't help it. His immediate reaction was confusion and a quirked brow, maybe a good laugh. Unasked questions already took up residence in the space between them. Nyla sighed, taking him in silently. Xander considered voicing his questions, but he swallowed them down. It was better that Nyla told him at her own pace.

"I don't think you're cursed," he replied with quiet sincerity. Nyla blinked, and if he wasn't mistaken, she'd almost smiled.

The silent seconds ticked by. Nyla drew her knees to her chest and tucked a few strands of damp hair behind her ear. After a deep breath, Nyla told him everything. She persevered through difficult memories and a cracking voice choked by grief and explained everything from the fire to the change of her hair and eyes to her fear of being stalked.

Xander listened intently. He nodded thoughtfully on occasion and even asked a few questions to clarify some detail, like if anyone in her family had magic. She didn't know for certain.

And then she'd told him about the vision that Fortune Falls had shown her from the day of the fire. Xander sat stunned, in more ways than one.

So that's what drinking from the Falls was like? That's what it did? Would he experience something similar if he drank from them too?

Or so that's why Nyla was alone. She'd left everything and everyone she'd ever known behind her.

He tucked all that information away for another time as Nyla continued on and told him about the second vision Fortune Falls had presented to her—about the man and the cottage and the crystal ball.

"And so, when the Falls showed me that there was a man who was watching me, I just wanted to run again. And I still do," she rattled on. "I can't stay here, and who knows what he'll do now that I know? You could be in danger now too, just for getting me here and being around me."

"Just to be clear, you want to flee from a place that might be the safest in all of Tenebris because you're afraid that this man will find you?" Xander paused long enough for her to nod. He pursed his lips and carried on, almost chastising her. "Nyla, that's a lot of hypotheticals. I mean, why not stay here? It's perfectly protected by the Shadow Forest, and very few people can actually find it or even know where it is."

Nyla tossed her hair over one shoulder, obviously anxious by what he'd said. She frowned. "Well…when you put it like *that*, sure. But I want to keep moving. Staying in one place for a long time only makes it easier for something, *or someone*, to find you anyway. *I have to go.*"

Xander knew the storm clouds had rolled in again and stood, desperate to get some fresh air before Nyla saw the flurry of emotions crisscrossing his face. She definitely didn't need his baggage right now too, but he had to say something. He couldn't bear it if something like that happened to someone else while he just stood by again and let them do something without thinking it through.

"Please don't make the same mistake that Issie did," he said, his voice raw with guilt.

"Who's Issie?" she asked, puzzled.

"Never mind that. Just be careful, whatever you decide to do." With that, he parted the leaves and began to exit the shelter.

"Xander?" He stopped, not turning to face her. A heartbeat passed before Nyla continued, "Whatever happened, you shouldn't blame yourself for it. It'll only eat you alive."

***

They had eaten a late lunch in silence. Xander spent a good chunk of the afternoon and early evening perched on the shelf by the Falls while Nyla gave him some space. Even with all she had going on right now between Fortune Falls' visions and her newfound magic, Xander's mysterious comments and actions served as a great distraction from her own troubles.

Who was Issie? What did she mean to him? Were they family?

Nyla would probably never know for certain, but she guessed that Issie was his sister who had passed. And she knew that grief all too well.

Alone in the lean-to, Nyla sat on her sleeping bag and drew the portrait out from her bag. She was tired of reflecting on the Falls' visions and hoped that some kind of answer would jump out at her if she stared long enough at the portrait. Its protective shirt was draped over her lap, by far the cleanest garment she owned. The creases of the portrait were smooth and as familiar to her as the lines of her palm. She traced the faces of her family with the tip of her finger, and not for the first time since she drank from Fortune Falls, Nyla explored the possibility that she was the reason the man had killed her family, to get to her. But the theory begged the question: why? Too deep in thought to notice the soft glide of footsteps over the grass, she barely managed to conceal the portrait as Xander poked his head into the shelter.

"I'm gonna go hunting for dinner before it's too dark. Don't kill me when I come back," he laughed.

"I can't make any promises," she responded with a small smile, her hands up.

When Xander came back, nothing happened other than a gloriously warm fire and a quiet dinner. Nyla didn't ask where he'd gone off to or if he'd drank from Fortune Falls. It didn't seem appropriate to ask such a thing, especially with how little they knew of each other. Instead, they discussed what they would do next. Neither had anyone searching for them or waiting for them in a cozy house with safe, warm beds. In the end, they decided to travel through the Shadow Forest together because there's safety in numbers after all.

With that decided, the pair settled as contentedly as possible in the lean-to. Nyla lay on her back, her eyes open but unseeing. To her right, Xander was stretched out on his stomach, studying the map by the light of a single candle he had lit beside himself.

"Do you have to go back to Halberry?" Xander piped up, glancing over at Nyla.

"No. Do you?" Jerked out of her thoughts by his question, she replied without looking at him. Nyla flexed her ankles to stretch her legs before drawing them up with her feet planted on the sleeping bag beneath her.

"Well…no, not really." He paused. "I was thinking of going north, to Caselle. It's a 'city,' if you could even call it that, but according to the map, there's magical archives there too. Maybe they could be a good starting point for you?"

Nyla only heard the word "city," and just like that, apprehension and panic wound their way through her mind. She finally turned her head to look at him. He'd rolled onto his side, his head propped up in his hand, waiting for her to say something.

"A city...with archives?"

"Calling Caselle a 'city' is more of a technicality than anything else in my opinion. It connects several trade routes, including some along the river, but it isn't very big overall. It's maybe half the size of Huntington."

Nyla felt as though Xander's eyes were boring into her soul and shifted uncomfortably. His gaze was just so focused, and she couldn't stand to keep eye contact any longer. Still, though, even half of Huntington was huge in her opinion. Nyla couldn't even begin to picture herself in a town with people, let alone a city. Her heartbeat began to quicken as memories of the places like Halberry she'd passed through surfaced in her mind.

"I mean, I don't know. I wouldn't want to drag you along with me. If you want to go north, then so be it—I'll go north too. And then..." She paused and bit the inside of her cheek. And then *what*? She shrugged her shoulders as best she could while laying down. "I guess I keep walking, maybe take a peek at those archives, but I keep walking all the same."

"It's just an idea. If you don't want to go north, that's fine. We'll get out of the Shadow Forest and move on with our lives. It's completely up to you how you deal with that magic of yours—just don't try and shoot me again!" Xander snorted, his dark eyes twinkling in the candlelight.

The apprehension instantly left Nyla's body as her face broke out into a smile. She laughed, turning her head to look at him. "Oh, so you're back to that again, are you?"

"All I'm saying is that I was *almost* shot today. It's pretty terrifying that you have such good aim for someone who didn't know they had magic." His words hung in the air, the easiness of the moment before gone with the realization that Xander was right.

The sudden awareness of the unknown magical potential inside her made sleep a stranger. Nyla's twisting and turning all night long hadn't bothered Xander, though. No, he'd lightly snored all through the night. Finally, when she couldn't stand being immobile anymore, Nyla quietly stalked from the lean-to and practically shook the bleary-eyed birds out of their trees before the sun even rose.

10. CASELLE

It seemed to Nyla that it took them longer to navigate out of the Shadow Forest's heart than it had to get to Fortune Falls. The cracked, black bark of the trees slowly gave way to the peeling, ashen trees that everyone in Tenebris associated with the area and the Forest's legends. The sheets of onyx dissolved into pebbles nestled in the fine, amber dirt before they disappeared altogether. The leaves overhead were no longer pale and lifeless, but bright sapphire. A few leaves even showed the beginning signs of Harvum in the tiniest hint of teal and mossy green on their tips. The weight nestled in the pit of Nyla's stomach lessened with the familiar sight.

All too soon, the rough and untamed paths through the underbrush morphed into real roads and traveled paths. These were clear and well-kept compared to the wild forest on either side, and the farther the pair walked, Nyla knew the well-worn dirt roads would eventually turn into travel-beaten cobblestone, a sight she hadn't seen for weeks. Naturally, that was by design.

Whatever peace that had soothed Nyla when they entered the familiar sights of the Shadow Forest had fled when they reached the travelers' roads. Her gut twisted the farther north they traveled. She fidgeted as they both stared at the wooden crossroads sign while Xander consulted his map and compass, something they did frequently as they navigated the roads. Beside her, Xander shifted from side to side in an attempt to get the best light for reading. Nyla nibbled on her lip, staring up at the wooden street sign. One sign pointed in the direction of the river and the other toward a town called Magnolia. Neither sign meant much of anything to her as she wasn't the one holding the map.

"Okay…we need to head toward Magnolia, and from there we can either take a trade route or cut through some of the more rural…" He paused; his eyes flickered over to Nyla and took in her worried lip and downcast eyes. "Rural it is then."

"Thank you." Her voice was laced with relief and satisfaction. The hum of her nerves faded away for the moment.

Xander folded up the map and tucked it in his back pocket to lead the way. Nyla trailed a few steps behind him. The drive and force of energy that had flowed through her after she drank from Fortune Falls dissolved the longer she worked through the scenes the water had shown her and the rude discovery of her powers. Throughout the entire hike through the Shadow Forest and even now, Nyla found herself wondering the same question, repeating it in her head to the rhythm of their footsteps: how could this possibly be happening to her?

This sentiment was often followed by a crestfallen puff of air that seemed to ask, 'why me?' If Xander had any inkling of the sullen thoughts swirling around in Nyla's mind as they marched on, he didn't say a word.

The countryside passed Nyla by, as she was too lost in thought to care much about the rolling hills with patches of wheat fields or pastures with bigger livestock she couldn't name. Sure, a handful of people in her community kept small livestock, but nothing this big, horned, or noisy.

The road was dusty, lined by these fields and the weathered wood of pens, framed by the end-of-Hugony hues of the Shadow Forest's fiery flora.

It seemed like a century had passed before the pitted dirt road morphed into uneven cobblestone. The sun had started to set, creating long, wiry silhouettes on the earth's surface.

"Shouldn't be much farther now," Xander said absently. "I think we're nearing the edge of Caselle."

Nyla only hummed in response. Her memory forced her to relive the stares and whispers that followed her in Halberry. Her gut clenched and seemed to curl up into a ball much like a petrified child. As if her own apprehension wasn't grating on her nerves enough, the pebble that Xander kicked across the cobblestone only served to further irritate her nerves with each *clackity-clack-clack*. She didn't say a word, though. Afterall, he was kind enough to travel with her, and though Nyla wouldn't ever admit it aloud, she was grateful for the company. Even so, she managed a small smile when he'd lost the stone for good.

They walked in silence, each lost in their own thoughts until they'd stopped for dinner and found an easy topic of conversation. It was getting too late to visit the archives and start searching, so Nyla relented to wait until morning. She argued that they could camp for the night outside the city, fighting every fiber of her being to not bolt into the woods surrounding them and never come out.

"Suppose it rains?" Xander inquired, a cheeky smile playing on his face.

"There's plenty of shelter. You just have to find it." Nyla fought the urge to cross her arms. Stubbornness wove itself into her bloodstream, flooding her cells and nerves. She bit back the wave that bristled in her core and forced herself to relax. She turned her head away from the fire and glanced at the ground, picking at a thread on her too-loose pants. Almost inaudibly, she added, "Besides, I don't have any money for an inn."

As if he hadn't heard that last bit, and it's quite possible that he hadn't, Xander sighed long and dramatically in a way that Nyla had come to learn meant he was about to weasel his way into getting exactly what he thought was best.

"You're right, I guess, though finding shelter in the rain and dead of night is extremely difficult and impractical. I just thought it would be nice to sleep in a nice, warm inn with a *featherbed* and running water and a hot meal, a *real* meal, at the inn's tavern. But it's your call, whatever makes you happy," he tempted with a shrug of his shoulder.

Put like that, there was no way anyone could turn down a real bed. The corners of Nyla's lips turned down. She couldn't ask this, but at the same time, Xander was making it difficult to say no.

***

Xander had let the quiet between them drag on all through their journey, even as he wracked his brain for *something* to say besides some idle chitchat when Nyla was up for it. But what could he possibly say to someone in her situation? That's largely why Xander kept his mouth shut. There wasn't much of anything he could say, and even if words of comfort *did* come to him, would they actually help Nyla? Probably not. If he were in her shoes, he'd be spiraling down a dark tunnel, never to see the light of day again…or at least for a long while.

Still, Xander always assumed that people with magic knew about their powers practically from the time they were born. Then again, he had been taught that some forms of magic don't manifest until the coming of age at sixteen. Cases like that were rare, or at least from what he understood. It usually had something to do with fairy magic and humans. Or a prophecy of sorts. Those were only part of legends and myths, stories told to explain events and natural occurrences before philosophy and science. He didn't really believe in legends all that much and chose to acknowledge the possibility of another explanation. After all, there *had* to be a reasonable explanation for everything—even magic.

He'd set all that aside for days. It wasn't really his business, but they were here now, and he couldn't just abandon her like this, so what was a little more time spent together? He put all his efforts into convincing Nyla to stay at one of the inns, safe and not entirely on her own. They didn't even have to stay at the same inn. He just figured they'd spent quite a time hiking, so what was the harm?

Besides, nobody could deny themselves a proper bed and a hot meal.

"Featherbeds?" Nyla echoed in response. Piqued interest dripped from her voice.

"Probably. Clean blankets too in a city like this."

Nyla bit her lip. She sighed. "Well, if you want to stay at the inn, then go ahead. Don't let me stop you." She brushed away the statement with a wave of her hand.

"Oh, come on, you must want a featherbed and a roof over your head as much as I do." He paused. Realization left a sizzling sting across his cheek as if he'd been slapped. Nyla wasn't merely being cheap; she *didn't have* any money at all. He cleared his throat, his entire angle changing course now that he'd realized why Nyla was refusing something as wonderful as a real bed.

He'd always assumed she didn't have much money on her, but the hard reality of her situation fully set in now that he knew. His heart pulled at his conscience. Xander knew, after all the miles they'd traveled to get to Fortune Falls and through their return to civilization through the Shadow Forest's heart, that he couldn't still consider Nyla a stranger. From pulling him up into that cave to forcing him to follow her with a ghostly trail of smoke as their guide, Xander owed her his life. If he'd had to trust in his map and his map alone, he might still be wandering in the Shadow Forest, lost and alone and hopeless.

It was the only gesture of kindness he could offer her after everything.

"Besides, what kind of gentleman—no, what kind of *friend* would I be if I just left you here? I just *can't* take no for an answer," he assured her. He'd saved plenty from his escapades in Halberry, and even from before the work he'd done there. And it wasn't about the money—not really anyway. What if something happened to her? Or with her magic? He'd never forgive himself if something were to happen and Nyla didn't make it out unscathed. She'd helped him into the cave that day, and again when the ogre appeared, so what was a little extra money for *both* of them to sleep comfortably tonight?

Nyla huffed, and he knew. Xander smiled, knowing full well that he'd managed to convince her of the benefits.

"Well, if you insist. I guess I can stay at the inn if it means that much to you."

"I know just the place!" He beamed, leaping to his feet.

In a few moments, their cooking fire was extinguished, and the pair was on their feet again.

***

Night fell long before the pair reached an inn. Caselle had three, apparently. Nyla couldn't imagine a travel hub so popular and big that it needed *three* inns, but then she remembered what Xander had told her as they traveled. Caselle was the biggest city for miles near the northern banks of the Union River, and it had access to the Shelton Bay, which flowed into the Sea of Harmony. The sun had only set about an hour or so ago, but the city's inhabitants had shuttered their stores and homes. Market stalls were dark and probably empty, no one to entice passersby to glance their way and buy their wares. While the city was mostly quiet, the few stragglers and empty marketplace with its darkened storefronts left a lot to take in. The barren market was a relief, but Nyla's skin still prickled anxiously.

She barely had time to study the inn before they entered. It was a flat building with large, oversized windows, one of which housed a carved 'vacancy' sign. She guessed that the building itself was four stories and still not the tallest building in the city center. Metal accents combined with the gigantic windows created a sleek appearance, both inside and out.

Upon entering, Nyla found that Xander had led her into a cramped foyer. Off to one side was a large, open threshold into the tavern, which, from what she could see, seemed to dominate the first floor of the inn. In the foyer, a host's desk stretched along the far wall beside a set of stairs. Nyla's stare flitted back to the tavern's entryway, lingering on the flameless chandelier dazzling from the tavern's ceiling.

It was easily the largest chandelier that Nyla had ever seen. As wide as she was tall, she marveled at the little glass bulbs in the shape of a candle's flame attached to cylindrical shafts. But they weren't candles at all. Nyla's father had once explained that they were beginning to use magic to light homes and inns and other places, like the royal family's palaces, but she could never figure out who he meant by "they." The sconces on the wall were also lit by magic, but the lanterns on each of the tables and on the host's desk bore the familiar sight of a burning, glimmering flame. Xander didn't seem fazed at all as Nyla quickened her steps to catch up with him at the host's desk, where a young blond stood. He couldn't have been much older than Xander was. Nyla's gaze fixated on the flameless wall sconce on either side of the desk, transfixed, as the host engaged Xander in a transaction she barely lent half an ear to.

"Can I help you, sir?" The man at the desk spoke over the rambunctious noise spilling from the open entryway of the tavern behind them.

"Do you have two rooms available?" Xander asked.

The man hesitated a moment, glancing at the paper in front of him before he addressed Xander again.

"Yes, we do." He turned and grabbed two keys off of their respective hooks behind him and passed them to Xander. He gestured toward the stairs and said, "Take those stairs up to the second floor, make a right, and your rooms, eight and ten, are all the way at the end of the hall. Is there anything else I can do for you?"

"That's all, thanks." Nyla peered over Xander's shoulder to see as he finished filling out the guest book and handed a few libacs over to the man to cover the cost of the rooms.

The steep stairs creaked embarrassingly with each footstep the pair took as Xander led the way to the second floor. Nyla pressed her lips together to hold back the wave of laughter.

"Guess they just renovated an old building to make it look new," Xander chuckled warmly when they reached the top. "So, do you want eight or ten?"

He paused and turned to Nyla, holding the two silver keys up for her to see. They each had a faded stamped leather tag to signify the room number.

"I don't care. They're both the same, right?"

"I guess. Suppose one has a better bed?" Xander inquired as they started walking toward their rooms again.

"I haven't slept in a real bed in forever, so trust me, *any* bed is a better bed than what I'm used to."

Xander didn't say anything to that, just handed her the skeleton key to room number ten when they reached their rooms at the end of the hall. After a moment, he mentioned that corner rooms tended to have the best view and watched as Nyla opened her door. He followed behind her and stood in the doorway as she stood in the middle of the room.

Nyla knew he was there and that he wanted to say something about what she'd said earlier, about the beds, but she didn't care because it was true. The bed in front of her could be as hard as a rock, and she wouldn't complain. A bed, after all, was a bed. And any bed was good enough.

"I figured we could drop our stuff and get a late supper? We haven't really eaten much in our travels," Xander piped up when she turned to say goodnight.

"Actually, I'm just going to get cleaned up and go to bed. I'll see you at breakfast." Nyla smiled tiredly as she shrugged off her backpack and set it on the floor.

He nodded and shut the door behind him as he walked the few steps to his room. Nyla breathed slowly, staring at the space Xander had taken up before she walked over to the door. The lock clicked into place, and she spun around. Her eyes flitted around the room.

Across from her stood a four-poster bed centered on the wall between the partitioned space and the exterior wall. The bed frame looked like a sturdy wood, but was simply made. A pile of blankets that appeared to be six inches high graced the bed enticingly. A grin tugged at Nyla's chapped lips. On either side of the bed was one of those oversized windows, though she was happy to see that they had thick curtains and a nightstand underneath, each with an unlit lantern.

In one corner of the room, the one that served as the exterior wall, was another window with the same navy curtains as the others and a writing desk. On the other side of the room was a floral dressing screen, which was mostly folded up. The folded screen revealed an amazing soaker tub and pedestal sink, as well as something she had only ever heard about but never seen. Her father had described it in the same conversation as the magic lights. A toilet, he'd called it. He said it was like a chamber pot, but it emptied itself.

He had been so excited to tell them all about the new magic plumbing, or 'plugic,' and sewer system and what they called the 'magicity' that he discovered on his latest business trip. He was practically bursting from the moment he walked in the door. He said that all you had to do was twist a knob, and hot or cold water came on demand through a system of pipes. Nyla didn't see how that was possible, but her father said that they used spells to defy gravity and set the temperature to your desire in order for it to work.

As Nyla stared absentmindedly at the corner of the room dedicated to function as a washroom, her grin only grew wider. She still remembered the wild energy and wonder in his eyes as he'd explained to them, his captive audience, all about the modern amenities he had discovered during his trip. Even then, Nyla had thought she'd never be able to try them herself, but here she was.

With the memory of her siblings and herself sitting at his feet as he sat in his favorite chair, listening eagerly to his tale, Nyla drew the velveteen curtains over all of the windows. Even with the small chandelier and its four little magic bulbs, the room was dim. She quickly searched for a box of matches and lit the lanterns on either side of the bed. After she had tended to the fire, Nyla went over to the tub and twisted the knob labeled 'hot.' A gasp escaped her lips when water actually came out of the spout, warm and getting hotter still. Her gaze lingered on the steady flow of water collecting in the stoppered tub, completely transfixed by the magic filling the tub. Steam rose from the water invitingly. With a half turn of the knob labeled 'cold,' the steam began to dissipate. Nyla undressed and let out a long exhale as she lowered herself into the warm water.

For a moment, she sat there, her legs stretched out and her head tilted back, cushioned by the cool lip of the tub. The *plop* of water droplets as they fell from the now-dry faucet echoed in the quiet room. All the laughter and shouting and thunderous conversations from the tavern below were gone. She soaked away days and weeks and seasons of travel in the warmest water she had felt in a long time. Her limbs relaxed, and Nyla was on the verge of a deep sleep if she didn't move soon. She let herself have a few more moments in that blissful state before she opened her eyes and began to scrub the dirt and grime from her skin and hair that she hadn't been able to before. Soon, her skin was the cleanest it had been in seemingly forever. Even her fingernails, broken and uneven as they were, were finally clean.

With much effort and resistance from her travel-weary body, she dragged herself out of the tub and dried off with her tattered towel as the water drained with a gurgled hum. Now ready for bed, she leaped onto it. The wood frame creaked from the sudden attack. A childlike giggle escaped her lips. And that's all she remembered. Nyla was asleep before her eyes even shut or before she could pull back the covers and burrow deep into the blankets.

11. THE SORCERESS

A sharp ringing pierced through the white static that filled Nyla's ears like cotton. All around her was a thick, suffocating darkness that swallowed her whole. She questioned whether or not her eyes were even open. Nyla tried to gain some feeling in her limbs by moving around, but to no avail. It only led to the curious sensation of trudging through molasses. She couldn't even wiggle her toes. There was a weight all around her like being dragged underwater while helplessly trying to claw your way back to the surface.

Nyla began to panic, fighting uselessly to move, to feel, to just open her eyes and see that she was safe in her room inside some inn. Each *thumpity-thump* of her heart boomed like thunder between her ears, each one louder than the last. An agonized scream was ripped from Nyla's throat. Searing heat blossomed in every joint. Her bones seemingly fractured and twisted as something pulled her apart limb by limb. It was like a wild animal gnawed and dragged her limbs away from her body, all while that sickly heat came to a crescendo within her. Nyla thought she was burning in hellfire.

Whatever was happening only got worse as her limbs were haphazardly fused together again. Her stomach swam to her throat, her heart fluttering like a caged bird's wings. She was falling, and there was nothing Nyla could do to stop it.

The heat slowly dissipated into a tingle that spread from the tips of her fingers and toes to her very core. Wind swept and swirled all around her as she fell freely in a way that she thought would never end.

The breath was knocked out of her. She gasped, swallowing lungful after lungful of air as something hard appeared beneath her—or was she leaned up against it?

Her ears popped, and the static was gone. Nyla stretched out, still unable to see anything other than a dark abyss before her eyes, and patted the area around her. It was a sort of fabric like felt or pilled cotton. Thin carpeting?

Slowly, light began to filter its way into her sight, banishing the darkness. She blinked and stared up at the eggshell-colored ceiling. Exposed beams came into focus, as did their intricate groupings of brilliant red tulips and Agergy-green *Moluccella laevis* that were stenciled on the beams. The beams formed an oversized grid pattern all along what was probably a hallway's ceiling. Between each grid square, the ceiling had a subtle ripple to it, like the veins on the underside of a leaf or petal.

Panting a little to catch her breath, Nyla traced the flowers and beams with her eyes. Her blood settled as her heartbeat calmed. After a few moments, warmth spread across her cheeks. Sheepishly, she at last got to her feet. Glancing up and down the candlelit hallway, relief flooded her veins as she found herself to be utterly alone.

But where?

Vague familiarity tugged at the far edges of Nyla's mind. Her eyes roamed over the walls on either side of her. There were paintings of all kinds and lit sconces that looked like the head of a raverin, a large and fierce bird of prey that was deeply rooted in the country's history. Little rectangular tables were positioned between every few paintings. Some of the tables had a vase of what looked like fresh lilacs, while others had lit candles set in sturdy silver candelabras.

With a frown, Nyla approached the largest painting nearest her and examined it. She hoped it would shed some light as to where she was, but even as she hoped this, the tiny voice in the back of her head squeaked, betraying her fear. The painting was hung in an ornate wooden frame with intricate, raised carvings. Nyla wanted nothing more than to run her finger over the smooth-looking cherrywood, but stopped herself.

The painting itself was an oil painting that featured a mountain range. She counted six mountaintops, some out in the distance, while others were closer in perspective to the painting's admirer. Some of the mountains were cast in the shadows of the taller mountains, but they were each a beautiful shade of luscious green. The different shades of green and even brown, along with the brushstrokes, gave each square inch of these mountains a distinct feature and outlined the trees. In the bottom corner, the artist's initials, G.H., were scrawled in a dark paint that marred the lush green of the trees.

In that moment, Nyla really began to question not only where she was, but how she had even gotten here, wherever here was.

With a final glance at the breathtaking scenery immortalized by the painting that made her heart ache for that sort of sunny tranquility and safety, she floated down the hall in search of somebody or some indication of where she was.

Nyla passed more paintings than she could ever remember seeing in her life, and several closed doors on either side of the hall. Though she considered opening them, Nyla didn't know what to expect on the other side. Friend or foe or more empty space, either way, she wasn't inclined to find out. She spared brief glances at the paintings, all of which were unique.

Some of the paintings had a different medium than the mountain one she had admired—though she did notice other oil paintings. As far as their subjects went, some were portraits of people probably long since passed, while others depicted battle scenes or interpretations of legends Nyla had never heard.

Just like the first, there were plenty of landscape portraits. From the countryside to forests to mountains to lakes or rivers to the desert, she fought the captivation that consumed her as she passed each one.

Despite the cheeriness of some paintings, others disturbed her. Those mostly depicted people Nyla couldn't name but looked oddly familiar. She knew she'd never met them, but their stern, unblinking painted eyes and thin smiles seemed expectant as she passed by. Nyla paused occasionally to appreciate one painting or another as she moved down the hall, but the portraits of royalty from long ago sent shivers through her body. Ghosts of the past might as well have been wailing down the hall in agony and pulling at her hair like some spirits were said to do.

It wasn't until she reached the very end of the long hallway that she found a door that was cracked open. Light poured out and illuminated the soft carpet in an elongated triangle. Nyla would've gone in, but just as she was about to, the painting on the opposite wall caught her eye.

It was another centuries-old portrait, but this one struck Nyla straight to her core. Three people stood in front of a fireplace in a room decorated with crossed swords and gleaming bits of old-fashioned armor. One of the portrait's subjects, a woman, stood behind two children. She had a hand on each of their shoulders as if to keep them from running off more so than as a nurturing touch. Nyla stood slack-jawed and frozen in place. Her eyes fixed solely on the two children with whom the woman must've been charged.

The boy with his blank stare and bored lips had become the focal point of Nyla's icy terror. His scarlet eyes bored into her. The discovery knocked—no, *stole*—the breath from her lungs until she didn't think she was breathing at all. In reality, her chest was heaving as much as her heart was beating like a drum signaling that the inevitable monster had come.

Her stunned gaze moved to the little girl who stood next to him. Draped over one shoulder in a pile of loose curls was hair as silver as Nyla's. Her grin held the tiniest hint of mischief and glee. The girl's shining lilac eyes that were so much like Nyla's had been painted with a twinkling gleam of someone plotting the world's greatest scheme.

Nyla couldn't help but stare up at those eyes, that silver hair. If she didn't know any better, she would've thought that *she* was the little girl in the portrait, but up until two years ago, her hair had been chestnut brown and her eyes as dark as chocolate.

Her ears pricked at the squeak of hinges as the door behind her opened with a groan. Quickly, Nyla schooled her features to mask the startled curiosity blooming in her chest and spared a glance over her shoulder.

Nyla took in the woman stepping out into the hall. Her breath stopped. She could've fainted.

Instead, her heart sputtered, and she fought off the quaking that started in the tips of her fingers. Any sense of calm she had forced was gone. Her hand slowly crept toward where her knife should be. She cursed silently, suddenly wishing she had tried harder to find an exit or that she knew where she was or that she wasn't alone. Her body tensed, waiting for a threat that didn't come.

"I remember the day that was painted." The silver-haired woman leaned against the doorframe and looked over Nyla's shoulder at the painting. She wore a soft, reminiscent smile that didn't quite reach her eyes before she met Nyla's. "We have a lot to discuss, Nyla, and very little time to do so."

Nyla took a step back, hand up to stop the peculiar woman from coming forward, or maybe to push her away. She didn't know what she wanted. Her mind spun around and around like a top. When she could finally speak, she drew herself up and narrowed her eyes.

"Who *are* you?" Nyla spat, her voice harsher than she intended.

"Astrid, the Royal Mage, or at least I was. I'm afraid I've," she paused and pushed herself away from the door frame, straightening, "moved on. Now please, we don't have much time, and I know you must have so many questions—"

"You mean like who is he and how are you related? Why do I look like you, and how come I suddenly have magic, and…" She rambled in exasperation, breathing heavily. The fact that yelling at this woman who might actually give her answers wasn't the best idea crossed Nyla's mind in the faintest of voices.

"Why am I *cursed*?" she finished with an abundance of exaggerated hand gestures that showed just how insecure and panicked she was inside. With a final heavy exhale, Nyla glanced up at Astrid from beneath her lashes, upset and mortified to have called her powers a curse.

Astrid frowned sympathetically, but as her eyes moved to study the portrait once again, they darkened into something that Nyla could only recognize as thinly veiled loathing. Behind that was bitter resentment.

"*That*," Astrid clicked, pointing at the boy, "is Cedric and our governess. She went by one name then, though I doubt it's the same now. I hold nothing but contempt for them anymore and am relieved to say that there is no relation there, only bad blood and broken trust. And as far as your magic goes, it is *not* a curse. Why don't you come and sit down, and we'll talk all this over?"

Astrid paused and extended a hand out to Nyla. Nyla nodded and stepped forward, but before she could take Astrid's hand, someone called her name. It came from a long way away like a garbled echo from the other end of a never-ending tunnel. Nyla turned her head, half expecting to see someone standing at the other end of the hallway, but she couldn't see that far because of a curve in it that she hadn't noticed before.

"Nyla?" it called again.

The disembodied voice pounded in her ears. That awful heat and bone-melting pain flared up again. Bits of the ceiling began to crumble. The painted wood beams cracked and splintered. The walls began to melt away.

Nyla panicked, jerking away from Astrid like a caged animal, and clutched her arms to her vibrating chest as every molecule seemed to rip itself to shreds. She didn't get very far when Astrid grabbed her by the shoulders with a bruising grip. Her eyes were wide and urgent.

"You need to find me again, but be careful. You hear me?"

Nyla barely nodded. Astrid's voice began to fade away like she was talking to her through water. "It is absolutely imperative that you practice caution because she's—"

Nyla's eyes rolled into the back of her head. Her body went limp, and she began to crumple. Astrid's grip on her shoulders disappeared, replaced by the sensation of every fiber of her being seemingly cleaved in half by an axe and forced together again. Once more, she spiraled down in a free fall.

Something cool was placed over Nyla's forehead. Her limbs were bound by a softness that wound and tangled itself around her body. Her whole body ached, and Nyla found that she had no desire to open her eyes. Where would she be this time? What could she possibly be forced to live through that she hadn't already been through? Would it be worse?

Nothing could be worse than that sickly heat or that sensation of shattered bones and contortion when her molecules fused themselves back together again.

With a deep breath, she reluctantly opened her eyes. Somewhere inside her jumbled mind, she knew that no matter how many deep breaths she took, she'd never be ready to face wherever she happened to be this time. Nyla blinked at the brightness of the room around her.

Xander hovered over her, worry drawn all over his features, asking her something. She only groaned, too exhausted to speak. The more she woke up, the more aches she noticed. Next came the clamminess. Nyla frowned, allowing herself to get her bearings. A wave of nausea overcame her. She quickly started to unwrap herself from the blankets on the inn's bed, brushing off Xander when he tried to get her to lay back down. The damp washcloth on her forehead slipped and fell to the side. Cool air enveloped her instantly. Almost frantically, Nyla swung

BRIANNA R. SHAFFERY

her legs over the side of the bed, stepping on the oddly squishy floor. She glanced down and saw the old comforter had fallen to the floor, and while the comforter itself was slippery, her legs were like jelly.

As she tried to make it to her bag, she nearly fell over. Xander caught her and righted her on her feet again, this time keeping a tight grip on her arms. Nyla glanced up at him and for the first time noticed that his mouth was moving. She stood there panting, grateful for his sturdiness, and tried to read his lips. Three, blurred Xanders were clearly talking to her, but the dizziness from standing and now the sickness that washed over her was overwhelming. Nyla blinked a few more times. Finally, one Xander stood in front of her, still frantically speaking to her.

"What?" she asked finally, her voice strained. "I can't hear you."

Xander paused, closing his mouth, and instead managed to guide her back to sit on the bed. His brows furrowed, and he started to speak again, but Nyla shook her head.

Instantly, the dizziness was back, and she lurched forward, a hand flying to her temple. Xander pressed a hand to her forehead and pressed his lips into a thin line. Nyla batted his hand away, not caring if she had a fever at the moment. Right now, her focus was on her lack of hearing and stability. Those, she knew, were not normal symptoms of the common cold.

"It's like there's cotton in my ear. I can't hear a single thing." She tilted her head one way and then the other as if trying to get water out of her ears. Nyla glanced around at the inn's room, just now realizing that the only light came from the fireplace. She thought the room had been so much brighter when she first woke up, taking in the dim glow of the fire and writhing shadows the flames cast over the room.

Slowly but surely, the rowdiness of the bustling tavern a floor below floated up to them. Nyla smiled dimly, glancing back at Xander, but the glistening key on her nightstand caught her eye, and her train of thought was lost.

"Hey, Xander? How'd you get in here if the door was locked?" she asked in a raspy voice, staring up at him. Xander went to the sink and got her a glass of water. Nyla sipped at it slowly, not wanting to further irritate her upset stomach.

"I, uh, picked the lock. But in my defense, I tried knocking and calling your name. When you didn't answer..." He trailed off and rubbed the back of his neck. He shook his head, his full focus on Nyla again. "What happened to you, though? Why couldn't you hear me just now?"

"I don't know. I thought it was just a dream or a nightmare, but none of it makes sense." Her hand floated up to her shoulder where Astrid's hand had been, her eyes puzzled. "I'm not really sure to be honest. It all felt so real."

"What did?" Xander waited patiently for Nyla to meet his eyes again and come back into the present moment.

Nyla bit her lip. She didn't know *what*. That was the problem. She quickly explained what had happened, leaving out the gruesome details of how her every being was ripped apart and put back together again. She didn't dare mention Astrid or the portrait of the little girl and boy, just that she'd found herself in a place she didn't recognize, as if she were actually there.

Xander listened patiently, but the longer Nyla spoke, the more fatigued she became. Maybe she was only coming down with something. That had to be it. She was sick, Nyla reasoned with herself. When she finally finished, she added, "I don't know. It's probably just a weird dream."

She waved her hand as if to cast away the notion that it could be anything other than a strange dream or a hallucination from her apparent fever.

"What if it's not a dream? What if it's a premonition or really anything to do with your magic?" Xander offered. Nyla scoffed.

"Then why now?"

"Just another possibility. Let's face it. Neither of us know a whole lot about magic. Maybe the archives will help." He shrugged.

As they stared at each other, Nyla wondered what Astrid had wanted to tell her and how they were connected. Were they related? She pursed her lips. Either way, it was probably for the better that she left Xander out of this, especially if *he* was watching.

Nyla nodded. After all, that was why she had come here, for answers. "Well then, to the archives."

She started to get up again, but Xander stopped her.

"You seriously can't mean that. You're not well and dizzy, and suppose you get worse while we're there? What if I go to the archives, check things out, maybe see if I can bring things back here, and come back?"

Nyla could only groan in response as her whole being lurched internally. Xander's voice was drowned out by the roar of her own blood in her ears. She fell to her hands and knees on the comforter, and just as swiftly as it had when she was speaking with Astrid, the heat reared its ugly head again. In the milliseconds it took Xander to reach her physical body, Nyla was already landing in a place far, far away.

12. DANGEROUS DREAMS

When Nyla's eyes popped open, they were met with the sight of a textured, cream ceiling. Her limbs slowly awakened, and the slight tingling sensation receded as she continued to catch her breath. Whatever was happening to her had taken a toll on her body far greater than she had anticipated. She shuddered, remembering the violent sickness that had overcome her moments before. Was that truly only a minute or two ago? She frowned. Deep lines creased her forehead as she contemplated this. With a resigned sigh, Nyla sat up on her elbows and glanced around.

The room she had landed in was circular, with pillars and tall windows and a grand chandelier lit in the center of the rippled ceiling. Nyla guessed that a giant would fit comfortably in here. On the far side of the great room, there was a large gap between the pillars in which an abandoned raised platform stood. There weren't any windows on this section of the wall, unlike the other three-quarters or so of the room.

A stage, perhaps?

The platform fit perfectly against the curved wall behind it, and Nyla could only guess that she was in a ballroom or a banquet hall of sorts. That small hint still didn't answer *where* exactly she was or if she was in the same place as before, the place where Astrid was.

She finally got to her feet, grateful that her legs held her weight. With tentative steps, Nyla made her way past the pillars on the perimeter of the expansive dance floor to one of the numerous, looming windows. The windows stood a few feet apart from each other with an ornate, though tarnished, brass sconce between them. Adorned with thick curtains of rich plum, the windows stretched from just above the decorative wainscoting to right below the crown molding above.

Lost in her musings, her fingers absently traced the corded gold rope that held the curtains at bay as she stared out the nearest window. There wasn't much to see outside. Stars winked, and the moon shone behind wispy clouds and leaf-covered branches.

Still, the shadowy surroundings, the brass sconces, the pattern of the stars in the night sky, and even the thick rope between her fingers were eerily familiar. It was like she had dreamt of this place once before and found it in real life, like a premonition of sorts. Nyla weighed the idea in her mind.

It tossed and turned and twisted around in her mind's eye, and as it did so, Nyla slowly turned on her heel. Her eyes leisurely traveled over her surroundings with a weighted gaze.

It was all so...curious.

The room was as it had been when she first put her back to it. As her eyes swept over each of the stone pillars and the rest of the ballroom, the sconces blew out one by one. Before the candles of the chandelier had extinguished with a hiss, Nyla caught a glimpse of someone leaning up against a nearby pillar.

"You know, I never thought you'd be here again," the shadow said as if they were old friends who had drifted apart.

Nyla didn't say anything. She *couldn't* say anything as her mouth went bone dry. The hair on the back of her neck prickled. Her skin began to buzz. Her stomach quivered before a lead weight settled deep within it.

The figure disappeared from her sight. Nyla tried to follow the voice with her eyes as he continued to speak in that same, even tone that would've hinted at vague disinterest had she not known any better. That tone held the same sort of patience and restraint that predators practiced when they baited their prey. And then, just before the prey realized they'd been duped, the predator struck. She wondered if he could see her through the dimness because any time she thought her eyes had caught a glimpse of him, the voice sounded from across the room. He was difficult to track, his voice flitting across the room with his unseen movement, seemingly surrounding her.

Nyla expected the worst at any moment now. Her fingers brushed against her hip, but found only the hem of her oversized shirt. The reduced visibility made it difficult to find exactly where the exits were, not that she'd been that concerned with noting them beforehand. At least she sort of knew where *he* was; that predatory voice and villainous monologue gave him away.

"I also didn't think you'd come into your powers; I mean after all: it's been *years* and no sign of them. I'd thought we were wrong about you. But then the ogre—now *that* was something! Reduced it—straight to ash!" The man paused, as if considering something. "It's a shame to waste so much power. And yet here we are."

Nyla could picture him extending his arms out to motion at the room around them, and when her eyes finally landed on the spot his voice had come from, he vanished into thin air. Unlike before, he allowed a lapse in his monologue, completely blinding her to his possible whereabouts. Nyla gulped. She needed him to say something or do something, just anything to make his presence known to her.

"How'd you know about the ogre?" she asked. Her voice was timid and exposed every ounce of fear that pounded in her veins. The shadow let out a maniacal howl that might've been a laugh. The sharp sound rattled Nyla's ears, but at least he'd responded. Her eyes flicked in the direction the noise had come from.

"Does it matter?" he sneered. "Besides, didn't the precious little Fortune Falls show you that? Surely, you must know who I am by now, Nyla."

She tried to place his voice to a time when she might've heard it, but no memory came to mind. The fact that he knew about the Falls and could guess what they'd shown her made her stomach flop. Scarlet eyes flashed before her memory. "You're...you can't be...no, it's not possible..."

"Isn't it, though? I mean, you're here." The voice came from somewhere off to her right. Nyla turned to face his voice as he stepped around a pillar there.

The soft, disjointed glow of the moon gave just enough light to catch the steely gaze of his scarlet eyes. Nyla sucked in a breath and held it. Her whole body went rigid. A hateful hum began to simmer just below the surface of her skin. Unadulterated loathing flooded her heart as he began to speak again.

"I'm Cedric, by the way. Though I suppose introductions don't really matter now."

He strolled closer, and with every step forward, Nyla took a step back until she was met with the firm hardness of a pillar. As she started to move off to the side in an attempt to keep some space between them, Cedric pulled a wicked-looking dagger from the hilt at his side.

Nyla's throat closed up, but she still managed to croak, "Why? Why me, my family? What could we *possibly* have done that warrants being murdered?"

"Nothing personal, really. Well, it's a little personal with you... with Astrid." He lunged at her. The knife glinted in the moonlight. Nyla barely whirled out of the way before it could strike her chest.

Cedric recovered quickly and swiped at Nyla again. He was too strong for her to deflect the blow entirely, and the blade sliced the skin of her collarbone and shoulder. She hissed through her teeth as her hand moved instinctually to staunch the flow of blood. Cedric never gave her the chance, though, as he attempted to stab her again.

The resentful hum in Nyla's core grew to a crescendo. Their movements slowed to the point where they barely moved, or at least it seemed as though to Nyla. She deflected his next attack, gripping his wrist with a sharp twist, and kicked at him. Consumed by the image of Cedric at her mercy, by her victory, by her need to survive, by the image of her *safety*, Nyla grasped the hatred sizzling in her bloodstream.

Just as she'd planned, Nyla landed a powerful blow to his gut.

A purple light exploded when her foot made impact. The hum that had built up inside her had worked its way through her body to her foot and disappeared with the light, the magic.

Time sped back to reality again. Shocked, Nyla lost her grip on his wrist as Cedric was sent flying backwards.

He landed on his side with a *thump* and skidded to a stop on the marble floor. Nyla stared at his form and waited to see the rise and fall of his chest. After a moment, he still hadn't moved, so Nyla turned and began to make her way toward an exit.

"Enough games!" Cedric's hard voice rang through the ballroom. Nyla turned. Goosebumps prickled her skin. "I am finishing this!"

Nyla didn't have time to ask what he meant by that. Her eyes widened as sickly red lightning burst from his fingertips and raced toward her with a ferocity she had never seen before.

She squeezed her eyes shut and threw her arms up in front of her to protect her chest and face. It didn't matter as the magic slammed into her with the force of hurricane winds. The air was knocked from her lungs as she went flying backwards. Nyla hit the wall behind her with a hard crash.

Pain blossomed in her back and head. It spread to every inch of her body. The plaster cracked, and bits dropped to the ground like snow. Even the sconce and windowpane, both of which Nyla had luckily avoided hitting, had rattled due to the impact. She crumpled to the floor, her eyes closed. The chandelier in the center of the ceiling swayed, the crystals quietly *tinkling*.

She must've looked pathetic, doubled over on her hands and knees as she wheezed. The stars behind her closed eyelids finally disappeared as the pain receded to an ache and instant bruising.

Part of her waited for the final blow; another simply struggled to gain some sense of feeling that wasn't throbbing flames of pain.

But the final part of her, the much stronger and stubborn part, needed to defeat him like her lungs needed oxygen. All of the grief and bitterness that Nyla had lived with for years now rose up like bile. It bolstered her and washed away the agony that made her body wail. Nyla forced herself to her feet. She was wobbly, but an iron-like determination flooded every fiber within her.

That grief and bitterness and abandoned feeling that she'd known for so long that it was almost a familiar friend morphed into a weaponized hatred that burned hotter than a thousand suns.

The air around her crackled and popped. Crystals from the chandelier above shattered. Shards of glass fell like rain. The victorious smirk that had graced Cedric's chiseled face was quickly replaced by an all-consuming terror.

Jagged bolts of static sparked from Nyla's fingertips. Her hands clenched and unclenched. Nyla's entire being tensed with an adrenaline and power she had never known before.

"You will never hurt anyone like you've hurt me. I might not know what the hell is going on, but that doesn't really matter because no matter what you do or how powerful you are, I am going to stop you, even if it means killing you!" she spat, each word punctuated with a venomous grit. She stalked closer to Cedric, who shrank and backed away from her.

He regained his composure and prepared to strike at her again.

Nyla lunged forward and wrapped her hands around his neck. Her weight dragged them both down at the suddenness of her attack. His hand ensnared her wrist while his other one came up to strike the side of her face. Nyla sprang up and out of the way, her better judgment fighting against the itch in her blood. It gave Cedric just enough time to turn over and sputter, coughing, heaving air into his lungs.

She kicked him hard in the side.

"Ya know, for someone who's supposed to be more experienced at using magic than me and apparently far older, you don't seem to be trying to win. But then again, who I am to judge how to be evil?" she taunted. The purple sparks returned to her hands. Her gaze shifted from Cedric's doubled-over and kneeling form to her hands.

She didn't know what it meant, only that she wanted to blast him like he'd done to her earlier. With her hands raised and arms outstretched, she hesitated. Her father had always said to fight back against your nightmares.

Was that all this was, a nightmare?

Nyla didn't know. Her mind seemed to scream that all of this, and Astrid too, was simply a nightmare. A long, exaggerated nightmare influenced by Fortune Falls' visions and heightened by the weariness of traveling.

Cedric slowly dragged himself to his feet. His eyes flashed as they met hers. Energy started to flow through Nyla's body and concentrated in her hands. Purple lightning leapt from her fingers, barreling straight toward her enemy, just as Cedric had fired his own scarlet magic at her. The red beam hit Nyla in her lower abdomen and sent her skidding across the floor.

All she heard was a booming *thud* of an impact on the far wall, almost instantaneously followed by the crumbling and rattling of plaster, the sconces, and the stone of the pillars. Bits of debris fell to the marble floor with a hard *plop*.

Nyla blinked away the stars from her eyes and inhaled. Sharp pain flared up all over her body. There was a moment that she lay there, a little stunned and breathless, contemplating whether or not she had broken anything. Surely, there'd be a lot of bruising and soreness.

She twisted herself until she could see how Cedric fared, but was met with an empty ballroom. It didn't appear as though he'd been hit at all, and it was, apparently, her magic that had caused the damage to the stone pillar across the room. Not sure if she was safe for now or not, Nyla ran her fingers over her body to see if she could feel any broken bones.

Her shirt stuck to her chest, the slash from Cedric's knife mostly forgotten until now. She groaned as she prodded the tender flesh there. At least the blood had stopped flowing. If Nyla could better see the gash, she would know that it wasn't deep enough to warrant stitches, but it would definitely leave a nasty, jagged scar.

Woozily, she got to her feet. Any adrenaline, magic, and energy she'd had had vanished just like Cedric. She struggled toward the nearest pillar and leaned against it for a while. While Nyla was certain now that she hadn't sustained any major injuries—which was a miracle in and of itself—there were several pressing issues that she still faced, one of them being where had Cedric run off to?

There was also the matter of where she was and how she'd gotten here.

With a long, ragged breath, Nyla pushed off of the pillar and slowly made her way toward a pale light that had appeared. As she got closer, she realized that it was candlelight from a servants' area adjacent to the ballroom. The doorway was a hidden panel directly behind one of the carved stone pillars by the musicians' platform. It must've been forced open during one of the blasts that shook the room.

Cautiously, she pushed the door open and stepped into a narrow, though seemingly endless, butler's pantry. Her eyes scanned the stretching room for danger. Sconces lit the way into a kitchen beyond the long pantry with its counters and cabinets on either side to stage things for great feasts and balls. She followed the lit chandeliers like she had with the smoke in the Shadow Forest. As Nyla tentatively strolled through the long pantry with weak footsteps, she peered at the contents of the cabinets on either side.

Fine sets of flatware for every season were stacked as far as the eye could see. Every so often, she passed a wheeled ladder that went from the base of the cabinets to the ceiling, which was maybe half the height of the ballroom's. Three-legged teacups sat atop their saucers, each pair stacked on top of another until there wasn't any more room on that shelf. Serving dishes of all shapes and sizes, some of which Nyla was certain weren't even Tenebrese, lined other shelves.

When the butler's pantry finally ended, she passed through a door-frame with a broken pocket door. Nyla had to turn sideways to fit through the narrow opening. She had no strength left to try and force the door back between the walls.

The kitchen was smaller than she expected, but it was still bigger than the entire first floor of her childhood home. Her eyes swept over the spacious center island and cupboards. Dust and cobwebs hung in the air. One web stretched from a pan that hung from a rafter to the corner of a window near the ceiling. The candlelight was dimmer in this room, as if the dust had squandered some of the light. Nyla continued on anyway.

The next doorway she came to led her into a long, stretching hallway. This must have been one of the main passageways, she reasoned. Like the hallway she had found herself to be in with Astrid, this one had paintings and tapestries galore between picturesque windows. Candelabras were lit on one end of the hallway, and that's the direction Nyla headed. She only hoped that it led her back to her bed at the inn...wherever that was now.

The hallway spilled out into a great foyer. On one side, presumably the front, towering oak doors with oversized, wrought-iron handles stood proudly. On either side of the curved steeple doors, a pair of medieval suits of armor stood at attention. One held a spear in its gloved hand while the other held a battle-axe in each hand, its arms crossed over its chest.

Nyla's eyes were wide as she crept into the center of the open foyer. She could make out a hallway on the other side, past the doors, but her attention was quickly stolen by the majestic staircase in the center of the foyer. The wide staircase dominated the back wall of the room. Its steps were covered in a plush, wine-colored carpet that led to a spacious landing before the staircase split into two.

Instead of continuing down the hallway into the other wing of the building, Nyla approached the steep staircase and began to climb. The soft light of the candles and lit sconces gave plenty of light to see by, sparkling off the wooden floors, warming the otherwise chilly room.

Nyla took her time on the stairs, weighed down by heavy limbs. It didn't seem like she had lost that much blood, but she also didn't know if magic would have any weakening effects on her body. And she'd used a lot of magic in her fight with Cedric.

What exactly was it that he wanted with her anyway?

Her legs protested another step. She gritted her teeth. Her hand grasped the banister until her knuckles turned white, frozen in place about halfway up the staircase. Her temple throbbed. When Nyla glanced up to see how much farther she had to go before she reached the landing, her eyes froze on the large stained-glass window.

The window was divided into four sections by wrought iron, with noble crests adorning the corner panes that flanked the wrought-iron circle in the window's exact middle. There, a single lilac bloomed eternally. The image struck a chord in Nyla's memory.

Hundreds of precious memories flooded her mind then. Things like when she'd stood on her older brother's shoes and they'd danced and laughed in the ballroom—the same ballroom Cedric had attacked her in—or when she and her twin had raced down the hallway of paintings, their laughter reverberating down the hall, thousands of games of hide-and-seek or tag, exploring every inch of the abandoned estate as if it were their own castle, spending hours in the library with Derek while he poured over tome after tome or—

Tears pricked her eyes. All this time, through all of these changes in her life, Fortune Falls and its visions, all of it had led her to her childhood playground. A place filled with memory upon memory of freedom and exploration and laughter. A place that was their secret, kept under guard by knowing smiles. A place she'd found by a happy accident when she'd gotten disoriented in the woods while playing 'predator versus prey' with her friends, a secret she'd only shared with her brothers. They would have brought Lydia one day too, but the walk was too far for her, and their parents weren't fond of their children playing in the abandoned estate they assumed to be only a crumbling ruin. She stared through bleary eyes and with an overwhelmed heart up at the window, torn and uncertain. Why would the Falls show her all of that? Why would her dreams bring her here?

That sickly heat and the sensation of twisting and snapping bones overcame her. Nyla collapsed on the stair, nearly hitting her head on the one before her.

Everything went black.

A different sort of heat, a clammy one, plagued her body. Extreme discomfort and sharp aches consumed her just like the nonsensical nightmares that filled her subconscious.

Hope

Metal clattered against the wooden nightstand and fell with a quiet *thud* to the floor below. Cedric's limbs were like anchors. He staggered, slapping a heavy hand down against his nightstand before he collapsed in on himself. The soft carpet jarred his knees. Cedric gingerly wrapped his arms around his torso. Every breath felt like it could be his last.

He knew it wasn't, but the assurance didn't soothe his cracked ribs or bruised back. His breath came in short, clipped pants. Cedric's lungs craved more, though.

Who knew Nyla had that much power? Cedric cursed himself. He should've known after she incinerated the ogre.

He cried out with what little voice he could manage. The hoarse wail was nothing like a human's, but rather, it was an animal's, trapped by injury while escaping a nearby predator. The searing agony of his own magic swept through his body. The buzz beneath Cedric's skin traveled throughout his limbs, fusing broken bones and healing bruises as it went.

Every time a bone was mended, Cedric's body jerked. He couldn't stop it. He had absolutely no control over how he reacted to the healing process.

Healing was a nasty business, but the alternative was worse. Patience wasn't one of his virtues, and time wasn't exactly on his side.

Sweat rolled down his pallid face. Cedric sat back on his heels and gulped down air. Ever so slightly, his cottage came into focus.

The pain was gone.

"I hope that wasn't more trouble than it was worth," Cedric grumbled as he grabbed the bloody dagger beside him and used the nightstand to pull himself up. He sagged against it.

At the sound of his trembling voice, Dia *cawed* once from his perch near the window. Cedric lazily looked over at the creature. The raverin's head was cocked, its unblinking black eyes fixed on him curiously.

"Don't ever underestimate Nyla, Dia," Cedric groaned. A weak smile graced his lips, eyes falling shut. "She's exactly like her. Strong."

Dia's only response was to click his beak. It was like the bird's way of tutting at him, reprimanding him for the obvious. With a grimace, Cedric straightened. Glancing down at the dagger in his hand, the pinch of his lips twisted tighter.

At least he'd gotten the blood he needed from her.

13. XANDER'S SACRIFICE

Dread. Panic. Guilt. Simultaneously, Xander had been struck by all three in the fraction of a second when Nyla hadn't answered his knock this morning. The voice in his head that had said she'd already gotten up and left went unheard as he frantically picked the lock. Strangers or not, in that moment, he'd only known that he had to be sure that she was all right.

That was then, though. And after the initial panic of Nyla collapsing on him, Xander made another hasty decision. But help had come—and chastised him through the whole process. But Xander didn't care. Now he could be certain that Nyla would be all right. Nan, as Xander affectionately called Gerri, would make certain of it. Even with the soulstone bracelets Nan had lent him, he still didn't feel comfortable leaving her, but also hadn't wanted to overstep any boundaries and move Nyla to George and Nan's home so Nan could better see to her.

So, they'd struck a deal: Gerri would sit with Nyla during the day while Xander "went to unnecessary lengths to secure their lodgings" as Nan had put it, and the soulstone bracelets would give him peace of mind as he could still monitor Nyla's condition through their healing magic.

And he'd have to visit George before leaving Caselle if he wanted Nan to keep this a secret.

Xander's knuckles rapped against Nyla's door. He wasn't all that ready to face Nan again, even if he was indebted to her.

The door opened quietly thanks to Nan's patient hand. She smiled mischievously.

"Tired of picking the lock?"

"How is she?" Xander peeked around the graying woman's shoulder.

Nan glanced over at Nyla, who was still unconscious on the bed. "Your mystery girl? She's fine, Xander. Stable."

Nan finally let him in and wagged her finger at him. "But you aren't, not until you answer some questions, young man."

Before Xander did anything else, he tugged off his muddy boots and set them in the corner by the door, crossing the room to wash his hands. He met Nan's bright eyes in the mirror above the pedestal sink.

"Which ones?"

"Well, we could start with where you've been all this time, but I know that would be like de-thorning a hellox's paw. So why not who is she, this Nyla? Where did you two meet? Why haven't you come to visit us, or why *didn't* you come to visit the moment you stepped foot in Caselle? Then you wouldn't have to work for your lodgings." Xander dropped his gaze to avoid her rightful criticism and ignored the rest of her born-from-the-heart questions. "Or even who is Nyla to *you*?"

The soapy water was stained brown by the time it swirled down the drain. Long lines of worry and exhaustion had etched themselves on Xander's face, but he paid them no mind as he worked out how to answer all of Nan's questions. Gerri was like a grandmother to him, and he knew she deserved the truth, but for some reason he couldn't bring himself to tell her. He didn't know if it was his truth to tell, but she deserved answers.

"Well?" she demanded softly once he'd turned to face her again.

"We met in the Shadow Forest, around Halberry," he offered quietly. The soulstone pulsed evenly at his wrist, so unlike the quiver in his own heartbeat. It had beat calmly and warmly all day, so at least Nyla wasn't in any danger, but Xander couldn't say the same of himself.

"And what brought you to Halberry, Xander? And no half-truths, please. My heart can't bear it." Nan grabbed his hand and squeezed hard.

Xander swallowed hard. "We were both heading to Fortune Falls and—"

Nan dropped his hand with a sharp gasp. "Fortune Falls!" she hissed quietly so as not to disturb Nyla. "What were you thinking?"

"I don't know, Nan, I really don't." Xander took her veiny hand in his, ready to beg her to understand if he had to. "I didn't know where else to go or what to do, and I wanted certainty, and I thought Fortune Falls could offer it."

"Did you make it?" she whispered.

"We did." Nan clapped her free hand over her mouth, but Xander carried on. "We made it, but when we did, I couldn't do it."

Nan whacked his arm. "You made it to Fortune Falls and didn't even drink from it? Stupid boy!" She whacked his arm again, more playfully than the first time. "Do you know how many people have *died* trying to get there?"

"I know, Nan." Xander pulled her in for a hug, not sure which of them needed it more.

"You smell like the stables," she grumbled, but squeezed him tighter. "Did your friend here at least drink from the Falls? Or are you not friendly like that?"

"She did," Xander said after a moment's hesitation. He pulled away from Nan slowly, once more peering over at Nyla. "You don't think this has anything to do with Fortune Falls, do you?"

"No. This is different magic. But I'm only a doctor. A Healer would know better."

Xander nodded. "If she's not conscious by tomorrow, we'll—I'll move her."

Nan's eyes twinkled in a way Xander sorely missed. "You're awfully kind to someone you've just met, Xander."

"She saved my life, Nan."

Nan nodded slowly and picked up her medical bag by the door. "Send word if you need me again tonight. I'll be here tomorrow, bright and early." She scrunched her nose, eyeing him from head to toe. "You'd better wash up before bed, dear."

Xander started to open the door for her. A quiet chuckle escaped his lips. "I'm planning on it, believe me."

Nan kissed his cheek before stepping out into the inn's hallway. Xander looked after her until she disappeared down the hall before he quickly washed up at the tub and changed his clothes. He'd just gotten done rinsing out the ring of dirt from the tub when Nyla let out a strangled cry, and the soulstone bracelet turned to ice on his wrist. The cold nearly sliced through his skin. Nyla's pulse quickened, thrumming madly from the soulstone.

"Nyla!" Xander shot to his feet, ready to rush to her side when he saw the blood blossoming near her neckline. He grabbed a washcloth off the sink's edge and rushed forward. Any thought he had about an easy night's sleep or time to read from the archive's resources was gone. "How the hell…" he muttered as he pressed the cloth to the gash at her collarbone.

Even through the washcloth, Xander could feel the heat that radiated from Nyla's skin. She burned hotter than the sun. It was a miracle that her blood wasn't boiling from the deadly temperature of her skin. He wondered if he should fetch Nan but was too afraid to leave.

So, he waited for the blood to stop. Nyla's skin had lost its pallor and was now a shade of gray not unlike death. His stomach clenched and buzzed with anxiety and the fear of the unknown. At last, the blood stopped, and he got up to grab a fresh washcloth as well as some supplies from his bag. He could handle a cut…maybe, with the grace of Balmae on his side.

Armed with a bottle of brandy and clean bandages, his hand hesitated over the pair of scissors, but he grabbed those anyway. He didn't have a clue how he was going to properly wrap her wounds.

Nyla's face was contorted in pain, her nose scrunched and lips pulled into a tight grimace. There was something darker expressed in her features, something Xander wasn't certain he wanted to name.

Absolute and unmasked hate.

For a split second, Xander worried about what was going on in her head, but with no way of knowing, he set his things on the nightstand and sat next to her on the edge of the bed. He swept the sweat-drenched hair from her face and paused for a heartbeat, the scissors held loosely in his hand.

Nyla's shirt was stained and sticky from her blood, and there wasn't any way that he could treat her without cutting away the neckline. Besides, he couldn't just leave her in bloody clothes. His brows furrowed as he cut away the sleeve and part of the thin shirt's neckline. He chucked the bloody scrap in the direction of the washroom and grabbed the brandy and washcloth.

"Sorry, Nyla, this is gonna sting, but the burning means it's working," he said quietly as he poured some brandy over a small patch of the washcloth.

Nyla didn't so much as whimper or fidget as Xander dabbed and cleaned the wound at her collarbone and shoulder. When he was satisfied that the gash was properly cleaned, Xander wrapped a bandage around her shoulder and taped gauze over her collarbone. He was certain that she didn't need stitches, but she'd have a jagged scar.

After Xander had cleaned up, he plopped down in the desk's chair with his feet up. A groan left him, as did whatever adrenaline that had appeared in his previous panic. The day had been long, and for him it had started before the sun even rose. And now there was nothing but moonlight.

"I hope you know that you owe me an explanation as to how you managed to cut yourself that badly while unconscious," he said dryly.

His eyes closed as he tilted his head back. He'd hoped to do some reading from the books he had brought back from the archives this morning after Nan had come on the heels of the page boy Xander had sent, but between the stable boys and Nyla's condition, Xander was absolutely worn out and slightly exasperated. He didn't know how much longer Nyla would be like this and wondered if Nan had been right when she'd examined Nyla this morning. With no way to change the past, Xander resolved to help move Nyla to Nan's practice and have a Healer come to examine her too. He trusted Nan, and if Nan said Nyla needed a Healer more than a doctor, then so be it. That's what he'd do.

Xander let out a breath he hadn't known he'd been holding and let himself have a few more moments to rest his eyes and aching muscles before he begrudgingly stood up. He set his sleeping bag up at the foot of the bed and settled in with only his worry to keep him company. There wasn't much he could do for her in this state, and he really didn't know if there *was* anything he *could* do.

A grim realization popped in his head as he focused on the even rhythm pulsing on his wrist from the soulstone.

What would happen if she got hurt again?

Another quickly followed.

What about food and water?

It's not like he could wake her up, let alone get her to eat or drink. He should've listened to Nan this morning. Moving Nyla was a risk worth taking so Nan could better care for her.

It took a while for Xander to relax enough to actually fall asleep, and even then, it was a fitful sleep consumed by a recurring nightmare he had only just begun to understand.

For weeks now, he'd had this realistic nightmare that completely consumed his subconscious. In it, he was always running toward a long field.

Bursts of energy, of magic as he understood it now, exploded and collided with each other. The air around him was charged as if the biggest bolt of lightning to ever strike the earth was about to come down from the heavens and smite everything in its vicinity.

Two figures slung magic as easily as warriors drew their bows or clashed swords with their enemies on a field of battle. These two

Casters fought with the same ferocity as any soldier. One of them had distinctly silver hair that whipped around her in the harsh wind that grew stronger with every second. The other was merciless.

He didn't know it when he first started to have this nightmare, but now Xander knew that the silver-haired girl existed and that this was probably no ordinary nightmare. Now, he knew her name: Nyla.

And now, when that final burst of scarlet and lilac magic collided with a thunderous rumble and *that* terrified shriek pierced the air, Xander fell to his knees. Every ounce of willpower was aimed at waking up, at fighting the nightmare's hold on him.

He didn't want to know. He couldn't bear to know what happened next.

Xander had never gotten to the end of the dream, and tonight was no exception as his eyes popped open at once. A cold sweat dotted his forehead.

Xander sat up on his elbows and glanced around the shadowy room before his eyes landed on Nyla. Somehow, she'd contorted herself in her sleep so that one leg dangled over the edge of the bed. The blankets had been completely thrown off and were draped over the footboard and floor. Xander got up and gently repositioned Nyla so she wouldn't fall off of the bed and pulled the thinnest blanket the inn had provided up over her. Relief flooded Xander's veins when he realized her bandages were still in order and that she hadn't fiddled with them in her sleep.

Any exhaustion that had plagued his body before was stamped out by the nightmare. As quietly as he could, Xander tiptoed over to the pile of books he'd brought from the archives and grabbed the first one, as well as a freshly lit candle. He settled back down in his sleeping bag and read until his eyes drooped shut again.

***

Nyla's tongue was like sandpaper when her eyes slowly drifted open, only for her vision to fall victim to her heavy eyelids. Aside from her dry lips and her parched throat, she only felt an aching burn throughout her body. Minutes passed; all the while Nyla failed to coax her eyes to stay open.

When she recognized the bare decor of her room at Caselle's inn, relief flooded her body. Pale pre-dawn light filtered through the tiny slit between the curtains and the windowsill. She rolled onto her side and carefully propped herself up. Her head swam at the movement and forced Nyla to rest there until her head stood still. Weakly, she swung her legs over the side of the bed. She hesitated before pushing herself up to stand on her feet. Though her legs wobbled, the dizziness had passed, and she managed to walk around the bed toward the sink.

It was then that she noticed a strange noise, like subtle snoring. She considered what in her room would drone on like that, when Nyla tripped over something by the edge of the bed. Luckily, she was able to catch herself, but the odd rhythm had been interrupted mid-snore.

"Nyla? Are you all right? What are…?" Xander sprang up. The book he'd been reading slid to the floor with a *thud*.

"Xander? What are *you…?*"

They both trailed off as they looked at each other in the shadowy light of the nearly burnt-out candle and weak fire. After a moment's pause, Nyla shrugged and continued on her path to the sink for a drink of water as Xander closed his book and got to his feet. A sharp throb started to pound in her head. Behind her, she heard Xander shuffling around, and soon enough, the room was bathed in a light that made her squint. She gulped down the water, not even bothering with a glass or canteen, and simply put her lips near the faucet like a cat to cream.

Once Nyla's throat was satisfied, she straightened and wiped her mouth with the back of her hand, catching a glimpse of herself in the mirror. Her silver hair was wild and tangled in knots. She had bags under her dulled eyes. She dragged her eyes down her waning face, landing on her collarbone and shoulder. Nyla lightly pressed her fingers to the bandages and lightly traced the cut neckline of her shirt.

"What happened?" Nyla rasped as she turned to face Xander. She blinked against the glare of the candlelight.

He stood with his arms crossed over his chest, but it wasn't out of anger or expectation. Instead, insecurity and deep lines painted his face, his lips turned down into a frown.

"I was hoping you'd be able to tell me. You've basically been in a coma all day, but it wasn't really a coma because you got hurt and..."

Nyla hesitated for a second, not quite sure how to respond to that. Her eyes went wide as the prospect of being in a coma-like state for a whole day sank in. None of it made sense: the dreams, the all-too-real gash, her unconsciousness.

"I thought it was just a bad nightmare, but now..." She trailed off and looked down at the covered wound on her collarbone and shoulder. "I'm not entirely sure."

"Well, start when you collapsed on me yesterday morning and walk me through what happened from there," Xander offered with a shrug.

Nyla nodded. She could do that. "All right, yeah. But first, I'd really love to wash up or change or something."

"Yeah." Xander scratched the back of his neck, "I'll just, uh, I'll be downstairs and see if anyone's manning the tavern and get some food. I mean, if you're hungry?"

"Maybe just some soup or something light? That'd be great. If not, don't worry about it."

Xander shuffled out of the room and locked the door behind him. Nyla waited the space of a heartbeat before she gathered fresh clothes and started to fill the tub with steaming water. Her aching body groaned as she lowered herself into the porcelain soaker. The groan quickly turned into a sigh as the near-boiling water worked to soothe her muscles. She noticed the soulstone on her wrist and fingered it with a frown. Where had it come from? Did Xander have the other? She'd have to ask him about it when he came back.

Still, though, where had he gotten them? Nyla idly wondered how much trouble he'd gone to on her account as she halfheartedly dragged a washcloth over her skin as if she could scrub away the...nightmares.

Before she got dressed again, Nyla twisted herself this way and that in front of the sink's mirror. Her back was already covered by a blackish-blue and eggplant-colored bruise. She winced as she angled her body to get a better look, but to no avail. After she'd tugged on some cotton pants, she examined the bruise on her stomach.

It wasn't as big or as severe-looking as the one on her back, but it hurt to the touch, and so she ceased her prodding and pulled her shirt on.

Xander hadn't come back by the time she'd finished, allowing Nyla to settle on the bed and gather her thoughts behind closed eyes. Where should she start? How was she going to explain everything to Xander, let alone herself? More importantly, should she tell him everything? What would happen if she didn't? She fingered the soulstone bracelet absently.

A few minutes went by before someone knocked thrice on her door. The soft but clear *raps* were followed by Xander's voice saying, "Nyla? It's me."

She shook her head. The worry faded from her twisted lips, and instead, exhaustion settled over her features. "Come in."

"I come bearing gifts!" Xander said triumphantly, holding up a small pot of soup and two lidded half-pints of something Nyla wasn't all that interested in.

"How'd you manage to open the door?" she asked as she took the pot of soup from him and lifted the lid.

"I'm incredibly talented. What can I say?" He smirked, all too proud of himself in her opinion. "Anyway, I wasn't sure if you drank tea, so I got a mint and a raspberry tea."

Nyla sat up, crisscrossing her legs, and considered this for a moment, not particularly a tea person. "I'll give the mint a go, thanks."

Xander smiled and clutched the raspberry tea close to himself. Nyla thought he looked like the hellox that caught the pollipes, both from the moment he entered the room and now that the raspberry tea was safely his. As he sipped, Nyla's eyes caught sight of the matching soulstone bracelet on his wrist, but said nothing. Instead, she unveiled the soup to her eager eyes and inhaled the hearty aroma wafting off the steaming pot.

Xander took his seat in the desk chair and kicked his socked feet up on the bed. Nyla avoided his expectant gaze, focused solely on her soup, determined to at least get one spoonful in before the questions started to fly.

"Oh fine!" She rolled her eyes, finally looking up from her half-way-devoured soup. She didn't think he'd last this long, but she knew she owed him some kind of explanation, even though she herself knew very little. "I…I finally figured out where I was in the…whatever that was."

Xander nodded encouragingly, and Nyla took a deep breath before she continued, "It's the Woodlane Manor…my brothers and I, when we were kids, we used to go there, to play. We'd spend hours just exploring or whatever."

Nyla stopped, staring wistfully into her soup. Her eyes glazed over as she lost herself in the memories again. Xander didn't say anything, only sipped his tea thoughtfully.

"And the cut?"

"Oh that?" Nyla took a keen interest in the now nearly empty soup bowl. "I got into a fight…in the nightmare thing…with Cedric…"

"Cedric?" Xander questioned. His feet slipped from the bed as he sat up and leaned forward. A squeaky floorboard *creaked* in protest beneath his feet.

"The red-eyed man that I saw in one of the Falls' visions," Nyla sighed, agitated by the thought.

"Are you all right?" Xander studied her intently. "I mean, besides the cut?"

Nyla considered that for a heartbeat, replaying the scene in her head, the image of the bruises on her back and stomach. "I'm fine. Just a little bruising. It's no big deal. Really."

At her forced smile, Xander quirked an eyebrow. "Really?"

She eyed the smooth, peach-colored stone ruefully. Her gaze flicked briefly to the matching bracelet around Xander's wrist before she forced the minor irritation from her mind. Nyla hummed in response to his concern, unflinching even in the face of Xander's hard stare or the reminder of how badly she ached. Xander folded his arms casually over his chest. Nyla's breath died in her lungs. Hopefully, he didn't press her for the truth. An air of thoughtfulness overcame him. Nyla sagged in relief. It didn't seem as though Xander would ask any further questions about her wellbeing.

"Okay, so what about this manor, and whatever it is that brought you there, has to do with that red-eyed guy and your magic?"

Nyla chewed her lip and looked down at her crossed legs. A single thread stuck up from the quilt on Nyla's bed. She took it between her fingers and pulled at it absently. "My family..." Nyla began with a hard swallow. Her throat had gone dry again. "I think he set the fire, but...why?"

The words spilled from her lips like a lead weight and sat definitively in the still air between them. She couldn't look at Xander and instead took a gulp of tea to soothe her parched throat. Xander shifted in his chair, and the next thing she knew, his warm hand wrapped around the one that had been playing with the bare thread on her quilt. His thumb drew circles on the back of her hand, and though Xander couldn't know it, the empathetic gesture chased away the bitter anguish that threatened to rise up inside Nyla.

"I know we barely know each other, but I'm here for you," Xander offered softly. His sincere voice coaxed Nyla to look up at him and meet his eyes.

Unlike her neighbors who had looked at her with pity and worry, though those emotions were there too, his eyes held pain and understanding. Just like that night after the ogre incident, she recognized that same hollow emptiness and steely or bitter grief she knew all too well reflected in Xander's eyes. On some strange, and maybe even twisted, level, it was relief and comfort that filled her when that mournful pity didn't consume his gaze.

"Thanks, Xander, for everything," Nyla started sincerely, "but you really don't have to stay with me. I have no idea where I'm heading, but I know Cedric'll be there, and he'll hurt anyone associated with me. I can't ask that of you."

"You're not, though. I'm offering to, and I really don't mind. Besides, I have nowhere to be, and *someone* has to make sure you eat and take proper care of yourself," he jested.

Nyla didn't know whether or not her guilt over his offer to help was made worse by the fact that he seemed to know good and well that he didn't have to stay or go with her, but was choosing to anyway. She pushed the concern away. That was a problem for tomorrow.

For now, Nyla's lips turned up into a small smile as she chuckled. Her eyes trailed away again, but the grief and agony had faded. Her gaze landed on their still-joined hands that rested on the bed. The tips of her ears heated, but she made no move to pull away. She teasingly met Xander's warm eyes again.

"I don't know. I'm pretty capable of taking care of myself. I mean, I've lasted this long."

"Okay, Miss Berries for Breakfast, Lunch, and Dinner."

Nyla pulled her hand away from Xander's and playfully swatted at him with both hands. He leaned back in the chair, effectively maneuvering out of her reach.

Nyla struggled to sit up, wincing as she moved. She hoped her lips hadn't twisted as her muscles groaned in protest at her attempt to follow after Xander to try and swat at him. She forced a laugh as she eased her jarred body back against the pillows. "Yeah, well, no one asked for your opinion, oh master game chef!"

If only he knew that she'd managed to successfully set traps for small game like pollies a handful of times when she wasn't on the move.

Xander put his hands up in mock surrender, despite the concern lining his face. Nyla fidgeted some and took a breath with her eyes closed, knowing she couldn't escape Xander's concern forever.

Xander was staring at her when her eyes flicked open. "Are you *sure* you're okay?"

"I'll be okay," she lied.

***

Xander narrowed his eyes but said nothing more. Nyla's assurance wasn't entirely convincing, but what could he do? He'd probably overstepped his boundaries already, what with calling Nan for help, but how could he have left Nyla like that? It was clear that neither of them knew what was going on with her, but Xander would bet whatever it was had to do with Nyla's magic.

As soon as she was better, she could go to the archives, and he could...He didn't know what he would do. He could stay in Caselle, at least for a little while. But the longer he stayed here and saw Nan and George, the more risk was in it. It wouldn't be long before he'd have to see someone he was actually related to, or worse, his grandfather, and then what? What would that confrontation bring?

No matter what Nyla decided to do, Xander had just about made up his mind. Caselle wasn't the place for him, no matter how much he longed for it to be some kind of salvation.

As his mind spiraled farther into itself, Nyla broke the silence that had befallen them. "Xander?"

He just hummed in response, his mind half surrendered to exhaustion.

"Why were you sleeping on the floor?"

Xander watched her slowly, carefully. "I didn't want to leave you like that. You really scared me when you woke up and couldn't hear me, and then you just up and collapsed. So, I called a friend of mine, Gerri. She lent me the soulstones and sat with you today to make sure you'd be all right." Nyla's stare didn't waver, so he went on. "That and I also gave up my room. Didn't know how long you'd be like that, so I figured it didn't make any sense to keep a room I wasn't gonna use."

"Oh." Nyla stared at him with wide eyes. He only shrugged.

He twisted around in his chair and peeked out the window to avoid her eyes even if only for a second.

It was true that Xander wasn't going to use his room at the inn, not while Nyla was like that. Even while he was abused by the lazy stable boys and doing the work of three men, he knew he had to stay close to her when he wasn't picking up a little extra money. It wasn't that he *needed* the money and couldn't afford both rooms. He had plenty from other odd jobs he'd had in different cities. He just—Xander swallowed. It was the right thing to do, and he could replenish his emergency fund.

When he turned back to her, his face had become difficult to read beyond the exhaustion of whatever toll the day had taken on him.

"It's still a little early, so we probably have a few more hours of sleep—and don't you dare give me that look and debate me on the sleeping arrangements. I'm fine on the floor," Xander scolded her with a wag of his finger.

Nyla huffed, feigning innocence. Her lips pursed. "What look?"

"That one—the one you're giving me right now." He snuck a glance at her as he blew out the candles and set the dressing screen up in front of the fireplace. "I'm not arguing or debating this with you, so stuff it."

"Fine then. Have fun sleeping on the hard floor," Nyla huffed.

Xander only rolled his eyes as he blew out another candle.

***

Nyla ignored Xander as she shifted the pillows around on the bed and consumed herself with the task of getting comfortable. She turned onto her side, her back to Xander, and closed her eyes. Pain flared up in her side, no doubt from the bruises on both her back and torso. A whine threatened to escape her lips, but Nyla managed to cover it under the guise of an annoyed huff.

"You're not going to sleep, are you?"

"Nope."

It was silent for a moment. Nyla began to think that Xander was going to leave it at that and she would have to stew not only in her discomfort but also her guilt over the fact that the person paying for the bed and the roof over their head and all their meals was sleeping on the floor instead.

"You really aren't going to be able to sleep if I'm on the floor?" he asked quietly.

She barely considered her answer before the words slipped from her tongue, "Not a wink."

"Oh, for the love of…" The *buzz* of his sleeping bag's zipper and the rustle of fabric reached her ears. The bed dipped under Xander's weight. Nyla glanced over her shoulder and saw that he'd placed his sleeping bag on top of the covers and was settling himself inside it once more. "There. Happy now?"

"No." She shifted onto her back and turned her head to face him, a goofy smile on her face despite the strained stretch of her abdomen.

"Nyla, I swear—" Irritation crept into Xander's voice.

"I can't sleep on my right side," Nyla answered sheepishly, fidgeting. Xander turned his head to meet her eyes in the dark and gave her a funny look that seemed to ask, 'why does that matter?'

"I usually sleep on my left, and it's weird trying to sleep on my right because of this stupid knife wound." She fought to untangle her hand from the blankets, and once she finally did, Nyla gestured angrily toward the mostly covered bandages on her collarbone and shoulder.

"I'm sorry almost being stabbed and killed is interrupting your usual sleeping habits," Xander replied dryly as he turned his back to her.

Nyla followed his example and tried to settle comfortably, but ultimately gave up and begged for sleep to take her.

14. MAGIC AND A RAVERIN'S LEGS

Somewhere, a grandfather clock chimed eleven o'clock. The loud *gonging* startled Nyla awake. It was the first time she'd heard it, and if she hadn't known any better, she would've thought that it was right next to her ear. She blinked a few times and rolled over onto her back.

Xander's sleeping bag was abandoned on the bed beside her. Nyla had nearly kicked it off the bed in her sleep. Her brows furrowed before she remembered what had happened the night before. She snorted and shook her head tiredly.

"Good morning, Nyla." Nyla jumped as a woman's gentle voice startled her. She bolted upright with a sharp intake of breath at the pain caused by her jerky movements. Her eyes landed on the woman in the chair by the fireplace. "Easy, easy. Don't want to provoke your injuries, do you?" the woman soothed her, standing slowly.

Nyla watched, her mouth dry, as the older woman approached her cautiously, unable to move away or call for help.

"I'm Dr. Geraldine, though you can call me Gerri," Gerri started. "Perhaps Xander mentioned me?"

Nyla wracked her brain for a moment before remembering what Xander had said about the soulstone bracelets and the friend he'd called for help.

"Yeah...yes, he did."

"So, he hasn't completely lost his mind then," Gerri chuckled softly with a shake of her head. "Well, anyway, to business. Do you mind if I examine you?"

Nyla hesitated, even though she knew she'd need *something* to help her heal. She nodded her head slowly, still not entirely convinced she needed a doctor or a Healer.

"Oh," Gerri said, "before I forget, Xander asked me to give this to you."

She handed Nyla a folded-up note before she reached for her practitioner's bag. Nyla unfolded it and examined the squished letters. Xander's handwriting was neat enough, but his letters were scrawny and sharp.

'Be back soon—had to do something, but will be back for lunch. There're some books from the archives on the desk if you want to take a look. I'm not gonna lie, I just grabbed whatever because I didn't know what to look for.' Nyla glanced at the desk and noticed the pile he had referred to before reading the postscript. *'Don't forget to rest and please let Nan take a look at you. I know you're worse off than you said you were.'* She rolled her eyes at this, mentally cursing the soulstones and their breach of privacy. She tossed the note back onto the nightstand where it landed with a fluttered rustle beside her knife.

Nyla sat silently as Gerri—or "Nan" as Xander called her—began her examination, listening to her heart and her lungs. She answered as many questions as she could about her family's health history, but there wasn't much she could say either way. Then Gerri took a look at her bruises and the knife wound on her collarbone. Tutting, Gerri gave her a Healer's tonic to help her regain her strength, both physically and magically, and some salve to help heal the cut, as well as some more bandages. Gerri also gave her an elixir to take if the pain bothered her too much.

While she offered to stay until Xander came back, Nyla sent her on her way, wanting nothing more than some time to herself to think things through...and another bath. After a moment's rest, Nyla got up and swung her bare feet onto the cool hardwood floor, wincing as she took steadying breaths to calm the spike of pain from her new movement. She hastily washed up and changed into fresh clothes. Unabashedly, Nyla stared at her reflection in the mirror above the pedestal sink for the first time in what seemed like decades.

A weathered and weary girl with bags under her eyes and a boniness she knew wasn't all that healthy stared back at her. At least the color had somewhat returned to her cheeks, but she was still considerably pale. Her lilac eyes were dull with fatigue.

Nyla frowned and splashed cool water on her face. A small spark of energy raced through her, refreshing her tired body. With a satisfied smile, she turned her attention to changing her bandages.

Nyla pursed her lips as she carefully moved the strap of her undershirt down her arm. The neckline stretched to accommodate the new strap position and allowed her better access to work. She grimaced as she slowly pulled the adhesive from her collarbone. A groan escaped from between her teeth at the sight of the gnarly gash. In some places, especially on her shoulder where the cut wasn't as deep, a yellowish scab had begun to form over the thin line. With the salve and a washcloth in hand, Nyla cleaned the wound and gently put some salve on it as Gerri had instructed. Just as she had set them aside and began to struggle with the rolled-up gauze, three knocks echoed through the room.

"Come in!" she called distractedly. The roll fumbled from her grasp, and through the short plummet, it managed to unravel and tangle itself together much to Nyla's waning patience.

The door clicked shut behind Xander. Mud and dirt trailed in his wake as he angrily ditched his boots in the corner by the door. Nyla watched him in the mirror and nearly dropped the twisted roll of bandages again. Her mouth gaped open.

"What happened—" she started with an exaggerated gasp before Xander cut her off with a simmering glare.

"Don't. Ask," he grumbled, shedding his dirt-splattered shirt off.

His usually neat hair was disheveled, and sweat soaked his flushed face. Xander stiffly pulled on the shirt from the night before and carelessly tossed the dirty one in the general direction of the tub.

Instinctively, Nyla moved over and made room for him at the sink. She refocused her attention on her wounds, even as part of her couldn't help but wonder what he'd been doing to come back with mud-splattered pants and a grumpy scowl. Xander came to stand beside her at the sink and began to scrub away at the dirt on his hands and face. Nyla quietly struggled to singlehandedly wrap the wound on her shoulder, aware that Xander was watching her out of the corner of his eye as he combed through his hair. As her irritation grew, a bemused smile replaced the dark, frustrated look on Xander's face.

"Want some help with that?" he teased.

"I got it," she mumbled halfheartedly.

Her tongue poked out between her lips, her eyes narrowed in concentration as the gauze twisted and slipped from her arm once again. A low whine bubbled up from her chest. Xander snickered and took the bandages from her hand without another word.

Nyla opened her mouth to protest, but stopped. She obviously wasn't succeeding in wrapping her shoulder herself and watched as Xander wrapped her shoulder and covered her collarbone with nimble fingers.

"Thanks," Nyla murmured as she readjusted the strap of her shirt into its rightful place. She slipped on a clean, albeit loose and faded, button-up. "If you want, I can leave so you can wash up."

"You know what? That sounds like a good idea, if you really don't mind. I'll meet you downstairs then."

Nyla grabbed her knife and took the first book from the pile on the desk before she headed out the door.

Nyla found a table in the far corner of the tavern and settled with her back to the wall. She had the best view of the tavern, and arguably the best light too, with a magicitric sconce on either wall beside her and a candlelit lantern on her table.

Proper reading light was the least of her concerns as she stared at the faded blue book in her hands. Her eyes traced over the gold lettering on the hard cover. *Magical Awakening and Talent* was stamped in the center of the cover in neat script, the book with its hard cover and aged pages feeling more and more foreign in her hands the longer she stared at it. Her fingers clenched the book tightly.

She didn't want this, any of this. She didn't want magic; she didn't want to have to chase down how to use her magic or the meaning of what Fortune Falls had shown her. She didn't want to be responsible for all that had happened to her family and herself. Things couldn't ever go back to how they were, before the fire, before her hair and eyes changed, but surely things could get better, could be easier for her. All Nyla wanted was to carry on with her life, or what was left of it anyway. She doubted the book in her hands would hold any true salvation for her, but it was a start.

Her self-pity was interrupted when a tavern lady came over to her table, and Nyla ordered a glass of water if only to stall herself. The woman returned shortly and set the glass down with a huff, disgruntled by the lack of money to be made off of Nyla. She didn't care what the woman thought and took a sip before she opened the book.

The table of contents stared up at her. Nyla debated whether or not she should start at the beginning as her eyes skimmed down the list of chapters. The chapter entitled "Dream or Not?" caught her attention.

Renewed hope swelled in her chest as she hurriedly flipped to page eighty-three. Nyla had begun to think she'd have to travel to the Woodlane Manor to find answers about her magic and an explanation for the events of the last few days, but maybe this was all she needed and she could go back to her life.

It wasn't much of a life, she realized with a glance at the tavern's entrance. Always on the move, looking over her shoulder—and with good reason now—and being utterly alone. She stopped the doubts that poured from the darkest edges of her mind into the forefront of her consciousness and focused on the pages before her, thankful for its straightforwardness and simplicity.

Nyla absorbed everything she read. The most helpful passages to her dealt with astral projection and clairvoyance. They even mentioned premonitions and how they all differed from regular dreams. It was with a relieved heart that she skimmed them. She read a few passages here and there as they seemed applicable to her, or if she were interested, though she predominantly focused on astral projection as that sounded like the most plausible scenario to her:

Astral travel is when your second body separates from your physical body to travel the astral plane. Astral travel is achieved through astral projection or the act of your second body leaving your physical body and traveling the astral plane or any other plane of existence, including our own. The second body is connected to your physical body by an ethereal cord and is how your astral body finds its way back to your physical body for reentry. Also called the soul body, the astral or second body, is best described as the representation of your consciousness while traversing the astral plane. During this time, your physical body gives the appearance of being unconscious or in a coma.

The astral plane exists alongside our plane of existence and is only formless astral light until it takes on a landscape or setting suited for the thought-form entities there. Consequently, anything that exists in the physical realm first exists on the astral plane and therefore has a duplicate that remains there.

Nyla paused for a moment before skipping ahead, not wanting to read about how astral projection was achieved, and read the chapter's conclusion.

Even though premonitions, clairvoyance, and astral travel are all different and at the same time can be used in conjunction with each other, the major similarity between all three, especially clairvoyance and astral travel, is that you can be physically harmed while doing so.

It is imperative to practice caution when exploring these forms of magick, especially with astral travel, because once the astral cord is severed, it means certain death for the physical body. Even in natural death, the astral cord will sever and allow the soul body to enter the afterlife.

Nyla bit the inside of her cheek as she reread that. Her fingers traced the bandage over her shoulder, hidden by the sleeve of her shirt. She stared absently at that last line, completely oblivious to the person who had since plopped into the chair across from her.

"So, find anything interesting?" A spotless and composed Xander smiled when Nyla jumped in her skin. The worried look in her eyes was replaced by a strike of fear that flashed to annoyance when she saw him in the chair opposite her.

"When did you get here?" Her eyes narrowed in a glare at being startled so easily.

"A few minutes ago, but you were so busy that you didn't even notice." He held a mug up to her. "Tea?"

A lopsided grin was plastered on his face, and Nyla rolled her eyes as she took the mug from his hand. She gripped it with both hands, savoring its warmth.

"Yeah. I mean, it's not enough to say I'm an expert, but at least I've got an *idea* of what's going on now," she started and instantly dove into a brief explanation of clairvoyance versus astral projection. She concluded by saying, "So I think I was somehow traveling on the astral plane or maybe traveling clairvoyantly. All I know for sure is that it wasn't a premonition because…because Astrid said she'd already passed on."

Xander took a gulp from his stein and nodded his head slowly. "And both of those can happen spontaneously?"

"Yes?" She shrugged.

Out of the corner of her eye, Nyla saw someone approach their table with a large tray of food. She shot a questioning glance toward Xander. He just tilted his head and held a hand up, though it could barely be seen above the edge of the table.

The woman stopped just before their table and set a plate of raverin legs and vegetables before Xander. A bowl of soup and plate of bread landed in front of Nyla before the woman set off as silently as she'd come. Nyla met Xander's eyes and quirked an eyebrow. He didn't seem to notice as he set his napkin on his lap and dug into the first of the two huge raverin legs.

Many people, Nyla's parents included, considered raverins, with their forked tongues and tails like snakes, to be a symbol of evil or bad luck, but they were also the royal bird. Loyal and fierce, the armies of Tenebris often trained the birds as scouts and messengers. It led her to question why raverins were considered a food source when they were so regarded.

Maybe because they couldn't be a bad omen if they were served on a platter.

Nyla didn't know how anyone could possibly eat a whole raverin leg and not be full, let alone make it through two without their gut bursting. She shook her head slightly and brought a spoonful of soup to her lips.

The pair made quiet conversation about this or that, the things they'd each seen on their travels, things that were easy and carefree. Nyla had long since finished her soup and had her fill of bread by the time Xander finished his plate. It was probably lean meat, but Nyla still found herself pondering how many people could eat two or possibly more raverin legs in one sitting. Her eyes trailed to the book she'd placed on the table beside her empty soup bowl.

"I think I'm going to head out tomorrow or the day after. There's something I need to see for myself, and it might hold more answers than these books," she said without meeting Xander's eyes.

"Okay. Do you want me to go with you? I mean, traveling together is better than going at it alone, right?" When Nyla finally glanced up, she saw genuine eyes despite the self-assured grin Xander shot her.

"You don't even know where I'm going," she pointed out with a smile and a wag of her finger.

"I'm up for a little adventure." He leaned back in his chair and placed his clasped hands in his lap.

Nyla considered this, and even though she didn't think she'd ever feel this way again, she had to admit that Xander was nice to have around. It was a relief to not be alone, to have someone there in the middle of the night when the night creatures howled and went on the prowl for easy prey. But she still didn't know why Xander wanted to come with her or what he stood to gain from staying with her. The only thing she knew for certain was that she felt safe around him. It was a sort of contentedness in her blood she hadn't felt in a long time. If she could trust anything about her life right now, it was her instincts—or so she hoped.

She shook her head with a laugh, easing the mild uncertainty from her mind. "Oh, this'll be an adventure! I'm practically going halfway across the country to the Woodlane Manor."

"A place I've never heard of and where you were attacked while possibly astral projecting or whatever, but go on." Xander waved the idea on.

"I know, I know: it sounds stupid and irrational to go to a place where someone might be waiting to kill you, but it's the best lead I've got. And if someone's there to help me, then that's great. I get a mentor *and* answers, maybe even a normal life again." Nyla paused and licked her lips. Her eyes dropped down to the table again. A rosy blush crept along her heated cheeks. "I just feel like I've been running away for so long, and I'm done. I've finally got a direction to go in or a path to follow, and I think I need to explore it, so if you want to come along, then fine. If not, I understand. I don't even know if this is a good decision or if I'm walking to my death."

Xander didn't say anything immediately, and as Nyla's heartbeats pounded in her ears like a war drum, butterflies were unleashed in her gut.

"We'll need a lot of supplies, so that means shopping in the market and a good night's rest," he started after a second or two. He scrunched his nose and frowned. "And I need to do laundry, so if you want to use the tub, I'd do that before I wash those clothes. You know what, no. I'll just burn them and get new ones. That's a better idea. I'll never get the dirt out anyway."

Nyla laughed and shifted forward in her seat. "That sounds like a plan. You go shopping, and I'll go ahead and do *my* laundry while you're gone."

"Oh no, no, no," Xander argued, "you're coming with me because you need new boots. It's a miracle your feet haven't fallen off yet with the state of those boots. And don't go giving me that look either. It's my treat, and trust me, I've got enough money." Once again, Xander scolded her by wagging his finger at her.

"My boots are fine, and I really don't need anything, but thank you anyway." She crossed her arms. "Besides, Gerri told me to rest."

Xander's eyebrows raised. His eyes gleamed with surprise. "And you're actually listening to her?"

Nyla huffed, crossing her legs as she leaned back in her seat. "Well, I mean...I was *thinking* about it, yeah."

Xander laughed boisterously. "See? Didn't I tell you you needed someone to make sure you took care of yourself?"

Nyla glared at him as he wiped imaginary tears from his eyes. "Bold words from the man trying to convince me to go shopping when I *should* be resting."

Xander only held his hands up in surrender, and that's how Nyla found herself following him down the street and into the first shop of what she hoped wasn't many.

15. A GLIMPSE OF THE PAST

"**I** don't need it, though." Nyla folded the shirt up and placed it back on the seamstress's display table alongside about a dozen other garments Xander had picked out. She'd aimlessly walked around the shop and admired the seamstress's magnificent dresses, a task that distracted her from the tight pull of her bruised body, until Xander had called over to her, drawing her over to the goods spread over the table. The woman who had been helping Xander watched from the other side of the table as the pair stared each other down.

This was the first shop Xander had dragged Nyla into, and while it wasn't as crowded as the cramped and jostling marketplace, at least twenty people milled about the wide shop, oblivious to the silent debate between two of the youngest patrons.

"Are you sure? Because I can think of at least one shirt that is absolutely destroyed and needs to be replaced," he started, but Nyla held her hand up. There wasn't a doubt in Nyla's mind as to which shirt Xander was referring to: the one he'd had to cut so he could bandage her up the other night.

"My clothes, while I'll admit they're old, are perfectly fine, thank you." She glanced down and fought back a grimace.

Of all the shirts she could've worn, it had to be the blouse with the frayed hem and missing buttons. The flowers that had once adorned the fabric had long since faded. She couldn't even look at her pants. Nyla's lips pursed into a thin line as she forced her hands to remain at her side.

Her eyes flitted back to Xander. Curiosity overwhelmed her mind. "Why? Why is this so important to you?"

Xander glanced back at the table with an almost remorseful glimmer in his eyes. He rubbed the back of his neck. Alongside the things the seamstress had apparently selected for her, Xander had also picked some things for himself. Xander's eyes barely flicked over to the smiling assistant before he'd taken her by the elbow and gently guided her off to the side.

"When was the last time you bought yourself something or had clothes that were in good shape?" he asked quietly. "If we're traveling halfway across the country, you need new things."

"That doesn't answer my question," Nyla pointed out. "I don't have mon—"

Xander shook his head, cutting her off. Nyla blinked, letting her mouth close silently, swallowing her protests as best as she could under the pleading gaze of her companion.

"Please just consider this, okay? I get it if you feel awkward or guilty or whatever if you can't afford these things, but I don't mind. Really, I don't. I'm fortunate enough that I can help you out, and I don't know. I just…it's not like we're strangers anymore, but friends, right?" He paused long enough for Nyla to nod. She supposed after all the days they'd spent traveling through the Shadow Forest, maybe they weren't strangers anymore. Xander's lips turned up in a small, relieved smile before resolution and a bit of mischief gleamed in his eyes. "I *want* to do this, and not just because I don't want to hear you complaining that you're cold or your feet hurt while we're traveling. I have no problem with this, but if you really don't want anything, that's fine too. I just thought it'd be nice to get some new things." He rambled on and shot another glance at the woman. Her smile had faded somewhat, and her eyes darted to the tinkling bell above the door, another customer for her to prey upon.

Nyla studied Xander for a moment and nodded slowly. "All right, but let's get one thing straight: I am *not* a complainer!" she hissed through her teeth.

"No, you're not," he chuckled, "but I thought it'd help you see reason, and it did. So, if you'll excuse me, Miss I'll Keep Walking 'til My Feet Fall Off, I have a seamstress to pay."

Nyla didn't even have the time to scoff at him as he strolled away, even if what he said was true. She'd definitely had her fair share of days when she'd gone too far without water or food or rest or all three. It'd been a miracle she hadn't died, though Nyla shook the memory from her mind.

It didn't do to relive that moment when she'd collapsed in the middle of a rare road in the Amber Dunelands of southern Tenebris. Or the throb in her head and the weakness in her blood. Or the way her tongue was as dry as sand, her throat like the desert itself.

It was another miracle that some old trader and his family were on their way home from the market. They'd picked her up on their way and even let her stay with them for a while, wanting to make sure she was healthy before they sent her on her way. Nyla's recollection broke up as Xander asked if she was ready to leave.

Xander, with their bags in hand, led the way back out onto the bustling street. All too quickly, they were swallowed by the throng of people in the busy marketplace. Xander navigated the packed cobblestone streets with precision and confidence. Nyla just followed in his wake, unnoticed by the mass of people. That minor relief didn't stop the pounding thunder in her ears that could've been her own heartbeat or the footfalls of thousands of people. She figured it was the former given the tightness in her chest and the panicked apprehension that swelled and vibrated in her throat.

It was hard to tell how far they had walked because everywhere Nyla looked, the city streets were teeming with new spectacles. She knew that if it weren't for Xander, she probably would've walked in one large circle with the way her head spun from the crowd and the endless stalls of eager merchants, all thirsting to sell their wares.

She witnessed passersby get nabbed by a merchant every so often, but it hadn't happened to her. It did little to comfort the fluttering heartthrob in her throat that seemed to taunt her to the beat of 'not yet.' She smiled with a long sigh when Xander held the door open for her when they reached the next shop.

Nyla didn't get a chance to really study the place before a wrinkled old man approached them. His eyes swept over her, immediately drawn to Xander as if he were under a spell. The man's face broke out into an excited grin and warm recognition, and both of them seemed to forget Nyla was there at all.

"Xander, my boy, where have you been? It's been what, three, four years since I've seen you last? You've gotten so big!" the man exclaimed and vigorously shook Xander's hand. Nyla wasn't entirely convinced that he hadn't dislocated Xander's arm, but the matching enthusiasm on Xander's face assured her that everything was fine. "Gerri will be so glad to see you! She's just upstairs, as luck would have it!"

"It's good to see you again too, George." Xander's voice had taken on an air of prim and properness, something she hadn't heard before. "George, I'd like to introduce you to Nyla. Nyla, George Remington."

Nyla politely shook George's hand, and the conversation that followed made her head spin even more than the crowd outside had. She listened as her eyes swept over the shelves of supplies.

George owned a general store of sorts, stocked with food and camping supplies and everything in between. It was definitely an outpost and probably one of the first places travelers stopped on their way out of Caselle.

Even with some of the odds and ends mixed in with the travel supplies and grocery items on the far side of the store, George had a neat shop from what she could see. As the two men chatted away, Nyla's attention wandered toward the empty shop. It seemed as though they were the only people in the whole place, besides the mess of goods that lined the shelves and aisles.

They spoke about how George's business was faring and his family, but Nyla didn't hear anything about Xander's, or even how they knew each other. All she could gather from their eager conversation was that George apparently had three grandchildren now, and his youngest, and only, daughter had married a respectable businessman.

Xander didn't say much about what he'd been doing all these years, dodging questions with vague answers and a skillful redirection of their conversation so that it was back on George. If George had caught on, he didn't press Xander for honest answers on the matter, much to Nyla's disappointed curiosity.

She didn't really start to pay attention again until George mentioned the strange occurrences out at sea that some of the sailors had spoken of. They'd been telling tales of islands appearing out of nowhere in the middle of the sea offshore. Even the shifting of the earth and the tides couldn't create or reveal these islands. If that wasn't strange enough, these islands were deserted, and not in the usual sense.

Usually when islands appeared due to the shift of the earth or changing tides, they were small sand banks close to the coast and had some sort of sea life cast about them. But these islands were completely barren and bone dry. Nyla raised an eyebrow, but didn't say anything. It's not like she knew much about islands or the sea to begin with.

"Ah, no more of that. Could just be more sailors' tales for all we know. But still, islands don't appear overnight. Something strange is going on, and not just at sea I'm afraid." George shook his head and smiled faintly. "If your father were here, he'd tell me not to put any stock in drunken stories told by sea-weary, homesick lads."

"My father had his stories too, though," Xander laughed. With a cock of his head, he continued more seriously, "But you're right. My father, though he was wily in his own ways, was a rational skeptic."

It was silent for a moment. Both men had their solemn eyes cast to the floor. Nyla glanced between them and understood their long faces entirely. They both still mourned the loss of what was probably a great friend and father, just as she still grieved for her own family.

George cleared his throat and began, "So what can I do for you today? Going adventuring?"

"Yes!" Xander confirmed almost excitedly. "And we are need of a lot of supplies. Do you mind if we start a pile on the counter?"

"Not at all! And remember, you're family, so anything you need, don't worry about it." George gave them each a hard look, one that Xander had used on Nyla a few times. She wondered if he'd learned it from George.

Xander began to weave his way down each aisle. Nyla trailed after him, staring wide-eyed at all the items on the giant shelves that nearly reached the ceiling. She couldn't even see the things on the topmost shelves without standing on the tips of her toes and straining her neck.

As she'd been studying the jam-packed shelves, Xander had grabbed a few items here and there until his arms were full. He went off to drop them on the counter, and Nyla continued to wander idly.

Left to her own devices as Xander hunted down whatever supplies he thought they'd need, Nyla stopped every so often to examine some of the more peculiar items, like the crystal balls on the shelf before her. The spheres sat on plush, velvet cushions.

One in particular captivated her with a sort of enchantment Nyla couldn't explain. As she stared at her distorted reflection, the glass began to cloud over with a billowing fog. Once it cleared, a mystifying lilac bloomed before her eyes. A soft, purple glow radiated from its bobbing form, but when she blinked, the image was gone.

Not even a glimmer of fog remained in the glass. Nyla looked up and down the aisle to see if anyone else had seen what had happened, but to her luck, no one was there. She hurried down the aisle as if nothing had happened, hoping that in doing so, she could shake the image from her memory for good.

It was an easy thing to shake as she was quickly captivated by the other items for sale. George had a large collection of magical items, including a plethora of dried herbs that made Nyla's nose tingle. She suppressed a sneeze and scurried down the rest of the long aisle and into the next. Her eyes swept over the shelves on both sides of her.

Daggers sat on similar plush cushions as the crystal balls, etched with strange symbols she couldn't name. Another housed candles of all colors, and sizes.

Farther down the aisle, Nyla spotted a large variety of wands. Chief among them were metal and wood types. Some were curved or twisted, while others were straight as an arrow. More than a few had carvings etched into the surface or crystals embedded in them. Nyla recognized some of the symbols as being the same ones that adorned the daggers from before and began to wonder if they were supposed to be a set, a wand and a dagger, or if these symbols were simply common in the world of magic.

She couldn't stop her lips from turning down into a perturbed frown. For the first time, the weighty realization of just how much she didn't know about her own magic, but rather magic as a whole, hit her.

Nyla shook the grim admission from her mind and stared wistfully at a few of the wands. These, compared to some of the others, were quite plain and carved completely from wood. One held the warm aroma of cedar, and she could smell it even without bringing it to her nose. She admired these for their natural beauty and simplicity.

Even though they were relatively plain, being only cylindrical shafts of wood, Nyla could feel the spark, the energy, the presence, the *potential* of the magic they could wield.

Were these stronger than the other wands? How did wands affect magic? Were they only as powerful as the person who used them? All these questions and more floated around in Nyla's head as she begrudgingly moved on to find herself surrounded by books of all subjects in the next aisle.

She delicately ran her fingers over the spines. Most of the books were newer, but a handful bore faded and cracked spines. Mostly, Nyla just floated down the row, awed by how many books George had, even if he were selling them.

When Nyla had finished with that aisle, she turned down the next one only to be met with the sight of dishes and varied kitchenware.

How did George organize his store?

This was something she found herself turning over in her head more and more often as she explored the shop. The shelves beside her were chock-full of household odds and ends. Among the mirrors, candlesticks, and lone dishes, her eye caught the sight of a bronze picture frame. Her footsteps hesitated and faltered to a stop as she finally turned to gingerly pick it up.

It was a dusty frame, about the size of the beloved portrait she kept with her. Nyla swiped a finger through the dust over one corner, exposing a delicate flower etched into the metal. It had five petals, much like the ones she used to draw as a kid, and a star in the center with a circle in its middle that touched the star's inner points. Nyla assumed that they were supposed to be forget-me-nots.

Through the dust, an inscription on the very bottom of the frame caught her eye. She cleared the dust from this too, curious even as practicality nagged at her. Disappointment flooded her as she stared at the newly exposed foreign words. The careful script was in a language Nyla didn't know.

Nyla reluctantly placed it back on the shelf.

"Oh, there you are!"

She jumped a little. Her eyes darted from the frame in a panic before the slight tremble of nerves subsided. A tiny voice from the recesses of her mind reassured her that she was safe, and it was only Xander. Nyla turned to face the boy leisurely strolling toward her.

She cleared her throat. "Did you get everything you need?"

Even though she hadn't done anything wrong, Nyla felt like a kid who had gotten caught with cookie crumbs on their shirt before dinner. Her hands burned. Sheepishness crept through her veins. Xander nodded and scratched the back of his neck.

"Yeah, I think so. I don't know if there's anything you need specifically, so just take a last look around, and *don't settle on anything*." He fixed her with that look, the one that shut down any protest she could possibly make. It was the same look she swore he'd learned from George.

"All right." She spared a fleeting glance back at the frame and chewed the inside of her lip before she hastily walked off to see if she needed anything.

*****

As she left, Xander followed where Nyla's gaze had been drawn to. He figured it wasn't the mismatched dishes littering the shelf that had caused the longing hesitation in her eyes. The disturbed dust on a bronze picture frame confirmed his suspicions.

He took it and cleared the rest of the dust away with his sleeve. The careful inscription sparkled in the light of the shop. Xander recognized the engraving on the bottom of the frame to be in Eurish, and though he was rusty, he knew it was an old expression that resonated strongly with Eurland's culture.

Love is for forever.

A slow smile spread across his face, and he brought it up to the counter where George was standing.

"Found something else?" George eyed him keenly.

"It looks that way." Xander shrugged. "Do you think you could hide this? As a surprise?"

"You care for her." George eyed him, but the way he spoke didn't seem like a question.

Xander swallowed. "We've really only just gotten to know each other, George."

"So? People who've only just gotten to know each other don't decide to follow each other through an unknown adventure."

"All right, all right," he agreed. "It just seems crazy, and I can't explain it, but maybe I do care about Nyla more than someone who's only known her for a short time should. I've never met anyone else who can make it feel like you've known them forever."

George nodded. "That's what true friendship is like. One day you meet, and the next you open your eyes and realize years have gone by. It's one of life's many wonders."

Xander didn't know about that, but he did know that being around Nyla made him feel whole again. It was like she was forcing him to face life again when for so long, he'd refused to. Yes, he knew she'd helped him during the storm and with Fortune Falls, but it seemed like she was helping him in more ways than he could ever repay.

That's what terrified him.

He had no idea where she would take him, or who he would end up being when they got there, but so long as the emptiness didn't consume him again, he didn't care. Nyla might very well prove to be the death of him, but at least he was living and maybe even coming into himself until then.

Silently, he and George began to package his finds up into bags, all the while Xander marveled at the changes he seemed to have undergone since meeting Nyla. The skepticism and jaded disposition had slowly melted away, and in their place curiosity and eagerness now bloomed.

Nyla returned a few minutes later with an armful of supplies as he and George went back and forth about payment. George refused to take Xander's money, and Xander refused to accept their supplies for free. In the end, they compromised. Xander promised to visit more often and write to them as much as possible.

"Ah, Xander!" Nan called from the stairs, a gleam in her eyes. "I thought I heard George talking to someone familiar!"

"Hello, Nan!" Xander hugged her and whispered in her ear, "Thank you for keeping the inn a secret."

"Nyla should be resting," she whispered back and pulled away with a smile on her face. "Why don't you two join us for tea before you head out? Going on an adventure, I assume?"

So, Nan led them up the staircase in the back hallway into their apartment, and Nyla, thankfully, played along as Xander made introductions.

***

Nyla didn't quite know what was going on, as she'd already met Gerri earlier, but she decided to let Xander sort it out, as it seemed like George hadn't known his wife was helping them—helping *her*—at the inn. All she knew from the moment they settled into the couple's living room was a whirlwind of tea and slices of freshly baked banana cake, Gerri's infamous banana cake apparently, and a barrage of stories and questions about how she and Xander had met.

As the sun set, George and Gerri called for their driver, William, to take them back, and Gerri had found a pair of boots that their granddaughter had no use for, much to George's disappointment. Nyla tried them on as they waited and walked around their apartment, but when she reentered the living room, her old boots were already gone. As if he could assume the picture of absolute innocence, Xander rocked on his feet and stuffed his hands in his pocket, humming all too suspiciously.

By the time William had pulled the Remingtons' sleek, black carriage around to the apartment's side entrance, she and Xander had been strong-armed into a promise to visit again shortly. Nyla smiled tiredly as she climbed into the carriage, full in more ways than just from the cake. She closed her eyes for a moment, savoring their afternoon with Gerri and George before she curled up on the bench and stared out the window. Across from her, Xander was quiet, his eyes withdrawn, but the light that had ignited in them the moment George had spotted him in the shop hadn't dimmed.

The sagittarii's hooves *clopped* against the cobblestone road. The steady sound soon mingled with that of merchants' voices, thousands of pounding footsteps, and the hum of conversations between the well-dressed people that strolled along as the carriage turned onto the main thoroughfare through the marketplace.

Nyla watched the passersby through the window. Her eyes closed for a moment, and she hummed in contentment. She could get used to a luxury like this. Especially now that she noticed the fatigue that had settled in her bones. She hushed the concerned voice in her head asking if she'd be well enough to travel in the morning.

Xander must've wondered the same thing, as he cleared his throat and started, "When we get back to the inn, you should rest up. I honestly didn't think we'd be that long, but George and Nan are…well, they're George and Nan. They're like grandparents to me. No one, especially family, leaves their place without food and forgetting the time."

"No worries." She stifled a yawn. "I didn't mind, and I fully intend to honor my promise to visit again…someday." The carriage was jostled by a rut in the old road.

Xander laughed heartily. "Then I guess you'll have to hold me to it too because I didn't think I would ever be back here."

Nyla wanted to ask why not, but stopped herself.

"Anyway, I have something to do when we get back to the inn, so I'll see you at dinner."

She nodded, further chewing on the questions his statements raised. She knew Xander had been doing *something* to pay or barter for the room at the inn, and that thought alone was enough to flood her with guilt.

But the fact that she'd never be able to repay him, for everything? That nearly drove her mad with shame, guilt, and most of all:

gratitude. And now he was willing to follow her to who knew where for Helpet knew what. Nyla shrugged the notion from her mind and went back to watching the mass of people that strolled through the marketplace.

***

She'd taken a long nap after she and Xander had hauled their bags of goodies up to the room, only to be awoken by a haggard Xander letting himself in. That's how she found herself at the table in the back of the tavern sipping on a cup of warm water and honey. A damp-haired Xander joined her about fifteen minutes later.

After a quiet dinner in which Xander again managed to eat two raverin legs, Nyla returned to the room to soak her weary body and wash up. The sweet aroma of bergamot faintly clung to her skin and hair when she was done. Whoever made this soap, whether it was George, his wife, or someone else, they earned her praises.

Nyla had just started on her laundry with the eucalyptus oil she'd gotten from George's shop when Xander knocked on the door.

"Come in!" She scrubbed at one particularly stubborn stain until the threads of the old shirt threatened to give way. With a sigh, she wrung the shirt out and hung it with the other garments she'd thought to save over the edge of the tub.

"I'd ask to join you, but some of my clothes are beyond dirty at this point." He flopped down on the bed and crossed his ankles, with his hands clasped over his stomach.

"And here I thought you were just going to burn them!" she teased, scrubbing at the dirt on a pair of pants.

"I really should at this point. It'd be a whole lot easier than try-ing to get all that mud and dirt out of 'em," he sighed. There was a moment of silence before Xander spoke up again. "It smells kinda flower-y in here."

Nyla froze and risked a quick glance in his direction. Had she gone overboard with the bergamot soap? It just smelled so nice and fresh! Her line of thought trailed off as the bedframe creaked as Xander got up.

"Smells nice…must not be lavender then."

Nyla slowly let go of the breath she'd been holding. She looked over at him, her body sagging with relief, but Xander's back was to her as he started to empty out the shopping bags along with his own backpack onto the floor at the foot of the bed.

A wave of calm settled over her as she laughed a little. "It's bergamot."

Xander hummed pleasantly as he began to focus on his intended task, and Nyla went back to finishing up her salvageable laundry.

Once Nyla was finished, her fingers shriveled and raw, she went to reorganize her own things and figure out what she no longer needed. Xander fiddled with something at the foot of one side of the bed, so Nyla took her bag and sat on the floor near the fireplace. The fire's warmth licked at her skin as she settled in her place.

Gingerly, Nyla took the top shirt from her bag, setting it aside with care, and dumped the rest of its contents, spreading them around her. There wasn't a question in her mind as to what to do with the old shirt she'd set beside her, as it protected the portrait, and there was no way she'd give up that little means of safekeeping.

She moved onto the jumbled mess of bandages. Nyla knew it wasn't right, though she'd had no choice but to clean them as thoroughly as she could on her travels and tuck them back into her bag to reuse if she needed them again. The ends were frayed, and the once-long strand of cloth was split into multiple pieces. It had been cut a few times, as she couldn't always clean it or didn't need the whole roll at once. This was further proof that miracles happened, as Nyla had rarely gotten seriously sick or even injured on her own.

She nibbled on her bottom lip and set these to one side. The next few items, mostly waning soap and a little square box of oils, were added to the pile with the portrait.

Unsurprisingly, there were plenty of rags and bits of old papers that she'd scribbled notes on. Nyla arranged the notes and read through each of them. Most of them were about towns she'd passed through or people who had helped her along the way. She kept these for future reference and the dwindling charcoal stick along with a few of the rags.

The rest of the bag's treasures, including old dried herbs, were added to the discards pile with the old bandages and rags. Even her faded, tattered towel and washcloth were added to that pile, as she'd gotten new ones from George.

After taking a quick inventory of everything, including the new items George had graciously given her, Nyla repacked everything in the new bag both he and Xander had insisted she'd needed. She stood and tested the bag's weight. It was only a little heavier than it was before, though more comfortable than her old bag, even with her healing bruises.

"I hope you still have room in there for this." Xander's voice came from behind her.

"For what?" Nyla questioned curiously, more confused than she'd like to admit. She turned to face him head on, setting her bag down as she did so, her eyebrows raised in question.

He handed her a rectangular package wrapped in brown paper. She took it and stared down at it before looking back at a nervous Xander. With a pinched inhale, Nyla gently unwrapped the firm object. Her eyes began to water at the sight of a smooth bronze corner. Her face broke out into a grin as she finished unwrapping the frame.

"Thank you, Xander, this is… this is amazing. Thank you," she said breathlessly. She ran her finger over the forget-me-not in the top corner of the frame. Her eyes floated down over the inscription again.

"It's Eurish. It says, 'love is for forever.'" She felt Xander's eyes on her as she admired the frame for a moment. He added softly, "I saw that you'd been looking at it and thought you might have something to put in it."

"I do."

Nyla went back over to her bag and eased the shirt from the top and unwrapped the portrait. She walked over to the bed and placed the frame face down on the soft covers. After sliding the backing from the frame, she slid the portrait in and replaced the back. Nyla turned it over and smiled warmly. The portrait was the same as it always was, but the frame put her mind at ease.

It was safe now.

Xander came to stand beside her, and she showed him the painting.

"Those are my parents, my older brothers Derek and Westley, and that's little Lydia," she whispered as she pointed to each family member in turn. Xander loosely slipped his arm around her waist and angled his head to get a better look.

"You and Westley have the same face."

"Yeah. Same eyes too…well, we used to anyway. But he got Pop's curly hair." She turned around to hug him. "Thanks, Xander. I really mean it."

"I know."

16. THE BREAKING POINT

About a week had passed since Nyla and Xander left Caselle. The roads they traveled made their path easy, and they'd passed few others on their way, something Xander assured her was unusual for this time of year.

Today was no different than days past: Nyla had stripped her jacket off before noon and had already pulled her hair back into a braid. Xander didn't seem as affected by the rise in temperature, or the cool morning air, as she was. He'd been comfortable in a short-sleeved shirt the whole time. Nyla threw a scowl toward the glaring sun and held fast to the whispered promise of cooler weather in the air. Despite this, it wasn't an exaggeration to say thus far, the weather had been fair, an utter blessing as Tenebris was in the midst of its rainy season.

Her heart ached to be back in the woods, protected by the uncivilized forest despite the things that haunted and prowled the dense woodland. The Shadow Forest was often cooler than the other forests throughout Tenebris, and the country as a whole. But once the sun set and the night life began to stir, the realization that danger lurked everywhere would sink in.

Nyla shifted her focus to their surroundings, not wanting to linger on dark speculations and visions or astral projection. Pleased to see the emerald tint that painted the sapphire leaves overhead, she basked in the knowledge that Harvum was fast approaching in these parts. After the other night, which had been particularly windy, Nyla was beyond appreciative of the tent and magic heat lamp Xander had gotten from George's shop.

Granted, it came as a bit of a shock that first night when Xander had set up the tent, but Nyla definitely wasn't going to complain about it. Besides, what was a little luxury on the road? Sure, it took a little longer to break down camp each morning, but it was well worth the comfort of being sheltered from the elements. Especially since Nyla still had some tenderness from the bruises on her back and stomach.

She imagined that they were now those awful yellow-and-purple splotches that bruises morphed into before they faded away. The first few days after the ballroom fight were difficult, but at least now the aching pain had dissipated, though she had the medicine Gerri had prescribed her to thank for helping her manage it. Nyla no longer felt like she was pulling a tendon every time she changed or bent over.

Her eyes swept over the narrow dirt road as she returned to reality. A few steps ahead of her, Xander hummed, lost in a world of his own, too.

They hadn't spoken much since they took to the road again, but that was okay. Nyla needed to contemplate a few things and hopefully avoid the things that troubled her. She ducked her head, lost in thought, absently watching her feet. Xander's humming made her realize how much she had secretly craved some form of human contact.

The desire had been buried so deep within her subconscious that she may never have noticed it if it weren't for the dark-haired boy that led the way. Her eyes flitted up to look at him before they reverted back to the ground beneath her boots. Her hands clenched and unclenched at her sides before she shook them out and forced them to stay still. That didn't stop the stormy tendrils that wormed their way through her mind in the form of questions she didn't dare try to answer.

How would she feel when they inevitably parted ways? Would it be understanding and acceptance that flooded her then? Or would it be anxiety and a crushing numbness that consumed her? She shifted her braid to sit over one shoulder and forced herself to stare straight ahead. Her mind still disobeyed, choosing to wander instead.

It brought her to times when she hadn't been alone. Her mind brought her back to that sacred kitchen table that could barely fit all six of them plus their dishes and meal. It led her to remember quiet breakfasts when she'd overslept and Derek would sit with her and they'd talk about what they thought were 'grown-up things.'

By the time she'd finished her meat and potatoes, they'd have the answers to all the pressing issues their parents whispered about at night. Those solutions were always so simple and in plain sight that she'd often marvel at how the idea hadn't occurred to the adults.

But Nyla knew better now. Things weren't simple. Sometimes, there were variables involved, things no one could control, that ripped and shred and tore reality to bits. They could leave a numb calm when there should be panic. Sometimes, they left only panic. Nyla shivered and let her eyes close for a second.

No. She refused to think about that, about the fire or the astral travel. Xander hadn't left her yet, and the other shoe hadn't dropped yet.

Who knew? Maybe he never would, and the Woodlane Manor would be the end of her life's greatest mystery. Instead of allowing the grim thoughts that began to swarm and buzz inside her, Nyla focused on the tune that Xander hummed.

It was an old, thought-provoking tune her mother had taught her years ago. She vaguely remembered the song and could hear her mother's accented voice alongside Xander's tranquil humming. The song was mournful and reflective. The more Nyla willed the lyrics to the forefront of her memory, the more surprised she was. It was almost as if they spoke about the war lost to time and the Shadow Forest, of the land, of how Tenebris came to be as it was, of how the choice of one Caster ruined her and those around her. She sang along in her head as Xander hummed and silently dissected the lyrics. It was easy to do as he seemed to be humming it on a loop.

Nyla turned her thoughts to the manor. A fresh wave of worry and apprehension filled her. She tuned out the steady beat of their footsteps on the dirt road and Xander's even humming as her fight with Cedric flooded her memory. She drew a deep breath. The images played on like motion pictures in her head.

Somehow in the heat of those harrowing and confusing moments, and in spite of the red-eyed man's taunts, she'd wielded her magic. She'd known exactly what to do, and by some miracle, she'd survived with only a minor injury and the bruises that had begun to fade.

Worry cast shadows over her vision. She absently traced the newly formed scar on her shoulder. The wound had healed nicely, and she had forgone the use of bandages several days ago. The deepest part of the cut, where the blade initially made contact with her skin, was still spotted with scabs, though it too had begun to pucker into a thin pink scar.

Xander gently bumped into her other shoulder. His assuring smile parted the shadows of her worries.

"You okay?"

She blinked, a little dazed at his intrusion. When had he slowed to match her pace?

"Yeah, I'm fine. Just thinking about something." Nyla turned to look at him and attempted a weak smile. The warm concern in his eyes deepened like the worst part of a storm, the only indication Nyla had that he didn't believe her. Nyla licked her lips and stopped in her tracks. Xander followed suit and turned to face her. She opened and closed her mouth before she found the words she'd been looking for. The world around them stilled as they stood in the center of the lane. Eventually, Nyla took a shaky breath and spoke first.

"By some grace of...I don't know *who* or *what* exactly, I managed to blast Cedric and use some magic in that...during that astral projection thing. But I don't *know* how I did that. I don't know *how* I did any of it. How do I just conjure up my powers and use them? What can I actually do? I have no idea how to control this or what I'm capable of and—what if I get hurt? Or worse, what if I hurt..." She trailed off and glanced away. The onslaught of questions made anxiety prickle her skin. Her vision blurred out of focus as the inevitable uncertainties consumed her. Nyla blinked against the emotional assault.

Xander grasped her by the shoulder and angled his head so his eyes were level with hers.

"You're not gonna hurt anyone. It's just not in your blood. So, you wanted to hit Cedric, but self-defense is completely different. No one would blame you for hitting back at *him*. That means you shouldn't either. And as far as what you're capable of, we'll find out. If the manor is a bust, I think I might know someone who can help, but you owe it to yourself to do it your way first."

"You think so?" she murmured hopefully.

"No, I don't think. I know so," he said confidently.

Nyla met his eyes and marveled at how much compassion was in them and the certainty that dripped from his voice. She nodded, too stunned for words. He squeezed her shoulder again and pulled away slowly.

Neither of them said anything for a long minute, and even though she should've, Nyla still couldn't find the words to thank him, an affliction she hoped wasn't permanent. She wiped at the tears that had collected at the corners of her eyes, and they pressed on. Their footsteps were infinitely louder in the silence that had befallen their surroundings. Nyla still considered what she could say to let Xander know how much his assertion had meant to her, but her mind refused to string two words together.

"What would you do, if you were me, that is?" She turned her head to look at him as they walked. Xander glanced at her and considered it for a second.

"I'd figure out what I could do and probably, completely by accident, set something or myself on fire." He kept walking as Nyla stopped dead in her tracks.

She caught up to him after her second of shock wore off. "Oh, my Helpet, you're serious."

"Yeah, I've, uh, *accidentally* set a few things on fire, but at least I can cook now. You know, without the whole 'fire and panic' bit." Nyla's jaw dropped at how casually Xander mentioned his unfortunate knack for pyro tendencies. She shook her head and considered his answer to her inquiry instead.

"So, you would immediately start to figure out how to use it and what you could do with your magic?" She bit her lip. It was risky, but it made sense. Why wait until they reached the Woodlane Manor to start? Suppose Cedric *was* waiting for them when they got there? He wouldn't attack her with a dagger again.

Or at least she wouldn't if she were him.

"Yup." Xander popped the *p* with a wry quirk of his lip. It left her wondering what could possibly go wrong.

All Nyla saw was Xander as he came out of the woods at Fortune Falls, much too close to the singed leaves, and barely suppressed a shudder. Nyla didn't say anything more and considered her options, even as the horror of one incident washed over her.

In the end, her curiosity won out. She also reasoned that the more she explored her powers and tried to figure them out, the more she'd know how to handle them, but also what she could do.

As Nyla began to plot what the best course of action would be to experiment with her powers, the world around her once again faded away. She'd have to start with small things, but what? All she knew she was capable of doing was blasting things—or people. She furrowed her brow. She definitely couldn't do that to start off with. It simply wasn't safe.

Her mind wandered back to Caselle. Somehow, someone, somewhere had managed to figure out a practical application for magic in the form of plugic and magicity.

Maybe that meant magic was more scientific and less mystical than she thought. Nyla thought about the bare necessities of survival: shelter, fire, water, and food. She sincerely doubted that her magic could build them a shelter. Food and water were another thing Nyla figured she couldn't conjure up with magic, though she did wonder if she could manipulate both water and sources of food.

Nyla shook her head. That left fire. Could her magic spark one? Would it be wild and unruly? Or tame? She contemplated this as a sickly heat began to worm its way through her gut. Nyla panicked, seized by terror. This was different than the all-consuming heat that signaled her unwanted astral travels, though. She glanced around.

The trees on either side of the road had drooping branches and limp leaves. They were muted in color, but not like the leaves in the heart of the Shadow Forest. These were on the verge of turning gray instead of the darker shades of blue that were nearly black. Nyla didn't realize she'd stopped walking to examine a tree until Xander was at her elbow.

"I'm glad you noticed it too. I was beginning to think I was going crazy or something." His voice was heavy with relief, but held a sort of tension that Nyla knew stemmed from caution and uncertainty.

"It could just be a disease." She bit her lip. She'd seen diseased trees, and this wasn't normal, even for something like fire blight. "Maybe it's just the Shadow Forest playing tricks or something."

The doubt in her voice seemed to take on a physical body as they each studied the trees around them. Their trunks were shriveled like prunes, but instead of that waxy texture, their bark was bone-dry and brittle.

"Maybe we should just keep walking?" Xander suggested.

Nyla nodded as she hid her shiver. There was something more going on, and she couldn't put her finger on it. A tingle ran down her spine, and fear had a firm grasp on the knotted pit of what most people called a stomach, though Nyla was beginning to think hers had been replaced by a cavity filled with only anxiety.

The farther they walked, the weirder their surroundings became. Nyla pulled her jacket back on and wrapped her arms around herself. She couldn't shake the chills that had overcome her despite the bright sunlight that pounded down on them. The leaves overhead waned until only fragile branches obstructed the sky. Then those too disappeared. That left shriveled, gray trunks and stumps where healthy trees once stood tall and proud. The hair on the back of her neck prickled as acid rose in her throat. Her eyes drooped just like the remaining branches on the poor trees lining the road.

They tread carefully on. A shadow passed over them, but the sun didn't seem to notice and kept smiling brightly down upon the earth. The dirt road beneath their feet gradually shifted into a fine, gritty sand. Nyla knelt and ran her fingers over what should've been the road. Like the leaves and healthy trees that should've been there, the road had melted away too, and their surroundings had morphed into an open desert that stretched on in all directions for as far as she could see.

Nyla stood and ground the fine particles between her fingers. In the far distance, she could see the beginning of the forest again and maybe even a proper road. Behind them, the faded leaves and trees would give the same appearance to people going south as Nyla and Xander had in front of them. A mere sign of life after the seemingly endless beige sand.

Her lungs drew tight breaths of air that never seemed like enough. It wasn't that she couldn't breathe or even that it was labored breathing; it was as if the air itself was too heavy to breathe. Nyla wondered if Xander felt the same way but didn't have the energy to ask.

Overwhelming emptiness like a void filled Nyla's senses. Even the wind had gone silent. Not even her own heartbeat thudded in her ears, even though it beat wildly against her chest. Her head buzzed with a hazy nothingness as lead filled her veins, rendering her fatigued. Or worse, like her body had been drained of all energy.

She turned to Xander then. "Do you *feel* that?"

"Feel what? All I feel is—" He hesitated. Nyla watched as he canvassed their surroundings, having already done so herself. "Is nothing."

"Me too." Nyla nodded slowly. It all came back to her. The memory sparked from the far reaches of her mind. "I've felt this before, this sort of nothing, when I traveled in the Dunelands. I thought it was just the heat and the fact that I... well, you know me. But I'm beginning to think it isn't like that at all. There's nothing here, no life, no energy, no..."

Her frown deepened as her brows knitted together. She thought back to the legend of the Shadow Forest, of how the evil sorceress was said to drain the magic from the land, of how some people thought that magic was tied to the land and gave it a sort of essence. "It's like there's no magic."

"You can tell that?" Xander asked, surprise clear as day in his voice.

Could someone actually *feel* the presence of magic, or lack thereof? And if magic *was* drained from the land, what did it mean? And for what purpose was it drained?

"I don't know," Nyla sighed. She stripped her jacket off again and began to walk across the desert that shouldn't exist.

***

As if there wasn't enough dread in Xander's bloodstream, a fresh wave flooded his veins.

Even so, he'd followed Nyla as they'd walked under the unblinking sun until they reached the other end of the sandy stretch. Even when they reached the edge of the desert land, they were met with the shriveled trees before they, too, faded away into the healthy trees of the Shadow Forest.

Neither himself nor Nyla had ever seen anything like this. But it was pretty clear to him that this wasn't a case of diseased trees or woodland. He even doubted that the Shadow Forest could morph into a partial desert on such short notice. It hadn't ever done so before, and most cases of the Forest's tricks could also be chalked up to a case of unprepared travelers.

Without a logical answer or explanation to satisfy him, Xander tried to brush it off. He went back to his humming. However, distracted as he was, he couldn't seem to pick a tune and stick with it. Nyla remained silent beside him, her head down, probably consumed by her own theories as much as he was.

By the time they'd stopped for the night, they were both agitated and unwilling to make conversation. Glares and eye rolls were easier to come by then a friendly smile or easy joke. Xander doubted either of them got any sleep at all.

Faith

Dia circled overhead. The *chitters* and *squeaks* of wildlife echoed through the trees on either side of the road. Cedric imagined the jewel-colored pollies hiding in the sapphire leaves. There would be hoffers hunkering in the underbrush, hoping to conceal their light gray fur, even though they could easily out-jump the raverin working hard to clear the surrounding area of all life forms that *could* flee. Of course, they didn't know Dia wasn't hunting for a meal, but it was for the better. If prey knew they weren't being hunted, his plan wouldn't work, and there would be a bunch of animal carcasses among the remains.

Cedric didn't know when he'd named the raverin, only that he had and that Dia seemed to respond to the name. The bird's delicate black wings dipped with the air current. Occasionally, the bird snapped his scaly tail like a whip through the air, but for the most part, the tail danced on the wind, dragging behind Dia without a care. He flew gracefully, confidently. Cedric envied the raverin. Its life was simple and quite possibly ruled only by its instincts. He supposed he should be grateful that the forked-tongued beast had tolerated him for the last few years that they'd known each other. Dia was the first raverin in a long time that Cedric was actually quite fond of. The others were… they were raverins. Dia was almost like a friend.

Or he'd gone truly mad after 600 years.

Cedric sighed. There was no way to keep putting this all off. Rolling up his sleeves, he couldn't believe he was about to do this.

Again.

To what end? It's not like he *wanted* to do this, just like he hadn't wanted or meant to do a lot of the things he'd done in his overly prolonged life. But yet, here he was, about to steal magic from the land all because *she'd* 'asked' him to.

Maybe a part of him was still afraid of her and for good reason. His mother wasn't a woman to be crossed. Especially since she'd—

Acid simmered in his gut. If he thought of that day and those flames for even a second longer than he already had through all of his waking moments these last couple of years, he was going to unravel.

Well, more than he already had.

The raverin overhead let out a sharp *caw*. Whatever remained hidden in the surrounding underbrush scattered. He waited a heartbeat and could only hope whatever critters had tried to hide were now far enough away. Taking a deep breath, Cedric drew his wand and the glowing, magic-filled quartz point from his cloak. He whistled a short note to the jet-black raverin overhead. The bird flew off with a *caw*.

There weren't any excuses left, except his own guilty conscience. All he had to do was walk away. He could forget about all of this and let himself fade—*die*—as he should've done 600 years ago.

So why was he standing here, ready to drain the land of its magic to make a potion he didn't even want to make in the first place?

The tiny voice in the back of his head that he should've listened to more often answered. He'd failed. He'd failed so many times throughout his miserable life, but there might yet be a chance, a spark of hope to do something right for once.

So maybe he had to play the villain. Maybe it would scare her, and then *she'd* never get her way to begin with. After 647 years, she hadn't gotten her way, so what would make this year, this season, this *day* any different from the ones that had already passed?

Cedric knew Fate was a fickle thing. It had let this petty grievance live on for centuries, and now that it had all but faded from memory, Fate had stoked the embers and relit a fire that wanted to consume the world.

And now he had his part to play.

He only hoped it was a better part, a more courageous part, than the part he'd allowed himself to play the last time around.

Of all his sins, of all his crimes, the worst was not being brave enough.

He hadn't gotten braver over the past six *long* centuries, Cedric knew that. But even cowards could do brave things once in a while.

If a potion was what she wanted, a potion she would get.

Satisfied he'd come to a reasonable solution for his cowardly heart, Cedric planted his feet firmly. It was time to get this over with. Holding the formerly clear quartz point in his hand, his brow furrowed in concentration. Keeping his wand arm aloft, the wind began to pick up. The breeze whistled through the trees, growing stronger until it howled.

The wind plucked the sapphire leaves from their weakening branches, muted in color and life until they shriveled on their stems and died, washed away in a streak of sapphire that the quartz absorbed. The dismal grays and charred ember color of the trees joined the color symphony, as did the rusty, amber coloring of the Shadow Forest's soil. Brilliant shades of green wafted up from beneath the earth's surface, and Cedric wondered if he was going too far.

As more magic flowed to him, he guided it with the wand to the crystal. The color of the sky, the wind's energy, swirled around him before it too was absorbed by the crystal.

Every color he'd ever seen was absorbed into the crystal. He fought against the urge to close his eyes against the blinding aura of the world around him, of the magic. But if he did so, the magic could smother him. He would lose control, and the magic would backfire and maybe even kill him.

Breathing heavily, Cedric slowed the pace of magic he consumed. As the flow reduced to a trickle, he was forced to take in the world around him, the new world. Just like yesterday, the Shadow Forest around him was reduced to a pile of ashy limbs and tangled remains where healthy trees had once stood. Where amber soil had once warmed the landscape, gray sand now choked the limp cluster of fragile twigs.

Cedric shut his eyes against the scene and the too-bright sun. Its rays mocked him, landing on his face and warming his skin, his soul. It gave him a hope he shouldn't—couldn't—have because all hope had ever gotten him was the idea that someone else would do something.

Someone else would stop her. Someone else would make a stand. Someone else would be the force that stood against the tide. Someone else would, someone else would, someone else would.

But that's not what happened, and it's not what would happen.

He was guilty, but most of all he was cowardly. He knew how to stop all of this without anyone ever knowing what had begun, but even after all these years of manipulation, of lies, of slander, and of cruelty, he couldn't bring himself to do it.

Someone else would, however burdensome it might be.

But that didn't mean he couldn't be someone who tried to do *something* brave, however miniscule.

17. LOSS OF MAGIC

Nyla slipped out of the tent early the next morning and made her way to the little oasis near their camp. She hadn't slept a wink thanks to the patch of desert they'd stumbled upon the day before and instead plotted to practice her magic.

The oasis was a spring pool hidden away in a small clearing and only a short walk from the relative safety of their camp. Rocks and boulders dotted the clear water and pebbled shoreline. Nyla perched herself on one of these sunbathed boulders, her legs dangling off the side. Her eyes fixed on the water that lapped at the boulder's base. The canopy of Harvum leaves opened to reveal a cloudless sky and beaming sun. The shafts of soft-white light sparkled on the water's crystal surface.

For a moment, Nyla lay back on her perch and collected herself. The sun shone brightly, even behind her closed eyelids. Even though the rock was hard and awkward to lay on, with all its bumps and pits, Nyla didn't mind as she steeled herself. She had no idea if this would even work or if she'd get hurt in the process. But at least she was isolated from anything or anyone else. With a deep breath, Nyla sat up and racked her brain.

When she was fighting Cedric, absolute hatred and the desire to hurt him had consumed her. That had resulted in something akin to lightning that would've struck him if he hadn't disappeared before she recovered from his attack on her.

Maybe that meant her magic was a feeling or something she had to envision. The notion sounded plausible enough to Nyla, and it was as good as any starting point.

With closed eyes and crossed legs, Nyla took a deep breath and slowly exhaled. Once her mind was clear, she cupped her hands in front of her and pictured a ball of light hovering just above her palms.

Warmth radiated outward from her chest, down her arms, and concentrated in her hands. Unlike the sharp burst of electrical energy that had flowed through her in the ballroom, this energy was calm and soothing.

The magic leisurely spread itself throughout her body. It was like that first whisper of a rejuvenating breeze on a hot day that swept over your face. When Nyla cracked her eyes open, astonishment fizzled in her veins. Her mouth hung open as her eyes went wide. Just as she'd pictured, a ball of light bobbed and glowed softly, hovering slightly above her hands. She moved her hands away, but the ball stayed and continued to hover happily in front of her.

Nyla willed it to move to the right, and it did. As her excitement grew, the ball began to waver and fade. She quickly tamped down her pride and focused her energy on the orb. Next, she willed it to move up slightly. Nyla played with it until she was certain she had control over it.

Staring at the sphere in awe for some time, she extinguished it by picturing it vanishing in her head. With a wide grin, she hopped off the boulder, only to sway on her feet. Nyla leaned against it for a moment before she quickly refilled their canteens at the water's edge, excitement shaking in her bones.

She turned to head back to camp. Her vision tilted with the onset of a vertigo spell, but Nyla managed to catch herself and keep her footing. She stilled until she was certain of her steadiness.

A branch snapped. Dull voices floated on the wind, though the low hum of their voices revealed it wasn't many, maybe three at the most.

As quietly as she could, Nyla slipped behind a boulder and concealed herself from sight. It was difficult to stealthily make her way back to the tree line, but she managed to without being caught. Carefully, Nyla peeked around the trunk of the tree she'd taken shelter behind to see who had entered her oasis.

A pair of men, too engrossed in their conversation to care much about their surroundings, held an animated conversation in hushed tones that steadily grew in volume as they came closer. Nyla melted farther into the foliage and had every intention of working her way back to Xander when the voices formed distinct words.

"...they're saying the magic was drained."

Nyla halted in her tracks and spun slowly back toward the tree line she'd just crossed. With a fleeting glance toward the general direction of where she and Xander had made their camp, she cautiously moved like a ghost over to a better position so she could listen in on the pair's discussion. Crouching low in the bushes near enough to the men, Nyla strained her ears to eavesdrop as they cast their fishing lines.

"Is that what the king's men are saying?"

"Yeah. I overhead one of 'em at the tavern yesterday. There's nine patches all together, and they're all to the south of town, spreading at least seventeen miles, so they say."

"Wonder what could do something like that. Do ya think it was man or monster?"

"No clue. I went to the one three miles that way." Nyla assumed that the man pointed in a specific direction, but her view was obstructed by the slender, webbed leaves of the bush she squatted behind. "It looks like someone dehydrated the land or something. Never seen something that made my blood run cold like that."

The other only hummed, and silence fell over the pair. Nyla waited a few moments to ensure that they wouldn't say anything more before she slipped back to her campsite.

When she returned, it appeared as though Xander had just woken up. He was sitting next to the fire and tended to a small pan, having caught something while she was gone. Nyla stopped, standing across from him, and instantly divulged what she'd overheard.

"We have to go! I just heard two men talking about the weird patches of land and the trees, and they said that there's nine of them, all to the south of town, though I don't know what town that is, and—" She gushed practically without taking a breath.

Xander stood and put his hands up, "Whoa, breathe, Nyla, remember to breathe. And go slower. It's *way* too early for this."

Nyla closed her mouth and blinked slowly. With a deep breath, she continued, slower this time as Xander had so requested. When she'd finished, Nyla added, "I think we should hit the next town, poke around, and just see if there's any truth to it."

"*You* want to go to a *town* and are actually standing there suggesting that?" He paused and studied her. "I need food or coffee or something."

With a little more grumbling, Xander fixed himself a cup of coffee and finished cooking their breakfast. Nyla tapped her fingers against her thigh and tried to get her eyes to focus on one thing. She failed, miserably. They darted around like her racing thoughts.

She barely remembered eating before she absently packed up her things and helped Xander break down the tent. He asked her a few questions about the men and if they said anything at all about which town they might be from. Seventeen miles was a lot of ground to cover, but in the end they both assumed it was Deering. Why else would the men have gone fishing at that particular pool? It was the closest town to their approximate location, and hopefully, it provided some answers.

Luckily, Deering wasn't too far off from the path they'd decided to take to the manor, but it would take the whole day to reach it.

All through their detour trip, Nyla couldn't help the recurring and all-too-persistent thought that the Woodlane Manor was a trap. It couldn't be a coincidence that the drained land was along their path, that they'd encountered one themselves, and would probably encounter another one before their journey was over.

What if it was *him*?

The more she thought about it, the more certain she was that it had to be Cedric. It was too coincidental, and she could see Cedric specifically sending her a message. He would want her to know he knew what she was up to and that he was getting ready to do *something*. But Nyla couldn't quite figure out what.

Why drain magic from the land, if that was even what he was doing?

All she knew for certain was that Cedric wanted her dead, and somehow, it was personal.

For both of them, apparently.

Nyla chewed the inside of her cheek but pushed her trepidation away. It was the only hope she had right now, and she'd be damned before she turned away from the manor. Her eyes flitted around and fell on a tree that looked all too gray.

The alarmed chirps and chittering from the birds hiding in the healthy foliage behind them reached her previously deaf ears. The Shadow Forest seemed more alive than it usually was, but the energy was nervous and full of fear. Everything was frantic, but she couldn't quite place why, especially since the last time they'd encountered a tree like this, it was an emptiness that blanketed the world. Up ahead, she swore there were scorch marks, but without the presence of smoke or a smoldering spark, Nyla knew it wasn't a fire.

"Is it me, or are the trees fading again?" Xander asked wearily.

"I really want to say no." Nyla grimaced.

They forged on, as the trees around them began to look sickly and dehydrated. With slow footsteps, they followed the dirt road until it turned to sand and the plants on either side were charred and shriveled.

Despite the sun beaming brightly overhead, Nyla couldn't help but believe they'd stumbled into a moonless night. While this patch of land was smaller than the desert they'd encountered the day before, it was still quite large, roughly a hundred yards in diameter.

Both Nyla and Xander bent to examine the crispy foliage. Nyla reached a trembling hand out to touch a shriveled leaf beside her. As soon as her fingers made contact with it, it shuddered and crumbled at the touch, transformed into that same gritty sand as the desert from yesterday.

"Maybe it's just a fresh wildfire?" Xander suggested weakly.

"I don't think so. There's no ash, only sand." She stood up and brushed off her hands. "But I do think you're right about this being recent, whatever this is. Why else would the animals…" Nyla trailed off as her eyes caught sight of something hovering over the tangled remains of a bush farther into the destruction. She drifted toward it. Everything that was once vibrant and now forced to the precipice of death turned to sand as she waded through the mass of recently drained foliage.

"Nyla, what are you doing?" Xander called after her.

She didn't answer as she stretched her fingers out to grab at the pulsating light. At her touch, it burst and displayed a single, purple lilac, before it too turned to sand.

Nyla pulled her hand back like it'd been burned. She couldn't stop the tears that flooded her eyes.

Her suspicions were right.

It was him.

Who else would leave a lilac there? What else could it mean other than this was all happening because of her? Her arms wrapped around her stomach. The sound of footsteps shifting through the remains made her flinch, even though Nyla knew it was only Xander. That comfort didn't stop the dam from crashing down in a single rumble of frustrated despair.

Xander crouched down beside her and wrapped his arms around her. She hadn't even realized she was on her knees until he tried to coax her to her feet. Just like that, everything came gushing out. The sobs, the gasping puffs of air, and the quivering words that had sounded in her head only moments before. Though Nyla's voice shook, it somehow portrayed the firm conviction her mind had given to each statement.

"It's all because of me," she mumbled against Xander's shoulder incoherently. He only shushed her and rubbed circles on the small of her back, stopping when she flinched at the ache of her healing bruises. "I don't know why, but it is. It's him."

"If it's really *him*, then we need to keep moving, okay? We need to get you somewhere safe, and at this rate, I don't think Deering's it," Xander murmured gently.

Nyla took a few deep breaths and steeled herself before opening her eyes and peeling away from Xander.

She let Xander help her to her feet. Neither one let go of the other's hand, and Nyla couldn't say she wanted to as Xander led the way back up the sandy path she'd created. They started a slow pace up the road. Fewer remains lined the road as they walked farther away from the outskirts of the drained land. Soon, a stretch of sand took its place where the lush Shadow Forest waited for them on the horizon beyond.

***

The pair made it to the outskirts of Deering before they stopped and made camp a long way off the road. The crackle of their campfire was a welcome rhythm as the nightlife finally settled into their symphony, even if it was plagued by the buzzing nervousness that Nyla knew all too well.

Other than that, the night was silent as they ate their meal. Part of Nyla wanted to go into town to investigate what the two men had spoken of that morning, but the majority of her senses agreed that a town like Deering wasn't the place for someone like her to pop up in, especially given the circumstances. Instead, she resigned herself to expand the efforts of exploring what she was magically capable of.

She peeked over at Xander, who was chewing slowly. When their eyes met, he swallowed hard and seemed to prepare himself for something difficult.

"I was thinking about going into town and poking around a bit. It shouldn't take me long, maybe an hour at the most, but will you be all right if I go?" he inquired softly from across the flames.

Always so polite, so subtle. Nyla wondered how he came to be that way.

"Yeah. It's probably a good idea to see what the townspeople know and what rumors are flying around." She put her plate to the side and drank from the mug at her knee, as she sat cross-legged on a blanket.

"Okay then. Maybe I'll run into one of the Royal Guard there."

They finished their meal in silence and avoided each other's gaze. It wasn't until Xander was about to leave that he turned to her and asked if she wanted his bow.

"I'm not very good at archery. Besides, don't you need something to protect yourself with in town?"

"I can handle myself if need be; I just want to make sure you have options in case…" He trailed off, his eyes distant for a moment.

"I have magic."

"I know, but…" Xander trailed off again, running a hand through his hair

Nyla's eyes glittered jestingly. "Well, if you're gonna leave your bow with me, I feel like it's my duty to warn you—you may not have any arrows left if I have to use it."

"Then I'll just have to make do then." Xander flashed her a lopsided grin.

With bow and quiver in hand, she waved him off and watched as he stalked through the woods toward Deering. She waited a second, her heart thudding against her chest with the rush of blood in her ears, before she settled back down on her blanket and cleared her mind.

Nyla needed to know what she could do, and it was with a grim determination that she set about her task.

***

The hollow sound of Xander's footsteps echoed in the cool night. Even though the stars twinkled brightly, and the half-moon glowed, an eerie shadow seemed to cast itself over the land. Every whistle of the wind through the leaves sent a chill over Xander, and he found himself wishing he'd listened to Nyla about taking his bow with him. He knew it would probably be useless against whatever threat she was so afraid of, and in a way, he recognized that he should be afraid of it too.

Rather than fear, he found a seething vengeance blossoming in his chest every time his thoughts fixated on what she'd said about the red-eyed man. There was so much hatred there that Xander couldn't even acknowledge the bastard by name.

Who targeted a teenager? A child's family? What in the world could possibly justify murdering a family like that? Or attempted murder?

He flipped the collar of his coat up around his neck. If he kept up this train of thought, he'd only spur the anger in his chest on and lose sight of what's at hand. So, he'd left his second-most prized possession with Nyla in the hopes that it didn't come to her needing it...

Or using all of his arrows and possibly losing them.

When Xander finally reached the center of the sprawling town, a hush hung over Deering. It didn't have avenues or streets with multiple houses like other places he'd visited. Instead, long fields separated the few houses that were nestled here and there. But even the least-populated rural towns had one street and a tavern. It was just the way of life in Tenebris. No matter how big or small a place was, it always had at least one tavern and a parish of sorts.

Every house he'd passed—well, all four of them—had dark windows. All of them were simple, one-story silhouettes with a pitched roof against the light of the night sky. Usually, rural folk would leave a lantern or some other marker for passersby, but not in Deering it seemed. Maybe they were all too afraid of the possible evil these signifiers would attract. Xander didn't blame them. He'd shore up his home—if he'd had one—given the circumstances too.

Light spilled from the tavern's window, the only building with any life in the town center, and illuminated three figures. The light glinted off the flash of armor hidden beneath indigo cloaks. Xander slowed, grateful that he could just make out what they were saying. One man drew closer to the other two, almost begging them to listen to him.

"I saw 'im with my own eyes! You lot have to believe me! He was jus' standing there—in the road this morning, drainin' the land!"

As Xander drew closer, he saw that the old man had a loose grip on the collar of the man, one of the two Royal Guards Xander realized, in front of him. The old man's knees shook with the effort of standing. His legs barely held him up.

"I think you've had a little too much to drink, sir." The soldier gripped the man's wrists and jerked them away. His grasp failed easily.

The pair of Royal Guards turned and left, leaving the old man to mumble under his breath. Xander halted and clung to the shadows of what was probably a closed general store.

After he'd kicked the dirt beneath his feet, the man entered the tavern, presumably not for the first time tonight. Xander approached the tavern and entered silently. His eyes swept over the mass of people, probably the population of the whole town—or at least the ones who didn't have the good sense to stay in their homes—until he spotted the old man at the far end of the barkeeper's counter.

Xander made his way through the throng of people and approached the bar. He quickly attracted the attention of one bartender and ordered two drinks. Leaning against the counter as he waited, Xander surveyed the room again. The balding old man had given up his seat at the bar, tired of the heckling from his fellow townspeople, and disappeared to a table in an isolated corner of the tavern. With a drink in each hand, Xander fought through the crowd again to the old man's table.

"Is this seat taken?" Xander asked, startling the man, who had been staring off into space, muttering something under his breath. He didn't have a drink in front of him, and Xander was relieved that his plan might actually work.

"Depends. Is one of those for me?" he questioned, eyeing the drinks greedily.

Xander chuckled. At least the easy part had worked. He pulled the chair out and sat down. The man across from him accepted the drink he'd slid across the table, and Xander set the second in front of himself. Now all he had to do was figure out how to bring up the thing with the trees.

It dawned on him. After all, every head had turned to look with the *tinkle* of the bell above the door when he'd first entered, so everyone knew he wasn't a local.

"I just got into town, and something's been gnawing at me, you know? I came across the strangest thing about four miles back. Has that patch of land always been like that? Sandy and all discolored or whatever?" Xander internally cringed at how awkward he sounded, but at least it broke the ice. Besides, he doubted the man at the other end of the table would notice how random his question was.

At first the man grunted and took a gulp from his drink as he studied Xander wearily.

"Whaddya think?" he spat. "Have ya come to make funnuva 'n old fool?"

Knowing he had little time to waste, Xander pushed the second drink toward the man.

"Look, I just want to know what you saw, that's all. I'm just trying to make sense of it is all, like you."

There was a pause, and the man eyed him far more intently than Xander thought possible for his condition. "Ya really wanna know?"

Xander nodded. The man shrugged and grumbled, "Yer not gonna bewewe me an'way."

He dove straight into his story within the next breath. Xander listened patiently and let the man's slow and sobering words fall uninterrupted. According to him, a man was standing in the middle of the field with his arms outstretched. At first, nothing had happened, and he thought the young man was basking in the sunlight, as the skies had been clouded over and dreary for the better part of a week. Then something started happening that "poor old Clyde" couldn't wrap his head around.

"It was like the ground was trem'lin' and every livin' thing was screamin'." Clyde visibly shuddered and took a long swig from the simple stein in front of him. "He was glowing! Like a monster! He musta known he was bein' watched, 'cause he turned 'round and stared right at me with blood-red eyes."

"Like bloodshot eyes—"

"No!" Clyde nearly shouted before he sobered once more. "The *color* of his eyes was red."

"His irises were…red." Clyde nodded at Xander's sullen revelation. Xander began to stand and dug around in his pocket for a midshade, knowing that a half of a libac could buy a couple drinks or maybe a decent meal instead.

He passed the coin to Clyde, figuring he'd definitely need it if Cedric didn't finish him off soon, and said, "Thank you, and for what it's worth, I believe you."

Xander made a mad dash for the exit. The night air was a welcome caress compared to the stuffiness of the packed tavern. Clyde's account had confirmed what Nyla suspected, but none of it made any sense to Xander.

Why drain the land? How was it all connected? Why would Nyla think he did this because of her? What had she seen in that last sand pit? He kicked the dirt road with his toe before he set off toward Nyla and their camp.

His head spun with the anger that buzzed in his hands. But the thought of how to tell Nyla about what he'd learned from Clyde brought a wave of uncertainty over him. She was already so convinced that all of this was somehow her fault. What would she think when he told her about Clyde's testimony?

He shook his head and shoved his hand in his pockets. How did you tell someone that their worst fears were legitimate and then convince them it wasn't their fault? That they shouldn't be afraid?

When Xander made it back to their campsite, the fire was weak, and Nyla was nowhere to be seen. He shoved down the panic that began to burn in his gut and ripped back the front flap of the tent.

Xander tried to regain control over his breath as the fear of a threat washed away. He ran a hand through his hair, letting out one long breath and, with it, the panic in his blood. He peeked inside the tent and let out a silent sigh of relief. She'd only gone to bed.

Stepping inside, he carefully removed his boots and settled into his sleeping bag for an uneasy sleep. For the most part, he nodded off for short bursts of shallow sleep, only to stare at the cloth ceiling of the tent until sleep claimed him again. The same question plagued his mind the whole night: How *was* he going to break the news to her?

18. A PAIR OF LIARS

The warmth of the fire rolled over Xander's skin. Meat sizzled in the pan he held over the glowing fire, but the *crackle* only added to his apprehension. He knew he had no right to be so protective over her, but the longer Nyla didn't come back to camp, the more anxiety clogged his veins. Had that *monster* gotten her? Was it her magic again? Or something else, something more *sinister*? His hand found the chain hidden beneath the neckline of his shirt, nearly pulling it out before he stopped himself.

Of course, the longer Xander waited, the more time he had to figure out how to tell her what Clyde had told him the night before. He still had no idea how he was going to tell Nyla everything while also assuring her that none of this was her fault.

He glanced up at the rustle of leaves and the heavy footfalls over the littered forest floor. Nyla came into sight shortly thereafter, pale, her eyes concentrated solely on the ground beneath her feet.

She picked her footsteps carefully, and chose a seat across from him with only a weak smile in greeting. Xander nodded in return, hiding the purse of his lips behind his mug as he took another sip. He couldn't think of any reason she'd be sick—unless something *had* happened. No matter how much he wanted to press her for an answer about what was going on, she'd tell him when she was ready to.

Right now, though, Xander had to pluck up the courage to tell Nyla about Clyde.

He handed her a plate of food and her canteen; his lips pressed firmly together. He knew it was now or never, and so he began, his eyes fixed on the flames between them.

"I met a man, at the tavern. Says he saw what happened to the land firsthand."

Nyla's eyes snapped up at this, but she didn't say anything and so he continued. Clyde, the magic, the red-eyed man, the drained land—all of it came flowing out, and Xander only hoped it made sense because he wasn't even entirely sure he was speaking properly anymore.

When he was finished, the air stood still between them, with the exception of the fire's *hiss*. They both stared into the flames, their faces drawn.

"So, it's Cedric then," Nyla said quietly, exhaustion and venom laced in her voice.

"Based on what Clyde told me, yeah. It's *him*," Xander confirmed with a curt nod of his head.

"Then I guess we should get going. The sooner we get to the manor, the sooner we might figure out what's going on." Nyla stood on shaky legs and stretched before she stumbled over to the tent to pack up her things. Xander could only shake his head and stamp out their campfire. At least Nyla had allowed them to eat something before determining to set off again.

Xander kept a close eye on Nyla as they hiked. Something was off, he just knew it, but her lips were sealed tight, and unless she wanted to tell him, he'd never know what was wrong. Of course, that didn't stop him from taking a few guesses. He kept those to himself, though. It didn't do any good to try and push her to talk if she didn't want to, and he couldn't hold that against her. Sometimes it was nice to have someone understand that. He knew from experience that not everyone did.

The memory that surfaced as a result of the sentiment was a nasty one, and Xander refused to let it play over in his mind for what was possibly the millionth time.

Instead, he glanced around to take in their surroundings, noticing that Nyla had stopped a few paces behind him again. She leaned against a tree and tugged off her boot—the other one this time—and Xander supposed a rock fell from it, though he didn't see it. Nyla promptly readjusted her sock. He wondered how many times she thought she could get away with this act, but the slight irritation faded away when she looked up at him with a hollow smile and dim eyes.

"Sorry, just had a rock in my boot or something." Nyla pushed off the tree and slowly began to make her way down the path again.

Xander only glanced up at the sky with pleading eyes. Maybe someone, somewhere would hear his prayer and actually answer. In the meantime, he matched Nyla's pace. His whole body was alert and ready, but for what? He wasn't exactly sure at this point, only that Nyla had already tripped or stumbled too many times in the short distance they'd traveled this morning.

And certainly not for the last time, Xander wondered where she'd gone off to that morning. He knew it wasn't fair, especially when most mornings he went off to find something substantial for breakfast and she never once questioned him about his whereabouts. Or that time at Fortune Falls after his mind had pulled the memory of his last fight with Issie to the forefront.

Xander racked his brain for a reasonable answer, but none presented itself. Maybe she'd astral-projected again and just needed a moment to herself? After all, the last time she'd been this sickly-looking was back in Caselle. Granted, Nyla was much better now than she was then, but it occurred to him that whatever was wrong might have been a precursor to something that was about to happen.

In front of him, Nyla lurched forward, her foot snagged on an arched tree root. He lunged after her with an exclamation and grabbed at her arm. She gasped, either at the near fall or from him jerking her upright, he wasn't so sure. Xander dropped his hand as Nyla regained her composure with closed eyes and gritted teeth.

When they opened again, she started off, only to be tripped by the same tree root. Xander caught her again. This time he didn't let go.

"Are you sure you're all right, Nyla?" Xander asked, his voice thick with worry. "Maybe we should stop for the day."

Nyla rolled her eyes at the notion, brushing him off of her, and snapped, "I'm fine!"

"Really? So, every rock in the Shadow Forest just *happened* to find its way into your boots? Or how about the fact that even now you can barely keep your balance? I bet a gentle breeze could knock you over right now. So, honestly, what's up?" he shot back. Irritation flared in his eyes. Guilt instantly wormed its way through every fiber of his being, and he softened up. Xander uncrossed his arms and let them hang loosely at his sides.

***

Nyla shifted her gaze away and pressed her lips together. She reminded herself that Xander was only trying to help and that she didn't have to be so short with him. And it's not like he was *entirely* in the wrong…just maybe a bit overconcerned. Standing there now, Nyla realized that maybe she should've mentioned she pushed her limits this morning, but she knew it wouldn't do any good to mention it now. All she wanted right now was to make it to the Woodlane Manor as soon as humanly possible, but if she killed herself in the process…it was all for naught anyway.

The longer they stood, the more Nyla swayed on her feet. The silence grew longer than the time that had passed.

"I'm fine, really. Just a little tired is all," she replied softly.

"Let's just stop for a while then. You can get some sleep, and I'll check out the map and get something to eat. It's almost time for lunch anyway." Xander took Nyla by the hand and led her to a rounded boulder off to the side of their path. "Sit. I'll pitch the tent."

"That's completely unnecessary, Xander!" Nyla protested. She sprang to her feet and instantly sank back onto the rock, but carried on anyway. "Especially since we're only stopping for an hour at the most."

"It's completely necessary if you actually want a decent nap. And suppose the nap doesn't help, *hmm*? We're not moving from this spot until you feel better." He gave her a hard look and turned his back to find a spot to pitch the tent, despite Nyla's quiet grumbling. Xander shucked off his rucksack and gathered up the package for the tent.

"At least let me help," Nyla called out when he'd finally picked a spot to set up the tent. He glanced over at her. She discarded her backpack and leaned it against the boulder she was supposed to be resting on.

"No."

Nyla opened her mouth to protest again, but Xander had turned his back on her and set about his task without another word. All the while, Nyla tried to offer her help. Her pleading fell on deaf ears and eventually turned into a fit of playful mocking, fueled in part by her irritation. Xander didn't seem to care, though, as he ignored her as he worked.

"I'm Xander," Nyla started after a final plea to let her assist him, "and I refuse help from people because I deem them too sick to lend a hand." Nyla rolled her eyes in annoyance, but kept going. "I'm Mister 'Let's travel together because two's better than one, but then I still go and insist on doing things on my own!'"

Nyla's mocking didn't stop there, and it became a constant hum. Her frustration grew with every laugh and amused smile he shot her way. The more she teased him, the more Nyla swore he dragged his task out by fumbling with this or that or not putting the spikes far enough apart or mistaking one piece for another, even though they'd had the last ten or so days to figure it out. Eventually, Nyla threw her hands up and drew a long, exaggerated breath.

"You're a real pain, you know that?" she huffed.

"So are you, your majesty," he beamed as he stepped aside from the now-assembled tent and bowed expertly. He smirked when he met her eyes as he straightened. "I mean, Miss 'Let's travel to a place where there might be a murderer waiting for me' and 'I'll even go alone because no one should have to come with me. I'm Nyla, and I push myself too hard sometimes and won't let people help me, even when my body physically refuses to keep going.'"

Nyla laughed at his admittedly awful attempt to mimic her voice. "Okay, I deserved that."

"Damn right you did! You didn't even *try* to mimic me!" He offered her a hand to help her stand, and she accepted it without any sass or debate.

"Wake me up in an hour?"

"Sure."

"Promise?"

"Yes, now go to sleep, would ya?"

Nyla rolled her eyes at him and disappeared inside the tent with her pack.

***

Even though he'd promised, Xander settled himself down for the long haul. He ignored the guilty conscience poking and prodding at his thoughts and built a fire anyway, gathering logs to keep it going through the night if need be. By the fire's glow, and the sunlight that found its way through the thinning canopy of sapphire and emerald overhead, Xander studied the map, tracing the route they'd planned with his eyes. All he knew for certain was that they had to get to Hart. From there, Nyla assured him that she could get them to the manor. That was another thing he'd wanted to ask about, but didn't think he should. After all, she'd said she and her brothers had gone there before. Maybe that was all there was to the story. Or maybe it wasn't.

Xander shook the creeping doubt from his mind. He turned his attention back to the map and the route he knew by heart. In a few days' time, they'd pass the outskirts of Huntington. Xander's eyes lingered over the city's outline. A lump formed in his throat, and he swallowed around it before he focused on the route once more.

His eyes lit up. Xander licked his lips and stared at a spot a few miles between Huntington and their path. It was maybe three hours out of their way, but it was well worth it. And who knew? Maybe a little break was exactly what Nyla needed. He supposed he'd find out in a few days' time. His lips turned up into a smirk.

With his scheme set, Xander folded up the map and tucked it back into the front pocket of his rucksack. The grumbling of his stomach interrupted the forest's song, but Xander ignored it. Instead, he reclined back against the trunk of the tree behind him and watched the flames flicker in the dimming light of day. He really should have gone hunting, but Xander wasn't too keen on the idea of leaving Nyla. After all, what if something happened while he was gone?

He shook the worry from his head and instead refocused on the thing he could actually do something about: food. Xander turned to his bag and unclipped the fresh bag from his pack. It wasn't as big as a true hunter's fresh bag, but it did the job for what Xander needed it for. It kept their meager food supply fresh for as long as it remained in the bag, up to a week if the weather was mild—as it had been for days now—and gave them the ability to hunt for the future and keep some edible plants from spoiling in the event that an area wasn't so plentiful. Other than that, Xander didn't care too much about learning how they worked, only that the fresh bags he *did* own worked properly. He was just grateful that George had one this small, the perfect size for adventuring.

As of right now, the fresh bag only had three pollies in it, but they would have to do for tonight at least until he was certain that Nyla would be all right if he went hunting for a while. He pulled the jewel-colored tree rodents out one by one and put the spelled bag away.

***

Nyla's eyes blinked open and promptly fell shut again. Her lips twisted in a silent groan. Just a few more minutes, she practically begged. Her eyes fluttered open again, and this time she forced them to remain open just long enough to get her bearings. She bolted upright. Her temples pounded at the sharp movement. Cursing under her breath, Nyla fought her way out of her sleeping bag. Rather than stand right away, she hesitated and grabbed her spare blanket before she pulled her boots on and stood awkwardly, stumbling out of the tent on heavy limbs that refused to work. She wrapped the blanket around herself like a cocoon, unable to storm toward Xander and his pretty little fire and neat campsite like she'd pictured herself doing in her head.

"Sleep all right?" Xander asked almost cheekily.

"You're such a liar," Nyla huffed and settled down beside him. "You promised that you'd wake me up in an hour and here it is: past dusk."

"You'll forgive me," Xander assured her without an ounce of uncertainty. Nyla snorted at this, even if she knew he was right. "Besides, don't you feel better?"

Nyla shifted next to him, considering whether or not she could ignore his question, and rearranged the blanket she'd cocooned herself in. A barely audible mumble reluctantly fell from Nyla's lips in answer.

"I'm sorry. What was that? I didn't quite catch that. I couldn't hear it over the silence," he snickered as he playfully nudged her.

"Oh fine!" Nyla burst, pausing for a long, exasperated breath before she continued rather shortly, "There. Happy now? I feel much better and less like a bumbling corpse…" She paused to readjust her blanket again, quietly adding, "Though I wouldn't complain if we just stayed here and didn't move for a while."

She nudged his foot with hers. Xander only hummed in acknowledgement, and Nyla found herself leaning against him and resting her head on his shoulder. And so they stayed like that until both their stomachs eventually growled.

"Hungry?" Xander asked.

"I could eat." Nyla nodded. As they'd sat, her energy had steadily perked up, though she still wasn't quite ready to move if she didn't have to anytime soon.

"Great. Mind if I steal some of those herbs you picked up?"

"Help yourself. They're in my bag, in the little tin, in the tent."

"Okay." Xander got up and came back shortly with Nyla's bag in his hand.

"You could've just grabbed what you wanted," she grumbled as she fought to free her arms from the blanket and accepted the bag.

"No way. I am not digging through someone else's bag. Not happening." He shook his head adamantly.

"Such a gentleman." Nyla handed him the rectangular box of packaged herbs and set her bag aside.

Xander busied himself with preparing their dinner as Nyla watched in quiet contentment. Soon enough, the sizzle of juices in a pan filled the air as the earthy scent of herbs tickled her nose. If she didn't already enjoy his company, she'd keep him around solely for his cooking, Nyla decided.

As they ate, Xander seemed absentminded, distracted by something Nyla dreaded if her suspicions as to its source were correct. She only hoped that he waited until *after* dinner—or never if that were an option—to talk about this morning and what she'd done. She'd barely taken her last bite when Xander cleared his throat. She fixed her eyes on her empty plate, only peeking at him through her lashes as the fire's crackle filled the static of the night.

"Can I ask about this morning?" he finally asked.

Nyla tilted the pan set beside the fire to peer into it. There was a little meat left, mainly roots and sprouts now. She took another helping anyway, as she couldn't technically talk with her mouth full. It wouldn't work for long; she'd have to answer him eventually.

"What about it?" she said after a minute.

"I don't know, really. Just are you okay, like for real?" Nyla chewed slowly as she flushed under his weighted gaze. She studied her booted feet intently, shifting them this way and that in the dirt. "I just want to make sure nothing happened is all."

Nyla finally looked up at him. Her eyes prickled with tears that wouldn't fall. She forced herself to keep an even tone, even as she felt her throat constrict against her mind's wishes.

"Last night, while you were gone and this morning before you were up, I decided that I needed to do something. With everything that's happened, I know that I need to gain some control over my powers, and even before you told me about that old man at the tavern, I *knew* it was Cedric. So, I decided to try it on my own. It worked a few days ago, and there weren't any adverse effects, but I needed to do more. So, I did."

"Did what?" Xander prompted. He scooted over to her so that they were side by side again.

"I used my magic, though I guess it was too much. But what else am I supposed to do? I have to know my limits because what if..." She choked. "What if he comes back, but for real? Not in some astral travel thing, but actually face-to-face attacks me? Attacks us? How am I supposed to defend myself when I can't even use my magic, let alone control it?"

"You'll figure it out. Besides, *he* hasn't shown his face yet. And maybe it's not about *what* you can do, but *how* you do it. Slow and steady wins the race, right?" For once, Xander didn't sound so certain, but Nyla guessed there wasn't really much he could say that he hadn't already told her. The truth was simple: they were both in the dark, about a lot of things, concerning the world around them.

"Like how, Xander?" Nyla closed her eyes and took a deep breath. Exasperation dripped from her voice. "How exactly do you control something you didn't know you had until weird things started to happen?"

"I don't know. Start small?"

Nyla laughed softly, but it sounded like nothing more than a wisp of air, before she leaned her head on his shoulder.

Xander wrapped an arm around her. "If I were you, I'd try to do small things, like lighting a fire or something. I also wouldn't push *too hard* seeing as we're trying to get somewhere too."

"Thanks for the advice," she whispered.

"Anytime."

19. THE CAT-CREATURE WITH THE SACRED DUTY

Shamira's eyes narrowed with the twitch of her whiskers and the prick of her ears as they swiveled to attention. The girl—*Nyla*—extinguished their small campfire. It was a cute display of magic, but Shamira knew the girl was capable of so much more. If the Elders hadn't said as much, Shamira could *sense* it, Nyla's magic. It hummed and thrived just below the surface, and Shamira wondered if the girl was just lying in wait to unleash her full potential or possibly conserving energy.

She hadn't intended to stalk Nyla, but now that she'd found her—and her human companion, Shamira reminded herself with a silent snarl—she didn't know how to approach the pair. For now, she resigned herself to waiting in the shadows, hiding amongst the foliage of the Shadow Forest as it faded away into its *Cresmuun* coloring, or Harvum as the humans now called it. Her tail flicked of its own volition. If she were to be amongst humans, Shamira needed to yield to them and their ways so as not to cause conflict between herself and them.

Especially with the pressing threats brewing against their kingdom, and the land—*especially* against the land and all of magic.

***

Nyla let out a slow exhale. The faint tingle of energy that traveled from her core to the tips of her fingers ebbed away. Her hand dropped limply to her side. Astonishment blossomed in her chest as she stared at the smoldering pile of charred sticks before her. Across from her, a slack-jawed Xander let out a long whistle. Nyla's lilac eyes flicked up to look at him, but he continued to stare at the freshly extinguished campfire between them with a quirked eyebrow. She beamed through the slight fatigue that began to weave its way through her body alongside the satisfaction that pumped through her veins. Seconds passed by. Xander finally met her gaze. His face was caught somewhere between a proud smile and confusion.

"What?" Nyla giggled innocently. "*You* told me to start small, and what's smaller than putting *out* a campfire? And," she added, "what are the odds of *accidentally* setting a fire if you're trying to put one out?"

"Fair point." Xander cocked his head to the side before he stood and hoisted his pack onto his shoulders. "Shall we?"

"We shall," Nyla said confidently.

***

About an hour or two after they'd left their campsite, Nyla's mind fell back into the now all-too-familiar groove of anxiety. At first, she'd focused on the other things she could do to help practice her magic. But every footstep Nyla took, and the closer they came to the source of either her salvation or doom, the farther her mind traveled away from thoughts of magic. And the farther into the recesses of her anxiety she traveled, the more waves of worry and the quiver in her throat persisted.

The only thing that kept the full-blown panic that threatened her at bay was the gentle breeze that swept through the long strands of silver hair that refused to cooperate this morning.

Nyla placed her hand on the rough bark of a low-hanging branch to duck under it. Her body stiffened. She froze.

Her skin prickled. Nyla staggered back a few steps as her head began to throb. If she didn't know any better, she'd say she was either getting a migraine or desperately needed to sneeze as her nose began to tingle. She blinked and stumbled after Xander, who hadn't noticed her recent lagging. Without thinking, Nyla grabbed his hand and held a finger to her lips as he turned to address her.

With a stiff nod, Xander waited for her to signal to him what was going on, but without actually *knowing* what was happening, Nyla just stared back at him with wide eyes as she let her free hand drop slowly. Silently, Xander reached for her other hand and grasped it. He leaned closer. Nyla's lips twisted into a thin line as the pounding in her temples slashed through her mind.

"Are you all right?" His voice was barely a murmur.

She shook her head, which only swished the pain around and aggravated it. She was definitely not okay, and she had no idea why.

Her lips moved of their own accord. "We're being stalked."

Xander reeled back a fraction of an inch as he blinked in confusion. "By whom?"

Nyla pursed her lips. "By *what*."

"How do you know? Did you see them?"

"I don't know. I just do." The searing pain in her temples plunged her vision into white static. She blinked rapidly, almost squeezing Xander's hands hard enough to break the bones.

With a deep breath, Nyla tamped down the panic thrumming in her blood and mentally dove headfirst into the murky depth of the pain consuming her. A few steady breaths later, and her vision cleared. She managed to attain the wherewithal to loosen her grip on Xander's hands and forced her mind to lean farther into the pain that had begun to subside.

She recognized the slight prickle beneath her skin as the hum of magic coursing through her veins. She didn't understand how it could know or how the magic had "activated" itself without her calling upon it or focusing her will, but it had, and it had something to tell her. And now Nyla knew. Her magic manifested itself in the form of an inkling that insisted some*thing* was stalking them. It was behind them, in the bushes, waiting. Nyla was certain of it.

Nyla took a deep breath and squeezed her eyes shut. She pictured gathering the magic up inside of her and exhaled. The magic flowed from her core and became the breeze that dragged her hair with it and forced the tree limbs above their heads to bend to it, their leaves laughing at the sudden wind. Nyla opened her eyes. The pain was gone, as if it had never been at all.

"It's behind us," she whispered, starting to turn in its direction. Xander stopped her. She nearly hissed, "What?!"

"Don't. Move," he answered through gritted teeth, staring over her shoulder.

Nyla studied his face. He'd gone as white as a ghost, his shoulders completely rigid. She hadn't the slightest idea what—or *whom*, if she was wrong about their stalker not being human—could be behind her that could make terror grip Xander as tightly as it had. Slowly, carefully, she turned her head, completely disregarding Xander's demand from a few seconds before.

Nyla blanched at the sight of the knee-high cat creature. Its coat varied in color, more like woven patches or stripes of black, brown, amber, and tan, a patchwork of cohesive color. She met the beast's murky, pale-green eyes and swallowed.

I didn't mean to frighten you. The cat's smooth voice flitted across Nyla's mind, and she raised an eyebrow. Definitely not a *normal* country cat then.

"Why are you stalking us?" Nyla's voice was much more composed than she expected it to be. She dropped one of Xander's hands and turned to face the cat creature. She smoothly positioned herself in front of Xander, not exactly certain if she could do much more than that. Briefly, she wondered if Xander could hear the cat too, or if this whole scene was a matter of absurdity to him. She brushed the concern away so as not to be distracted.

"It can—You can hear it too, right?" Xander sputtered under his breath as he came to stand beside her.

It was not my intention, the cat began. *But I was uncertain on how to approach you, Nyla.*

Nyla staggered backwards. She forced herself not to panic as her heart sank to her stomach. As if snapped out of a daze, Xander whirled in front of her, and in a flash, he'd nocked an arrow and drawn his bow. The hair on the back of her neck rose. It never boded well for her when a stranger addressed her by name. As if she were zapped by static, Nyla recovered from her shock and knew she needed to do *something* before one of them did something they'd regret.

"Xander, wait!" Nyla gripped his arm, reaching for the bow over his shoulder at the same time as the cat began to speak again.

This doesn't concern you, human. The cat hissed. Her fur prickled as she slunk low to the ground in a way that Nyla knew was a precursor to an attack. *This is between Tenebris and Nyla.*

As Nyla halfheartedly watched the scene before her, Xander shook himself out of her weakened grasp. All Nyla could do was stand there, slack-jawed and trembling.

Why would a *cat* be looking for *her*? And what did this have to do with all of Tenebris?

"That's where you're wrong." Xander answered the cat with as equal a snarl as she had directed at him. "You see, it *does* concern me because I'm standing here, and we're traveling together, and you've been stalking us."

Nyla forced the words from her dry tongue, drawing the cat's attention back to her. "How do you know I'm the one you're looking for? It could be anyone."

Lilac-colored eyes, silver hair, how many women have that? The cat stared at them with quizzical eyes. She tilted her head as if considering something, and Nyla waited for the creature to say something more. *Besides, your magic has a specific signature all its own. Just like pumpkie magic, human magic has its own individual aura or wavelength unique to its wielder. All magic is like that, even the land's. Now, are you Nyla or not?* The cat bared its teeth and narrowed its green eyes.

Nyla barely shifted her gaze to the side, and Xander shot her a look she couldn't decipher. Everything inside her raced. Nyla could barely hear anything over the booming of her heart in her ears or the storm raging in the form of rolling waves inside her stomach. The warm hum of magic spread through her once more, but because it wasn't actively channeled toward a specific use, it only bubbled beneath the surface of her skin. Her mind was flying, and not in a good way.

"What happens if I am the girl you're looking for? Then what? You already said my magic holds a specific signature, so surely you already know the answer." Her voice quivered.

The cat relaxed and sat tall. Its black-and-gray striped tail curled around her legs, tapping the ground languidly. The creature blinked, but to Nyla it seemed like a wink of approval. Its voice sounded like a smirk when the cat started next. *Clever girl. I just wanted to see if you'd admit who you are, and I suppose in a way you have.*

I am Shamira. I have been tasked by my clan to find you. And now that I have found you, I am here to assist you in your journey and help guide your use of magic. She looked at them expectantly.

Xander finally relaxed and put the arrow back in its quiver. Nyla met his eyes and tried to gauge his reaction. His muddied eyes were just as conflicted as her own thoughts.

"You said this was between me and Tenebris." She looked back over at Shamira and licked her lips. "What did you mean by that?"

Only that you have a lot on your shoulders and much to learn. As you should well know, pumpkies are the sacred guardians of Tenebris. We have vowed to protect this country, but our numbers dwindled, and so we hid ourselves away. We could afford to, as the threat was contained. It appears now that the threat was only weakened, much like ourselves, and lay dormant all these years. Until recently.

"What do mean, 'recently?'" Xander asked accusingly, his eyes narrowed.

Within the last two or three years. Shamira blinked.

"Two years?" All eyes turned to Nyla. "No, this is…this is crazy! There has to be another Nyla with silver hair and purple eyes. You've got the wrong one. I mean how rare is my name?"

Xander turned to her and gripped her by the shoulder. Nyla forced herself to take a breath and look him in the eye. Her mouth refused to shut. The familiar prickle of panic and the urge to flee buzzed through her veins until she was physically vibrating under his touch. Xander only gripped her tighter and stared back at her with concerned eyes.

"What happened to you two years ago? And more importantly, does it tie you to some centuries-old, big, bad evil?"

"Fire…" She sobbed, but no tears came. The overwhelming terror only gripped her throat with an icy hand and made her voice hiccup.

"A fire or…" Nyla shook her head. Xander knew instantly what she meant by the gesture and whirled around in an instant with a knife Nyla didn't know he'd had. Nyla watched blindly and wrapped her arms around herself.

"And what, exactly, is your part in all this? What happens to Nyla?"

I've already told you. I am a protector of Tenebris, and I have been tasked with finding Nyla. And now that I've found her, I am to assist her with her magic and protect her because she is the only one capable of stopping this war. Shamira's voice grew more agitated as she went on. Her ears twitched as she snarled, her sole focus on Xander now. *And for what it's worth, you've threatened me several times already, and I have spared you. Consider that a favor as an ally of Nyla's.*

"Xander?" Nyla started weakly. She eyed the cat warily, but Shamira seemed inclined to wait for her to come to terms with all of this.

Xander barely glanced back at her, but hesitantly followed her when she walked a few paces up the path.

Once Nyla was certain that they had some privacy, she nervously turned her eyes toward Shamira one last time. She hissed frantically through her teeth, "What do we do?"

"I don't know," Xander admitted. He ran a hand through his hair, sheathing his knife. "Do you think it's worth trying to outrun her?"

"Do you really think that'll work?"

"Not for long."

"So, we really have no choice then, but to trust her?" Nyla's heart sank. Any glimmer of hope she'd had had abandoned her. Her eyes glazed over with tears. Xander took a step toward her and wrapped her in a tight hug. She limply wrapped her arms around him. "I can't do this."

"I'll run if that's what you want to do. Might not last long, but hey, it would buy us *some* time," he offered sincerely.

"Why put off the inevitable?" she mumbled into his shoulder. She took a shaky breath and reluctantly pulled away.

The bitter prayer that if she couldn't physically see the problem in front of her, then it didn't exist, came crashing down around her as she saw Shamira a few yards away, simply watching them.

All set then? Shamira asked evenly.

"Hey, Xander?" Nyla whispered, barely moving her lips. She dipped her head in a stiff nod to the cat as a way of acknowledgement.

"Yeah?" He hummed, not taking his eyes off of the approaching pumpkie.

"Do you know how to kill a pumpkie? I mean, would an arrow to the heart or lung work?" The idea made her choke on the acid that sat in her throat.

"Let's hope we never have to find out." He put his arm around her shoulders and steered her back along the overgrown path they'd started off on that morning. Neither one needed to look over their shoulders to know that Shamira trailed after them.

All through the rest of their hike, a fresh wave of horrified curiosity gnawed at Nyla. Did Shamira really mean to help her? Why would a pumpkie clan want to find her? What even were they?

The worst part of the new arrangement was that she didn't feel it was safe to consult Xander about her new worries, for the fear of alerting Shamira of her suspicions if she really did work for Cedric. All Nyla knew for certain was that all of this, all her problems from the magic to the pumpkie sleeping right outside their tent, it all came back to that cursed fire.

20. A MUCH-NEEDED BREAK

Nyla watched the wavering spiral of smoke. Gradually, it grew thicker in her mind's eye as she moved on to urging the pile of sticks to spark and glow bright orange. Her brows twitched and furrowed as she concentrated even harder until a soothing heat kissed her skin. She knew it wasn't the result of the magic that hummed through her veins, but then again, she wouldn't know for certain until she opened her eyes. With a long, slow exhale, Nyla peeked one eye open. The sight of a bright, brilliant fire greeted her.

Even though the sight should've filled her with warmth and giddiness, it couldn't quell the fresh anticipation that had taken root inside her. The flow of magic dissipated. Any flicker of pride Nyla might've had in the moment when she'd opened both eyes was outmatched by the growing pit in her stomach.

For the last twenty-four hours or so, all it did was twist and churn, until her nerves pressed against her lungs. The knots choked off not only her air flow, but her appetite too. And if the amount of sleep, or rather lack thereof, from the night before was any indication of what the state of her life had become, she was certain Xander had gotten even less. Sure, it wasn't *his* life that had been turned upside down and reflected in a broken mirror, but he was part of this now—whatever *this* was.

Nyla's eyes flicked over to Shamira. She didn't even have to stop and ask Xander what he thought of the cat-creature. Nyla knew by the tightness of his jaw and the irritated glint in his darkened eyes that he was wary of the pumpkie. As if Nyla didn't want Shamira to know what she was thinking, she fixed her eyes back on the fire she'd created.

The cat in question was a stark contrast to the image of a war-mongering beast that Nyla's darkest fears had conjured up. Shamira was peacefully curled up with her paws tucked under her cheek, her eyes closed. But by the minute twitch of her irregularly striped ears, the cat was anything but blissfully asleep. Nyla wasn't aware of the cat's attention until Shamira's gruff voice tickled the forefront of her mind.

Why not use your magic for more than lighting a fire? The cat's voice had a little bit of a lilt to it, but Nyla couldn't quite place the emotion behind it. Either way, it was a different quality than what she'd heard in the cat's voice before.

"I don't know," she started and licked her lips. Xander glanced between them from the other side of the fire, catching Nyla's gaze. "I guess it's better than running myself dry."

But how do you expect to build up your endurance if you don't push yourself a little harder each day?

"Is there a reason I need to be able to use a lot of magic at once?" A hot prickle of irritation traveled the length of Nyla's spine. She pursed her lips as she waited for an answer. Shamira only closed her eyes and resettled herself into a more comfortable position. Nyla threw her hands up in exasperation and let them fall to her lap with a *thump*.

"So…is that a 'yes?'" Xander pressed. Even the most oblivious of people could hear the snark in his voice.

Shamira remained silent.

Nyla and Xander shared a brooding look over the flames before he handed her a small plate of whatever rations they had left.

She pushed the dried meat around on the round plate before she tore a piece off and popped it in her mouth and chewed. And chewed some more. She forced herself to swallow it. The rational part of her knew she needed to eat. The other part of her, the part that was consumed by the torrential storm of anxiety and growing terror, wanted nothing to do with the already less-than-appetizing food in front of her.

"We have to make a very important stop outside of Huntington tomorrow." Xander burst out of the blue. Nyla almost dropped her plate, too far gone to remember that she wasn't alone.

"Okay?" She waited for him to say something more, but he didn't. She handed her plate back over to him and figured he'd finish the rest of her portion off. "Goodnight then."

***

"*This* is your 'necessary,' 'crucial to our journey,' 'an absolute do-or-die' stop? You're, you're…" Nyla growled in frustration, "You're such a liar!"

"Oh, calm down, would ya?" Xander glowered. His features soon turned coy, and he smirked. "And I *technically* didn't lie. This stop is absolutely essential to our overall journey."

"How is *this*," Nyla jabbed a finger toward the calm lake and sandy beach that all but glowed in the dazzling sunlight, "*absolutely essential*' to where we're going?"

I think the boy's right. You have been a little tense lately, and I've only known you for two days. Shamira sauntered over to a sunbathed rock and hopped up to circle its top.

Nyla seethed, her fists clenched at her sides as she watched her potential ally settle in the warm sunlight.

"See! Even the demon cat agrees that this is a good idea!" Xander gestured widely toward the cat, temporarily accepting Shamira's presence.

Shamira's green eyes narrowed in a glare as she bared her teeth, a look that Xander received fairly often.

Watch your tongue, human. With that final warning, Shamira curled up as still as a statue to bask in the glowing rays.

Nyla turned back to Xander, but he'd already started to walk away toward the water. He quickly peeled his shirt off and threw it in the general direction of Shamira's boulder before he waded out into the crystal-clear water. Nyla groaned and dragged a hand across her face. She knew that there wasn't any use in trying to fight them on this.

Her eyes swept over the landscape of the vacant beach and landed on the rock face that protruded over the water like a cliff. With a final glance out over the water, she spotted Xander floating on his back. If tranquility had a human form, it was that picture right there. And that's what did it.

Nyla hurried over to the cover of the trees and changed into a loose shirt and shorts. When she emerged, she stuffed her clothes into her bag and dumped the pile near Shamira. The cat's ears twitched, but she didn't acknowledge Nyla beyond that.

Despite the slight irritation that had been bubbling in her blood the last few days, Nyla forced herself to move and to embrace some semblance of normalcy even if only for a moment. The sand was soft beneath her bare feet. They sank into it with every step, but the smooth feeling of being encased by the sand was so peaceful, Nyla was almost content to let it drown her.

She wove a path up to the ledge. The sand soon mixed with smooth pebbles that stuck to the bottoms of her bare feet. It didn't matter, though. Nyla was too intent on forcing herself to enjoy this day that Xander had seemingly planned so meticulously.

Once she reached the top, Nyla glanced over the edge. It looked safe to her. No rocks or obvious shadows lurked beneath the surface of the water below her, and she silenced the nagging voice in the back of her mind. Xander didn't notice her looming above him on the cliff's edge. He was too relaxed just drifting in the water, and if she timed this right…Nyla grinned deviously.

It was perfect.

She retreated a few yards and took a deep breath. Cool wind caressed her body and soothed away any worries that lingered in her head. With another breath, Nyla darted toward the edge.

Freedom wrapped around her like the bright sunlight as she leapt with a smile on her face.

For one glowing second, Nyla remained suspended in the air. Much too quickly, the weightless freedom was over. Her eyes squeezed shut. Wind rushed around her and snagged at her hair, her clothes. It wasn't a particularly high ledge, but the fall seemed much longer than it had looked from above. Maybe it was only her mind playing tricks on her. Nyla screwed her eyes shut even tighter.

Her toes hit the cool water first. The shock of it knocked the air from her lungs, and she quickly gulped in another lungful before she was completely submerged.

Nyla let herself sink down for a moment before she kicked her legs and opened her eyes. The water bore a mild sting, though it was a minor irritation to her eyes compared to the bite of the cold water on her skin. But at least it was clear. She broke the surface of the water and wiped at her eyes. Xander waded a few feet away from her with a reprimanding scowl on his face.

"What is *wrong* with you?" he shouted. "I was just floating here, all nice and peaceful, soaking up some sun, innocently trying to relax and enjoy the water, but *no*…no, *someone* had to go and dive off a cliff and send a tidal wave at me!"

"Oh, calm down, would ya?" Nyla mimicked him.

"I will do no such thing. This means war!" he declared, breaking the surface of the water with a thrust of his finger before he splashed her.

The water hit her square across the face. By the time Nyla opened her eyes again, Xander was farther away and quickly putting more distance between them.

"Fine, war it is, then." The words were barely a whispered threat under her breath. Nyla focused her eyes, squinting against the sun as she zeroed in on Xander. The motion of her legs kicking beneath the water was all but forgotten, same with the smooth ripple of the water from her movements as she pictured a wave of water crashing down on Xander. The water obeyed her whim.

Xander turned to look behind him as the shadow loomed over him, only to be met with a wall of water. The hum of magic receded from Nyla's veins, replaced by giddiness and laughter. She slapped a hand over her mouth in an attempt to dampen her giggles, but to no avail. Xander stormed toward her as fast as he could in the deep water, but the look of him determinedly swimming toward her only made her laugh harder.

Before he could reach her, Nyla swam off. She reached the part of the lake where her toes could just barely brush the gentle slope of sand beneath the water's surface and started to run toward the shallow water to use that to her advantage.

Strong arms wrapped around her waist. She panicked and tried to pry them off of her, but it was no use. All she could do was let Xander drag her through the water as she pushed at his arms in a futile attempt to get them to budge.

"You're it!" Xander shifted his arms until he had her waist gripped in his hands. Nyla barely had any time to register what he was doing before he'd lifted her nearly out of the water and tossed her through the air as if she were weightless.

Squealing, she forced some air into her lungs before she hit the deep water again. She resurfaced and parted the curtain of hair in her face.

"That was just uncalled for!" she shouted after him, not even trying to hide the amusement from her voice.

"Yeah, well, that look in your eyes says otherwise!" Xander called back over his shoulder.

All through their game, he kept heading back into the deeper waters, obviously relying on his swimming skills to win the war. A dirty trick, in Nyla's opinion, though she supposed it wasn't as dirty as using magic to help her swim faster.

Once she was close enough again, she launched herself at his back. Nyla wrapped her arms around his shoulders and clamped her legs around his hips like a vise.

Xander tried to pry her off of him, but it was no use. His legs kicked twice as hard under the water to keep them both afloat. Nyla giggled and squeezed her legs tighter around him. It didn't even matter to her that she wasn't doing anything at all to keep them from sinking, and maybe that would work to her advantage and burn him out a little.

After all, Xander couldn't swim *and* fight her off. The harder he struggled to keep them both afloat and free himself, the harder Nyla laughed. Ultimately, her grip failed, and she was forced to abandon ship or be caught.

Nyla didn't make it very far when Xander's fingers wrapped around her ankle. She kicked at him as she tried to use her arms to swim away. It didn't do her any good. He was too heavy for her to tow and too strong for her to break his grasp. All Nyla could do was let herself be dragged backwards. She kept her head above water and twisted in his grasp so she was gliding across the water on her back. With her free leg, she used her magic to urge the formation of an arc of water and kicked it toward Xander.

The water hit its mark. But Xander hadn't set her free, so Nyla was forced to think bigger. She channeled her magic, gathering all she could manage to summon as she continued to struggle in the hopes of freeing herself.

Xander used his free hand to wipe his face, and at this rate Nyla had managed to wade upright and use her captured leg to keep some distance between herself and Xander.

She breathed in and sent a huge wave in his direction. Xander set her free as he braced himself for impact, sinking down below the surface. She didn't wait to see the water smack into him, if it even did, and again tried to make it into shallow water.

Relief flooded Nyla's veins when she reached her goal and could somewhat run away. But somehow, she wasn't fast enough. Xander tackled her.

They fell in a heap in the water. She'd somehow ended up sprawled across Xander on her stomach. She pushed herself up onto her hands and grinned down at him.

"Did you just tackle me?" She laughed breathlessly.

"No…" Xander's guilty eyes shifted away from her own gaze.

Nyla moved to sit in the water beside him and drew her knees up to her chest. She was almost completely submerged in the water, but she didn't mind. It was actually sort of soothing. She glanced behind them and saw Shamira watching them with keen eyes.

The sun had dipped low in the afternoon sky, but it was the perfect position to warm her back and to cast a tangerine glow over the surface of the water.

The longer they sat in the water, the cooler it became until goosebumps had erupted across her skin. She knew her teeth would start to chatter soon.

"Maybe we should get out and dry off. It's way past lunchtime now," Xander suggested softly.

Nyla hummed lazily in response. She was satisfied just listening to the happy bird chirps and the rustle of small animals in the trees to really care about the cold or even her empty stomach. It was with a great effort that she begrudgingly agreed with him.

She dragged herself over to Shamira's boulder. The sun's warm glow had slowly shifted off the cat. Nyla plopped herself down and sat against the boulder. Her fingers and toes had turned into wrinkled little prunes from swimming for so long. Her skin glistened with water droplets, but that didn't matter. What did bother her, though, was the chill of being wet in the setting sun. The exhaustion of all the fun they'd had seeped into her blood.

A shadow fell over her, and she peeked one eye open. It was too late. Xander dumped a towel over her head and snickered.

She dragged it off her head and grumbled, "Really?"

"Yes, 'really.' I can see your goosebumps all the way over here. Now are you hungry or not?" a fully clothed and dry Xander teased as he built a fire, including some driftwood so the flames would change color.

"Not if I have to move." She wrapped the towel around herself and resumed her almost nap-like state.

"Care to do the honors?"

Nyla whined, but flicked her fingers in the general direction of Xander's voice, where she assumed he'd built the fire. A cozy, warm fire crackled in her mind before it became reality. The promise of real, tangible warmth coaxed Nyla into getting up. She groaned as she twisted her body in a stretch and made off for the cooler tree line to change. A shiver raced through Nyla's body. It took all of her willpower not to throw random articles of clothing on just to keep what little warmth her body had.

When she emerged, Nyla darted to her bag and desperately searched for her jacket and possibly another blanket. Satisfied with the layers she'd found, Nyla stretched out on her towel by the fire and looked up at the clear sky. Out of the corner of her eye, Nyla saw Shamira leap off of her perch and stretch herself in a slow, slinking arch.

I'll be back, she said.

Nyla almost asked where the cat was going, but thought better of it. In the end, the only thing that mattered was that Shamira wasn't an ally of the red-eyed man's. With that grim consideration, Nyla watched the cat stalk toward the trees and disappear.

"What'd'ya think that was about?" Xander murmured as he stood over her, blocking the sunlight that poured over the tops of the Shadow Forest's trees.

Nyla squinted up at him and motioned with her hand for him to move to the side. "Don't know, don't really care so long as she's not rendezvousing with you-know-who."

Xander obliged and sat on the opposite side of the fire to cook what was left in the fresh bag. Today, it was a pyrosa, a nocturnal creature of the flames that could spit fire. Their charcoal eyes could set your soul ablaze and bring about your damnation.

Nyla didn't want to know how he'd managed to catch one. He said it was from a trap he'd set the night before, but she doubted that. Besides, Nyla knew he hadn't set any traps the night before…or any other night, now that she'd thought about it.

The pan sizzled with the meat's juice, filling the air with a savory aroma that made their mouths water. For a moment, everything was still. The only noise was that of the Shadow Forest's creatures and the crackle of their fire.

"Do you really think Shamira's with him?" This time, it was Xander who asked the million-libac question.

"I don't know, and I honestly couldn't say if I did. I don't know much about pumpkies, only what you said when we found her and what she told us. But I do know one thing for certain: if Shamira wanted to kill us or was told to kill us, she would've done so already. So I'll take that small comfort and go out on a limb and say maybe not." Even as she said it, Nyla chewed the inside of her cheek. It was a dangerous slope she had to climb for that conclusion. One false move and they were both goners.

"Yeah, I guess. We'll see." Xander removed the pan from the fire and fished the pyrosa meat from it.

Nyla forced herself to sit up and graciously accepted the plate of food passed over to her. Xander came and sat down next to her, speaking around a mouth full of food. "I hope you know you're never gonna get all the sand off this towel."

"Isn't it one of yours?" she asked sweetly despite the mischievous quirk of her lips.

Xander glanced down. He cursed foully.

"Well, *you* were the one who *dumped it* on my head earlier, so really the sand's your problem."

Xander paused, his glower softening. "Fair point."

They ate and spoke softly about what they expected from the remainder of their trek. The meat was tender with a hint of smokiness from having been cooked over the campfire. There still wasn't any sign of Shamira, and Nyla shoved aside the voice in her head that compelled her to up and leave. She figured that the cat would only find them again anyhow, and so she forced herself to enjoy the moment. It was an extremely easy task to do as the day's activities bore down on her.

Nyla and Xander had just finished cleaning up their meal when Shamira's presence was announced by the rustle of bushes and the tension that floated in the air as Xander looked over Nyla's shoulder. Nyla turned and locked eyes with the cat. She sauntered over to them. A few aquaerials, birds that were a watercolor mixture of glimmering teal and silver, hung limply from Shamira's mouth. As she came closer, Nyla could see that the fur around her mouth was stained with blood.

I figured you two would be running low on your food stores, so here. Shamira dropped the ethereal fish-eaters at Xander's feet. Neither Nyla, nor Xander could get a word of thanks out before the cat turned and headed away from them.

"Hey, wait!" Nyla called out once the shock wore off a second later. Shamira paused and barely glanced over her shoulder. "Thanks."

The cat bowed her head and continued to a spot a little farther away from them. Nyla watched as she settled and gazed out over the land. Whatever Shamira was watching for, Nyla wasn't certain she wanted to know. Instead, she stretched her legs out alongside the fire again. The towel beneath her kept the soft sand at bay. The sky was alight with hues of dusty blue and lavender. In the nearing stretch of the sky, Nyla could make out the faintest hint of indigo.

The sensation of water rippling over her skin lulled her into a state of overall contentment. This sort of inner peace was vaguely familiar to her, only a distant memory now. Her eyes fluttered shut. For the faintest of seconds, Nyla ached for this to last forever. And why couldn't it? A shiver ran through her. She pulled the blanket around her shoulders tighter and twisted her hands in it. Red eyes seared into her consciousness, and a fire flashed before her memory.

"Still cold?" Xander asked.

Nyla opened her eyes. He was prepping the second aquaerial for the fresh bag. She shook her head and studied the sky.

Not another word was said for a long time. Stars slowly winked to life. Xander got up and came back with another towel. He lay beside her and clasped his hands over his stomach. The pair sat quietly for a moment longer.

"I can't remember the last time I was this exhausted," Nyla whispered.

"That can't be true. What about the other day?" Xander glanced over at her, obviously referring to how she'd overtaxed herself by using too much of her magic.

"This is a *good* exhausted, not a 'you've just discovered what astral projection is' exhausted. There's a distinct difference, and I quite like the way I feel right now. It's..." She trailed off and traced the constellation of Ursa Minor. Nyla moved on to trace her own constellations, ones she thought were easier to spot and imagine than real constellations. "Peaceful."

Xander chuckled, "That's true, I guess."

"I feel like there's waves crashing over me. And do ya know what? I'm okay if they sweep me away. It's nice just sort of...floating." Nyla's voice dripped with the sort of whimsy that only came from tired satisfaction.

"Long time since you've gone swimming, then?"

"The last time I went swimming, for fun, was to teach my younger sister, Lydia. We went down to the creek behind our house because it's pretty shallow—well, except for the pool down by our neighbor's. Westley and I ended up goofing off while Derek tried to teach Lydia. She was so afraid of the water." Nyla laughed, remembering Lydia's shriek when Westley had disappeared behind a rock to scare her.

It was cruel, she knew that now, but they'd howled with laughter until she couldn't see through the tears. "She refused to go in the water, and we ended up going back home for the day. Westley and I chased each other all the way home and almost didn't make it back until dusk, long after Derek and Lydia. My mother was so miffed that we came home covered in dirt and leaves, but more so because we'd missed dinner."

"That sounds like freedom," Xander replied wistfully. His voice was barely above a whisper, a secret between himself and the night sky. "My parents took my sister and I sailing a lot. It was mostly for my parents' business, but Issie and I managed to get into some mischief. Not a lot, because there's only so much you can do on a ship without jumping overboard."

Nyla turned onto her stomach so she could rest her head in her arms. She hummed, encouraging Xander to go on. He was silent for a heartbeat longer. "Have you ever been sailing?"

"No…well maybe when I was little, but I don't remember it now."

"It's pretty fun, with the wind in your face and the endless sea. It's kind of like this. A whole new world of possibilities and things to explore." Nyla watched him curiously, but didn't interrupt. "I actually grew up in this area. That's how I knew about this place. Coming back here was like a new world for me, and for Issie. No stuffy governesses, no expectations, and more importantly: no prying eyes. Our parents loved us, but they expected a lot from us too, but here, we could be anything. It was a nice little break from the same old things. Sometimes, when they could, my parents would come with us and we'd camp here for the night."

The crackle of the fire soothed the silence. Shamira appeared beside it and stretched out near their feet. Xander piped up, "Do you remember that terrible snowstorm about seven years ago?"

"Yeah, we couldn't leave the house for weeks. The crop was pretty bad that year too."

"Okay, well, it wasn't that bad in the city. They got things up and running pretty quickly, after a couple days." Xander turned onto his side and propped his head up so he could see her better. "The magicity was weakened by the storm, and we didn't have enough oil to fuel the house for more than a day or two, so we rationed it.

"I had never seen my house so empty before. It was just the four of us. That's the only time my parents slept in. I think it did them a world of good, personally. And we had these massive snowball fights in the garden, right up until the rest of the world got up and running again about a week later.

"One time, Issie beaned our father in the face. She ran off and hid, but he found her because she couldn't stop giggling. He dumped at least a pound of snow on her, and we were all soaked by the time we went in. My mother's hair was so frizzy. I'd never seen it like that. My grandfather stopped in on the second day—I guess because the snow had been cleared.

"He found us in the kitchen, trying to bake a cake. Issie had flour in her hair. Somehow, I had egg and sugar streaked across my face. Grandfather wasn't so happy to find us so disheveled, but my parents didn't care. He left shortly after we put the cake in the oven." He paused, a breath stuck in his throat. "It's one of the best weeks I've had."

A gentle breeze swept through the trees and rustled the leaves. Nyla smiled at Xander. She stretched out her legs, her eyes heavy-lidded. A yawn escaped her lips.

"We never set up the tent."

"Do you want to? I mean, I will, but I kind of don't want to get up now…" Xander laughed slowly.

"I say forget the tent and just sleep, right here. No moving required." She yawned again and nuzzled her head in her arms.

"Suppose it rains?"

"Then we get a little wet. Besides, you know as well as I do that there isn't a cloud in the sky."

"Sleeping bags?"

"Not moving. Quite content right here, just like this. That and just thinking about setting everything up and then having to take it all down tomorrow is *exhausting*."

"We're so gonna regret this in the morning."

"Just don't think about how we're never gonna get the sand out of these towels and you'll be fine."

"Thanks for that, Nyla. Hadn't thought of it until now."

"No problem! Now shut it, so I can go to sleep."

The air was still with only the chirps of niphonies, little insects that almost looked like they were miniscule chips of the night sky, to fill the silence. Their campfire was beginning to die, until Shamira stoked it with a simple, unspoken urge of magic that tickled Nyla's newfound intuition. Nyla was almost asleep, her consciousness floating away on the sensation of water gently rippling under her skin.

"Hey, Xander?" she started quietly, her words slow and thick with sleep.

"I thought you wanted me to be quiet," he whispered back.

"Thanks for today. I needed this."

"You're welcome."

Courage

Their laughter shrieked from the crystal ball. Cedric had half a mind to shatter it, but he stayed his hand. It wouldn't do to lash out and whip it across the room until it smashed against the wall in a glorious display of raining glass. He'd only have to clean up the mess and procure a new ball—something he didn't have the time nor the resources to do.

Instead, Cedric refocused his attention on what he should've been concentrating on to begin with. All the while, the girl's antics with the demon cat and that insufferable boy played like a soundtrack in the background of his thoughts. Cedric took a long, pinched breath and pursed his lips. He should just let the image go.

But he couldn't.

Cedric stared at the hunk of quartz in his hand. It was once clear, but now it glowed and swirled with all the colors of the universe. That was the magic he'd stolen from the land, trapped inside this neat quartz point. His mind finally stopped the ever-present barrage of speculation, mesmerized by the enchanting hues that danced within the crystal.

Why was he doing this?

That was a question Cedric had asked himself a lot over the centuries. Except now it had a different context, one that Cedric understood even less than the previous—if that were even possible. And ever since Astrid's magic had resurfaced…

He swallowed.

Why, why was he doing this again?

Cedric told himself it was to set things right, and this time, that actually meant something to him. A promise, he vowed. He'd set things right, and do absolutely anything to do so.

What was another sin atop the heap he'd already committed?

With his wand now in hand, Cedric extracted the land's magic from the gemstone point. His brow furrowed with the hardship and the resistance he toiled with when it came to controlling the fickle essence. He guided the wavering tendril until it was absorbed into the batch of potion stewing in the smallest cauldron Cedric had ever worked with.

But it got the job done.

As the last of the land's magic was absorbed by the milky potion, it flashed. Cedric stumbled back and blinked hard. The potion sparked and sputtered as it had each time he'd added more magic. Cedric brought his hand up to keep the light at bay.

It didn't work, even with his head turned away and his eyes screwed shut.

The popping and bubbling of the brew fizzled out. Cedric cautiously opened his eyes and let his hand drop.

Nothing happened.

Hesitantly, as if the cauldron could explode at any second, Cedric inched toward his workbench and peered into the squat, black pot.

The potion inside was as dark as night. Cedric set his wand down as well as the quartz point. Now all he had to do, Cedric mused, was add his blood. He grabbed the athame and twirled the blade's point over the tip of his finger. Without so much as a blink, he pressed the blade into his skin and let a few drops of blood drop into the cauldron's depths.

Cedric healed the pinprick and stirred the potion with the dagger stained with Nyla's blood. The black liquid picked up a red undertint that shimmered. Its sheen almost looked like iridescent garnet dust in the inky vat. Almost, but not quite.

It was better this way, Cedric told himself.

She wouldn't know it wasn't as it should be.

21. HAUNTED HUNTINGTON

The water was almost like a sheet of glass far below him. It would've fooled Xander if he didn't know better. Each time the breeze dragged over the surface of the water, it created gentle ripples that disturbed the otherwise still lake. He didn't feel much of anything except for the warm silver ring between his fingers. Serenity used to embrace Xander when he was here, but when he woke up this morning, there was only emptiness.

Any happiness or peace of mind was gone.

Not only was every single memory Xander made here bubbling up from the far reaches of his mind, the dread of what might happen when they reached the Woodlane Manor plagued him. Between Issie's laughs and lazy days of lounging on the beach, the plain silver ring twirled around and around. The heirloom was a simple band with a modest onyx gem embedded in the band that flashed in the sunlight. But it was so much more than it appeared. Xander's fingers twisted the silver chain around his neck. The ring was forced to move with it as he relived everything. His brows furrowed. His eyes fell shut. What should've been happy memories were shrouded with guilt.

The warmth of Pagmas, a joyous holiday on the cusp of Harvum and Serenmae, had become cold with abandonment. The flickering candles and holiday feasts with family and business partners had long since dimmed. The end of the year was no longer a celebration but another tick of the clock. Another mark on the calendar.

The quiet Pagmas mornings spent with his parents and sister were doused in silence. He'd come to realize that there's a distinct difference between quiet and silence.

Silence was lonely and riddled with guilt.

Quiet was comfortable and vibrant.

Silence was filled with a sort of static that didn't even exist.

Quiet boasted a hum that spoke volumes, that spoke life.

Silence came from a void somewhere beyond this world, whereas quiet lived.

Xander missed those precious moments on Pagmas morning, sitting in front of the roaring fire. The delicate scent of pine tickling his nose from the fresh tree in the corner of the room. It was almost like the calm before the storm.

Pagmas morning was always the first morning in a few weeks when his house was still. All the preparations were done, and he always suspected that was because his parents wanted a simple morning with himself and Issie before having to mingle with guests and navigate complex social dynamics of industry and loyalty—and the unspoken competition to outdo the other families.

While it's true that his parents had expectations passed down from his grandfather, they also didn't seem to care about their social standing in the same way as the other families. His parents commanded respect and only gave it when earned. Xander supposed that's why so many people tried to build relationships with his parents. From business to social bonds, his parents always seemed to be at the center of it.

But, at the end of the day, they were Mother and Father. The sort who would tuck their children into bed and seek nothing more than their eternal happiness. Sure, they weren't always around once he and Issie had grown some, but they were there when it mattered most. Like Pagmas.

Tears dotted Xander's vision when he finally opened his eyes. The sun crested the tops of the trees. It bathed him in a heavenly light he didn't want. But he didn't want darkness either.

He'd already dwelled there and didn't want to crawl back from it again.

The pebbles on the dirt path behind him crunched under light footsteps. Xander tucked the warm ring and chain back under the neckline of his shirt. Quickly, he swiped at the wetness collecting in his eyes and clenched his jaw.

"Hey," Nyla chirped. She came to stand by his side at the edge of the cliff and looked out across the water. "Whatcha doing all the way up here?"

Xander didn't look at her, preferring to let Nyla remain a shadow in his peripheral vision. He cleared his choked-up throat.

"Just thinking."

"Oh."

The new silence stretched on. Xander could feel the weight of her gaze on him and balled his fists. He only hoped the mask he'd donned worked. She didn't need his heartache too. His lip trembled, and instantly, the mask fell, and the dam broke.

"It's funny, you know? I never thought I'd come here again. Didn't think I could. It didn't hit me yesterday, but now, with everything so... still, and standing up here, it's like I'm looking at it from a distance."

"Well of course you're looking at the beach from a distance. I mean you *are* standing on a ledge high above it," Nyla joked, her voice light.

Xander's lips twitched in what might've been the precursor to a laugh on another day, but not this time. Nyla shrank from her failed attempt at lifting his spirits. His heart clenched at this. Xander knew it wasn't fair to burden her, but he couldn't stop himself.

"I know it shouldn't be this bitter. It should be comforting or heartwarming or something like that." Xander's face fell into a dark shadow of guilt and anger.

"You blame yourself?" Nyla asked. Xander let the silence be his answer as tears slipped from the corners of his eyes. She gripped his hand and squeezed. "It's not your fault."

"You don't even know what happened." Xander's voice was strained as he turned to meet her purple eyes with a burning gaze. "Issie and I were fighting, and she ran off. I chased after her, and a hellhound attacked her. If I had been a better brother, Issie might still be alive."

"How do you know that? That's like saying if I was never born, my family would still be alive, and Cedric wouldn't have started the fire. You just don't know that. So what if you two were fighting? I believe our families know exactly how much they mean to us. You can't be angry at yourself for things you *think* you could've or should've done because you just don't know. You need to stop blaming yourself." Nyla tugged his hand to get her point across as she brought her other hand up to wipe away Xander's tears. "Love doesn't disappear just because people pass away. It's always there, even when we hate ourselves."

"Do you really believe that?" His voice was only a cracked whisper. Nyla's callused fingers were gentle and soft as she swiped them over his cheekbone, almost like she was afraid he'd crumble under her touch.

"Yeah, I do. Our families love us, no matter what happened. None of this is in any way our fault, and no matter how many times we force ourselves to relive it, there wasn't anything we could've done." She glanced away for a second. Xander's eyes softened. When their eyes met next, Xander didn't have time to process anything as Nyla wrapped him in a fierce embrace. "I'm here for you just as much as you are for me."

"Thanks, Nyla," Xander murmured into her hair.

After a moment, Nyla slowly pulled away, and Xander let her, letting his arms fall limp at his sides. Neither one of them moved for a long time, and Xander was grateful for it. He was at peace with the way the water glowed in the sun's light and couldn't bear the thought of breaking down camp or facing the road ahead.

His mind wandered back to the memory of the day before. He stared wistfully at the water. His heart longed for the ability to relive that day over and over again, or at least something like it. To be that carefree and content…it was something anyone would envy. Xander wanted to be in a bubble like that for as long as he lived.

He had, for a while anyway. It was so long ago, and when that bubble had popped, it exploded, shattering like glass.

What a shock it had been too.

Gone was the peace and easiness of a weightless life. Gone was the bright, clouded gaze of innocence. That wholesome sentiment was soon replaced by the belief that it was only a child's ignorance that the world could be so free.

But maybe that wasn't the case either.

Neither innocence nor ignorance, but rather a jumble of beliefs and moments that morphed into one life. What exactly was that life then, with all that was good or bad, blessed or full of sorrow? Or even virtue or blame?

Xander couldn't answer that.

Unable to settle the matter himself, Xander went about breaking down their camp alongside Nyla. No matter how hard he shook out the towels and blankets from the night before, sand remained embedded in the soft fibers. There wasn't anything more he could do about it without rinsing them out, so he rolled them up and strapped them to his bag, stealing a glance at Shamira. The cat was still sunbathing. His eyes shifted over to Nyla. She was already packed up, her bag on her shoulders. She stood at the edge of the lake with her bare feet in the water.

"Almost ready?" he called out, squinting against the sun.

"Yeah," Nyla drawled reluctantly as she turned and made her way over to a rock to dry off her feet and pull her boots on.

Shamira stood and stretched before she bounded off the boulder.

Once they set off, Shamira stalked ahead of them. Her head swiveled from side to side, a true hunter. Xander watched her with equal parts curiosity and uneasiness. Even if she was on the alert for threats, wasn't she one herself?

It was true that the cat hadn't done anything to harm them, but was it only a matter of time? Xander shook his head. He continued to keep a keen eye on the cat as he too observed the fading Shadow Forest for any present dangers.

***

Over the course of the next week, the Harvum-kissed leaves of the Shadow Forest bled together with the scarlet-splotched leaves of the Godberd Woods until the Shadow Forest was behind them. As they sat around their lunchtime cooking fire, Nyla couldn't help but stare anxiously at the canopy of scarlet and plum leaves overhead. Somehow, the sapphire leaves of the Shadow Forest to the south were more of a comfort than the familiar sight of the northwest's Harvum foliage. She'd always loved the change of season between Hugony and Harvum, but the last two years were different, and this time, the sight of the Godberd's turning leaves brought only worry. If her mind could stop whirling, Nyla would be able to wonder how she hadn't split her lip open from nibbling and biting it so much.

Perhaps you'd feel less uncertain if you were more skilled in wielding your magic? Shamira spoke as if she could read Nyla's thoughts.

Could she?!

Nyla blinked out of her daze. Fresh terror consumed her, but she tamped it down and leveled her eyes with the pumpkie's unwavering gaze. She didn't even know what to say or what to think. Everything came to a grinding halt, and Nyla found herself glancing away from Shamira and seeking out Xander's eyes. He gave her a guarded look that was rife with skepticism and flicked his eyes over to the cat. Nyla swallowed the rocks in her throat and tried to wrangle a response, as Shamira was still watching her.

Before she'd had a chance to respond, Shamira shrugged. *It's just a thought, and one of the few ways I might assist you.*

Nyla cocked her head to the side and carefully considered Shamira's insight. "Maybe you're right. Maybe I should seriously practice my magic."

And I would be happy to help, even if pumpkie magic differs from human magic.

"How're they different?" Nyla asked.

You have much to learn and little time, Shamira chided ominously. *In short, pumpkies are more powerful than humans, drawing magic from an infinite wealth of our history and energy from the land by way of revival. Humans draw magic from their own energy stores, much like they do when performing physical activities.*

"That's all fine and dandy, but can you actually teach Nyla to use her magic without it being dangerous?" Xander piped up as he stamped out their cooking fire.

Possibly, and no, it shouldn't be dangerous. Though I must admit, the potential is there seeing as we're working with different magics.

Nyla glanced between Shamira's composed and certain posture and Xander's perturbed frown. Her lips pulled into a grim line. "It couldn't hurt, right?"

Shamira's lip curled. *Then let's begin—unless you'd rather keep moving?*

Nyla's eyes cut to Xander. He only offered her a shrug and a curt nod. It was her decision, and faced with it, Nyla couldn't say for certain which option seemed worse. Pressing on meant reaching the Woodlane Manor, but letting Shamira teach her about magic at this very moment meant many things. It meant trusting the pumpkie, a species Xander had quietly seethed were nothing but ruthless killers when they'd had a moment alone. It also meant *not* reaching the Woodlane Manor just yet. And it meant that Nyla would have to accept all that Fate had recently thrown at her.

"Where do we start?" Nyla held Shamira's gaze with a resolve she didn't know she could muster.

With the basics. Shamira smiled. *First, you need to know that magic is all around us. It's an energy that belongs to the land we travel, to the air we breathe, to the water that sustains us, and the light that guides us.*

For humans, magic is a part of you, just as much as your blood or bones are. And your strength comes not only from endurance training, but from your will. Magic is an extension of yourself, something you seem unwilling to accept. Shamira studied her with calculating eyes.

She swallowed and shrank under the cat's gaze. "And *how* do I do that? Accept it when I didn't even have a choice?"

No one chooses magic. It just happens, Shamira explained. *Do you question your free will? The reason you need to breathe? To eat? To drink?*

Nyla shook her head. Those things simply were. But could she consider magic—her magic—as something so inherent and simplistic?

Stand up, Shamira ordered. Nyla rose to her feet slowly, uncertain if she really wanted to follow the direction. *Now close your eyes and focus. Draw on your magic.*

"And how do I do that?" Nyla huffed.

Magic is about imagery, Shamira started, *and intent. You have to know what you want to do with it in order to use it effectively. How do you want to use your magic, Nyla?*

Nyla's breath stuttered. How *did* she want to use her magic? She swallowed thickly and forced herself to look Shamira in the eyes. "I don't know."

I don't need a long-term answer. I just want to know what you want right now. Shamira remained undeterred, steadfast in her purpose.

"I just want to make it through all of this," Nyla answered honestly, her voice solemn.

You want to protect yourself then?

Nyla nodded.

There are five elements that make up magic and, in a lot of ways, make up the world around us. You have already worked with fire and water, but you could also utilize earth, air, and energy. Energy is often forgotten by you humans, or not recognized as such, but that is the core of everything around us. It cannot be destroyed or created, only manipulated, replenished, or dispersed. Shamira paused for a moment and only began again once Nyla had nodded for her to do so. *To protect yourself, you need to focus your energy, the most primal form of your magic. Picture a shield in front of you.* As she spoke, a shield of sage-colored magic appeared in front of the pumpkie. *Its strength is yours. Are you strong, Nyla?*

Nyla didn't answer. She didn't know how to. Instead, she closed her eyes and pictured a shield in front of her. A strong shield. An unbreakable shield. When she opened her eyes, a translucent wall of lilac-colored magic—*her* magic—shielded her from the world in front of her. She stared through it, grinning at Shamira. But the cat's lip was curled, and there was a gleam in her eyes that had Nyla's stomach rolling.

Before she could blink, a bolt of sage magic shattered her shield and struck her in the chest. Xander shouted at Shamira as Nyla landed on her back with a groan. She blinked her eyes open as a shadow fell above her.

"Are you okay?" Xander held out his hand and pulled her up.

"Don't get hit in the chest with magic. It's not fun," Nyla grumbled as she rubbed her sore bottom. Her chest stung, but the sting receded with every second that expired.

Again? Shamira asked with a lilt of amusement in her voice.

"Do you intend to shoot me again?"

Only if your defense fails again, the pumpkie answered honestly.

Nyla glanced over at Xander. "You might as well pitch the tent and get comfortable. I think we're gonna be here for a while."

Xander nodded. "I'll go find something to eat. Maybe try to replenish our stock."

It was with that that the rest of the afternoon passed, with Shamira directing Nyla through different exercises and reasons to call her magic. Sometimes, Shamira would only have her conjure energy—her magical essence, as Shamira called it—and expel it. Other times, Shamira would instruct her to form a magic shield. And then she'd attack Nyla's defenses until they wavered, which was often much too quickly. She'd order Nyla to focus, and Nyla would try her best, but she was quickly becoming fatigued.

At the mere mention of being fatigued, Xander suggested they stop for the day and rest. Nyla relented, and watched with dulled eyes as he set about cooking dinner. Shamira said she'd need more food—and more practice to build up her endurance. By the time they'd cleaned up dinner and Shamira was done lecturing for the night, Nyla was convinced she could fall asleep standing up. She didn't know how long she would be able to keep up with Shamira's high expectations, or when she'd even meet the pumpkie's baseline expectations, but if she was training her that hard, then maybe she didn't want to go to the Woodlane Manor after all. Maybe they were better off heading back to Fortune Falls. After all, Xander had once asked her why she wouldn't just stay at the safest place in all of Tenebris. Maybe he'd had the right idea, and Nyla should've listened to him then.

Prudence

Cedric swallowed hard as he stared back at the raverin. It hissed at him with a forked tongue. He *tsk*ed it and snatched the miniature carrier from its leg. The bird nipped at him, but Cedric was certain that its bite would hurt less than the guilt of sending the letter he had yet to write.

"You aren't the only one that's unhappy about this," he muttered, glancing over the letter. Dia only ruffled his feathers and puffed out his chest. Cedric gently brought his hand to rest on top of the bird's head, scratching Dia fondly. The bird nipped at his fingers sharply, obviously displeased.

Or was it in disapproval?

Cedric couldn't be certain which the action was meant to portray, only that Dia was most definitely passing judgment on him and his actions as of late.

"At least you can fly away from all of this. I certainly wouldn't damn you for it," he murmured, dropping his hand by his side.

But this time was different, and no punishment could ever be worse than the one he'd lived with since that one pivotal decision he'd made 647 years ago. So, Cedric did what he had to do now. He'd finish playing his part and hope that wherever that got him, it was enough to set things right.

His fountain pen scratched the thin strip of paper. This update had to get done, and the faster he completed it, the better. When it was gone, maybe he'd be able to breathe again.

Cedric sat back in his chair and looked over the scrawl he called handwriting.

They are close—should be there within the day.

His eyes flicked over to the raverin still on his windowsill. Dia had one wing extended, picking at its ruffled feathers, grooming itself. Cedric whistled two short notes, and the bird looked over at him. It was a glance short of an eye roll.

"Don't give me that. You know exactly why I'm doing this." He stuffed the letter in the carrier and walked over to the raverin. Throughout the whole rest of the ordeal, Cedric avoided the bird's eyes. He knew it wouldn't talk back, but a responsive animal wouldn't be the first.

But raverins couldn't speak.

In some ways, Cedric wished they could. It would be nice to have *some* sort of interaction, but maybe it was for the best. At least Dia had some personality other than being a trained messenger and scout or whatever other human directions it understood.

Cedric felt like this bird was everything that he wasn't 600 years ago and still wasn't.

"There." Cedric took a step back, and the bird ruffled its feathers. He knew that it didn't like the little carrier tube, but that was the only way. "Woodlane Manor, please."

Dia squawked sharply before he flew off with a rustle of its wings. In the blink of an eye, Cedric was alone again.

22. MATTERS OF HART

Another dash of ethereal light streaked across the star-studded sky above the Godberd Woods. Nyla lay awake with only a blanket draped over herself and a towel beneath her. Bands of turquoise, teal, indigo, and lavender light swirled above. It was like they were caressing the sky and stars with each pulsating ebb and flow. Soft snores came from the tent behind her. She could barely hear them over the crackle of the warm fire beside her. Shamira was also fast asleep, a state Nyla knew she should be in too. No matter how hard she tried, her mind wouldn't stop, and neither would the anxiety that gnawed at her insides.

She hadn't realized how close they were. Sure, Xander had said that there were only two or three days left when he double-checked the map this morning, but she didn't want to believe him.

Yet here they were.

They had passed the road signs for Glendale and Covington sometime after lunch. Nyla knew a shortcut that would get them to the manor a day earlier, but something had made her lips clam up. She didn't know why she'd kept this information to herself. Maybe it was because they had also passed the weathered memorial that was built forever ago. It was yet another marker that they were closer to the Woodlane Manor than she'd anticipated.

Her father had told her that once upon a time, noble and well-loved governors controlled the region of Hart. The lord and lady's daughter lived in the country's capital with the royal family. Nyla's brow furrowed as she remembered the tale. Her father never mentioned what the daughter did or why she didn't live with her own family, but for whatever reason, it was important that she stay at the royal's palace. Nyla supposed that it wasn't relevant to the three stone obelisks along the side of the road. They were staggered in height, the tallest among them no taller than her father himself. The smallest was about even in height with her shoulders.

Nyla watched the lights that danced and the Wishing Stars that fell across the sky as her father's story washed over her memory.

The Lord and Lady of Hart had left their holding to visit their daughter and attend to grave matters at the palace. The people of Hart saw them off, cheering and waving banners of the nobles' rich colors. Even though the country had fallen on hard times, the governors had done everything they could to help their people. For that, the people of Hart were grateful, especially after the war. Even though the war was over, its grip hadn't failed yet, and the consequences were still making themselves known.

The Lord and Lady of Hart never made it to the palace, to their daughter.

Some said that the Lord and Lady were captured by the deviant survivors of the failed uprising. Her father had speculated it was either bandits or a terrible accident, but that didn't make for good gossip—or stories.

No matter what their demise ultimately was, Lord and Lady Hart, along with the driver of their carriage, had disappeared for good. The only proof that their ill-fated journey was more than a centuries-old tale of caution were the lamentations of those who mourned them and the three stone obelisks.

Once she was a little older, Nyla's mother explained that the Lord and Lady's expansive holdings had been split into different towns and cities, including Glendale and Covington. The few square miles that surrounded their seat as the authority over the hilly and quiet county remained known as Hart. She said that it was a reminder to cherish every day and honor the last Lord and Lady of Hart. Over time, the title of governor had been retired and the idea of city-states broken up all together.

Nowadays, Tenebris was unofficially divided up based on its geography. Politically, the country was broken up into smaller counties overseen by elected officials from the region, though they were still mostly of noble birth. The Shadow Forest region, known for its sapphire leaves and specters, was overseen by a panel of the lords and ladies that had holdings there. The Godberd Woods, which was larger than the region of Hart used to be and distinguished by its plum leaves, was split between a panel much like the Shadow Forest's and the royal family, as the capital city of Mageffery was nestled in the heart of the Godberd Woods. The Barrier Plains and Amber Dunelands that the rest of Tenebris was comprised of were ruled in much the same manner as the Shadow Forest.

A sad smile pulled at her lips.

Even though the memory of her father's story and her mother's history lessons brought with it the embrace of a warm home, surrounded by her family, the sight of the three obelisks sent a tingling shiver of foreboding through her. The knots in her stomach had pulled just a little tighter. The itch of trepidation plagued her. Now more than ever, Nyla wished for everything to turn out all right, for someone to help her through the shadows that threatened to swallow her whole.

Her eyes fixed on one of the falling stars, the telltale streak of iridescent light from the heavens, and her heart beat faster. Nyla squeezed her eyes shut and gripped the blanket tighter around herself, the soft material desperately clutched in her balled fists.

"Please," she murmured, her lips moving silently. Her whispered plea couldn't be heard over the timid crackle of the fire beside her. "Please, just one little miracle, for me, or guidance or *something* to protect us. *Please.*"

Nyla didn't know exactly what she begged Helpet for, only that she craved some sense of security or a sign. She didn't know what she was looking for or what significance it should hold, only that a sign from the heavens might soothe her weary soul. And who better to pray to than her goddess, the one who stood for guidance and wisdom?

The goddess of old was the protective force they all prayed to in these parts. There were older religions, sure, and newer ones that emerged, but Nyla and her family looked to Helpet for all things. And what Helpet couldn't aid them with, it was left up to Fate.

Or Corruptio, Helpet's opposite and Her shadow.

Heavy footsteps thudded behind her, crunching some fallen leaves as they fell. Nyla sat up on one elbow and twisted herself around. Every muscle in her body coiled tight like a spring ready to pop up and strike.

Xander emerged from the tent with the rustle of fabric and a yawn. He brushed the chunk of hair that had fallen across his face aside and looked in Nyla's general direction.

"You're still awake?" In the dim light of the fire, Nyla could see that Xander's eyes weren't even open. He rubbed the sleep from them and stumbled over to her. "Come on, come to bed."

"Are *you* even awake right now?" Nyla looked through the flames and caught Shamira's narrowed eyes. The cat sniffed the air, and after a moment, she shrugged before she resettled in her spot.

If he's truly sleepwalking, he's your problem, Shamira grumbled, presumably asleep again within seconds.

Nyla stood and faced Xander. She poked his cheek, not sure what to expect. He only twitched and staggered away from her. With a heavy sigh, Nyla cast one final, longing glance at the Wishing Stars she remembered so fondly. Carefully, she guided Xander back inside the tent. Relief flooded her when he managed to find his own way back to his sleeping bag. As she snuggled deeply into her own, Xander turned toward her, still very much asleep.

"It'll be okay, you know."

Nyla blinked, but before she could even respond, Xander's snores resumed, and his body fell captive to a deep slumber. He'd managed to leave her wondering what just happened and how mentally present he was in his sleepwalking.

***

"So, how long have you been a sleepwalker?" Nyla asked hesitantly the next morning. She'd had a fitful sleep plagued by nightmares of a shadow stalking her from the darkened edges of the Woodlane Manor's circular ballroom.

"What do you mean? I don't sleepwalk." Xander glanced up from his plate and briefly paused to study her.

"Really? 'Cause you were sleepwalking last night. It was kinda creepy too." Nyla's voice was filled with skepticism.

"Sorry, but I'm pretty sure you were dreaming. The only thing I know I do in my sleep is snore."

That's not true. You sometimes mumble incoherently in your sleep, and Nyla, I've seen you bolt upright in your sleep. Shamira stated this as if it were perfectly normal for someone to watch another in their sleep. *Besides, I sensed another form of magic last night. It was like...divinity.*

The cat's eyes narrowed as she considered this for what was probably the millionth time, but for Nyla and Xander, it was the first.

"I'm sorry, but did you say '*divinity*?'" Nyla hissed. She swallowed hard. Venom crept into her voice as bile rose in her throat. "If you 'sensed' something last night, why not mention it before? Why not wake us up? I thought you were here to help us!"

"Nyla—"

I am here to help, to help you! Shamira shot back.

"Really, because for all we know you're trying to kill us or you're working with *him*!"

I haven't the slightest idea whom you're speaking of! I'm trying to—

"For the love of Balmae, what do you mean by you sensed another form of magic?" Xander burst out. Both Nyla and Shamira turned to look at him. Nyla met his eyes sheepishly like a scolded child.

Shamira glared at him and snarled, *I mean something happened last night, and then a wish was granted.*

"A wish?" Xander repeated.

I don't know. Ask Nyla. She must've been the one to make it. Shamira nodded her head in Nyla's direction. *You were walking in your sleep, and then the only magic that was left was my own, Nyla's, and the faint trace of the Wishing Stars.*

Both sets of eyes turned to Nyla expectantly. She glanced down at her nearly empty plate. Her heart pounded in her chest as she searched for answers. Not a single explanation could be conjured by her imagination.

"So, Wishing Stars, huh?" Xander prompted.

"You know, I think it's about time we got going, don't you?" Nyla sprang up from her seat on the ground and practically hurled the plate, utensils and all, over to Xander. She turned on her heel and tried to appear calm as she forced her shaking hands to still on her near sprint to the tent.

"As you wish, Miss Question-dodger," Xander called after her receding back.

It wasn't long before Xander and Nyla were all packed up, and Shamira's tail had stopped tapping the ground impatiently like a human might tap their foot. Nyla's head buzzed. Her insides twisted tighter and tighter. As if Shamira's lengthy training session hadn't been enough last night, the fact that there was the presence of 'divine' magic made Nyla's blood run cold.

Cedric was evil—there was no doubt about that—but could he be more than human? A god?

The very premise sent shivers through Nyla's body.

What had she gotten herself, and now Xander, into? How could she fight a god, hellbent on something terrible, that killed her family? She swallowed thickly and remembered all Shamira had taught her thus far about magic—and how much they'd practiced over the last few days.

She glared at the pumpkie who glided a few paces ahead of her and mulled over what she'd learned about magic. Despite the differences between pumpkie and human magic, the principles were apparently the same. Magic was an extension of will, grounded in the elements.

Magic was the use or balance of energy, manifested by an exertion of choice or desire. She said that someone had to wish to use their magic in some way or form, and just like humans, pumpkies had a varied degree of magical ability or aptitude.

Shamira had stressed that it was important for Nyla to realize that it wasn't about controlling her magic so much as it was about embracing it as an extension of herself rather than a means to an end or an entity of its own.

Besides all of that, Shamira had mentioned that Nyla shouldn't be afraid of her own magic because it was hers to wield and hers alone.

Magic was nothing without a conductor, just as a bow and arrow was nothing without its archer.

Rationally, Nyla knew that even this bit of information should help her, but her fury about Shamira not mentioning the different magic that had popped up last night sooner than this morning bothered her. As she trailed after Xander and Shamira, Nyla reanalyzed what the cat had said and was left with a burning curiosity.

Who exactly was Shamira? If she, Nyla, were so important to the pumpkies, why send only a cub to find her? Why not teach her more about magic and why not do something sooner?

There was something Shamira was withholding. Xander knew it. Nyla knew it. It was only a matter of what, exactly, Shamira was hiding.

Nyla narrowed her eyes, watching the cat move gracefully through the purple-and-red flora. The ease in which Shamira floated through the brush fueled the uneasiness spreading through her body, and before long, Nyla had convinced herself that Shamira was another enemy. The farther away the odd safety of the Shadow Forest became, the more Nyla ached to go back and change her mind.

Every footstep brought them—brought *her*—closer to either salvation or damnation. The longer her thoughts dwelled on how much she didn't know, how little control she had, the more Nyla wondered about the shadow that had stalked her dreams.

Nyla's breath hitched. Her heart beat faster. Her footsteps faltered. When had they left the sanctity of the Godberd Woods' plum-and-crimson leaves? When had they stumbled onto this road? Nyla couldn't answer that. The paranoia that plagued her had consumed her entirely by the time she found herself nearing a crossroad. Her body started up again with a shudder. She half expected to fall through the roadway or worse.

The closer they got to the fork in the road, Nyla felt as though she were walking on broken glass, trying not to get cut. But there wasn't any demon patiently lurking behind the wooden post of the road signs, ready to pounce and snatch her away. Instead, her eyes were met with the sight of the two road signs, each in a different state of rot.

The first was in better shape than the other. It had probably been replaced within the last year or so. Through the weathering of the wood and cracked paint, Nyla could just make out the faintly recognizable letters of 'Gossamer.'

She remembered Gossamer. It was the last port between Tenebris and Eurland. The town wasn't nearly as big as the port cities, but Gossamer was the perfect place for a Tenebrese fort, as her father had once explained.

Gossamer and its wooden sign didn't matter, not when the other sign was rotted beyond recognition, and yet so much more distinctive.

Nyla knew that once upon a time, the rotted sign had read 'Hart.'

The sight of these two signs rooted her to her spot. A hand gripped and squeezed her heart. The faded sign slunk closer to her. It edged closer and closer until it surrounded her. The sign taunted her, asking her why she would come back after all this time away. Her heart thudded like thunder between her ears, the only sound she could hear over the sign's cackling. Her limbs turned to lead. All Nyla could do was succumb to the icy chill that ran up and down her body. Something had a harsh grip on her bones. If she could think properly, she'd know its name was grief-stricken guilt.

"Nyla?" Xander's soft voice, laced with concern, broke through the daze. "Are you all right?"

She shook her head, her eyes glued to the remnants of Hart's sign. Any noise Nyla could've made in that moment died in her throat. She glanced down when Xander's fingers brushed her wrist. Her lilac eyes were oddly dry no matter how horribly her heart wailed as their fingers laced together. Nyla wasn't certain whose hand was squeezing, but she was certain that her hand was about to break. It was like she was made of the same brittle, rotted wood as Hart's sign.

Xander stepped in front of her, blocking the road signs. For the first time in a few days, Nyla's mind was silent. Every fiber of her being was heavy and exhausted. Her head hung as she tried to shake off her inner demons, the ones that had commanded the wooden signs.

"Talk to me." Xander brushed away the strands of hair that had fallen into Nyla's eyes. She glanced up at him, finally aware of reality again.

She took a deep breath, the aching throb in her heart gone for now, and looked between her companions. Shamira watched them curiously. Nyla couldn't meet Xander's eyes, preferring the view of her own feet and the ground beneath them.

"This was a mistake."

Hurt and confusion laced the undercurrent of Xander's quiet words. "What was? Taking this route? Skipping breakfast? Traveling with—"

"No." Nyla shook her head again. Fatigue and faintness settled in her bones. "Coming here in the first place. This," she pulled her hand free of his and jabbed a finger toward the road to Hart, "was a mistake.

We came all this way and for what? I was sick, and I'd just found out I had magic. I have no control over any of this and—and..."

You have more control than you think. Maybe not as much stamina as you'd hoped, but your magic is strong. You are strong. *You just have to learn to trust in yourself, in your magic. You've already done so much, keeping yourself safe all this time. The only limit is your own fear.* Shamira's cold nose nudged Nyla's hand reassuringly. *That's the best I can do to help you with your magic.*

For the first time since the sage-eyed cat had found them, Nyla felt a hint of fondness for the creature. She nodded her thanks and met Xander's eyes. "Then maybe it's time we get going again, and finally put this all to bed."

"Are you sure?" Xander asked slowly.

"No," Nyla answered shortly, "but if I don't decide now, I will always talk myself out of seeing this through. I can't stand in front of these crossroads forever." She paused, considering her companions in turn. "Are you both sure you want to come with me? You don—"

I'm not afraid for myself, Nyla. I'm not much afraid of anything, Shamira assured her.

Nyla nodded solemnly, silently thanking the pumpkie for her resolve. She met Xander's eyes next and started to ask again if he was absolutely certain, but he spoke before she ever got the chance.

"If that's what you really want, then okay. There's no way I'm leaving you alone now. I promise. You don't have to deal with this all on your own."

Her heart was still weighed down with dread, but at least their words of comfort had made each step forward a little easier. As the trio traveled farther into Hart, a different sort of bitter sadness swallowed Nyla whole.

23. THE WOODLANE MANOR

The sun had hardly risen, but Nyla didn't need it. Just like that day outside of Deering, Nyla focused her energy until a ball of light bobbed in front of her. Even though she was proud of this small accomplishment, she didn't smile. She didn't think such an expression was possible right now, not with the tightness in her chest or the tears that were on the brink of filling her eyes at any moment. Nyla steeled herself with a few deep breaths through her nose and hauled her bag into her lap. Elbow deep, she dug around the disheveled contents when her fingers brushed the hard package of the wrapped picture frame. Once free from its protective shirt, Nyla relaxed against the rough bark of the tree trunk behind her.

She brought her knees close to her chest and laid the bare frame against them, staring at the portrait. The tightness in her chest constricted again. This time, the stab of pain went straight down to her lungs.

She'd done it. She'd come home.

But was it really home anymore?

Nyla wasn't sure why she was certain that the portrait had changed. Their faces still smiled. The corners were still faded, torn, or blackened where the flames had lapped at them. Flakes of gray ash clung to the glass. And right there in the middle was Nyla, beaming like a little ray of sunshine. Nothing had changed. Her eyes skimmed over the rest of her family. They lingered on her twin.

Westley had a round face and a mess of curly hair. Nyla's lips pulled into a genuinely warm smile. Her twin's hair was so wild, so untamed, so unlike him. Alone, Westley could be quiet and patient. Sometimes, he'd disappear for hours, a book tucked under his arm. She never could figure out what he hid in there, no matter how many times she'd tried to sneak a peek.

Tears pricked her eyes. Nyla would never understand how the painter had grasped each of their expressions so perfectly. The brilliant smile that graced her twin's soft features sparkled in both life and in this captured moment. The way her father held her mother close, like he was afraid she'd disappear into thin air, or the grip Nyla had on Lydia's little hand to keep her from wandering off. How Derek was almost the spitting image of their father. Her eyes moved to focus on the frame instead, not wanting to reduce herself to tears she thought she'd cried out.

The inscription glowed in the pulsating light of the orb beside her. 'Love is for forever.'

Bitterness rose in her throat. Her love for her family might never die, and while they had passed on, she knew their love for her hadn't passed with them. But the sentiment didn't bring much more comfort than that. It didn't fill the void and ever-present emptiness that had consumed her since their deaths. All it left her with was loneliness. And grief. Guilt. Resignation. Emptiness.

Her life was empty. Or at least it was until Fate had thrown a storm in her path and a boy with a map. A pumpkie too. Her eyes fixated on the forget-me-nots etched into the bronze frame.

A single vow flitted across her mind: She'd never forget her family. She'd make sure their stories lived on in her heart.

Nyla latched onto the part of her silent vow that promised them she'd make a life for herself, a better life than the existence she'd sprinted through for the last two years.

She clung to the hope that the portrait gave her, not truly knowing if those were promises she could keep, but she would try. Its survival was nothing short of a miracle.

If something like this portrait could survive that fire, then maybe there was a miracle waiting for Nyla as well. After all, she'd survived too. She'd changed from that young girl, in more ways than one, but maybe she could get some part of that life back—or at least some semblance of that life back.

The crunch of fallen leaves brought her attention to the approaching footsteps of a barely awake Xander. He was already dressed, though his messy hair stuck up at odd ends.

"Dare I ask if you slept at all last night?" he asked groggily, taking a seat next to her on the soft ground.

"Dare I say the answer is barely?" She rested her head on his shoulder and continued to stare at the gleaming faces before her.

"We don't have to set off right away if you don't want to," Xander offered softly.

"Good, because I really don't want to. Not yet anyway."

"You wanna talk about it?"

"Not really. It's just..." Nyla swallowed, not sure what 'it' was exactly. "*Complicated.*"

"Okay."

Nyla took in their surroundings. If she let herself, she could almost believe that they were anywhere. Except the bark wasn't cracked or ashen like it was in the Shadow Forest. There wasn't a blanket of sapphire leaves that obscured the sunlight above. Instead, the trees were a golden brown like honey, and sunlight danced between the loose canopy of bright scarlet and lingering hints of plum.

In some strange way, the familiar sights of home filled Nyla with a sense of ease and comfort. But the bitter grief and anxiety greatly outweighed any sense of homecoming. This was just another forest.

Another day. Another place. Another little trip in all of her endless wanderings. It's not like she could stay here.

Even as Nyla thought about how she'd be gone again by the week's end, a timid voice piped up and asked, "Why not?" Why couldn't she stay here? This was home after all. This was where she grew up, where her family had lived and died. Hart was where her roots were laid.

Had the fire scorched them?

Had those roots been severed completely?

Nyla walked with a heavy heart as the late morning and early afternoon passed before her unseeing eyes. Xander and Shamira followed her down roads she still knew by heart. Memories of the neighbors that had come to help put out the fire led to more questions. Would they remember, let alone *recognize*, her if they saw her now?

Nyla bit her lip. Her feet led the way of their own accord, her mind too consumed to pay attention. The kind gray eyes of the neighbor who had taken her in, the one Nyla had stolen from when she'd fled, pained her memory. Were all these people still here in Hart?

Or were they gone in some way too?

Nyla was so focused on getting to the manor that she'd lost sight of everything else. And for what? She couldn't answer that because she simply didn't know anymore.

If Shamira was right, and magic was about embracing it, trusting yourself, then the manor didn't have much more to offer her.

If only she'd realized that sooner. Maybe then Nyla wouldn't have found herself somehow passing through once-familiar fields of farmland before they reentered the shady coolness of the Godberd Woods.

As Nyla's memory led the way, Xander fell into step beside her. He hummed a quiet melody that calmed Nyla's mind. Whether or not he knew it, it gave Nyla something to latch onto and ground herself with. Nyla could tell that Xander was anxious too by the way his fingers often brushed his quiver, like he was subconsciously reaching for an arrow.

She glanced over her shoulder and met Shamira's eyes. The pumpkie's green eyes sparkled like the hardest metal known to Tenebris and beyond. Nyla admired her two companions, even as regret wove its way through her core. She should've never come here, and to make matters worse, she'd dragged two friends along with her.

Even though Nyla was ready to break out into a sprint until she reached the Shadow Forest again, her companions' resolve and dedication to her urged her forward. Turning around now would be like turning her back on them—especially Xander. He didn't ask to be dragged into any of this. Yet, for whatever reason, he was helping her.

No matter how much it felt like the earth was collapsing in on her, Nyla continued to lead the way through the Godberd Woods she remembered so fondly.

The trees and plants grew wilder here than they had before. Branches and twigs were intertwined with each other, as if they wanted to form a wall to stop travelers in their tracks. Tree roots twisted together to form large knots on the forest floor. Thorns snagged Nyla's clothes and tangled in her hair. Irritated by the sharp fingers that grabbed at her, Nyla gathered up her hair and braided it as she led Xander and Shamira even deeper into the untouched woods.

Her eyes flitted over their surroundings. They were close; she could feel it in her aching bones. Each breath was a hardship with how tight her chest had become. Even so, she was able to recognize the relics left behind from centuries of use before the manor was abandoned.

Crumbling stone statues wrapped in flowering vines and ivy lined a long-deserted path. Nyla gulped at the sight. Her heart hesitated half a second before it beat steadily beneath her chest. An odd calm consumed her nerves. For the first time since they'd entered Hart, her hands stopped shaking...for the moment anyway.

Walking down the long drive that used to welcome esteemed guests did nothing to cultivate the calm Nyla fought to bolster. Her nerves turned to jelly once more. She forced her breaths to steady. Just like the stone statues of creatures from myths and legend, she felt as though ivy tightened around her. Nyla kept moving, even as those vines tightened around her heart and throat, strangling her.

The threesome continued on the path as the canopy of the Godberd Woods parted above to expose the late afternoon sunlight.

Nyla's stomach flipped over and over again as Shamira led the way up the path. As antsy as she was, her curiosity piqued. Maybe all her fears were wrong. Maybe she could come home, and all of this was just a crazy quest thrust upon her by a twisted turn of Fate.

Or maybe Fortune Falls wasn't all it was acclaimed to be. Maybe it was actually a curse, a force of Corruptio. A test of morality or will.

Goosebumps ran up and down her limbs at the realization. For so long, Nyla had clung to myths and legends, to stories, for company or a sense of hope.

Were they all simply a child's wildest dreams? A false reality that gave hope to those who were otherwise empty?

She shuddered. Her mind clouded with renewed doubt as the sight of two stone figures stood guard before the first gated wall—the *closed* gate. Almost in unison, the trio stopped in their tracks. Out of the corner of her eye, Nyla could see that Xander had stiffened before letting go of a withheld breath. She turned to look at him. His eyes were no longer worried, but hardened with perseverance. She glanced at Shamira. The pumpkie's tail flicked as the cat regarded the gate with a slight tilt of her head. Nyla knew she was on edge by the constant twitch of her listening ears. But in the end, to her human ears at least, it was Xander who broke the quiet.

"Is this it?" He nodded toward the gate up ahead.

"Almost. There's an inner gate farther up, but yeah. Welcome to the abandoned Woodlane Manor of Hart," Nyla replied with an air of resignation.

"Then I guess we should be ready for anything. Shamira, you lead the way. I'll take up the rear." He paused and looked up at Nyla, already drawing an arrow from his quiver as if he expected to need it in the seconds that followed. "You ready, or—"

Nyla drew her knife.

Still using that old thing? Shamira brushed past Nyla. *Don't forget that you have magic at your disposal too. There's something here. I just don't know what. It's an old magic, but there's something hidden, like it's being masked or restricted or bound to something, like the manor itself. Be ready.*

"You need to teach me how to 'sense' things all the time like you do," Nyla huffed as she fell into line behind her. All the same, she heeded the pumpkie's warning and began to gather her magic, imagining the fine essence spooling around her fingers and down her arms.

The cat's laugh was gruff, still out of place in the afternoon's resounding silence.

Nyla's eyes darted from side to side. Each step they took was a surprise to her. Where was the attack? The danger? The trap?

Was Cedric only a figment of the Falls' visions, of a fever-induced hallucination that left a scar across her collarbone and shoulder?

Or was he waiting, biding his time?

Nyla fought off the shudder that threatened her guard. Her skin began to hum as every evil possibility lingered at the edges of her mind. She glanced down long enough to see the sparks of lilac-colored magic leap and crackle from the fingertips of her free hand. She took a slow breath and wrangled the magic inside her. She couldn't let her emotions get the better of her mind right now.

The gate before them opened with a *screech*. Torches on either side of the stone guards and gated archway came to life. Shamira tossed a look over her shoulder at Nyla. The pumpkie arched an eyebrow in question, much like a human would. Nyla supposed this was the ever-knowing cat's way of checking in with her and shook her head. Neither she nor Shamira had opened the gate. Nyla didn't know if that was a good sign…but it wasn't necessarily a bad one either, she supposed.

One after the other, they passed through the gate. Nyla held her breath as she crossed through. Nothing happened. Xander followed close behind her, and together they followed Shamira's lead.

The gates ground closed behind them with a thunderous *clang*. Frozen in her spot, Nyla stared at them. A dread of finality bore down on her spirits. Xander met her eyes with concern swimming in his own, his bow beginning to lower. Nyla nodded her head in a silent answer to his unasked question and moved on.

Flameless torches lit themselves as the trio worked their way up the path. They didn't illuminate the dim light of the waning sun so much as invite them farther down the path. Nyla eyed the torches suspiciously. Every nerve ending along her spine buzzed. Rather than keep her magic localized, she let it spread throughout her body and wrapped it tighter around herself like she would a blanket. At last, a minor comfort battled the grimness in Nyla's heart.

In the dancing light of the strange magic, Nyla stole a glance at the stone statues that stood guard on their blocks of granite on either side of the wide path. They were raverins. Each one stood on a clawed foot while the other talon held a wide, shallow bowl, which lit itself as the trio approached.

The second wall and guard gate were feet away now. Unlike the first gate, this one had scrolling detail set into the wrought iron. Once regal, the gothic elegance did nothing but grate on Nyla's persistence.

Just as the other gate had, the wrought-iron structure in front of them drifted open with a pitiful *creak*. Its *screech* filled the air and sent an eerie chill up and down Nyla's limbs. She gritted her teeth. The Woodlane Manor stood before them. The dirt path that led them through the last part of the Woods was taken over by a stunning driveway of colored pavers laid out like a mosaic.

Her eyes followed the obscured pattern she knew was best seen from the courtyard balcony up to the front steps of the Woodlane Manor. Ivy climbed the pillars of the entryway and covered one portion of the manor house. Windows were blocked by the thriving plant life. Magic leapt with eagerness in its sconces throughout the grounds until its excitement reached the manor. Then it too was graced with light.

The fountain in the center of the front courtyard sprang to life. Water flowed with a gentle trickle that would've soothed anyone's nerves. Nyla tossed a look over at Xander, who had come to walk beside her now. He had his bow at the ready. Still, nothing happened. Not even as Shamira neared the fountain and slunk past it with the precision of the predator she was.

Nothing appeared to lie in wait. All Nyla could see were hedges and once-prized garden paths leading around the back of the manor. Despite the ivy that claimed parts of the manor, it seemed as though the place wasn't as abandoned as it should've been.

They pressed forward. Tensions eased, even though acid rose in Nyla's throat as she climbed the stone steps with Xander by her side. He'd relaxed a little, but Nyla wondered just how on edge he really was. It couldn't have been more than she was.

Nyla gulped as they came to stand face to face with the carved oak doors. Both doors were adorned with an ornate brass knocker. The knockers, like the statues that lined the path, were modeled after raverins. One had its mouth open in a silent but fierce cry of attack with a ferocity she must've imagined in its tarnished eyes. A ring was clutched in one talon, while the other talon was poised to strike an unseen enemy. The other smirked. Victory gleamed in its eyes. A ring was clutched in both talons. Both knockers had their wings spread wide.

Nyla shot Xander a stiff smile. "I guess no one's actually home."

"Do we knock?" Xander glanced around.

I suppose we—what is it you humans do? 'Kick the door down?' Shamira shook her head. Her pointed teeth sparkled in the waning light.

"Or we could pick the lock." Xander slung off his bag and began to dig around inside it.

Nyla grasped one of the rings and knocked thrice on the door. The clang of metal against solid wood echoed in her ears like cannon blasts. The sense of finality Nyla had come to know all too well within the last day or so pounced.

The tall steeple doors swung open. Xander glanced up at them with his lips drawn in a tight line. He turned and gave Nyla a bitter look of disappointment.

"Oh sure, take all the fun out of breaking into an old, abandoned manor, why don't you!"

"Sorry." She peered inside.

Shamira hesitantly stepped across the threshold, stalking inside of the entrance hall, and drifted toward the right side of the foyer.

One. Two. Three steps. Nothing happened to her.

Xander brushed by Nyla with his bow and arrow once again raised. He instantly strode to the left. Nyla shoved aside the hesitation bubbling up inside her and crossed the threshold into the entrance hall like her companions had. The only thing that stopped her one hand from shaking was the white-knuckled grip she had on the hilt of her knife. If the buzz in her veins was any indication, there was most definitely magic sparking from the fingertips of her other hand again.

Nyla neared the stairs when two figures approached her out of the corners of her eyes. She whirled in the direction of the taller one. Relief flooded her when she met Xander's resilient eyes. Shamira came to stand beside them. They all looked up at the stained-glass window that graced the stairs' landing.

"Is that the window, from your astral projection thing?" Xander murmured.

"Yeah." Nyla regarded the staircase, uncertain of what to do now that they'd all survived walking through the front door.

"What now?" Xander asked.

Nyla turned his question over in her mind and glanced up at the window. "I don't know. I'm not dead, so that's a huge relief," she laughed bitterly. "I can't believe we actually came here. And for what?"

"The adventure of a lifetime?" Xander offered with a lopsided grin. Nyla laughed for real this time, the butterflies in her throat gone. "What do you want to do about dinner?"

"I'm not all that hungry, so maybe just a snack unless you and Shamira want a real meal. There's a proper kitchen down that way," she nodded her head toward the hallway on the right side of the foyer, "but I don't know..." In truth, Nyla realized she didn't know a lot of things, but the state of the kitchen was not one of her foremost concerns.

If you two wish to eat and rest a moment, I'll ensure the manor is secure, Shamira offered as Nyla had trailed off. *But other than old magic, I can sense nothing.* At this, the pumpkie's whiskers twitched in an obvious sign of annoyance, or tension, as Nyla had come to learn since meeting Shamira.

"Perfect. Nyla and I'll wrap our heads around what comes next over a bite to eat, which will really do *you* some good," he looked pointedly at Nyla and continued, "and we'll meet back in the kitchen?"

Perhaps. I may be a while, but I'll find you two once I've finished. Shamira began to pad away toward the other wing of the manor, the part that had always set Nyla's nerves on edge. Before she'd gone too far, Shamira turned back and met Nyla's eyes with a piercing gaze. *And then maybe you could tell me about that astral travel you spoke about before, with the window?*

Nyla nodded, her tongue too dry to answer. With things seemingly decided, the trio went their separate ways. Nyla led Xander toward the kitchen as Shamira stalked away in the opposite direction with intent purpose. All the while, Nyla's heartbeat quivered in her throat. There were so many things she wanted to discuss with Xander, but she didn't dare begin until they were in the sanctity of the kitchen.

"What do you think she's up to?" she asked quietly, taking in the space. Since her astral travel—if she were ever actually *here* in the literal sense—the kitchen had been cleaned spotless.

"I really don't know." Xander laid his bow and quiver down on the counter. He unclipped the fresh bag from his belt and started to prepare the last of his spoils. "It could be nothing, or it could be the game master setting their trap. Either way, food first until there's a problem."

Nyla rolled her eyes at that. At least with Xander around, she wouldn't go hungry. As he prepared the meat, with great flair and sweeping gestures, she lit the fire pit that was set deep into the counter like a burrow. The tips of the flames licked over the top of the square hole, and she found a grate that fit over it. With that set over the lip of the hole, Xander could set his pan down over it.

As they ate, Nyla and Xander discussed what they should do next. They were here, but now that they had made it, Nyla didn't know what to do other than show Xander around the manor so he wouldn't get lost. She was exhausted, in every sense of the word. Helping herself to another helping, she answered as many of Xander's numerous questions about the Woodlane Manor as she could. No, she didn't think it was actually haunted. Yes, she found it creepy now. Yes, there was a library.

"Xander," Nyla reached over and scooped a third helping of roots and the last of their meat onto her plate, "please."

Xander chuckled sheepishly. "Sorry."

"We have all day tomorrow and the next and the one after to find what answers the manor could offer me, if any, so can we just…call it a night?"

"Sounds like a plan to me." Xander tilted the pan toward himself and frowned.

It was Nyla's turn to look sheepish. She gently cleared her throat around the last forkful. "Sorry."

Xander only laughed and brought the empty pan to the sink basin Nyla had filled while he'd been cooking. "This just means you owe me a tour of the manor before we settle in for the night."

Nyla groaned. She supposed it was only fair. He hadn't spent *his* childhood here, after all. "As you wish."

24. WHAT LURKS IN THE SHADOWS

Urgency and panic shone in Astrid's lilac eyes. Her fingernails dug into the skin of Nyla's shoulders. Her voice was wild, desperate even. "You have to be careful! *She's here.* I know I told you to find me, but I was hoping it would be on the plane, not here, not now! Find the box and *leave!*"

Nyla's eyes popped open. Her heart pounded against her chest as her eyes swept over her surroundings. She licked her parted lips, only to find that her tongue was as dry as her throat was parched. She twisted herself around and took in her surroundings. Xander slept soundly off to her one side. His snores brought an odd mix of relief and comfort to Nyla's frayed nerves. Her chest rose and fell with her rapid heartbeat as Xander's constant snores helped quell the fear.

She glanced at her other side where Shamira had settled the night before. Instead, she found only empty space. Even though Xander had insisted before bed last night that none of them go off on their own, the pumpkie had done just that. Twice now. And Nyla was compelled to do the same.

Astrid had told her to find something—a box. While Nyla was certain that the woman was a manifestation of her dreams, she had to at least consider the possibility that there was *something* here to help her. There had to be, especially since they had come all this way.

With as much stealth as she could muster, Nyla slipped out of her sleeping bag and eased open the aged door. Her eyes went wide as the hinges made not a sound, not even a whimper of protest. Whatever, or whoever, had kept the manor in such a clean state had also seen to the doors, and Nyla wasn't sure if she should thank them or run from them.

Shrugging, Nyla maneuvered her way out of the library where they'd made camp for the night and toward the foyer. She paused at the base of the grand staircase and stared at the stained-glass window. Her face scrunched in a mixture of curiosity and eager apprehension.

The window was as it always was. The lilac floated in the center of the wide steeple glass pane, glowing in the early morning light. Old crests floated in the four corners of the window, though Nyla couldn't determine which noble house they belonged to, if they still survived. Nyla turned away from the breathtaking artwork. A bitter scowl darkened her face.

Somehow, lilacs followed her. She didn't know why or how the flower was connected to her, but they always seemed to pop up where her magic or Cedric were concerned. The image of the lilac from the drained field sprang up in her memory. Why would he leave it for her? It's not like they symbolized hatred or the desire to murder someone. In fact, it was quite the opposite. Lilacs were a symbol of first or old love. The people of Hart, and she supposed the Godberd Woods as a whole, had a tradition of laying them on funeral pyres. So it came to be that lilacs were a gesture of mourning and remembrance to Nyla.

Tears pricked her eyes. She blinked them away, but the memory that surfaced couldn't be held at bay so easily.

When Nyla had fled from her neighbor's home in the days that followed the deaths of her family, she'd picked a large bouquet of lilacs. Before she'd left Hart for good, or what she thought would be for good, Nyla had made one last stop where her home once stood. When she got there, the sight had all but broken her. Beside the rubble and ash from the fire, the neighbors had left a heaping pile of lilacs. She knew it was a custom in Hart, though she never expected anyone else to leave them for her family.

Nyla wiped at the wetness on her cheeks, her grief along with it, and let her feet carry her back the way she'd come. But instead of returning to the library as she'd absently intended, Nyla found herself pausing outside a different set of tall double doors. They opened as she stepped forward, just as the manor gates had last night. Nyla's breath caught in her throat.

All it had taken was one glance inside the room to turn her insides into a stormy sea. Her blood ran cold. Compelled by a trance that demanded she kept going, Nyla was dragged forward against her struggling will.

Nyla's legs gave out in the center of the room from the violent shakes that racked through her body. Her breath came in short, strained *hics* that fled just as quickly as they had come. The round room closed in around her. She fought the acid that rose in her throat. The burning didn't stop there. Sweat gathered along her brow. An earthquake rattled her bones.

Why had she come here? Of all the rooms she could've wandered into, it had to be this one, the ballroom.

Her tear-blind eyes closed against the beaming sunlight that streamed in through the towering windows.

Scattered moments flashed before her eyes. Cedric's smooth voice washed over her, and there was nothing Nyla could do to stop it. Every fiber of her being fixated on that one specific instance when the moonlight had glinted off of his dagger.

Nyla could feel the rapid beat of her pulse in her chest. Her stomach collapsed as if she had just been hit in the gut with magic. The resounding *thud* and *rattle* of the crystal chandelier echoed in her head as her memory slammed her into the wall like Cedric's magic had. Heat spread from her collarbone as if blood pooled there, below the surface of her scarred skin, waiting to spill over. Nyla's face twisted with a flash of agony.

A tiny voice in her head tried to tell her that she was safe, but all she could hear was Cedric coolly telling her: *It's a little personal with you...with Astrid.* His scarlet eyes flashed with the tempered flame of bitterness.

The disjointed scenes flooded Nyla all at once. Those scarlet eyes mocked her, filled her vision until that was all she could see, all she believed existed. That gaze consumed her until it suffocated her. Nyla struggled and fought, could feel the hum of something violent and restless in her stomach. She wasn't certain whether or not it was sickness or the heat of astral projection or the power that fueled her magic all those days ago when she faced Cedric, but it gave her something other than red eyes to focus on.

They were the last thing Nyla saw behind her closed eyes, the burning heat in his eyes when he'd said Astrid's name.

Her eyes popped open. Nyla gasped for air. She shouldn't be here. She should've heeded Xander's insistence that they stick together. It was too late now.

It was all real: the fight, the astral travel, her magic, the faded bruises on her back, the *danger*.

Cedric.

Nyla forced air into her lungs and fought to regain her bearings. The room stood still. Nyla looked around.

Plaster and glass littered the floor. Pillars were cracked. Blood, *her blood*, speckled the tile floor. Her hand found its way to her collarbone. Even though the cut had long since sealed itself, a jolt of pain sliced through her skin at the touch. The pain seared down her arm into the tips of her fingers.

She closed her eyes and tilted her head toward the rippled ceiling. Her hand dropped to her lap, and Nyla forced herself to breathe evenly again. With one final glance at the fractured pillars and splintered walls,

Nyla stood. The room was once again filled with bright morning light. She turned, more than ready to leave.

A shadow lingered in the doorway. It bobbed in the air, waiting. The hair on the back of her neck prickled. Every muscle in her body tensed. The ice crept back into her veins. Nyla didn't think her heart could take another shock or punch of panic.

The darkened figure disappeared down the hall. Nyla darted after it. She was barely able to keep it in sight as it turned corners and dashed up the main staircase. She lost the shadow by the time she got to the landing. Thrown off balance by her short stop, Nyla jolted forward before her body caught itself. She stood on the landing, her chest heaving as her head whipped back and forth between the two wings of the staircase in the hopes of catching a glimpse of the shadow. The sunlight that streamed in through the lilac window gave her a golden crown as she stood there, panting. Her head snapped toward the set of stairs on her right. The tail of the shadow caught her eye, and off she went again.

Nyla barely made it up the stairs in time to see the edge of the shadow round the corner into a side passage meant for servants, one Nyla had been down many times before during brighter days. Through each twist and turn of the maze of passages, both known and unexplored, Nyla followed the shadow until she found herself barreling out into the library's balcony. Lost among the stack of books and unable to catch sight of the shadow, Nyla flung herself around a corner, slamming into something like a ton of bricks.

Strong arms wrapped around her. A groan left Nyla's lips. A solid *thump* echoed between the bookcases like thunder. Her wrists stung as she pushed herself up and snapped her head up with a wild look down the aisle. Shelves of books, and a grimacing Xander, were the only things to be found. Not an anthropomorphic shadow in sight.

"Good morning to you, too," Xander grumbled groggily.

Nyla glanced down at him with wide eyes. A gasp escaped her lips, finally registering that she'd run into him and knocked them both down in her hunt for the ghostly silhouette.

"Sorry! I just…there was this…and I…"

Scrambling to her feet, Nyla helped Xander to his. Heat crept along her cheeks. She took a few steps back.

What happened? Shamira burst up the winding staircase from the library's ground floor, her tail fluffed out and ears pointed.

Xander rubbed his elbow. "*Someone* decided to go off on their own and knocked down a barely awake bystander."

Nyla shrank away at the pointed look he shot her. "I thought I saw something, and I ran after it, and then, well, you can guess what happened next." Nyla turned fiery eyes on Shamira. "Besides, I wasn't the *only* one who went off on their own. Where were you off to, Shamira?"

I was hunting, if you must know. She grinned, her pointed teeth stained red. Nyla's stomach churned at the sight.

Both companions turned their eyes on her. The weight of both their gazes bore down on Nyla.

She opened her mouth to say something but immediately clamped her lips shut. The din of dishes clinking against each other floated up from below. Silently, Shamira strode to the loft's railing with Xander on her heels and Nyla reluctantly following after them to peer down over the library. Shamira growled low in her throat. Instinctually, Nyla gathered her magic, something she was certain Shamira was likely doing too.

Below them, an older woman with not quite silver, but also not quite white, hair carried a tray of dishes and petite foods toward a coffee table in the center of the main seating area. The porcelain teapot and three-legged cups rattled with each step the humming woman took.

"Oh!" She gasped, glancing up at them. "I didn't realize the three of you would be awake! I hope I didn't wake you."

Nyla's heart beat between her ears. It was a steady *thumpity thump*, a stark contrast to the adrenaline that barreled through her veins. The woman ambled forward a few steps, never quite leaving their line of sight as she stared up at them expectantly. Shamira growled openly, pouncing forward. It was like she dared the woman to approach them. All Nyla could do was stare curiously.

"I'm sorry. I don't mean to scare any of you. I just thought you'd all be hungry after such a long journey." The woman's voice was sweet and gentle, even if it was brittle and crackled with age.

Nyla shared a look with Xander. How could this woman know they'd had a long journey? Xander furrowed his brows and addressed the woman.

"Who are you?" Xander asked.

The woman smiled softly like a grandmother would. "I am Dinora, keeper of the Woodlane Manor. Now, I'm sure you have a lot of questions, but for now, why don't you settle in and eat a little something, and then we'll chat."

Dinora's eyes twinkled as she glanced pointedly at the tray. Nyla swallowed. The food *did* look delicious, and she *was* hungry. But accepting food from a stranger in a strange manor was far from the best decision any of them could make. She'd rather starve until they found something else.

"Well, if you need anything else, just help yourselves. I'll be around to check on you later." Without another word, Dinora disappeared into thin air with a *pop*.

Nyla blinked. The hairs on the back of her neck stood on edge with the static that filled the room. "Where…"

She's still here, in the manor. I can't pinpoint where exactly *she is, though.* Shamira stalked down the stairs and headed straight for the tray of dainty breakfast things. She sniffed them cautiously. *It might just be residual magic from Dinora's presence and disappearance, but there's traces of it on the tray.*

Numbly, Nyla followed Xander down the winding staircase as he let out a string of curses under his breath. She wished she could do the same, but she knew it wouldn't help anything. Instead, Nyla wondered if it was better to leave the manor before or after breakfast or if it was worth poking around first.

"Great, just great. So not only do we have no idea how this place is connected to your magic, but now we have a demon cat and a grandmotherly old lady who may or may not be trying to kill us too! That's it: from now on, you're not going anywhere alone." Xander balled his fist and ground his teeth.

"*Excuse you?*" Nyla glowered. "That is so not fair! What about you, huh? You're just as defenseless as I am against her, maybe even more so because *I* at least have magic!" Her blood boiled. She wanted nothing more than to turn around and leave.

Xander whirled on her, his eyes flaring like his bristled temper. Nyla crossed her arms and waited. Her bare foot tapped against the soft carpet in expectation.

"Fine! Then neither of us are going anywhere alone until we figure out who's trying to kill us and who isn't." He softened, his eyebrows unknitting themselves. "At least then we'll be safe."

And what about me? Am I not a concern of yours? Shamira snarled.

"Like you'd actually listen to me anyway," he spat, whirling on the cat. "I don't know what your goal is, and you can gift us as much meat as you can catch, but that still won't change the fact that you're hiding something." Xander wound up like a top again, and Nyla watched helplessly as the two became locked in a furious battle of glares. Shamira's fur bristled, and she bared her teeth. She slunk low to the ground, and Nyla was certain that the two would come to blows if she didn't do something.

"All right, that's enough!" Her voice pierced through the library. She flinched at the volume of it. Much more softly, Nyla continued on. "Xander, you and I'll stick together and watch each other's backs. Now obviously we can't be together *all* the time, but close to it." She fixed him with a look that made him wither, and Shamira snickered.

Nyla's eyes flicked to the pumpkie. "Now, Shamira, you're more than welcome to join us and stick with us or come and go as you please, but first, you have some explaining to do, starting with why you're the only pumpkie sent to look for me and why none of you have come for me sooner."

The cat glanced away when Nyla fixed her with the same expectant glare and bowed her head in shame. *I apologize, Xander. I only want to protect the kingdom and try to do my best by Nyla.*

"Well, then, at least we can agree on that. I accept your apology," Xander relented. "And I...I'm sorry for being untrusting of you."

A silent agreement passed between the two of them, their gazes murky. Nyla didn't quite understand it, but if it stopped them from skirting around each other and taking jabs at each other, then so be it, she supposed.

Your mistrust wasn't unwarranted, Shamira admitted. *I have kept things from the both of you, out of shame, out of...uncertainty.* Shamira's gaze flicked between them. The tip of her tail bobbed slowly.

"And the whole truth is?" Nyla prompted, sinking into an armchair by the coffee table.

The Elders didn't send me. No one sent me, except myself. But you have to understand—after the war, my species was decimated. Only a small number of us survived, and we went into hiding. While we continued to watch over Tenebris as we have always done, we grew our numbers and vowed to never interfere with human affairs again, even if the balance of magic and the universe would be gravely affected because of those affairs.

For a long time, we didn't need to. Things were quiet. Other wars were fought, sure, but none of them were exactly consequential. *But then, about two decades ago, things started to change.* She paused, gathering her thoughts.

Xander shifted on his feet. Nyla stared wide-eyed at Shamira, her mind reeling. How did this all fit together? How could she *possibly* be involved in any of this? She slipped farther into her chair, crestfallen.

Shamira continued stiffly, *I have been attempting to contact the Elders. It took a few tries as I…I left the colony without their consent or blessing. There was something, a feeling if you will, that pulled me to you, Nyla.*

We knew that the leader of the Corvids was imprisoned, though our exact records were destroyed in the Dark Fire, and not even the Elders are old enough to remember the war anymore. What records did survive mention that the Royal Mage willed her magic to another in her bloodline. The spell she used was complex, and as the centuries passed, we deemed her magic lost forever and, with it, the threat that the Corvids would rise again. But then, something akin to the Corvid leader's essence resurfaced a few years ago.

For generations now, we have lived in an ignorantly blissful solitude, watching over Tenebris from afar. When I sensed that magic, and recognized it for what it was, and then I sensed yours, I knew our greatest fears were on the horizon.

Tenebris hangs in the balance, especially with the land being pillaged of its magic once more. I tried to warn the Elders, but they were hesitant to believe me. So, I left because I knew I had to find you.

A stark silence overcame the three of them. Xander finally sat across from Nyla, scrubbing his face with his hands as if to wipe away the speechlessness Shamira had left them with. The pumpkie's downcast eyes were dark with a storm of worry and shame. Emptiness consumed Nyla. Her brain couldn't wrap around what Shamira had said, and while she could feel a million questions bubbling to the surface of her mind, words were a distant memory.

"You're telling me that a Royal Mage, who I may know as Astrid, left her magic to someone, *to me*, like someone would leave a family heirloom to another after their passing?" Nyla found herself asking eventually.

Yes.

"This is crazy! This is all one giant mistake. There's no way. I'm just… Shamira, you have to be wrong. No way would Astrid's magic gravitate toward me! I'm too young for this!" Nyla burst to her feet and began to pace the length of the room, having walked around her armchair to do so. Her hands shook. "And a war?" Nyla threw her hands up. *Nyla, I—*

"No, give her a moment to process all this her way." Xander swatted his hand in Shamira's direction as if he could stop her words in midair like flies.

Nyla's mind was jumbled and not so much a linear stream of coherent thought but rather a heap of words and sensations. Adrenaline coursed through her veins until it was an itch she couldn't scratch. The energy pulsed and flitted through her body, but couldn't find any escape. Nyla was trapped by her own crippling hysteria.

She could accept her magic and all of the other crazy things that had happened to her since the fire, but war?

If Nyla could be certain of one thing, it was that no one decent wanted to declare war.

"Why, though? Why would Astrid's magic manifest in Nyla?"

Nyla stopped short at Xander's question and turned wide eyes on Shamira.

I don't know.

"Why not tell us any of this sooner?"

She didn't particularly care about that, but was glad Xander asked anyway. If she had known any of this, Nyla was certain she would've never come here in the first place. As her mind raced to wrap around everything she'd learned over the last several weeks or so, her thoughts came to a grinding halt. Chills ran down her spine. Her body stopped in the dead center of the room. She turned to them with terror in her eyes. "What about Dinora?"

"What about her?"

"You said that the Corvids' leader was imprisoned, right?" She pointed at Shamira, who simply nodded with narrowed eyes. "What if that 'prison' is here, and Dinora's actually their leader? I had a dream last night about Astrid, and she told me to leave, that 'she' was here."

Both of Nyla's companions gawked at her. A stiff, uncomfortable silence darkened the room. Lightning shocked Nyla's core. "Shamira, you sense things, so what can you sense about her?"

The pumpkie straightened at her question and considered it. She closed her eyes, a blank expression on her face. *There's too much clouding her own essence for me to see anything distinguishable. I have to trace it to the source.*

Xander scrunched his nose. "The source?"

The source of the signature. It's here somewhere. Shamira turned her head away. Her ears twitched, and the air filled with static. A low grumble disturbed the quiet that had befallen them. Shamira's eyes cracked open like little slits. *I'm terribly sorry if getting to the bottom of this has interrupted your plans for breakfast.*

Xander shifted and scratched the back of his neck. "Not at all. The blame lies fully on Dinora for that. Continue."

"No, your stomach's right." Nyla shook her head. "We need to eat and make a plan. There's a greenhouse outside of the kitchen that I'm hoping is in good shape, so let's get changed and figure out our next move."

"What about your dream?" Xander moved toward his bag and gathered some clothes into his arms.

"She wanted me to find something, but for all we know, it doesn't even exist. I think the best thing to do is leave." Nyla glanced at him, apology and regret written plainly on her screwed-up face.

Perhaps I should find the source first. Maybe that would give us a better idea of what we're doing next? Shamira offered. Her tail curled and uncurled at a pace that Nyla had come to learn meant that her patience was wearing thin.

"Maybe. Let's eat first. Nyla, I'll meet you in the kitchen." Xander grabbed his bow and quiver of arrows, a bundle of clothes already tucked under one arm. He yanked the door open and stopped. "Shamira, whatever you're about to do, be careful."

The pumpkie blinked at the sincerity of his concern, but nodded at him in assurance anyway. Nyla watched with a lump in her throat as Xander closed the door behind him. She could faintly hear his footsteps padding along the hallway toward the kitchen. The air was still around her. Forcing herself into action, Nyla hurried to change her clothes, not wanting Xander to wait alone for too long.

It'll be all right, Nyla. Astrid's magic wouldn't have chosen you if you didn't already have some magic of your own. Magic can't bloom in people, or anything really, where it doesn't already exist.

"Why are you telling me this now?" Nyla pulled her shirt down over her head and turned to study the pumpkie.

Because you need to hear it. If Astrid is the Royal Mage and the Corvids are rising again and this all comes back to the Corvid Uprising, then you need to know that not only are you worthy of Astrid's magic, but that you are *strong.*

Nyla finished lacing her boots up and straightened. "You're putting a lot of faith in someone you barely know."

So are you. Shamira turned. The door to the library eased open at the behest of Shamira's sage-colored magic.

Nyla followed in the cat's wake as Shamira led the way to the kitchen. Thunder rumbled in the distance. A shadow fell over Nyla as the storm brewing outside echoed in her gut.

It seemed as though the three of them wouldn't be able to leave today after all.

***

Shamira was grateful for the hush that blanketed them as she led Nyla down to meet the boy in the kitchen. It gave her time to gather her thoughts.

The jumble of magic trails or essences was a puzzle to her. How could one place have such an enormous amount of energy, all of which seemingly intertwined? And so old? She brushed the inquiries aside, her sole focus on reading the energies around them. It was the same as everywhere else in the manor.

No matter what room she had walked through or stood in, the energy was always the same. At first glance, it was oppressive and overwhelming, all tangled and tied together like the knots on an abandoned noose.

Under that puzzling surface was another layer, a barrier of old magic. It must've been nearly invincible for it to have survived this long. Perhaps Nyla was right to believe that Dinora wasn't who she said she was.

Then there was the darkness, twisted and gnarled. Some might mistake it for good if they saw its brilliance, but Shamira could taste it. It was sour like spoiled fruit. Outwardly appealing in certain lights, but rotten all the same.

It was this strange combination of energy that furrowed Shamira's brows. When she'd spoken to the Elders about it this morning, they weren't able to offer much guidance on the matter. The only thing they seemed capable of was to offer their word that they would consult the clan's archive and Seer. Maybe he'd be able to shed some light on the issue and bring some clarity to the whole of Nyla's situation.

Rain began to tap against the windows of the drafty manor. Fluffy storm clouds blocked the bright sunlight. Fierce wind bent tree branches to its will as it gained strength. Shamira couldn't help but wonder if this storm was a sign of what was to come or if it was just an average end-of-*Belsuun* storm.

Nyla walked ahead of her. A nervous hum radiated off of the girl in waves. Shamira wasn't sure if it was possible to help her, but it seemed to her as though Nyla was always in some state of distress.

As they passed a set of double doors, Shamira paused. There was an abundance of signatures inside, but they were fresh. Her eyes flicked to where Nyla had stopped a few paces away.

"It's the ballroom." Shamira waited for her to say something more, but Nyla continued on their trek to the kitchen.

With a final glance at the ballroom doors, she followed after Nyla. The girl knocked on a closed door and hesitated half a second, worried and confused. She shoved the kitchen door open and started with a frayed sigh.

"Guess we're no—Xander?"

Shamira bounded into the empty kitchen after a frantic Nyla. The girl completed a single twirl in the center of the room before her wild lilac eyes landed on her. "Can you find him?"

The words had barely left Nyla's lips before Shamira was off again, hackles raised. Nyla followed after, wholly accepting the fact that there wasn't any time for her to explain. Through some kind of narrow storage hall, they raced toward the ballroom.

The pair burst through a panel in the wall with a clamor of heavy footfalls. Shamira slowed. Her green eyes settled on Xander, who stood in the center of the room. *And what do you think you're doing?*

Xander flinched and whirled around, his bow raised. Once he realized it was only them, his eyes locked on Nyla. He instantly gravitated toward her until he stood in front of her. Shamira watched with a mixture of curiosity and irritation.

He said he'd wait for Nyla in the kitchen. Her annoyance faded when the overwhelming mixture of fear and grief hit her.

"You didn't tell me it was this bad." His voice was soft, barely above a whisper.

"I'm fine, promise. The room makes it look worse than it was." Nyla tried to brush him off and steer them back toward the kitchen.

Shamira took in the rubble that littered the floor. From glass to chunks of scattered stone to the faint speckles of blood. Her eyes flicked to Nyla's collarbone and shoulder. She nodded toward Nyla's arm. *That happened here?*

The girl glanced down at the scar and nodded slowly. "Yeah."

"Did you even check for broken bones? For—"

Who was here with you? Both humans turned to look at her.

"It was just me. But then, he showed up and attacked me. The red-eyed—would you stop that! I'm fine!" Nyla swatted Xander's prodding hands away with a huff.

"Oh, I'm sorry. My *deepest apologies* for trying to make sure you didn't break anything in a *magical battle* with an *evil murderer* that left this much damage to a room with *stone pillars* and lots of sconces and glass and apparently left you with bruises you never *actually* mentioned before we set off on a long trek to a place where said murderer could've been waiting. I truly beg your pardon, your majesty." Xander continued to examine Nyla even as she kept brushing him off with a glare.

What's his name?

Nyla swallowed thickly and brushed Xander off one final time. "Cedric."

I have a hunch, but I want to be certain before I send you both into a frenzy. I'll meet you later. Shamira turned, her tail sweeping high through the air.

Confusion floated through the air, radiating off of the two humans as she left them behind. She knew that they had turned to look at each other. They did that a lot. She'd come to realize that they were checking with each other, a silent communication that held no real significant meaning outside of the two of them.

She brushed the distraction away. Shamira wove her way through the manor in search of a stronger connection to the traces she sensed all around her. The energy was similar to the second trace in the ball-room, but different than the underlying essence that lurked in the Woodlane Manor's shadow. Shamira latched on to that essence and began to search from room to room for any trace of its source.

Each new room was well-kept whether it was a study or a servant's quarters. It was odd how Dinora, if she was truly imprisoned here, had maintained the upkeep of the manor. Like everything else about the Woodlane Manor, Shamira recognized Dinora as another piece of the puzzle. Perhaps she was a separate puzzle all together in a series of tangled plots.

Rain pounded on the roof. Shamira found her way into the manor's attic. Relics of a rich past collected dust and grime, forgotten in heaps of dishevelment. She stalked through the remnants of times gone by. The trail she followed grew stronger with each step. Shamira's fur bristled the closer she got to the source. But what was it?

The hulking furniture surrounded her. Old portraits were distorted by their improper storage or torn in their travel. She traveled up and down the rows of things until she was certain that the items stored in the attic were laid out like a maze. This was all just another obstacle to keep prying eyes away from the source.

Thunder rattled the abandoned china. Her ears swiveled in the direction that the twinkling dishes sang from. With a shake of her head, Shamira began to walk along the wall of the attic. It was strange that while the room was nearly as long as the manor, it wasn't anywhere near the same width. She pawed at the wall, her nose twitching. Why would someone build such a stately home with insufficient storage space? It didn't make sense, especially given that the roofline allowed for a space twice the size across of what was built.

A faint purple aura seeped through the corner of the wall. It ebbed and flowed like the lights in the night sky above Hart. Shamira stared at it with narrowed eyes.

Passion and grief, love and hatred, agony and sacrifice. All of this and more rolled off the fading magical residue.

At last! Something vaguely akin to the source!

Shamira growled. Frustration sank in her heart. She needed to find a way into that room. With a resigned sigh, Shamira stood on her hind legs and placed her front paws on the wall. She closed her eyes and let the tension fall from her body. Her breathing slowed to a rate not unlike sleep. The beating of her heart calmed until everything around her melted away.

Freedom wrapped its wings around her, and Shamira left her corporeal body behind. A sage astral cord connected Shamira to her physical body, but it was lost among the lines of the astral plane. There must have been hundreds of them, if not thousands. They were all connected in a way, but Shamira needed to narrow down her field of search because she couldn't possibly follow every strand of this spider's web.

No, she needed to focus her energy on the source, the one that was right on the other side of the wall.

Shamira floated over to the lilac essence seeping through the wall and allowed herself to pass through into the other room. It was difficult to penetrate the wards that hid the room from intruders, but they ultimately let Shamira through.

Shelves and bookcases were lined with scrolls or random pieces of parchment, books, and potion bottles. Crystals and other magical aids were scattered throughout the cluttered room. Shamira glanced over these objects, her gaze instantly drawn to the looking glass across the room. Like a bolt of lightning, she made her way to hover before the grimy pane of glass.

It was hazy and clouded over. Years of neglect had drained any magic it once had, but the presence of it was still there. While the magic was unable to be harnessed, Shamira had no use for it outside of tracing the line back to the origin of the magic that plagued the manor now.

After a quick inspection of the glass, Shamira's eyes fluttered shut. The clouds parted as the glass came to life. Beams of sage danced and twirled on the surface of the smooth pane. Shamira focused her efforts on deciphering the looking glass's history.

Looking glasses, as her clan's Seer had once explained to her, not only allowed the viewer to see out into the world, but they were also a primary source, a witness to events in the owner's life. A magical archive that was virtually all-seeing.

The downfall of a looking glass, though, was that it had no magic of its own. It relied solely on the magic its owner imbued it with. Once that magic wore off, it was as useless as a mirror. No longer able to see or archive, unless someone was willing to tangle with the original owner's lingering energy.

Shamira peered through the thick layer of grime as the image of her own sage magic misted the glass before it cleared. Before her lay the astral plane of the manor, as it was captured by the looking glass. She assumed that the glass showed her what the manor's plane was like at the time when the web of magical essences began.

The looking glass might not have been *the* source, but it was as close as Shamira could get. Someone had once worked in this room and wove such a tangle of magic that it survived to this day. *They* were the source of the manor's tangled energies.

Her ears swiveled and stood on alert as the squeak of a door opening in a room somewhere below broke through her concentration. Shamira gritted her teeth.

One more second, she pleaded mainly to herself, but also to Moerae, the pumpkies' goddess of Fate and Time. With that silent plea, Shamira plunged head first into the image presented by the looking glass. Her astral body sprinted across the pulsating crimson and lilac lines. They crisscrossed and wove together in a jumble of magical strings. Other colors were mixed in with them, but the web was predominantly comprised of these two magics and, presumably, the same two magic users.

Shamira sniffed, her heart sinking. Nyla's face, paled by fear and aged by grief, flashed before her mind's eye. It was as she feared. The energies that were bound to the manor, that were familiar to Shamira in a way she couldn't explain, were almost a genetic match to Nyla's signature and the red-eyed man's energy, the ones from the ballroom.

She raced along the intricate web without a sound, following the cardinal line of magic, the one that she guessed had started it all. It was lilac, like Nyla's essence, which in a way was a relief.

A meek voice spoke from the shadows of Shamira's consciousness: what if Nyla's ancestor was the Corvids' leader and not Dinora? What if they were looking about it all wrong?

Shamira shook those fears off. All of her efforts were focused on getting to the end of this line. She assumed that the other lines linked various other magical items or key locations and memories from the looking glass's owner, but she didn't have the time to trace every line.

Not now at least.

The sick pulsating of the lines blurred her vision, but Shamira pressed on. There was no way she could lose sight of the cardinal strand. She was so close to answers, and she couldn't fail.

Her surroundings grew brighter the closer to the center of the web she got. The cardinal line stretched before her. At this rate, the lilac trail seemed endless. Hope was beginning to leave Shamira, her eyes desperate to see the fruit of her labor.

Light flashed up ahead. The cardinal line fed into a brilliant sphere of lilac which several other lines extended from. Shamira came to an abrupt halt.

This was it.

The absolute center of the tangled energies that clouded the Woodlane Manor.

She took one step forward. Her front paw stopped midair. Shamira's lean body froze with hesitation. The looking glass had given her a way to see the truth.

What if it wasn't as Shamira had hoped?

She swallowed. As it was, Shamira faced the prospect of banishment for disobeying the Elders. But this could prove that she was right, about everything. Or it could prove quite the opposite.

Shamira gingerly touched her paw to the ball of magic. It flashed again, but the blinding light only lasted a fraction of a second. She was plunged into the sort of night that was like spilled ink, a thick, engulfing darkness. Before her stood an arched door. It swung open with a *creak* as she approached. Slowly, Shamira crossed its threshold.

"Go on then. Kill me."

Shamira's surroundings rippled until the picture cleared.

A woman with striking silver hair stood in the manor's courtyard with her arms stretched out to either side, waiting expectantly for the man across from her to do something.

She was challenging the man that stood opposite her, Shamira realized.

Shamira walked toward him as she observed the scene before her. As she neared, she saw his scarlet eyes. Curiously, they were obscured by tears even as he clenched his jaw.

"Why didn't you leave with the others?"

"And miss the opportunity to say hello? Now that's just rude." The woman glared against the setting sun and dropped her arms. *"Although I suppose it's much crueler to betray someone who loved you. It's cruel to use them and deceive them and use what they've taught you to hurt innocent people!"*

She slung a fierce bolt of lilac magic at the red-eyed man. He threw his hands up. A translucent shield of scarlet magic blocked the woman's assault.

"You want to talk about betrayal and innocent people? Fine, let's talk about it then! What about Corvus? What about us?"

"And waging this war is supposed to fix that?" The woman whipped attack after attack at the man opposite her.

Shamira figured the woman was the looking glass's owner and Nyla's ancestor, Astrid, based on the fact that her magic looked so much like Nyla's. She had little to go on, but she had hope. That's about all Shamira could hold onto as she continued to gather information. She only prayed the memory gave her something more concrete than her own speculations.

The man sent his own attack at Astrid, though the magic wasn't nearly as strong.

Shamira circled him. Why provoke someone leagues stronger than yourself?

That wasn't the matter at hand, though, Shamira reminded herself. She needed to figure out who he was, how he fit into all of this, and in the end, she assumed the man must be related to Cedric based solely on the description Nyla had started to give her in the ballroom. Shamira snarled.

The air crackled, and another woman appeared beside the red-eyed man. She looked between the two and rolled her eyes. Astrid's chest heaved. Everything stilled.

"What have you done?" Astrid seethed. Her hands balled into fists. "Do you have any idea what fury you've unleashed upon the land?"

"Oh, how cute. You think I care. Did Tenebris care what they unleashed upon the Corvids?" the woman shot back.

Shamira studied her with narrowed eyes. There was something off about the woman, something she didn't need to sense to know. It was like her body could barely contain the energy within it, like a lively hornet's nest. Magic sizzled in the air around her. This woman had somehow amassed more magic than she could possibly handle.

"And stealing the land's magic, killing innocent people, going against Corvid law, you can justify that? Convince yourselves you're not doing exactly the same things, worse things, than what happened during the Ten Years' War?" Astrid argued.

"As lovely as this has been, Astrid, dear, Cedric and I have places to be." The woman tossed her hair over her shoulder and made to turn around.

Shamira stared at the man with wide eyes. If this man was Cedric, and Nyla's red-eyed man was also Cedric...could they be the same person? She desperately wished she could read the energies of the people in this memory, but knew it was impossible without tangling with the trace residue of the looking glass's owner.

Astrid's nostrils flared. With one deep breath, she blasted her opponents. She centered her magic in her core, like a singer would bolster their voice with their diaphragm.

Bright lilac magic flashed across the earth, met by a flash of crimson magic that was all too powerful for it to have come from one person.

Impressed that a human could draw so much power without burning themselves out, Shamira was all but blinded by awe and the sheer amount of magic involved in Astrid's attack. The two magics clashed. All the colors of the rainbow filled the air, a sign that magic was released in abundance.

Shamira knew that the worst was yet to be unveiled.

When the air cleared of dust and magic, the other woman was barely conscious. Blood stained Astrid's lips.

The far reaches of the memory-scape began to fade and cloud over.

Astrid struggled with one last breath.

Shamira was plunged into that same dark night as before. The arched door closed with a groan behind her. The *thud* was that of eternity, like the final, mournful note of a bagpipe. Shamira's heart still beat between her ears, a steady beat that couldn't bear to move on, even as desperation wove a path to her core. With one last glance at the arched doorway, and a reflection on the things the looking glass had shown her, Shamira darted off back the way she had come through the astral plane.

Shamira's fur rippled as she let go of the magic coursing through her veins and let her astral body rejoin her corporeal form. Adrenaline sped through her like lightning.

Nyla! Xander! She telepathically screamed their names as loud as she dared to without jarring their minds. The attic passed by her in a blur. Her paws pounded against the carpeted floors like the thunder that rumbled in the sky outside. She needed to find them. Quickly.

Through darkened hallways, Shamira sprinted until even her own heartbeat was lost to her ears. Her lungs burned.

When she passed an ajar window, she didn't stop, even as the faint scent of fresh rain and crisp wind tickled her nose.

A raverin's scent.

Shamira tucked that information away because as of the present moment, her only concern was to find the boy and the girl.

The closer she drew to the main staircase, the stronger the pull on her senses from Nyla's energy became. With relief and hope, Shamira surged forward, even as that strange, tangled signature closed in around her.

25. TIME LAPSE

"Should we be concerned?" Nyla stared in the direction Shamira had gone, even though the cat was probably long gone in the seconds that had passed since her departure.

"Definitely." Xander resumed his study of Nyla, all too stunned that she was physically fine, despite the room's destruction.

He couldn't believe that she hadn't come out of that fight against Cedric without any broken bones. It seemed impossible. None of it made any sense to him. How had Nyla remained marginally unscathed when the room around them bore the scars of a horrific battle?

His stomach twisted as the night of the ogre attack replayed before his mind's eye. Nyla had unknowingly obliterated that beast. She'd almost, albeit accidentally, shot him at Fortune Falls. She was powerful—and terrifying. Or at least she *would be*, if she were that sort of person, like Cedric. But Nyla wasn't like that.

The epiphany solidified the feeling that Xander had had since he met her: Nyla was going to be the death of him.

One way or another, he was certain of it.

Nyla's eyes flicked up to meet his. "You're still staring."

"Sorry," Xander said with the flash of a smile. He shook his head and with it the line of questions he'd wanted to ask. The ogre. Fortune Falls. This ballroom.

Nyla turned away, her face unreadable, and began to move toward the open panel in the wall that led back to the kitchen. He reached out and touched her shoulder softly.

"You *are* okay, right?"

She turned to look over her shoulder at him. A shadow fell across her face. "I'm all right, really. I just don't want to be in here is all, so let's go."

Xander nodded and followed her back to the kitchen, but not before he had taken one last, long glance around the ballroom. Whatever he thought he had heard or seen was gone. Rationally, Xander tried to argue that his mind was playing tricks on him. He was only unsettled by Dinora's appearance and being in an old, abandoned manor. Somewhere deep down, a self-conscious voice wondered if the manor itself was playing tricks on him and using his worst nightmares against him to do so.

Either way, the thing, the girl, the *sister* Xander swore he'd heard, and had led him into the ballroom, was gone. Now, he let Nyla lead the way through an arched doorway at the end of the kitchen. The opened door revealed a lush—and wet—pathway through the manor's gardens to its greenhouse.

The rain pounded against the path's stepping stones in a deluge of rapid *pitter-patters*. Its assault was backed by the force of the howling wind that came in frequent, short gusts. Lightning flashed in the distance. Thunder rumbled lowly. Nyla hadn't even hesitated before she stepped out into the downpour, and Xander had no choice but to follow her.

Xander couldn't help but think maybe the manor *was* haunted, in a sense, and it used visions of its visitors' past to haunt them. Like Issie.

Thwack! He swatted a stray twig out of his way. The leaves snapped like a whip against the air. Droplets of water splattered his already rain-drenched shirt.

Nyla glanced over her shoulder at him, and he smiled sheepishly.

"It had it coming, I swear!" A laugh bubbled up from his chest, and Nyla rolled her eyes.

"Oh, I'm sure it did." She approached the double doors to the domed greenhouse and reached for the handle. Xander walked up behind her and waited as she stood there and jiggled the handle again. "Dammit!"

"I know! Why don't you use the creepy raverin knockers and knock on the door?" Xander suggested sarcastically and pulled his lockpicking kit from his back pocket. "Or you could let me have my moment and pick the lock."

He moved to crouch eye level with the lock. Nyla shifted beside him. Her nervous energy rolled off of her in waves, to the point where Xander almost believed that *he* himself was anxious.

"I'm not sure how I feel about the fact that you know how to pick locks. Like, why or where did you learn to?"

Xander glanced over his shoulder at her and grinned mischievously. "Why not?"

"Please, Xander, why?" Nyla's curious gaze burned the back of his neck as he worked. He looked at her once the lock clicked open and opened the door for her.

"After you." Xander bowed and motioned with his hand for her to enter.

She strolled through the door. "You didn't answer the question."

Xander made the mistake of inhaling too deeply as he crossed the threshold into the greenhouse. His nose scrunched at the floral and herbaceous scent that wafted through the enormous, though crowded, building. He swept his damp hair from his face and huffed. Nyla fixed him with a piercing gaze, and he knew then that she wouldn't let this go.

"All right, all right. I'll tell you over breakfast." Xander clapped his hands and rubbed them together eagerly. "Now, what's good here?"

"If memory serves me right, most of these plants should be edible." Nyla's head swiveled, her eyes scrutinizing the plants around them.

Xander hesitated, watching as she plucked the leaf off of a plant and plopped it in her mouth. "Most?"

"Yeah, most. Peppermint?" She offered him a leaf from the same plant she'd taken one from. He accepted it slowly.

"And you know what you're doing, right?"

"I basically grew up in the garden."

"So…yes?"

"For the most part, yeah. I've only gotten sick from *suspicious* plants a few times."

Xander froze, his fingers stuck on the plant he'd been playing with as he sucked on the leaf Nyla gave him mere seconds ago. The supposed peppermint leaf burned like acid on his tongue. "I'm sorry, what?"

Nyla shrugged and plucked a hopple from a nearby tree. "It happens sometimes. A lot of plants look alike."

"You know, the more I get to know you, the more I wonder how you're even alive right now. I mean honestly, you just admitted to surviving poisoning yourself!"

Nyla twisted around, her lips turned up in amusement. "I guess I'm just lucky."

She resumed her path through the winding rows of plants. Xander trailed after her, all the while paying attention to any signs that that leaf may not have been peppermint. Even though he was fairly certain it was, Nyla hadn't exactly inspired much confidence in him.

The rain hammering on the glass ceiling above lulled him into the belief that everything was fine. And it was that familiar rhythm that made him pause to study a plant whose leaves looked like dragons in flight. He stood in front of it, half tempted to sniff it, but refrained from doing so. Maybe Nyla knew what it was. Xander looked over the leaves one last time and turned to ask her, only to be met with an empty aisle of flora.

He swept a hand through his hair and cursed himself for getting distracted. This wasn't your average stroll through the garden, and yet

Xander had fallen into the trap set by the soothing music of the storm and curious greenery around him.

***

Nyla hummed as she walked up and down the aisles of the manor's greenhouse. Xander's shoes scraped the stone floor, and she took comfort in the fact that he shuffled along behind her. The rows of herbs and flowers, fruits and vegetables were another comfort all of their own. It reminded Nyla of the farms back home. Between her parents' fields and their neighbors, they had everything they needed to survive.

It was with that gentle memory that Nyla floated down the long, winding rows, completely lost in a sort of peace she knew she shouldn't allow herself at the present moment. After all, they still had Dinora to figure out and Cedric to deal with. Then there was Shamira's ominous theory about 'the source'—whatever *that* meant—looming in the distance.

Nearly every plant she'd passed was edible or medicinal, with only a handful she couldn't identify and a few plants she knew to be deadly. The sight of these plants tied knots in Nyla's stomach.

Her head snapped up from the plant she was examining. A torrent of lighthearted giggles floated down the greenhouse's row and echoed in her ears. Nyla looked up and down the aisle. Any hope of Xander's assurance that he hadn't heard anything had disappeared along with him. She started to call out for him, only for her voice to die in her throat.

"Catch me if you can!" A girl's merry shrill bounced through the glass walls of the greenhouse. The sound had an ethereal quality that made it seem as though someone had shouted down a well. A chorus of laughter and rapid footsteps followed the girl's taunt. Nyla started after the voice, drawn to it.

Bang!

"Nyla!" Xander called from a few aisles over. His pounding footsteps came closer, as did the rustle of him crashing through plants and leaves.

"I'm okay!" Nyla answered, her eyes wild. Nothing around her had fallen, not even the vegetables and herbs she had gathered into a spare shirt, and certainly nothing that could've shattered like *that*. Her grip on the bundle tightened until her knuckles turned white.

Xander rounded the corner with a burst of disturbed plant life. Laughter continued to fill Nyla's ears, but no ghostly specters came into view. She jumped at the clatter of leaves and hurried footsteps. A relieved puff of air left her lips at the sight of Xander, and she trotted over to meet him halfway down the row.

"What was that?" she gushed. Her eyes roved over Xander in search of any apparent injuries.

"No clue. You're all right, though?" Xander's eyes gravitated up to meet hers.

"Yeah. Now let's get out of here before something else happens." Nyla practically ran through the greenhouse and burst through the door onto the soaked pathway, back to the kitchen. She assumed Xander was hot on her heels, but didn't dare chance a look back at the aisles of plants, too shaken by the specter she'd only heard.

Nyla shoved the door open and shut it tightly against the howling wind once Xander crossed the threshold. Plopping the bundle of food down on the counter, Nyla's brows furrowed ever so slightly, all but lost in lonely contemplation.

"You okay?" Nyla looked up and found Xander watching her from across the island.

"Yeah." She swallowed. "I just have no idea what you can make with all of this."

"Liar." Xander cocked a half smile. Nyla opened her mouth to tell him what she thought, but he held up a hand, turning his attention to the food before them. "You don't have to tell me. I get it. This place is obviously haunted, and it's going to drive us both crazy."

Nyla pressed her lips together. She wanted to tell him, but was glad that she didn't have to. Not right at this moment, anyway. Eventually, they'd talk about it, and maybe then she'd find out why she and Shamira had found him in the ballroom earlier.

"Now, about breakfast…"

She nodded, leaning against the wall as she watched Xander mull over what to make. He moved his folded-up nightclothes off of the island to the table in the corner and scouted around the drawers in search of something.

Things *clinked* and *clanged* as he rummaged through each drawer, his eyebrows knitted together in concentration. Nyla was afraid to ask if he wanted help for fear of distracting him from his thought process about breakfast.

At last, he cried out in triumph. From the depths of one drawer, he pulled out a long knife. The light in his eyes diminished almost immediately at the blunt and tarnished blade. Xander brought it closer to his face with a frown.

"I don't suppose you have your knife on you?" Xander threw the knife down on the counter with the air of someone who had just been disappointed in the worst way possible. Nyla bit back a laugh and passed her knife over to him. "Thank you!"

He twirled around, his eyes in search of the next thing he needed. Nyla watched, unable to help him without knowing what he actually sought to do with the foods she'd collected. Her stomach grumbled, and she pressed a hand into it. Xander's eyes landed on her again.

"There's no plugic here, is there?" Again, the light in Xander's eyes dimmed.

"Nope, no fancy magic running water here. There's a well right outside, though. I can fill the basin over there like last night if you want," she offered, pushing herself off the wall.

"No, I'll get it. Can you light the fire pit?" He pointed toward the hole in the countertop that they'd used the night before.

"Sure."

323

Xander grabbed the basin from the opposite counter and braced himself before he headed out into the storm again. Nyla flicked her fingers in the direction of the fire pit. Soft flames crackled and popped in the pit. She smiled and placed the grate over the hole.

Once Xander came back, he set about washing and prepping the vegetables and herbs Nyla had gathered. Her mouth watered when he finally set them in a pan over the flame. A warm aroma filled the air as the pan sizzled, and it wasn't long before Xander took the pan off the flame. Nyla extinguished the fire and dusted off a couple of stools for them.

They dug into their plates eagerly. Not a word passed between them. The scrape of their forks and knives against the plates filled the air.

As she ate, Nyla wondered what Shamira was up to and when they'd hear from her again. Whatever the pumpkie had considered earlier had called for immediate action, and Nyla wasn't sure what that meant exactly. All Nyla knew was that Shamira was looking for a 'source.' It must have had something to do with how Shamira could sense things, but either way, the meaning was lost on Nyla.

After her second absentminded helping, Nyla pushed her empty plate away.

"There's more if you want some." Xander stuffed another forkful into his mouth.

"I'm good, thanks. I just want to know what Shamira's doing." Nyla bit the inside of her cheek. "And Dinora."

Xander nodded and shoveled the rest of the roasted vegetables onto his plate. "Well, we can't do anything about that, so what do you wanna do in the meantime?"

Nyla shrugged. What could they do? Astrid wanted her to find some box and leave. That was all fine and dandy, but suppose the box didn't actually exist? Besides, they couldn't leave with the storm waging war outside.

She jumped in her skin. Thunder boomed like cannon blasts. The pots and pans that hung on the wall rattled angrily. Nyla and Xander exchanged sullen glances.

"I guess that means we're not leaving today." A flash of lightning illuminated the room. Nyla sighed and gathered her hair over one shoulder. "Wanna start in the library? Search through the rooms?"

Xander collected their dishes and set about washing them. "When will I ever get the chance to explore a creepy old manor, inhabited by a creepy old woman, who may or may not be an imprisoned traitor trying to kill us, with a cat creature that mysteriously goes off on her own to find something you or I can't possibly see on our own? Sounds like fun to me."

"We could brave the storm and leave all three behind," Nyla offered as she came to stand beside him with a towel in hand.

"Think it would work?" He shot her a lopsided grin.

"I wish." She dried off a plate and stacked it on top of the other.

The pair finished cleaning up their breakfast things and decided on where to start their search on the manor. Nyla's mind journeyed toward Astrid's insistence that she needed to find the box and leave. As the morning drew on, the clouds grew darker until the sky was covered by coal dust clouds. Lightning became the only source of light left in the sky.

"So, the library?" Xander suggested as they stood at the kitchen window.

"Yeah. My brother Derek spent a lot of time in there. He probably knew more about this manor than Dinora." Nyla frowned, the storm outside reflected in her eyes. "Too bad Astrid didn't tell me where this box is or what it looks like."

"Even if she did and you found it, would you leave in this storm?" Xander turned his head to look at her.

Nyla chewed her bottom lip. The specters she'd seen and heard within the last few hours gathered at the forefront of her mind. "Maybe."

A bright flash of lightning split the sky. Thunder boomed like a thousand church bells, and not so sweet. The window's pane of glass rattled and shook.

"So…the library?" Xander repeated hopefully.

"Afraid of a little storm?" Nyla teased.

"'Little' is a bit of a subjective term, don't ya think?"

Smiling, Nyla shook her head and set off for the library. Shadows plagued the windowless corridor from the kitchen to the library. Not even the lit sconces gave enough light to chase the apprehension in her gut away. But Nyla didn't have to dwell in the shadows anymore. She conjured up a pair of light orbs and illuminated the odd shadows of the Woodlane Manor's hallways until the double doors of the library stood before them.

Nyla pushed the doors open triumphantly and inhaled the comforting scent of aged paper that tickled her nose. Her eyes roved over the plush loungers and inviting bookcases as tall as the ceiling. The wide window on the far side of the room was graced with a plush seat that served as one of the coziest nooks Nyla had ever sat in. She brushed the memory away and approached one of the bookcases.

"I'll start here and work my way toward the middle."

Xander nodded in agreement. "Then I'll work my way toward you from here."

***

The storm served as a background symphony as the pair worked their way through the bookshelves. Nyla didn't bother with the library ladder. She figured that if they couldn't find what they were looking for, whatever that was exactly, at eye level, then she would put more effort into finding it later.

She ran her hand along the shelf of books as she skimmed over each title. Her head was crooked at an odd angle that made her neck stiff. The candlelight from the sconces and candelabras throughout the room cast an eerie, flickering glow over the library.

At some point or another, Nyla had drawn her knife as they searched the shelves. She still absentmindedly flipped and twirled it between her fingers to keep her nerves occupied, switching her grip with each pass. The storm had put her on edge, and she needed to do something with that nervous energy. The dancing shadows from the candlelight didn't help her anxious imagination.

Her stomach clenched. Breakfast had worn off at least an hour ago. Nyla figured it was just the uneasiness from the storm and being forced to stay in the Woodlane Manor another night or two. Her lips pressed into a thin line.

Every now and again, Nyla found a book that looked like it could be useful and turned it longwise so it stuck out from the shelf. Xander had adopted the same method on his side, and soon the two of them met in the middle.

"Looks like a lot of history and magic encyclopedias." Nyla straightened and rubbed her neck.

"I wish I could say the same. My side was mostly epics and old ballads until I got a little farther down," Xander replied, his nose scrunched.

Nyla chuckled and swatted his shoulder playfully. "And what's wrong with that?"

"Nothing, just not really helpful. Besides, who needs six different copies of the Ballad of Godberd? The only acceptable answer is no one." He shook his head.

"Well, they say perspective matters."

Nyla jumped in her skin and snapped her head in the direction that Dinora's voice had come from. The woman lounged in an armchair in the center of the room, a teacup and saucer in her slender hands. Without another thought, Nyla threw her knife at the older woman.

The knife froze in midair. Nyla's blood turned to ice.

What had she done?

Dinora took a sip from her teacup, a wry smile just barely hidden by the delicate china. The knife dropped with a *clatter* and *thump* against the wooden floor beyond the seating area's rug. The woman placed her cup on the saucer and turned her twinkling eyes on them.

"Now then, would you two like to join me?"

"Why? What for?" It was Xander who spoke. Nyla's throat had gone dry. It was a miracle she could even hear anything above the *thud* of her heart between her ears.

"For perspective, of course. You're looking for something, and judging by the books you've singled out, it has to do with the war and Nyla's magic." Dinora's gaze fixated on Nyla. The sweet, innocent lilt in her voice sent a quiver through her.

Nyla couldn't explain it, but she felt like an animal that had caught a whiff of something they didn't like that made their fur stand on edge.

"And what kind of 'perspective' is that, exactly?" Nyla piped up.

"The kind from *someone who was there*." Nyla and Xander exchanged dark looks. Dinora sighed. "I'll explain everything, if you'll let me."

Nyla shrugged. What could go wrong?

It's not like they could do anything about her magic or this war that kept getting brought up or even about leaving the manor today. She slowly stepped toward the couch opposite of Dinora's plush armchair, picking her knife up along the way, and took a tentative seat on the edge of the soft cushion. Xander joined them soon after and sat with a heavy sigh, his arms crossed over his chest. He reluctantly set his bow beside him.

Nyla watched Dinora expectantly, waiting for something. The teapot and a pair of teacups floated over to herself and Xander, serving them each a piping hot cup of tea that made Nyla's nose crinkle. The teapot returned to its place on the coffee table that served as a barrier between Dinora's armchair and the couch that the pair sat on.

"Now." Dinora cleared her throat. Nyla placed her cup on the table beside her and let her hands fall to her lap. Xander shifted on the couch. Tension rolled off him in waves. "Where do I begin?"

Dinora's piercing blue eyes flitted back and forth with her thoughts before they flashed brightly and looked up at them with a forlorn smile. "I've already told you that I am the keeper of this manor, but it didn't come by choice. Not really anyway. I was once the Royal Mage until the time of King Harrison, when I sought out an apprentice to replace me so I could retire." She paused, her eyes downcast.

"But then the war happened. You know the one, the Great Tenebris War." Dinora faltered when she saw Nyla's raised eyebrows and puzzled stare. The woman gasped, "You don't know about the war?"

Dinora tutted to herself and straightened in her chair. Nyla stole a glance at Xander. He didn't seem fazed as he listened to her continuation with a chilling, neutral expression.

"Let's see, let's see." Dinora began again, her lips quirked down in a frown. "It was such a long time ago, over 600 years ago, give or take. It's hard to tell time when you've been trapped for so long, but I can remember it like it was yesterday." Dinora's eyes misted over with shadows of the past. Her voice was hollow and yet weighed down by sadness.

"600 years ago, our country suffered from a grave uprising that evolved into an all-out war. Some, the Corvids from the east, rose up against the king and nobility because of a conflict that had happened years before...the Ten Years' War.

"They plagued the country and brought chaos wherever they went. Their leader grew desperate and began to steal magic from the land, harnessing its magic to bring about Tenebris's damnation in her quest for justice. She even stole magic from other users. After some time, they stormed this very manor.

"By then, of course, King Harrison had ordered the evacuation of Hart. A few of us here at the Woodlane stayed behind, myself and my apprentice included. We needed to salvage what we could of the manor's archives. Beyond that, the manor has a rich history and deep roots in magic as the seat of the Royal Mage for centuries. It even served as the center of Tenebris's government after the country split from Corvus.

After that, the others left at my behest. It was too dangerous for them to be here. My apprentice and I combined our magic to protect the manor, and our spells proved fruitful. But the Corvids' leader was a powerful Caster and would stop at nothing to enact the justice she sought." Dinora's lip twisted, and she paused. Nyla studied her. She seemed almost bitter when she began to speak again.

"But she couldn't harness the manor's magic, its essence. As her powers waned from trying to break the protections, she grew desperate and began to turn on her own people. Slaughtered them, *all of them*, for magic, for power. She threw off the balance of the land's magic, its essence.

"Once she was satisfied, she unleashed a hellish fury over the land. Blast after blast of magic energy scarred the country like a curse. The abundance of magic and the consequences of stealing it from the land resulted in aftershocks that even she wasn't able to predict. Those aftershocks transformed the land into what it is today, forming places like Fortune Falls, where there's an overabundance of magic, and areas where there's very little magic at all. Because the Mage had drained the magic from the land, it didn't go back from whence it came, but rather rolled over the land from the epicenter until there was nothing left to return.

"That's why Tenebris has such an unbalanced climate. Her means of attack violated the fundamental laws of magic, and I suppose she suffered for it." Dinora was silent for a second, her eyes once again fixed on her lap. She pursed her lips and continued in the most exhausted, bone-weary voice Nyla had ever heard. It was the voice of someone who was beaten down over and over again until nothing of their spirit was left to salvage.

"I soon found out that the land wasn't the only thing she cursed. She cursed this manor, and me with it. I'm bound here forever, however long that is."

Dinora's words sank in. Nyla sat back on the couch. A crippling ache of sorrow spread through her. Out of all the things Dinora had said, the thing that struck her most was the part about being cursed. How had she managed being in the Woodlane Manor for six centuries? How was she even still alive? None of it made any sense.

Nyla looked over at Xander. He was fidgeting with the shaft of an arrow, spinning it between his fingers. She could see it in his eyes that he had so many questions that he wanted to ask, but he was holding back, his jaw clenched firmly. She glanced back at Dinora. The older woman was lost in her own reminiscence.

The storm outside rumbled on, filling the quiet that had swallowed the library. Nyla flinched. Beside her, Xander's hand flew to his temple, his face screwed up in a wince.

Shamira's frantic voice boomed louder than the thunder outside. *Nyla! Xander!*

Nyla's eyes were wild as they flew to the library door.

One breath. Two breaths. Three breaths.

Shamira didn't burst through the door like Nyla expected her to. Instead, the echo of the pumpkie's frantic call rattled her brain.

"Well, it's been great, but we have somewhere to be," Xander said coolly.

Nyla took his cue and popped up, giving Dinora a feigned smile. "Yeah, thanks for the, uh, the perspective."

The pair rushed out of the library. It wasn't until they passed the ballroom that Nyla burst out into a sprint.

"Shamira!" she yelled as loudly as she dared.

Stormy light filtered through the stained-glass window at the main staircase's landing. Shamira's claws *clicked* against the floor as she came into view on the opposite end of the grand entrance.

Nyla jarred to a stop. She panted for a second or two before she looked at her companions, who were in much the same state as she was. "What's wrong?"

26. BEYOND HELP

Nyla's heart clenched as she listened to Shamira and what the looking glass had shown her.

What had she gotten herself into? What had she dragged *Xander* into?

I'm still not certain who killed Astrid, but your concern that Dinora may not be who she claims to be is looking more and more likely. I'm sorry, Nyla. Shamira concluded her tale of confrontation and betrayal with a somber expression. *If it's any consolation, I don't believe that Astrid was a Corvid, given her position against Cedric and the other woman in her memory.*

"That..." Nyla swallowed thickly. Her mind was carried off by her own fear and the overwhelming gravity of the situation. "That helps."

Xander draped his arm around her shoulders and rubbed her arm. "So, about that storm, you think it's worth the risk?"

"And what would we do if we left?" Nyla looked up at him, her pale face drawn. The hopelessness and emptiness she'd managed to rid herself of for too short a time came back like old, unwanted friends. She'd lost everything in that fire all those seasons ago, and for the briefest of moments, Nyla had allowed herself the solace of hope, of answers, of what legends could offer her.

The visions from Fortune Falls' waters had given her something to believe in, a way to figure her life out, and she'd trusted that. But they'd led her here.

This wasn't the saving grace she'd hoped it would be.

"No, we have to stay long enough to find that box, and then we can go." Nyla numbly pulled herself from Xander's attempt to comfort her and rounded the stairs, headed for the passage behind them.

Where are you going? Shamira trotted next to her as Nyla hurried down the new hallway.

"I just need a minute. I need space—I need," Nyla groaned, her pace slowing as if any and all of her energy had been drained in the time it took to blink. Xander's hand slipped into hers, and she stopped. Tears began to flood her eyes. She glanced over her shoulder at him. "I just want to be alone right now if that's all right."

Dark looks of uneasiness passed between her two companions, and Nyla understood that. She was sure that the same was written plainly on her own features. The longer each second stretched on and they were stuck in the middle of the hallway, the walls seemed to close in on her.

Xander squeezed her hand. "Holler if you need anything, okay? I'll start with the rooms along this hallway then and see what I can find."

Nyla nodded and pulled her hand away. "There's a veranda, down this way. I'll be there."

With the confirmation of each other's safety, Nyla sped down the remainder of the hall, breathless and with a constricted chest. Heaving air into her lungs at the sight of the glass door, she heaved it open and hauled herself through. The scent of the rain-soaked earth washed over her. Water dripped down from the overhang of the veranda's tattered awning, occasionally dripping onto the wood planking below.

She shut the door firmly behind herself, half leaning against it as her body sagged. The solid door wasn't enough to keep her standing, and she crumpled to the wooden treads under the weight of her own limbs.

Murdered.

Astrid had been murdered, just like her family.

And what for? It sounded like a petty grievance to Nyla, one that she not only suffered for, but others as well. Whatever had happened centuries ago during the Corvid Uprising was happening again.

Everything came back to the Ten Years' War, which she knew nothing about really: Cedric and his ancestors, herself and her family, the fire, the draining of the land's magic, Dinora.

The worst part was she didn't know who to believe anymore. Was Dinora an innocent woman or a ruthless killer? Was Cedric twisted by the atrocity and aftermath of war or just as heartless as the man Shamira saw in the looking glass? Was he the *same* man? Was Astrid noble and righteous or wicked and deceptive? What about the pumpkies? Which side did history write them on?

And what did all of that make Nyla? Was she a monster, a pawn in someone else's game, or something of her own free will and design?

Nyla hiccupped. Every breath caught in her throat. She barely managed to choke it down to fill her starved lungs. Her face burned, and that was the only way she knew that all of this wasn't some long, convoluted nightmare.

This time, she wouldn't wake up on some forest floor, drenched in her own cold sweat, clammy and shaking with a terror that lingered, brought on by her darkest nightmares.

She brought her knees up to her chest and buried her head in her arms. It didn't matter to her that this position squeezed out every drop of oxygen she managed to take into her lungs. She wanted to hide, but didn't have the strength to move.

Goosebumps formed on her skin. As flushed as Nyla was, the icy chill that rolled over her was anything but a relief from the onslaught of heat caused by her sobbing fit. Cold air in the shape of hands came to rest on her forearms. Nyla gathered the last of her willpower and picked her head up off her arms.

Her mouth dropped open in a silent shriek. Crouched before her was a boy with a round face and a mess of curly auburn hair.

"Why are you crying, Nyla?" Westley asked her. His eyes shone with a reflection of the small, lopsided smile he offered her.

"You're not real. You're—you're…" Nyla closed her eyes and swallowed hard. "You're gone."

Her voice was barely above a whisper, choked with tears. It wasn't her twin before her; it couldn't possibly be.

No, he was a cruel trick of the manor's or a test sent from Corruptio to see what path she'd take, whether she was good or evil. Whether or not she still believed in hope and morality, or if she'd drowned in pity and vice.

Westley glanced away. A blush crept along his translucent cheeks. "I don't know what I am, but I know you need help right now, so talk to me."

"I can't. I don't know if you're a spirit or a trick. I don't even know if I can trust myself," Nyla sputtered. Her teary eyes began to dry. She sniffled, her nose still clearing.

"If you don't think you can trust yourself, then can you even trust at all?" Westley tilted his head to the side and studied her. "You know what, I don't think *you're* real. My sister would never doubt herself. You're the one who isn't what they seem."

Westley rocked back onto his heels and stood. He brushed his knees off, and Nyla couldn't help but notice the pearly aura that radiated off of him. She scrambled to her feet and reached out to him. "Please stay. Don't leave me again."

He looked at her with a bemused smile. "You're taller than I am now. I don't like it."

"What?" Nyla shook her head. A pitiful laugh crackled its way from her chest. "What does that have to do with anything?"

"Nothing at all, but it made you smile a little." Westley opened his arms to her, and she ran into them. Instantly enveloped by cool air, Nyla let herself believe that instead of a ghostly presence, Westley was alive and well. For one precious moment, she desperately believed rather than cold, empty air, it was really his arms that wrapped around her.

"I miss you," Nyla grumbled, unwilling to open her eyes. "All of you."

"We know, but we're here for you. Anytime you need us, just remember us," Westley soothed her and pulled away. The presence of his touch lingered on her hand, pulling her toward the door. "There's something Derek asked me to show you. C'mon, it's in the other wing."

"I can't." Nyla tugged her hand free of the cool air's grasp.

"Why?" Westley looked back at her, his nose crinkling. "Don't tell me you're still afraid of the other wing."

Nyla glanced down at her feet and wrung her hands together. "It's not just that. It's Dinora and Cedric and Astrid and this war that people keep talking about."

"I don't know about any of that, but Derek really wanted me to show you this, and I don't have much longer to be here." Westley's form wavered.

The cold air wrapped around her hand again, and Westley tugged her forward. Nyla relented and let the cool draft that radiated off of him guide her as the apparition of Westley glitched.

Together they raced through servants' passages Nyla hadn't even known existed until this moment. Westley floated ahead of her, and Nyla followed him. All the while, his form sputtered and disappeared, only to reappear farther away until he'd led her to the hall of paintings she'd found herself in during her first astral travel.

This all started here, where she'd first met Astrid. Glancing over the familiar portraits of old on either side of her, the same regal and expressionless faces stared down at her. She fixed her eyes back on Westley, who hovered in front of her, leading her to who knew where. Hopefully, Nyla pleaded with Helpet, it wasn't back to that painting of the red-eyed man and Astrid down at the end of the hall.

Nyla's breath hitched. Westley turned to her, his face twisted with guilt and grief. He faded, his form disintegrating before her eyes like sand blown away by a determined wind.

"I'm sor—Ny—find the…" His voice cut off in a gurgle. "Green…fire…"

"No! Don't go, don't leave me!" Nyla rushed forward, her arm stretched out as if she could hold him here.

Her hand grabbed only empty air. The chill that had come with Westley's presence was gone.

Nyla wrapped her arms around herself and stared at the empty space. He was right there. He'd spoken to her, and he'd held her, and he'd tried to comfort her. Whatever Westley was, a ghost or manifestation of the Woodlane Manor, he'd led her here and tried to tell her what to look for: a green fire. But that meant nothing to Nyla. Fires weren't green. And what did that have to do with this wing of the manor?

Dismayed, Nyla slowly started to make her way back to where she'd left Shamira and Xander. As her feet carried her away from what Derek had wanted Westley to show her, she tried to recall everything she knew about the Woodlane. From its rooms to her own memories, to places her brothers spent most of their time and where she liked to hide out. Against her better judgment, Nyla started back the way she had come. While she couldn't draw up any images of the rooms that resided behind the few closed doors that called this wing of the Woodlane Manor home, she tried to figure out what any of them had to do with a green fire.

Given how difficult it was to hear Westley's last attempt to help her before he was called back to wherever he'd came from, Nyla figured that she'd missed the bulk of his message. He never spoke in riddles or tried to be tricky when something was important. Whatever 'green fire' meant, it had to be something significant and obvious, an identifying feature of where she needed to go.

She groaned. The answer had to be right in front of her. Now more than ever before, Nyla wished with every ounce of energy she had left in her that her family was here to help her.

Westley's words from before echoed in her ears. All she had to do was remember them. But how? What was she supposed to remember exactly, or did it matter? Would any memory serve the purpose of helping her? Nyla stopped dead in her tracks and closed her eyes.

Maybe this was all a long, convoluted diversion, a distraction.

Her mind replayed the brisk and dark Serenmae nights when her home was plagued by an inescapable draft and the fields were blanketed in a freshly fallen snow. They'd all gather by the fireplace and spend the day there. Sometimes her father would be away, and her mother would busy herself with quilting. She said it helped with her nerves and burned up the worry in her hands of him traveling in such weather. Other days, when her father wasn't on an errand for the businessman he occasionally did work for, they'd spend the day playing games.

Her mother had stitched games onto old pillowcases, and they used little trinkets or stones as game pieces. They'd spend hours shrieking with laughter or teasing each other over the game. Some of her favorite memories, however, were spent sprawled out by the fireplace with her entire family, listening to stories or her mother's songs. Everything centered around their fireplace, loose brick and all.

Nyla couldn't count how many times she'd slipped on it because it shifted under her foot if she ran through the room too quickly.

"Of course!" she whispered excitedly to the empty hallway. Her eyes popped open and went wide with the realization of how obvious Westley's clue was. Nyla could've slapped herself. He'd tried to tell her to find the green fireplace. If their fireplace at home had a loose brick and they hid things in its cavity, then surely one of the fireplaces here had a loose brick too.

Nyla darted off toward the spot where Westley had disappeared for good and rushed past it. She pulled up short on a door near the end of the hall, almost across from where she'd met Astrid.

The door opened with a *squeak*. Heavy curtains were drawn over the twin windows on the opposite wall. She breathed in the stale air and focused her energy. A ball of light bobbed in the air in front of her. Nyla peered through the dimness of the small room. A simple wooden desk was centered between the two windows. Nyla could faintly hear the storm still raging outside over her pounding heart.

At her beckoning, the sconces sparked to life. Her fingertips tingled with the magic that flowed through her, and Nyla had to admit that she was beginning to like that feeling. Shamira must've been right—she really was stronger than she let herself believe, and Westley was right too. She needed to trust herself.

And she did.

Nyla trusted the things she saw with her own eyes, how the sight of Westley made her heart swell. She trusted herself, and she trusted in the details that crisscrossed between the different perspectives she'd uncovered. While the brick-shaped emerald tiles couldn't speak, Nyla knew what to look for, and that they had a story to tell too. She had to have faith that the green bricks before her could tell a story that those around her couldn't—or didn't want to.

The ball of light beside her bobbed over the fireplace and split into two at Nyla's urging. They gave off a bright light that filled the shadowy corners of the room and dispelled the dancers created by the sconces' flames.

She studied the fireplace before her, trying to find any bricks that looked loose or didn't quite line up with the others. Cracked mortar was usually a good sign, but as far as she could see, the fireplace was sound. Each brick was exactly where it should be.

With a huff, Nyla ran her hand over the wooden mantelpiece. It didn't even wiggle.

Next, she ran her hands over the surface of the fireplace, or as far as she could reach, anyway, to test the soundness of the bricks. The glowing orbs hovered over her. Their light glistened over the tile bricks of the fireplace, and if there were any imperfections, their light would show it. But Nyla didn't see any and turned her attention to the hearth.

She knelt on the cold wood floor in front of it. The orbs followed her, and, in their light, she saw a brick that didn't quite fit in its cavity.

Nyla touched a quivering finger to it. The brick shifted ever so slightly. Grinning, she pried the tile out of its spot. One of the lights came closer, and she leaned forward to peer inside the cavity.

"How in the world did you manage to find this, Derek?" she mumbled in astonishment.

The cavity was truly a hiding place. The mouth of the hole was a hair's breadth larger than the brick in Nyla's hand, with a ledge that the brick sat on to keep it at the right height so it lay even with the others. The hole opened up wider after the depth of the brick, and that was where Derek had hidden his treasure.

She placed the brick beside her and reached down into the hole to grab a package wrapped in a burlap cloth to keep the grit and dust away. This too she placed beside her and leaned forward to get a look inside. The orb of light beside her nudged her aside and dove down into the cavity, lighting up the rest of its contents.

A few miscellaneous items that Nyla knew to be all Derek's sat atop another package, also wrapped in a scrap of burlap and bookish in shape. For some reason or another, he'd kept a perfectly smooth, oval-shaped stone that glittered and shimmered in the light. Nyla guessed it was an opal, but her focus quickly shifted when the dulled glint of a thin silver line caught her eyes.

Her breath hitched.

It was impossible for it to be here. It was supposed to be lost, long gone and forgotten in a pile of ash, if it even survived the heat to do so.

Nyla plucked the blackened silver chain from the cavity and wiped away the grit from its round pendant with the hem of her shirt. She brought it closer to her face and studied the smooth pendant. Through the burned and tarnished metal, Nyla could just barely make out the surviving etching.

Lilacs.

A bouquet of lilacs was etched onto the surface of the round silver plate.

Tears flooded her eyes. This shouldn't be here. It *couldn't* be here. And yet, in a world that had proved to her that the impossible happened all the time, it was. The necklace her parents had given her when she was about ten was clasped in her hands, clutched to her chest. Nyla wiped her eyes and studied the necklace anew. Despite the tarnish and the places where the flames had licked at it, the necklace had survived, melted clasp and all.

And somehow, it had found its way here.

Nyla slipped this into her pocket, along with the opal, as she gathered the second book out of the cavity and replaced the brick. With both books tucked close to her chest, Nyla made her way back to the other end of the manor.

She glanced over her shoulder every so often, as if she expected someone to pop out of the shadows and attack her. Whatever was in these books, Derek had thought it was important enough to hide them and had asked Westley to show her.

Nyla hurried back through the halls, swerving into a servants' corridor she knew would put her back in the same corridor as Shamira and Xander. Light flooded out of a room down the other end of the hall, but Nyla ignored it. She wanted to take a peek at these for herself. For all she knew, these books had nothing to do with Cedric or the war, but everything to do with what she needed to hear right now. She darted into the first room she saw, shutting the door behind her.

Safely inside an abandoned sitting room, Nyla sat down on the sofa and bit her lip. She supposed it didn't matter which book she looked at first and blindly chose one of the bundles.

Wrapped carefully in the burlap, the first book was thin and worn. Nyla knew it instantly. It was the book Westley had sometimes carried with him, the one she could never get a peek at. Something inside her sparked.

After all these years, she could finally solve the mystery of Westley's book. On the other hand, Nyla felt like she should respect the fact that he'd wanted to keep it private.

In the end, the fact that Westley had insisted she find Derek's hiding place convinced Nyla that whatever lay hidden in Westley's book was fair game. If it wasn't meant for her now, it wouldn't have been in that cavity.

With a deep breath and a silent apology, Nyla opened the tan leather book. Westley's messy scrawl greeted her. Her eyes fell over the angular letters, and, for the first time in a long time it seemed, Nyla let out a hearty laugh.

N–

If you so much as breathe on this book, I'll tell Ma and Pa about what happened at the manor when you collapsed on the staircase and Derek had to carry you home. You really scared us, but we kept your secret anyway, so I'm asking you to let me have this—just this one thing that's mine and mine alone.

If you love me even the slightest bit, you'll put this book down and walk away now before I find you (and I will find you)!

–W

She grinned and flipped the page carefully. He'd expected her to sneak a peek sooner, but she hadn't. After all these years, Nyla would finally get to see what her brother did when he stole away with his little book and disappeared for hours. The first page was a sloppy and crude portrait of their mother. Nyla couldn't believe her eyes.

All that time, Westley had spent his moments alone drawing. The farther into his sketchbook Nyla wandered, the better his drawings got. His lines were less shaky and depictions more accurate, or a reflection of how he saw things. He drew portraits of their family with twinkling eyes and the world as seen by himself. Nyla took it all in with a swelling heart.

About three-quarters of the way through, Nyla came to an incomplete rendering of the Woodlane Manor's Serenmae garden during a gentle snowfall.

Nyla flipped the page only to find a blank canvas. With a strangled breath, she thumbed through the rest of the pages.

Empty.

Just like the drawing of the garden, Westley never got to complete his sketchbook.

"Oh, Westley," Nyla murmured, "why would you hide this, especially from me?"

Nyla flipped back through the book and drank in Westley's sketches, hoping to commit them to memory as she had her family's portrait.

Eventually, with a heavy heart, Nyla closed Westley's sketchbook and rewrapped it. She sucked in a long breath and eyed the other book with weary eyes.

Nyla? May I come in? Shamira's tentative voice skirted over her consciousness.

Nyla took a deep breath. "Sure."

She watched as the oval knob turned, and the door gently swung open as Shamira slowly came into the room.

Xander wanted me to check in and see if you needed anything or wanted something specific to eat. The pumpkie's green eyes narrowed at the sight of Nyla's treasures. *What's this?*

"Oh." Nyla looked down at her lap. "These are just some things I found. Um…"

Shamira nodded and approached the sofa, leaning her front paws on the soft cushion to get eye level with the book in Nyla's hand. She nosed the book Nyla was about to unwrap and sniffed. *This one's old. I think it belongs to Astrid because I can sense her magic on it.*

"Should I look at it?" Nyla's stomach churned.

What's the harm? It's just a book, right? Shamira blinked nonchalantly.

Nyla tilted her head. She couldn't argue with that. It's not like the book was cursed or something. She peeled away the protective burlap to expose the smooth, lilac-colored cover. Her fingertips grazed the cover, and her mind started with a spark. Nyla was vaguely aware of falling back and sagging into the cushions behind her as her whole body flinched.

Her vision clouded over, and Nyla blinked. Nausea rose in her throat. Shamira called out to her, but her voice was garbled and sounded from a great distance. Nyla's eyes fluttered shut, and her vision filled with a memory not of her own making. The image was faded and blurry, with muted voices that reverberated in Nyla's mind.

"You all need to leave, protect the other villages. The Corvids are on a rampage, and with the magic she stole from the land, it will be near impossible to defeat her."

A woman's voice rang clear in the room that formed around Nyla. She had cropped, silver hair and a thin frame.

Astrid.

The memory came into focus.

Astrid leaned forward on her hands, a solid round table in front of her. Heaps of scrolls and parchment were piled or laid flat on the table.

"And you, my lady?" a man dressed in armor asked.

"I will stay here and try to stop her," Astrid answered solemnly.

"You'll die," another woman, also fashioned for battle, interjected grimly.

"You'll all die if you stay here. If I can stop her in her tracks, and save the rest of Tenebris, even if I lose my life in doing so, then so be it. That is an oath we've all taken, and I will not let any of you remain here only to be killed for vengeance. We all know why she is doing this, why Corvus is. Let's not make more bloodshed than there has to be." Astrid straightened, and while her voice was weary, she held a resolve that couldn't be shaken. The others nodded and filed out of the room.

Astrid bent her head and whispered what could only be a desperate plea before she too left the room.

The memory skipped, and Nyla forced her eyes to adjust to the new scene.

Once she had seen the others off down the manor's main road, Astrid returned to the foyer and stood in the center of the room. Her hands glowed with a lilac light as her pulsing magic engulfed her. Tendrils of magic extended from her aura and spread through the room, through the Woodlane Manor, like crawling vines.

The light grew to a bright shock of plum as it hugged every crevice, every corner of the manor inside and out until it was blinding to watch. Just when the light became unbearable, it disappeared.

Astrid slumped against the banister of the main staircase. She panted and used the last of her strength to hold herself up. Three heavy breaths later, she sat with a thump *upon the bottom stair and drew a bottle from her pants pocket. The cork came free with a* pop *that echoed in the empty manor. Astrid stared at it with a grimace and hopeless, hesitant eyes. She drank it anyway and shuddered.*

The image wavered and skipped, and Nyla saw a shaking, slender hand close the lid of a carved, wooden box before Astrid carried it away, and the image faded completely.

Nyla's back arched off the cushions against her own volition. She gasped for air like a woman nearly drowned.

Nyla, hold on. Xander's coming! Shamira's panicked voice sounded like an alarm bell in Nyla's head.

Nyla's body shuddered as she sputtered for air and consciousness. In her struggle, Astrid's book slipped from her clawed grasp. It fell to the floor with a *thump,* and her body went limp against the soft cushions of the couch.

Her eyes fluttered open slowly, and Nyla blinked against the light. She brought a shaking hand to her temple and struggled to sit up. Shamira's eyes were wide with worry.

Maybe you should lay back down? Shamira suggested, her voice laced with uncertainty.

"I—" Nyla began, but the book moved and opened with the rapid rustle of pages. Tendrils of lilac light spiraled out from the floating book.

Nyla scrambled off of the sofa. She tripped over her own feet and fell back against its edge, her legs shaking as she watched with wide eyes as the magic unfurled, searching for something. The lilac magic wafted throughout the room and beckoned to her.

Without so much as another thought, Nyla got to her feet and moved toward the magic.

Where are you going? You should stay here and rest for a minute.

"No, I have to follow it. Astrid, she's trying to show me something." Nyla stumbled to the door and grasped the handle with a weak hand. After some fumbling, she managed to open it, and the thin trail of magic spilled out into the hallway.

Nyla staggered after it with Shamira by her side. She hugged the wall in an attempt to keep her balance, but the weight of her limbs became her anchors. Nyla knew it was only a matter of time before she fell. Shamira nudged her hand, and Nyla glanced down.

You can lean on me a little if you need to, the pumpkie offered.

Nyla blinked and set her hand down on Shamira's back. The cat's fur was soft and silky beneath Nyla's numb fingers, and together, they slowly ambled down the hall as guided by Astrid's trail of magic. Only a few feet later, Nyla stumbled over the carpet and fell to her knees on the plush floor.

"Nyla!" She forced her head up. Her eyes could barely make out Xander's form rushing toward her from around the corner.

"Xander!" Nyla breathed with relief. She tried to stand, but couldn't find anything to help pull herself up off the floor.

Xander's booted feet came to a stop just in front of her field of spotted vision. "What are you doing? Shamira said—"

"Astrid. We have to follow the light." Nyla stared up at him with determined, wild eyes. Xander looked over at Shamira, who nodded in confirmation, and back at Nyla.

"All right, sure. We'll follow the light only you and Shamira can see. Sounds like a good plan." Xander huffed as he reached his hands out to help Nyla stand.

Like a fawn just learning how to walk, Nyla stood on unsteady feet. If it wasn't for Xander's firm grip on her waist and hand, her knees would've given out again.

"Can you walk?"

"Barely," Nyla grumbled as she leaned into him with her eyes shut tight. The hall around them spun and shifted like a top as Nyla swayed on her feet. The sensation of air rushing out from under her didn't help as Xander swept her off her feet. "What are you doing?"

"You wanna follow a mystical light sent by Astrid to who knows where, even though you can't walk, so I'm carrying you. Deal with it," Xander said resolutely. Nyla swallowed the protest on her tongue, and before she knew it, Xander was telling Shamira to lead the way.

Oh, I can't actually see *what Nyla's talking about. I was just following her.*

"Oh." Xander turned his head to look at Nyla. "Well in that case, where to?"

"You don't have to carry me." Xander fixed her with a reproachful, scolding look, and Nyla swallowed. "Fine. That way."

She pointed toward the way Xander had come and directed them back to the foyer, up the main staircase, and down a wing Nyla hadn't spent much time in if she could help it—a hall that Fate seemed determined to make her peruse. The three of them started off again, with Nyla adding directions as they went until she finally perked up.

"That room, the one right after the table on the left!" Nyla shifted in Xander's arms and glanced at him.

"Do you know what's in there?"

"It's just another bedroom...I think."

I think you might be right, but there's something in there. It's something of Astrid's.

The three cautiously made their way into the room. Shamira urged the candles and fireplace to life as Xander set Nyla down on the bed.

Nyla's head swiveled as she looked for any sign of the lilac light. With nothing in sight, her lips turned down into a frown. While the room was a decent size, certainly bigger than the first floor of Nyla's home, she'd expected more.

Astrid had only a simple four-poster bed with a hope chest at its foot and a plush chaise lounge near the fireplace to serve as items of luxury. The only other furniture in the room was a plain desk and dressing table with a matching armoire. None of those things sparkled with magic or seemed like a decent hiding place for much of anything.

"It's gone. The light." Nyla glanced around as if she expected to catch a glimpse or spark of lilac. But there was nothing.

"So, we search the room then. You just stay there and rest." Xander made his way over to the desk and pulled a drawer open.

"That's not fair. I can help!" Nyla whined.

Xander's right. With what you just experienced, you need your rest. Just give yourself a little bit of time. Shamira eyed her sternly.

Nyla fell back on the bed with a dramatic sigh and draped an arm over her eyes. "Fine. If it gets you two to stop acting like concerned parents, I'll rest up a minute."

Xander chuckled, "That's the spirit."

Nyla listened as Xander and Shamira rummaged through every surface of Astrid's chamber. Xander hummed quietly under his breath. Whatever the melody was floated over to her from somewhere behind where she lay. A door clicked open, and the rustle of fabric reached Nyla's ears next.

"What do you think of this?"

"Of what?" Nyla moved her arm and opened her eyes. An upside-down Xander beamed down at her, a dress held aloft in one hand. She turned onto her stomach and stared at the emerald gown in disbelief. Nyla pushed herself up and sat back on her heels, still not believing the gleam of pride in Xander's eyes as he looked from her to the dress. She reached out and pinched the delicate lace of the skirt between her fingers.

"You don't like it?" Xander's eyes dimmed.

"It's beautiful, but…" Nyla bit her lip and tilted her head. "I don't think we're looking for a dress."

"Maybe not, but it brings out your eyes." Xander replaced the dress in the armoire and sat down on the edge of the bed.

If you two are done discussing fashion, I think I found something, Shamira piped up from beside the dressing table.

"Is there a book of spells in there or something?" Xander studied both the table and Shamira with quirked eyebrows.

Better. Nyla, I need you to focus your magic, let it flow through you, and touch the mirror.

"I thought I needed to rest," Nyla quipped as she stumbled over to the vanity. Xander snickered behind her. Shamira fixed both of them with a glare and tutted, but otherwise remained silent.

Nyla took a deep breath and closed her eyes. With each steady and calm breath, her muscles loosened, and soon a comforting warmth spread throughout her body. When her fingers began to tingle, Nyla opened her eyes and reached a hesitant hand out to touch the mirror. Her hand glowed with the faintest of lilac energy, and when the tips of her fingers brushed the surface of the mirror, the wall and attached vanity *creaked* open.

A set of steep, dusty, and cobweb-covered stairs led the way toward what must've been the hidden room Shamira had found in the attic. The hair on the back of Nyla's neck stood on end, reminded of the presence of her two companions as they came to stand beside her.

Xander whistled lowly. "And here I thought we'd be eating lunch soon."

Nyla glanced at him out of the corner of her eye. "And here I am thanking the stars above that this didn't end like how touching Astrid's book did."

"Astrid's book?"

Nyla went exploring on her own and found one of Astrid's things. It seemed too personal to be a record or something of that nature.

"You rat!" Nyla burst.

I beg your pardon!

"You did what now, Nyla?"

350

The three of them stood staring at each other. Nyla sent a nervous glance toward an overly concerned Xander before her gaze simmered at Shamira's indifference.

"So, we have a lot to talk about then, but first things first: where's that book now?" Xander asked.

Downstairs, fifth room on the right, Shamira answered matter-of-factly.

"I'll go back and get it then. No way am I going to leave it in a place where Dinora could get to it. Until we figure out who's who, whatever we find stays with us if we can help it." Xander made for the door.

"Can you grab all the stuff around the sofa? I don't want to forget anything." Nyla chewed her lip, half focused on Xander and Westley's abandoned sketchbook while the other half of her consciousness eyed the staircase leading to who knew where.

"Yeah, sure. I'll meet you two up there." Xander stepped over the threshold of the door and disappeared from sight, only to poke his head back into the room. "And be *careful.*"

Nyla cracked a smile and shrugged. "What could *possibly* go wrong?"

Xander glared at her and started off again. As Xander's footsteps faded down the hallway, Nyla was forced to stare up and into the hidden space. Warily regarding the uneven staircase, she shrank at the insecurity mounting inside of her.

"There's…there's nothing dangerous up there, that you can sense, right?" she asked Shamira.

Not that I can sense. Shamira brushed past Nyla and started up the worn stairs. *And if this is the room I believe it to be, then there is nothing here that can harm us at all.*

Wordlessly, Nyla followed after the cat. Her nose crinkled as she breathed in the stale, dust-laden air.

Nyla placed one foot on the landing before the turn in the narrow staircase and gasped, "It's back!"

The wisp of lilac magic led the way up the stairs. She pushed her way ahead of Shamira in the tight space and darted up the rest of the staircase. Nyla was blind to the cramped and cluttered room around her as she eagerly followed the lilac trail to the mirror hung on the opposite wall.

"This is it?" Nyla murmured.

Why would the magic lead her here? She pursed her lips. Maybe she needed to touch it with her magic for something to happen like she did with the vanity in the bedroom below. Transfixed, Nyla reached a trembling hand toward the smooth glass.

Nyla? No, don't touch that—

It was too late. Nyla's hand had already reached the surface of the looking glass that Shamira had told them about. She didn't even have time to panic at Shamira's sharp warning.

The smooth surface of the magical glass rippled. Nyla's hand went straight through the clouded-over pane. The cloudiness cleared, and Nyla was greeted with the sight of her hand reaching out to a wooden box.

"Shamira, look!" Nyla exclaimed, half in awe and half in disbelief. She reached farther into the looking glass and stretched her hand out to grasp the carved, wooden box that Astrid must've hidden all those centuries ago and just now told her to find. Her fingers met the smooth wood, and she pulled it free of the looking glass. "I hope this box was worth the trouble…"

Shamira stared at her with wide, fearful eyes. *Are you all right?*

Nyla cocked her head to the side. "Should I *not* be?"

Usually, mixing energies with a looking glass as someone who isn't the original owner can have grave consequences.

"I…I feel fine. Is there something off about me that you can sense?"

No. I'm just as stunned as you are.

"Well, maybe because I'm related to Astrid somehow or supposedly inherited her magic, it thinks I'm her or accepted me as a surrogate? Or maybe she gave it special instructions to let me pass unharmed? I don't know, but I do know that we have to go find Xander. Whatever's inside this box is too important to just stand around and worry."

Agreed.

Nyla and Shamira pounded down the uneven staircase and made their way down to the sitting room to meet Xander. Nyla frowned, having fully expected to meet Xander along the way but said nothing until they were greeted by an empty room. Disbelieving, she ran into the room, her eyes roving over every surface before she stopped short of the sofa and frantically patted the cushions, flipping them over.

"They're gone!" Nyla clutched the box to her chest. "Shamira, please, can you find him? *Please*!"

Shamira's hackles raised before she shook her head, presumably to clear her mind. She settled into a sitting position and closed her eyes. Nyla waited as patiently as she could in spite of the desperation boiling in her blood as Shamira searched for his trail.

I found him!

The words had barely passed between them before Shamira was bounding off toward wherever to meet him, with Nyla racing after her a few paces behind.

27. INNOCENTLY GUILTY

Xander shook his head as he made his way back to the sitting room downstairs. Why would Nyla ask such a question? Of course something was going to go wrong.

"It's not like we're in a centuries-old, haunted manor or anything," he grumbled under his breath.

He had no right to be upset with Nyla going off on her own, even if she *had* gotten hurt in some way in doing so, according to Shamira at least. He wasn't responsible for her. He wasn't in charge of her. Xander was just barely even her friend based on how long—or rather how briefly—they'd known each other.

Yet, they'd gotten closer, and Xander did feel a little bit of responsibility toward her. He had to admit that he cared for Nyla.

Maybe it was his guilt over Issie's death. True, Issie and Nyla were wildly different people, but, in some ways, Nyla did remind him of Issie. They both tried to make their own way in the world. Perhaps Issie would've succeeded as Nyla had if she'd been given the chance to.

If only he hadn't fought with her. If he hadn't gone after her and tried to control her, force her to come back, if she hadn't—

"No. I'm not going there again. I have to focus." Xander forced himself to let go of the breath he'd been holding and stalked into the sitting room.

A book lay spread open on the floor, dumped unceremoniously, to expose the neat, slender handwriting within. Another sat comfortably on the sofa, carefully bundled up in burlap. Xander did as Nyla asked, his sole focus on getting back to her, and tucked the books safely against himself. Maybe he ought to grab their bags from the library too. It would be foolish not to be prepared for anything, especially leaving, at any given moment should they need to.

He couldn't help but wonder if both books belonged to Astrid and how exactly they'd hurt Nyla. In the end, Xander could only assume that Nyla would tell him what she needed to as soon as they were all relatively safe.

Doubt wove its way into his mind. The Woodlane Manor wasn't the pinnacle of safety. Strange things had already happened to them, practically from the moment they'd arrived. Xander shook his head. He couldn't dwell on things he had no control over.

With one last glance around the room and a hard look at the sofa to make sure he hadn't forgotten anything, Xander briskly started for the library. He'd just grabbed their bags from the floor and stuffed Nyla's found treasures into her bag when the hairs on the back of his neck stood on end. Goosebumps erupted along his arms. He attempted to rub the chill away with his free hand, but the cold hungrily persisted. He tried to shrug the chill off as a draft in the room. Xander hadn't forgotten what happened this morning when the air had turned to ice.

Xander wasn't going to fall for that trick again.

No.

He was going to head straight back to the room where he'd left Nyla and Shamira, and pretend like nothing strange had just happened to him. He was going to get Astrid's books back to the one person who had the best chance of protecting them and forget about the fact that the last time this chill had overcome him, Issie had appeared out of thin air—and led him into the ballroom.

Determined, Xander placed one foot over the threshold of the library doors. Issie's bored voice floated over to him, forcing the hair on the back of his neck to stand on end.

"You can't ignore me forever, Alexander Hun—"

"Issie, that's enough! You're not real," Xander snapped and whirled around to face the apparition.

Issie leaned against the back of the couch in the center of the room, her arms crossed. A smug grin graced her face. "Someone's touchy. What, you forget how to have fun without me, Xander?"

"What are you? How are you even here?" Xander studied her with narrowed eyes.

Issie pushed off of the couch and considered this for a moment. She cocked her head to the side and looked down at her hands, the ones that glowed softly. "I'm not sure exactly. All I know is that I had to see you, to try and show you what you're getting yourself into with her."

"Trust me, I think I've got this pretty much figured out, but thanks." Xander turned to leave again. He barely made it one step out into the hallway.

Issie appeared in front of him. He glanced behind him and back at her in bewilderment before his features hardened again. She put her hands on her hips, scowling, her lips pursed. Xander fought the tremors that started in his fingertips. He couldn't look her in the eyes, could barely even look at her at all, but he forced himself to because if he didn't, then he'd have to admit that this was only a trick of the Woodlane Manor and not really a specter.

A ghost.

His sister.

"Oh, that's right, I forgot: You're the great Alexander the Third, the only one capable of protecting and caring for others, all while bearing the weight of other's guilt and burdens on your shoulders! Well, have I got news for you: My death wasn't your fault! Taking care of me when our parents died shouldn't've been your responsibility! And Grandfather's own pride, and selfishness, isn't something you should feel guilty for! He made his choice, just like I tried to make my own." Issie paused, her chest heaving. Despite her translucent appearance, and the faint glow that radiated off of her like an aura, Issie's face was flushed with her frustration and anger.

"That girl isn't your responsibility, and *you don't need to protect her because you feel like you couldn't protect me,*" Issie finished quietly. Her words stung despite their softness.

Xander balled his fists and clenched his jaw. He tried to stamp down his flared temper but still seethed through gritted teeth, "First of all, me helping Nyla is not about trying to make up for failing you, and secondly, I'm not fighting with a trick."

He stepped around her and stalked down the hall. The icy chill that radiated off of Issie followed close on his heels. The cool air wrapped around his wrist like a hand would, and Xander stopped. His body quivered with something that wasn't quite anger, but also not exactly guilt. The grip he had on Nyla's bag tightened around the fragile threads of the handle until they threatened to pull loose from the fabric.

"That's the thing," Issie began in a sobering whisper. "I don't think I'm a trick. But I do know that I'm tired of watching you destroy yourself. You want to help this girl out of the kindness of your heart, then fine, but if you're doing this because you're still punishing yourself for things you shouldn't be or things you can't change, *then you're just using her.*"

Xander whirled around. There was no one in all of Tenebris, all of creation probably, who could get under his skin like Issie. Her cold grip on him faltered and broke. The warmer air of the manor greeted his skin once more.

"I am *not* using Nyla to help myself."

"Then where do you see this all going?" Issie questioned. "Truly, Xander, where? What's your plan here? How do you think you can help her? She has that cat now anyway."

"Issie, you're not really here." Or was she? Was she a ghost? Xander wanted to reach out and grip his sister by the shoulders, but didn't dare to. He was terrified of what would happen if he did.

"*Look* at me, Xander! Do I look real—" Issie paused, her mouth opening and closing, her eyes wide. Softer, as if she remembered herself, she said, "It wasn't your fault."

"Wasn't it, though?" Xander glanced away, his jaw twitching with tension.

"No," Issie said, stepping closer to him. The cool air around her licked at Xander's skin and seeped into his clothes. "It really wasn't. You didn't tell me to leave, you didn't tell me to go out in the middle of the snow storm, and you aren't our grandfather. But you do need his help now."

Xander's eyes snapped up. "I—I…We don't need him. He can't help us."

"He can, Xander. And you can help him too," Issie asserted. "Promise me you'll go to him?"

"Is—"

"Xander, *please.*" Issie's shining eyes widened with her plea.

"All right, all right." Xander waved her off, and she smiled.

"I love you, you know," Issie looked away with a frown. When she met his eyes again, Xander's heart broke. "Be careful, okay? I don't want you to show up where I am anytime soon, you hear?"

"Where—no, Issie, don't you dare disappear on me now!" Xander reached out to grab at Issie's fading hand, but his fingers were met with a lingering patch of cool air. Issie stood up on the tips of her toes and placed an icy kiss on his cheek.

"I miss you too, you big softie." Issie faded away for good and left Xander more perplexed and hopeless than he was before.

Where was Issie? Was she a specter, a ghost from somewhere beyond this world? Or was her appearance only a trick of the Woodlane to derail him, like he'd initially thought?

Xander glanced down the hall in both directions. With a heavy sigh, he took off for the main staircase and began to climb. His stomach knotted itself into a tight bundle of stormy foreboding. Still, Xander placed one foot in front of the other.

She'd led him into the ballroom earlier this morning. *She* was the only reason why he now knew just how terrible Nyla's confrontation with the red-eyed man had been.

Deep down, Xander had already begun to see the foreboding clouds in the distance around the time Nyla had disintegrated the ogre and nearly shot him at Fortune Falls. Granted, he didn't know it at the time of the ogre incident, but he managed to do the math after Fortune Falls, and Caselle only confirmed his suspicions that something heinous was afoot.

Then they'd come to the Woodlane Manor.

"Oh, how things change," Xander grumbled ruefully as he paused on the landing.

He wasn't convinced that his grandfather would be willing to help them, to help Nyla. Even if his grandfather *could* help them, the real question to Xander was *would* he? Things… things were complicated all around between Nyla's situation and the way he'd left things with his family after Issie's funeral. And the more things that came back to the Ten Years' War and the Great Tenebris War, the more seeds of skepticism were sowed in his mind. It was an endless puzzle, and half of the pieces were missing. Some may as well have never existed at this rate.

Xander raked his hand through his hair. Nyla's bag knocked into his knee as he turned in a slow circle in the middle of the landing. He licked his lips and glanced over his surroundings. He didn't know what he was doing, what he *should* do, but he did know one thing: they had to leave the manor. As soon as they possibly could, they all had to leave, even Shamira. Xander was even willing to risk traveling through the storm if Nyla was still up for it.

"Xander! What are you doing here?" a breathless Nyla called from the base of the stairs. "Are you all right?"

He shook himself out of his thoughts. "Yeah, I'm fine. Did you find anything?"

Both Nyla and Shamira bounded up the stairs to meet him in front of the stained-glass window. It was Shamira who answered him, though. *We found the box. Astrid had hidden it inside her looking glass.*

Xander's brows furrowed. "Inside...like *in* the glass?"

"Yeah." Nyla held up the box in her hands. It was small, maybe about the width and length of a hand. It certainly wasn't an object of notice, even with its detailed carvings.

"Have you opened it yet?"

Nyla shook her head. "No, we wanted to meet up with you and get everything in one place."

Xander nodded and handed over Nyla's bag into her waiting hand. "So, what now?"

Thunder boomed overhead. Nyla jumped in her skin beside him. "We go somewhere safe?"

"Right. The kitchen, then?" He shifted on his feet. Xander's head spun with a surge of new questions with even less answers than he'd had before. He doubted the kitchen was all that safe, but it *was* getting late, and the storm was picking up in ferocity again, as if it could tell one or all of them wanted to leave.

And who knew? Maybe it could. Maybe...

No, Dinora had said that her powers were bound, that she was stuck here. But still: she'd used magic to disappear and appear, so what about a storm? Did she have the strength for that?

Or was it Cedric?

And more importantly, how had Dinora known they were in the library both this morning and this afternoon? Could she sense things like Shamira could? What else could they both sense?

Xander didn't have any good answers. Instead, he'd garnered a few new suspicions he hadn't asked for. Ultimately, between Issie's pleading and these new puzzle pieces, Xander resigned himself to seek out his grandfather come first light.

***

"You've been staring at that box all afternoon. Are you going to open it?" Xander kept his head down as he glanced at Nyla from beneath his furrowed brows.

They sat opposite each other at the kitchen island, both halfheartedly picking at their plates. It'd been a long afternoon since their meeting on the landing—as well as his silent resolution—and though he'd tried his best to squash down the agitation in his chest, it still boiled over. The skies weren't the only thing that were stormy, he'd realized. Shamira was stiffer than usual, her fur bristled like her composure. Nyla was like a ball of spun anxiety, something that seemed to buzz off of her like static. As for himself, well, Xander knew that dark clouds churned angrily around his mind.

Nyla pushed her plate aside with a heavy sigh. "Truth is, I'm a little afraid. I know I have to open it…eventually…I just don't know if I'm ready to today."

Are you afraid you'll have a seizure like when you touched Astrid's book?

"Wait," Xander started. He set his fork and knife down with a *clink* and fixed Nyla with narrowed, concerned eyes. "That's what happened? You had a seizure because of that book?"

"I wouldn't say it was a 'seizure' exactly, more like a violent shock, and then I saw something, and then the light, and, well, you know the rest." Nyla bit her lip. "I think touching it triggered one of Astrid's memories from when the manor was invaded, during the war."

Why didn't you tell us this sooner? Shamira scolded. Xander threw a glare in her direction before he met Nyla's wide eyes.

"A lot's happened today, cat." At this, Shamira hissed at him, a gesture he returned with a growl of his own. "I think what we all need is a good night's sleep, though that probably isn't going to happen tonight." Xander stood and brought his cleared plate to the sink basin, not wanting to look at either of them for a minute. The clouds around his head had broken for just a second, but returned all too soon.

He knew what he had to do. Whatever was going on with Dinora and Astrid and Nyla's magic was much bigger than a couple of teenagers and a growing pumpkie cub.

I suppose. Shamira huffed in agitation. *Well, why don't you tell us what you saw? It might be important.*

Xander scrubbed and scrubbed as Nyla explained how she saw Astrid and a bunch of other people in a room, all talking about the Corvids and their impending attack on the manor.

"And then, after they all left, Astrid did something with her magic. I don't know what, but it just engulfed the whole manor! It was kind of amazing, though it seemed to take everything out of her." Nyla paused. Xander turned his head to look at her over his shoulder. "I think she planned on sacrificing herself because when that was done, she drank something from a vial."

What happened next?

"Nothing. Something happened, but the next thing I saw was her closing the lid of that box, and then I was me again."

Xander stopped, his hands still occupied with the washcloth and plate in the soapy water. His back stiffened. "Did you see what was inside?"

"No."

So why not open it? Whatever's inside is obviously important.

"Well...here's my third confession for this afternoon: I don't know how to," Nyla admitted. "I've tried everything, but no luck. There's no keyhole, but it's locked. My magic can't open it. I can't find any hidden buttons to open it. Hell, I don't even know if there's a spring mechanism *to* open it. Or if it's rusted or..."

"Let me see." Xander finished drying off his hands and returned to the island. Nyla stared at him with questioning eyes, and he'd rather face her than the daggers Shamira threw at him. He pulled his stool around to sit beside Nyla as she slid the box in front of him, and Xander actually studied it for the first time since she found it. Shamira came over and stood on her hind legs so she could put her front paws on the island to get a better look. Xander ignored the cat and the impatience that rolled off of her.

He pursed his lips. The cherrywood was carved with flowers and vines, but even with the delicately ornate design obscuring the practical aspects of the box, Xander was certain that there wasn't a latch. He turned it around in his hands, grateful for the sight of hinges cleverly fitted into two hollows in the wood, and turned his attention back to what he now knew was the front of the box. Two thin lines interrupted the pattern of leaves and vines. Curious, Xander rubbed his thumb over the strip of wood between the two scars. The wood shifted beneath his fingers, and he slid the section of wood until it stopped.

The lid opened easily after that. Xander exhaled a long, slow breath. He hadn't even realized that he'd been holding it. But he had to admit the craftsmanship of this box was that of a master. Once the lid was open, he could see the sliding mechanism that 'locked' the box by sliding over a nail in the lid, like a bolt.

Nyla's hair tickled his arm as she leaned closer to peer into the box.

"Careful, Nyla, we don't know if touching what's inside will hurt you or not yet," Xander warned as he shifted in his seat.

"Right." Nyla leaned back and gathered her hair over one shoulder. "So, what did Astrid hide all those years ago?"

Xander's eyes moved over the cylindrical-shaped package that was nestled in the center of the box's plush velvet pillow. He gingerly picked it up and unwrapped it. The candlelight from the kitchen sconces bounced off of the tarnished gold shaft.

"Is that a wand?" Nyla asked, a lilt of excitement making her voice a little higher than normal.

Yes. And it's definitely Astrid's. Her signature is the only one I can sense on it. Shamira sniffed.

Xander turned the wand over in his hand, the minute emerald studs glistening in the candlelight. On one end of the wand was a chiseled sphere of clear quartz settled in the crook of a golden crescent moon. The opposite end of the wand formed a star with a clear quartz point that jutted out from its topmost point. Much like the box that the wand called home, it too was covered in raised carvings of delicate vines and leaves.

Xander stared at the short thing. It couldn't have been much thicker than a pen and about the same length, but it was heavier, definitely solid. He looked over at an enchanted Nyla.

"You know, I never understood the purpose of a wand."

He turned toward Shamira, but the cat frowned at him. *Don't look at me like you expect an answer. Wands are an entirely human device. No other magic users have need for a wand that I know of. If anything, I'd think they're cumbersome.*

"So, this is basically useless then?" Nyla asked, crestfallen.

I don't know. For now, let's just keep it safe.

Xander tilted his head as he wrapped the wand back up and placed it back in the box. "Well, you heard the cat. We keep it safe for now. You want this in your bag or mine?"

"Mine. Might as well keep everything together, right?" Nyla held her hand out. Xander hesitated, looking from her to the box. Nyla huffed. "Xander, I've already touched the box, and it was fine. *I'm fine.*"

"I know...I just...what if..." He trailed off. What if *what*? Nyla was right. Nothing had happened when she'd first touched the box, so there was nothing to worry about. Still, Xander hesitated before finally handing the box back over to its new, rightful owner.

Nyla slid off of her stool and bent over her bag to stow the box away. "I hope this storm passes in the night."

"Me too."

It was the truth. Xander wanted—*needed*—the storm to pass. His plan depended on fair weather and a few hours that he could sneak away. His hand brushed the scraps of paper in his pocket, and he swallowed hard. He couldn't find the words to tell her, and even if he could, Dinora could be listening.

Xander got up and hauled his own bag onto his shoulders. He'd just started after Nyla to follow her back to the library when something made him pause. Heat simmered in his stomach, and he glanced over his shoulder. Shamira glared at him, her eyes alight with a fury he hadn't yet received from her.

You're not telling us something, and it's causing some inner turmoil that is rolling off of you in bitter waves. So, whatever you're going to do or say, don't, and move on. Shamira turned away sharply and swished her tail through the air in such a way that Xander was reminded of a knife slitting someone's throat.

He stared after the pumpkie. A chill ran down his spine and settled in his gut. At least this icy grip wasn't indicative of another Issie sighting. He turned on his heel and quietly made his way down the hall and into the library. His feet dragged along the floor. He dreaded just about everything, especially the wand inside the wooden box that Astrid had hid so well.

Shamira was nowhere in sight.

"Everything all right?" Nyla sat up on her elbows and stared at him with tired eyes. She looked half ready to pass out and not wake up.

Xander guessed he looked the same too. He felt old.

"Fine." The word barely escaped his dry throat.

Nyla hummed, skepticism barely hidden in her arched brow. "See you in the morning?"

Xander nodded and shrugged off his bag so he could unroll his sleeping bag. Xander barely heard her mumble goodnight. She might as well have said it to the floor. He almost smiled.

Instead, his chest ached, and the guilt wormed its way through his veins. "Night."

28. THE WOMAN WITH THE LILAC-COLORED MAGIC

Xander's stomach churned with guilt, only to tie itself in tighter knots when he reached into his pocket for the paper and charcoal stick. Setting them on the table in front of him, he struggled to find the right words. It wasn't like he was *leaving*, so much as running an errand. The assurance didn't quench his shame. The paper, smoothed out on the table, stared up at him, completely blank. What was he doing, really?

He didn't have a clue. Whatever plan Xander had wanted to form never came. And the longer he sat, the worse the knots in his stomach got. He didn't know what Dinora would do if they all tried to leave the manor or what kind of magic she could wield. If their theory held true, and Dinora was the evil sorceress from the legends about the Shadow Forest, then there was absolutely no assurance in anything. She obviously wanted Nyla, but could Xander quiet his conscience long enough to leave her behind with such a deranged woman? Sure, she'd have Shamira, but it still didn't sit right in the pit of his stomach.

Xander's mind churned with what he considered to be every possible scenario that might befall them if they tried to leave the manor without Dinora's blessing—a blessing he doubted she was inclined to give. He didn't think they could avoid confrontation, and he was terrified at the prospect of it. Would they manage? Would they survive a fight against Dinora? Xander wasn't certain and came to the conclusion that it was best not to find out.

Either way, Xander knew he needed to leave the manor. Someone had to get help from the outside world, and it seemed to him that he was the only one with the connections to get any sort of significant help. While Shamira was in contact with the Elders, he didn't know too much about the pumpkies and therefore didn't know if they could be considered reliable help. Nyla trusted her instincts, but that would still leave them alone. And besides, instinctual feelings and notions were left up to interpretation. He didn't blame Nyla for their current situation, not in the slightest. By all accounts, she'd assumed the manor to be abandoned.

None of that helped him figure out what to do. They needed to leave the manor, but they had to do so safely and without crossing paths with Dinora's wrath. But how?

In the end, Xander ended up writing three notes, and finally, he had a solid plan in mind. It came to him like a bolt of lightning, sudden and electrifying, but it was a decent plan. He only hoped it worked out like he needed it to.

***

She knew that Xander had gotten up, too anxious to sleep, and Shamira would be lying if she said she hadn't lain awake too. She wasn't entirely shocked by that fact. Xander had been strange for the better part of the day. Anxiety and guilt rolled off of him in waves, and it drove Shamira's senses insane. If she didn't know any better, she would've believed that these were her own feelings. But they weren't.

Her eyes darted to the double doors of the library and back over to Nyla. The girl hadn't moved since she settled in for the night, but Shamira knew she wasn't asleep. Her heartbeat was too fast, her breathing too shallow to be indicative of a deep sleep.

That couldn't be helped.

Shamira needed to speak with the boy.

Her paws made no sound as she snuck out of the room, only to hover in the doorway. She glanced over her shoulder at Nyla. The girl hadn't noticed that she'd moved at all, and it was for the better.

A dim light fell into a weak puddle just outside of the kitchen's threshold. Shamira stalked down the remaining stretch of hallway and strode confidently into the room. Xander sat at the island, hunched over something she couldn't yet see.

Trouble sleeping? Shamira's lip curled into a smirk as the boy jolted in his seat and whipped his head around to glare at her. *Sorry, I didn't mean to startle you.*

"You and I both know you did." He turned back to the table and hastily covered up whatever it was that he was doing.

True. But I'm not the only one that's lying or at least withholding something. Shamira narrowed her eyes and studied him for the millionth time since they'd met. *What do you think of this storm?*

"It's an inconvenience." Dark eyes fell on her. "Are you interrogating me?"

I don't need to. And frankly, I don't particularly care what you plan on doing, only that you take your stress and shame with you. It's sickening.

Xander pursed his lips. Shamira strolled closer and jumped up onto the stool opposite him. They stared each other down, neither one willing to wilt under the other's gaze.

Why are you here, Xander?

"Why are *you* here?"

I think I've made that clear. At least I'm not the one writing a goodbye note.

Xander stilled, and Shamira knew she had him.

369

Didn't think I could read your human language? Shamira paused and glanced over Xander's rigid features. *Or maybe you didn't think I'd figure it out.*

"What do you want from me?" he asked through gritted teeth.

I'll ask you again: why are you here? Is it to help Nyla, or yourself?

Xander glanced away, his eyes drawn to the window. Shamira's eyes flicked over to gaze at it too before they shifted back to him.

When Xander finally looked back at her, he was fuming, his rage barely controlled. She admired that. Even when his temper was boiling over, he tried to contain it, to stop it from making him blind.

"You want to know why I'm here? Well, so would I," he spat quietly. "I saw a girl in a tavern, she needed a map, and the barkeeper couldn't tell her where to get one, so she left. Don't know where she went after that, but when I left the tavern, I still found myself wondering about the girl with silver hair and why she didn't have a map, or if she ever did find one. I couldn't help myself. I don't know why. It wasn't like I could find her anyway, not without putting myself at risk.

"The next day, I'm off traveling to Fortune Falls, and the deeper into the Shadow Forest's heart you go, the worse it gets. And what would Corruptio have for my luck other than a torrential thunderstorm?

"I walked for *hours*, soaked to the bone, trying to find any form of suitable shelter. I finally found it, but of course, it was up a cliff face. So, I climbed up." Xander paused, his anger simmering now. "I'd just reached the ledge of what I hoped was a cave, when someone grabbed me and helped pull me up."

Nyla?

"Yeah. I opened my eyes, and there she was, the girl with silver hair and no map." He paused, looking down at the table. His features softened. When he spoke again, it was reflection that painted his voice. "Turns out we were both going to Fortune Falls. And I guess I just felt like I needed to help her. You weren't there when she discovered her magic."

So…you're here because…because you want to be, and you have nothing else.

"I guess so."

So why are you leaving her?

The mask fell onto Xander's face again. He glanced all around, and Shamira understood. His brooding, secretive nature all day made sense now. Something had happened, and it was *that* which had led Xander to his conclusion. Xander wasn't leaving because he couldn't or didn't want to help Nyla anymore. In fact, Shamira was willing to bet that Xander wasn't leaving at all.

You've figured something important out? Shamira bristled at Xander's nod. *Then you should know that this storm is only over the manor. Once you pass the driveway and the grounds, it's clear skies and fair weather.*

Xander quirked an eyebrow, and while Shamira didn't know why humans used this as a way to express a question, she finally recognized it as such. The only thing she couldn't figure out, was what, exactly, he was asking her now. She'd just have to tell the whole story.

I've known since this afternoon, but I couldn't figure out why. Then between Nyla's glimpse into Astrid's memory and the memory from the looking glass, I figured it out. Dinora and the leader of the Corvids are the same woman. I'm certain of it, and I'm willing to assume that she's the reason why this storm is so localized.

Xander's eyes shifted to the doorway and back at his notes.

I'll keep her safe. I don't know what you intend to do when you leave, but it must be something you feel will help. Shamira leapt off the stool and bounded off toward the library.

At least their little chat had been of some use. Relief wove its way through Xander's aura and eased the negative emotions emitting off of him. Shamira smiled. Now, she could have some peace.

***

Nyla turned over onto her other shoulder. For hours now, she'd been chasing sleep and not so successfully either. It wasn't the storm that kept her awake, or even hunger, but general uneasiness.

She opened her heavy eyes slowly. One thought persisted through her jumbled mind and fitful sleep: she was leaving.

Today.

If the storm moved out before this afternoon, they'd leave. *She'd* leave. Nyla knew that with every fiber of her being. Xander and Shamira could do whatever they wanted, but one way or another, she was leaving. Today. She'd go right now if it weren't for the low rumble of thunder overhead, or the fact that it was sometime before daybreak.

With a long, silent groan, Nyla shifted onto her back and turned her head. Xander was on his stomach, his head in his arms. Beyond him, Shamira was curled up by the dying light of the fireplace. As carefully as she could, Nyla sat up and pushed back the cover of her sleeping bag. Her joints cracked and popped as she stood. She froze, her eyes searching for a sign that she was caught.

Her body sagged with a silent sigh of relief. Being that she was the only one awake, Nyla grabbed her bag and walked out of the room as quietly as she could on the tips of her toes.

Nyla had no idea where she was going to go. She didn't even want to be on her own at the moment, but no one else was awake and she couldn't stay still anymore. Tired from not sleeping, tired of lying awake, and tired of all this magic and war business, she let her feet lead the way.

This wasn't what Nyla had wanted when she went to Fortune Falls. Sure, she'd wanted answers, but how was any of *this* the answer to what she was looking for?

Nyla shook her head. She didn't even know what she was looking for anymore, or what she'd had in mind when she drank from the Falls.

She didn't want this.

Every step drove her farther away from the library, and somehow or another, Nyla's feet brought her to the main staircase in the entry hall. She stopped and stared at the lilac window on the landing, ignoring the four noble crests of old. The singular flower was a rich purple in the predawn hours, so unlike the true lilac purple that it was when the sunlight streamed through it during the day.

With the way it looked right now, with its rounded petals and curled edges, Nyla realized that it was the same color as Astrid's magic in the vision she'd had when she touched the book. When the window was basked in sunlight, the color of the lilac looked like her own magic, the magic she'd apparently inherited from Astrid.

Nyla was beginning to hate lilacs. Somehow, everything that was happening to her now came to remind her of lilacs. The flower had become a symbol of her anguish and bad luck.

She moved on, having decided that some fresh air might do her some good. And the best place was the veranda—though she preferred the upstairs balcony that overlooked the courtyard, she didn't want to go too far from her friends. Nyla told herself this was only to gather her thoughts and occupy the time. But to what end?

She shrugged her bag off of her shoulder and set it beside her on the deck's wooden boards. The torches sparked to life at her urging, and Nyla didn't have a clue as to what she was doing.

The longer she stared at the backpack, the more temptation flooded her. Nyla was meant to find those things, so why shouldn't she look at them? Astrid *wanted* her to find that box, and Derek had *wanted* her to find those books in the fireplace hearth. Her fingers twitched.

They itched to reach out and open her bag, and that's exactly what Nyla did. She wasn't sure if it was of her own accord or what, but in a few seconds, she found herself unwrapping the lilac-colored book that had given her such a horrific episode. Nyla bit her lip. Her eyes skimmed the smooth leather cover.

With a deep breath, Nyla reached a finger out to poke the cover. Her hand trembled, and she squeezed her eyes shut. Nothing. She peeked one eye open. Still nothing.

Her finger had touched the cover of the book, and there was no spark, no crippling vision, no seizure-like experience that whisked her away into someone else's memory.

Nyla let out a shaky sigh of relief. She straightened in her chair and opened the book to glance over the flowing handwriting. It wasn't particularly neat, but legible enough that it wasn't messy or scrawled. It was a strange mixture of somewhere in between chicken scratch and perfection.

She struggled through the first page, the 600-year difference in their language a distinct obstacle in Nyla's path, but she understood the gist of what she realized was Astrid's journal.

The entry evidently began after the war had already started, as it detailed some kind of war meeting and preparations, but because Nyla didn't know when the war started, the dates at the beginning of each entry meant nothing to her. The clues scattered within the pages she'd started to skim weren't all that helpful either. She'd need more time to properly read through it. Her head just wasn't in it today. She packed up Astrid's journal and traded it for Westley's sketchbook.

At least that was a happy distraction.

***

The sun began to fight against the stormy clouds outside. It was like the sun served as a backlight to the curtain of clouds in the sky. Nyla replaced the sketchbook in her bag and went to stand by the veranda's railing. The wind still howled, beating the trees with each powerful gust. Dark storm clouds hovered beyond the treetops, another wave of chaos in the battle that consumed the sky. Nyla wondered if it was only a matter of time before the thunder and lightning started back up again.

She turned away and scooped up her bag, resigned to spend another day in the Woodlane Manor if the hazardous storm began anew. Or maybe it was better to risk it. They hadn't been able to find many answers about her magic here, or the war, and Nyla didn't like all that they didn't know about Dinora. Her mind was made up. Coming to the Woodlane Manor was a mistake, one that she didn't want to have to face the consequences for if their suspicions about Dinora being the evil sorceress from the legends proved true.

Nyla moved through the halls at a snail's pace. There was no sense in rushing around, only to end up waiting around for something that might or might not happen. At least walking was something.

She turned into the entryway. Footsteps echoed through the foyer. Her heart began to pound between her ears. Her eyes flicked to the source, to Xander.

He froze when their eyes met. Even from where Nyla stood at the edge of the foyer, she could see him swallow hard. Nyla's eyes fell to the bag on his shoulders, to how ready he was to leave. With a fist clenched at her side and the other twisted around the strap of her bag, her eyes never once left him as she crossed into the foyer, stopping in the middle of his path to the steeple doors.

"Are you leaving?" she asked quietly.

Nyla wasn't sure if it was hurt and betrayal that ached in her chest or envy. Hurt that he was leaving and she'd probably end up staying because she didn't know what to do next. Envious because he could just leave all of this behind.

"I'm sorry, Nyla." Xander took a few steps closer. His eyes shone with guilt. That's when Nyla knew that it was anger and betrayal that simmered in her blood. "I have to go."

"Were you even going to say goodbye?" She gritted her teeth.

A shadow moved in the corner of her eye by the hallway. Her eyes flicked over to see Shamira hovering there, watching the scene unfold between her and Xander. Nyla ignored her and finished closing the gap between herself and Xander.

He gulped, glancing at the arched doors mere feet away. "I left a note. You...you weren't there when I was getting ready, so I left it for you."

Nyla narrowed her eyes and studied him. She knew it was wrong for her to be upset. Xander didn't have to come all this way with her. He didn't have to help her. He shouldn't even have been wrapped up in all of this anyway—whatever this turned out to be.

"Okay." Her blood boiled over. Nyla forced herself to smile. She didn't need a mirror to know that it didn't reach her hardened eyes or that it was pinched and sickly sweet, the sort of sweet that was fake, a trap, a façade. "Safe travels, then."

She started to walk away, to return to the library. Xander's hand slipped into hers, and Nyla stopped. Her temper wavered when she realized that it wasn't the skin of Xander's palm, but something dry and malleable that had greeted her own. A scrap of folded paper. Xander needed to tell her something, but wouldn't say it.

Or was it that he *couldn't* say it?

Her eyes flicked to Shamira again before she glanced at Xander over her shoulder. There was pleading in his eyes. The piece of paper, and the careful—no, *sly*—execution of how he gave it to her was a sign. Xander needed her to be hurt, he probably had a plan, and she needed to roll with it.

And that was easy because she *was* hurt. Betrayed. Angry.

And now confused.

Nyla stared Xander down, waiting for him to say something more, see how he wanted to play through this little scheme of his. She quirked her lip into a flutter of a smile, just so he knew she understood before the anger twisted deeper in her eyes.

"What?" she snapped, even though it was more exasperation than anger in her blood anymore, and tugged her hand away from his.

Nyla spun around to face him. The paper crumpled in her clenched fist, nice and safe, and she only hoped that this was what Xander had meant to happen.

"Nyla, I—" Xander started and took a half-step away, his hands up. "I'm sorry to just leave like this, but I can't handle this—any of this. *I* can't help you."

"So go." Nyla shrugged. "I'm not stopping you. You didn't have to come with me. You didn't have to help me or anything. I never expected you to. *You have nothing to be sorry for.*"

She needed to tell him that he wasn't obligated to help her and that he didn't owe her any sort of apology. They were still technically strangers, even with everything they'd been through. Nyla needed to give him a way out, especially with how difficult her situation seemed with her magic and Astrid and Cedric and the war and how they still didn't know how, *exactly*, Dinora fit into all of this. Nyla tried to convince herself that she'd be okay on her own again. And the fact was Shamira would still be with her. But she was a pumpkie. Tears blurred Nyla's vision. She tried to blink them away.

Xander looked at her with soft eyes, even as she tried so hard to play the part he'd cast her in. For whatever reason, he'd thought it best to leave like this, even if it hurt her.

"I'm sorry, Nyla," he said again, somehow even softer than before.

Nyla's face twisted into a frown. The longer they put this off, the more she'd want to actually scream at him. Her heart pounded in her ears, alongside the echo of Xander's voice when they stood before the crossroads to Hart, when he promised she wouldn't be alone.

Nyla swallowed the lump in her throat and straightened. It was the only hope she had of not breaking down and begging him to tell her everything, right this second. She struggled and clawed at the anger in her blood, latched onto the fear and desperation in her heart, and hissed the words that an overwhelming inkling told her could be some of her last.

"You should go."

Xander nodded. "All right then. Bye, Nyla."

Just as he'd reached the doors and put his hand on the knob, Xander turned and met her eyes one final time. Nyla tried to hold her head high, as if none of this bothered her in the way that it did, but rather as if she was bitterly hurt. He gave her a pointed look, and she knew whatever came next was genuine. "Stay safe, okay?"

She nodded stiffly. It was as if her head hadn't moved at all. "You too."

The door opened with a groan, and Xander stepped over the threshold. Nyla couldn't help the tears when they finally rolled down her cheeks. She stood there and pleaded with whatever higher powers were listening that Xander would turn back around and, if he didn't, that he'd be safe in whatever it was that he was doing.

He didn't come back to her. Instead, the massive steeple doors creaked open, and Xander walked out into the storm and, with him, the crushing realization of everything she wanted in her life.

The doors shut behind Xander with an ominous echo, leaving Nyla and Shamira alone. A sob escaped Nyla's lips. Her legs shook, but she fought it off. She didn't have time to let her emotions get the best of her. Even now, Nyla realized that the sensation that coursed through her body was magic. She glanced at her clenched hands. They glowed and sparked faintly of purple. She prayed that the note hadn't been incinerated in her palm and fought to control her magic.

It'll be okay, Nyla, Shamira tried to reassure her.

Nyla crossed the remainder of the foyer. "I hope you're right."

The note Xander had slipped her, much to her immediate relief, was still clutched tightly in her hand. It was the only thing that grounded her as they walked back to the library. Sure enough, there was another rolled-up note waiting for her on her sleeping bag.

Nyla strolled over to it, sitting cross-legged on her sleeping bag with Shamira following close on her heels. Carefully, Nyla unfurled the note Xander had left for her there, all the while conscious of the note concealed in her hand. As nonchalantly as she could, she unfolded the note he'd slipped her in the foyer over the one in her hands, wanting to read that one first.

Nyla—

First let me just say I'm sorry to leave like this. I know someone who might be able to help us figure out what to do next, but I need to send a letter to them first. I'm heading to the port just north of here, in Gossamer (he often has business there, so it'll get to him faster than the regular couriers).

I should be back in a few hours.

I'm sorry I had to leave like this. I just don't trust Dinora—I was afraid of what she would do to us—to you—if we tried to leave. Hopefully, I'm wrong, but if not, now you and Shamira don't have to worry about me if Dinora exposes herself for what she is.

Shamira leaned over Nyla's shoulder to get a better look at the note. *So that's what all this secrecy is about?*

"It looks like it." Nyla shifted the note down to expose the beginning of the second one. It looked like a crude map. Xander had probably drawn it or traced it from his own. Nyla huffed, slightly amused. Maybe he *had* thought of everything. Seamlessly, Nyla crumpled the first note back into her hand without ever really moving.

Her eyes studied the map, recognizing the roadways and path he'd intended to take to the port town of Gossamer a few miles away. Toward the bottom of the crude map, Xander had written another little note. His handwriting was cramped in the corner of the scrap paper, but Nyla was glad to read it.

If you want, we can meet somewhere along this route if you're not comfortable staying at the manor. Stay safe and I'll see you soon.

Another little "I'm sorry" was wedged into the tiniest bit of what was left of the corner, but Nyla barely glanced at it.

"Well, I guess if there's nothing else for us to do here, we should head out too." Nyla paused and took one last look at the map Xander had drawn for her.

It looked like he was going to H&R Trading, as it was the only major merchant company that worked out of Gossamer's port. The rest, Nyla remembered her father saying, were fishermen and Tenebris's navy. She shrugged away whatever lingering questions she had about Xander's adventure and crumpled up both notes.

The fire popped and crackled when she tossed them in, and for good measure, Nyla urged the fire to make certain no trace of them survived.

Shamira was ever watchful as Nyla dressed and repacked her things.

Are you sure there's nothing else you need to do here? The pumpkie's tail curled and uncurled, tapping the floor like a human would their foot.

Nyla paused. Her eyes lingered over every surface of the room, looking for anything that they might have otherwise forgotten. "No, I don't think so."

Another pause. Nyla met Shamira's eyes. "Could we take Astrid's looking glass? Is it worth taking anything from there, from her workroom?"

It's worth a second glance. Shamira blinked, already on her paws.

Shamira led the way toward Astrid's hidden workroom. Nyla's bag was heavier than she could ever remember it being. She shouldered it and hiked after Shamira. While the storm outside thundered on, the sun had managed to break the clouds a little and let its light shine through. Nyla basked in the sunbeams that streamed through the lilac window as they climbed the main staircase. All too soon, the world was plunged back into a stormy gray. Yet another violent-looking cloud blocked the sun.

Her stomach grumbled. Nyla pressed a hand to her abdomen to quiet it. She was in no mood for this sort of distraction. All she really wanted at the moment was to take one last look around Astrid's things and leave so they could meet Xander on the road to Gossamer.

Hungry? Shamira glanced back at her.

"I'm fine." Nyla tried to shrug her off, but the cat blocked her path toward Astrid's bedroom.

You need to eat, Nyla. Not only to keep up your physical strength, but also your magical strength, Shamira nagged, giving her a maternal scowl.

"Okay, okay. I'll grab something to eat." Nyla turned on her heel. "You and Xander are impossible, you know that?"

You can't change the fact that we care about you. Nyla heard the sly grin in Shamira's smooth voice. *Do you want me to come with you?*

"No, I got it. It'll only be a quick run down to the kitchen, and then I'll be right back up."

Be careful.

Nyla waved the pumpkie off with a roll of her eyes and begrudgingly headed down to the kitchen. She had barely made it down the one wing of the main staircase and down onto the landing when the wide oak doors groaned open for the second time that morning. She stopped and stared. Had Xander changed his mind?

And if he had, why?

Nyla's smile and confusion faded. Illuminated by a bolt of lightning and the pale stormy daylight, the shadowy silhouette's blue-gray cloak billowed out like rolling waves behind them.

Ice ran like blood through Nyla's veins.

Cedric strolled into the brightly lit foyer. His bored scarlet eyes sparkled with agitation. The doors closed behind him with a *thud* that echoed in Nyla's ears alongside her frantic heartbeat.

Her mind screamed at her to run, but her legs were like anchors. She wanted to look away, but she couldn't. There was nothing she could do, other than let the ice crystals creep and crawl across her skin. The backpack on her shoulders burned, and Nyla didn't know whether it was an anchor or a balloon. No matter what her mind tried to tell her body to do, it wouldn't listen. All she could do was watch as Cedric strolled toward the stairs. His deft fingers undid the clasp of his cloak and he draped it over the banister.

"You know, I'm a little disappointed that there isn't more of a reception." He fingered the wet material, and Nyla tried her best to swallow.

This wasn't happening.

It simply couldn't be.

***

One step, inhale. Another step, exhale. Keep walking, keep breathing.

It was all Xander could tell himself as he walked down the drenched path of the Woodlane Manor, the path that was still assaulted by buckets of water from the volatile storm clouds above.

Thunder rumbled overhead. Xander pulled his hood farther down over his eyes. He kept his head down and his hands free for his bow, but there was nothing he could do against the gusts of wind that slammed into him. He knew his bow was a useless defense.

Guilt settled in every bone inside his body, but Xander pressed on anyway. Through the first gate and onto the slick, muddy path that led to the second gate, the one he could barely make out through the blurred wall of rain all around him, Xander's feet carried him farther away.

The howling wind nipped at his heels, as if it made to push him along the path and away from the manor—away from Nyla. The paranoid assumption wasn't very reassuring when Xander remembered that this storm wasn't natural.

He picked up the pace. The sooner he got to Gossamer and sent his letter off, the sooner he could meet up with Nyla.

It had to be done, he kept telling himself. His inner voice wasn't very convincing, though, especially as goosebumps spread up and down his arms upon crossing through the second gate. The gate groaned and *clanged* shut behind him.

Just as Shamira had said, the storm was somehow confined to the Woodlane Manor and its grounds. With each step, the rain slowed. Xander walked on until he crossed through a drizzling curtain of rain out onto the clear and lush, winding paths of the Godberd Woods. Old and crumbling statues lurked in the shadows of the scarlet blotted plum leaves that were dry and curled in on their edges. Droplets of rain *plopped* onto the ground behind him, the thundering storm only a hollow echo in the near distance.

The farther away he walked from the manor, the more the sunbeams poked through the canopy of Harvum-kissed leaves overhead. Xander welcomed the sight, but the miniscule sense of relief was easily shaken. Even with his self-assigned mission, his resolve was beginning to chip away with each footstep. He considered the strange behavior of the storm and the story Dinora had told them in the library.

By the time Xander was through working out what they knew, and especially what they didn't know, he had half a mind to turn back around and beg Nyla to come with him.

But the look in her eyes…

Xander shrugged the thought away. He wouldn't blame her if she were actually angry with him.

He wanted to do this alone. There was no way for him to know who would be at H&R Trading, or if they'd recognize him, or *worse*: call him by name. But there was one thing Xander knew for certain, and it was that he didn't want Nyla to know just yet.

Rationally, Xander knew she'd find out eventually, and it was more than likely that Nyla would find out sooner than he could ever want, but that didn't mean he wasn't terrified. How would she react? Would things change between them?

If he *did* go back, how would his life change? Would it all be for the better? Or worse?

Xander wasn't ready to face any of that and honestly believed he'd never have to.

After all, he'd vowed to never return home. Disowned and estranged. Good riddance, he'd declared upon his departure.

And now?

Now, Nyla needed more help than he could give her, and Issie was right: he had to reach out to their grandfather. Xander grimaced at the thought. His grandfather had a lot of reach, a lot of friends, and a lot of say. No matter what was going on, his grandfather always had a finger on the pulse and sometimes was the very heartbeat of current events. He had to have some idea, at least, on how to help Nyla and stop Cedric.

It was that hope that kept Xander's feet on the northern path to Gossamer. No matter how badly he yearned to return to the manor and say 'damn it all,' his feet brought him forward.

Either way, he knew he was being selfish. He wanted to remain as the Xander he had become, the Xander who met Nyla.

Issie's use of his full name yesterday came to mind just as the path through the heart of the Godberd Woods opened up to reveal happy, sunlit fields of grain. The gentle hills in the distance were illuminated by golden daylight. By all means, it was the picture of peace. But its beauty was lost on Xander.

Fine dirt crunched beneath his feet, the only noise that he could hear besides the quaint chirps of the birds and the rustle of grain swaying in the breeze. His footsteps were hollow compared to the pleasant din of the life that flourished all around him.

Over the tops of the trees, Xander could see a few tendrils of smoke curling up into the sky. He smiled at that, knowing that somewhere not too far away was some semblance of civilization, of people, people working hard to make a living, of families, of homes with happy memories.

Xander kept on the path, figuring that he'd find a road sign or something eventually. Until then, the only choice he had was to stay on this nameless country path. Xander kicked a stone across the path and took comfort in its skipping and *skittering*. The stone's *clacking* kept his mind off of the fears and worries that held tight to his thoughts. He spared a dark glance over his shoulder at the way he had come.

"This was a stupid idea," he muttered to the empty field of overgrown weeds and what looked like an abandoned farming field.

Wild tangles of vegetables grew on vines that strangled the fruits growing on squat trees. A rotted fence sat disheveled on what was probably once a property line.

He squinted against the gleaming sun. Six piles of stacked stones stood in the only cleared patch of land. Taller weeds grew between and over the mossy stones. His mind flashed back to the three stone obelisks they'd passed on their way to the manor, right outside of Hart. Nyla hadn't mentioned anything about them, but Xander was beginning to wonder if these were a tradition in Hart, memorials of some sort.

Against his better judgment, Xander let his curiosity drive him forward. One of the stacks had a pile of dried flowers on them. They were barely clinging to the stone, withered away by only Balmae knew how long.

As he got closer, Xander noticed the crumbling remnants of a stone foundation in the shape of a small home. The fireplace and part of the stack were mostly intact, though its weather-aged masonry was scarred by flames.

A bone-chilling realization turned his blood to ice. Was this...No, it couldn't be. Plenty of houses burned down. Besides, Nyla never *said* where she was from.

Or had she?

Xander shook his head. All she said was that she and her brothers would go to the Woodlane Manor as kids. Maybe it was like the beach he and Issie went to outside of Huntington. Maybe the manor was out of the way, but close enough to be an escape?

The weeds on the other side of the stacks rustled and shook. Xander glanced up, his fingers already on an arrow. He faltered and let go of the breath that had caught in his throat. The older man had raised eyebrows and a crooked smile.

"Well, hello there." He came and stood next to Xander. He held a bushel of lilacs in one hand, and that only bolstered the ice in Xander's veins even more. "I didn't think anyone would be here today because there never is."

The man took his hat off and brushed away the dried remains of what used to be flowers off of the stack one away from the end. Solemnly, the man placed the fresh lilacs on the rough surface of the stone and let his hand rest there for a moment. That's when Xander knew for certain that this was a memorial, and he really shouldn't be here at this particular moment. He should leave and let this man mourn. Even as the thought skirted across his mind, his feet remained planted firmly where he stood as if they were rooted to the earth below.

"What happened here?" Xander heard himself asking. It was pretty obvious, but he needed to hear it, even as his mouth ran dry.

The man paused and took a step away from the stack of stones. When he spoke again, his voice was soft and quiet, delicately crackled with age. His voice was fragile and haunted as he started, "There used to be a home here. A home with a family, a good family.

"A couple years ago," he went on, stopping to wipe his forehead with a handkerchief, "the house went up in flames one day. It was just a normal day. A normal day...until I saw the plumes of black smoke blowing above the tree line. It was like a furnace." The man shook his head. "Everyone was inside, except for one of the girls. She tried to save them, ran right into the flames."

Another pause, and any strength the man's voice had gained was lost as he began again. "She ran right into that burning home and refused to leave the rubble when it was all over.

"She was the only one who survived that day." The man kept his head down, his eyes cast down to stare at the ground. But Xander knew better. "I don't know how any of us didn't melt. I don't know how *she* didn't melt when she ran in."

The man's eyes were vacant, oblivious to the world around them, but Xander knew that they weren't unseeing. The man probably saw the flames that had long since been extinguished and the image of a girl left with nothing. Another heartbeat passed, and the man looked around them before his gaze once again landed on the six stone monuments. "This is all that's left now. And this is all that will ever be here until a few decades have passed and someone who doesn't know comes along and rebuilds. This land has a curse upon it, but I think it's just tragic grief."

"How?" Xander asked.

"I don't know. No one knows how the fire started. There's no evidence of anything. Local investigators couldn't find anything other than some trace of magic, so the king's men got involved and sent their people." He pursed his lips. "They never said anything, only assured us that everything was fine. But that didn't stop people from talking."

Xander considered all of this and let it turn over in his head. There wasn't anything he could think of to say, but somehow, the question he wasn't sure he wanted an answer to was asked. "What happened? To the girl?"

The man looked down with sad eyes, eyes that were haunted by age and regret. "I don't know. My wife and I, once the fire had been put out, we took her home with us and thought she might stay with us. There wasn't any family that we, or anyone else for that matter, knew of that could take her in, so we thought she might stay with us."

He paused and eyed the stack of stones in front of him. "She ran away a few days after that."

"I'm sorry," Xander said numbly. He clenched his sweaty hands.

Coincidences didn't happen.

Xander studied the man for the first time. He had gray speckled hair and a face that was beginning to wrinkle. His eyes were plagued by a perpetual dullness, the sign of a man haunted by the past, by things he couldn't change.

"She just left," he whispered seemingly to himself, or perhaps his words were meant for the stacked stones. "No rhyme or reason, no goodbye. She just left, a girl with no family, not a libac to her name. And the worst part isn't that she left or didn't feel safe with us. It's that she was so young, and now I have no idea if she's okay. For all I know, she could've died, and there was no one to save her."

A shiver ran through Xander. His blood couldn't run any colder. "What was her name?"

The man gave Xander a hard, skeptical look through narrowed eyes. They softened after a moment, and the man smiled sadly. "Nyla."

Xander's mouth opened and closed. He swiped a hand over his mouth, wiping the sweat from his upper lip. "I—"

From the corner of his eye, Xander saw a large blur. An animal barreled toward them, and his heart fell to lay at his feet. The man beside him, upon noticing how stricken by fear Xander was, turned to look at the thing that was hurtling toward them as well. Xander couldn't speak, much less move, even as desperation and urgency filled every fiber of his being. His body jolted, and his fingers freed the piece of paper from his pocket.

***

Nyla took a step back. A scream bubbled up from her core. Her throat was too dry, her tongue too dumb-stricken, and her lips too numb to allow its escape. The only reasonable thought that was able to flit through her still mind was that she was dead. It was the only way Nyla could explain this sort of situation. She was dead and somehow ended up in the worst possible afterlife.

"Ah, I see you two have met." Dinora's voice was like a cannon blast in Nyla's ears. It clawed and scratched at her until she thought she'd bleed.

Nyla's head snapped in the woman's direction. Fear ran through her veins at what she saw. Dinora was no longer the image of a feeble old woman with kind eyes. Instead, she was a severe woman with cold eyes and a sort of bristled pride in the way she carried herself. She was a walking nightmare, and Nyla realized that she stood between not one but *two* living, breathing nightmares.

Dread sat like a lump in her throat. Below her, Cedric straightened and glanced up at Dinora. Nyla tried to look at both of them and quickly found herself frozen, backed into the corner of the landing, pressed up against the windowsill of the stained-glass window. Her fingertips tingled, and it was everything she could do to remember to breathe, to control the magic that pressed up against the underside of her skin, wanting to burst.

"Hello, Mother." Nyla might've been surprised by the veiled condemnation in Cedric's voice, but all she heard was the rapid beat of her heart and the scream in her head to *run*.

"You're late." Dinora clicked disapprovingly. "I hope, at the very least, that you brought what I asked for?"

Cedric held up a vial filled with a thick, dark liquid that vaguely shimmered red in the candlelight. "You mean this?"

Dinora's eyes lit up with satisfaction as Cedric examined the small bottle. The weight of Dinora's venomous eyes landed on Nyla. Nyla could barely gulp as she peeled her eyes away from the bottle in the red-eyed man's hand to meet Dinora's glare.

"For centuries, I've been trapped here, and all that time I've been thinking about what Astrid did to me, what she did to Corvus," she began slowly, thoughtfully. "Of course, it was immediately apparent what she had done to me: bound me here and put a blocker on my magic to prevent me from using the extent of it.

"But then I came to find out that she stripped herself of her own magic and passed it on to someone in her bloodline.

"For centuries, I've had to live with that. Not only had she stopped me from setting things right for Corvus, but she put a failsafe in place to prevent us from doing so in the future!

"And all the while, I've had to sit here and delegate all the footwork to a failure of a son." Dinora paused and looked Nyla up and down with disgust and a wicked interest that sent shivers down Nyla's spine. "For centuries, I've wanted to spill your blood, *but that's not good enough*."

Dinora's lips curled up in a devilish sneer that made Nyla's knees turn to jelly. Magic hummed and pumped through Nyla's veins, but she didn't know what to do with it. Even if she *did* unleash the power that had built up inside her, Nyla knew she was cornered between two people who had years—centuries, even—of experience over her. The fight she'd had in the ballroom with Cedric was a fluke. Even with the way she'd wielded her magic then, it didn't seem to have any lasting effect, if any, on the man. She glanced his way again. He still looked bored, as if he was one eye roll away from leaving. Nyla focused on Dinora again.

"It's a real pity that you're Astrid's heir. You have so much raw talent, so much potential, and yet you can't be of any use to me." Dinora shrugged and took a step down the stairs.

Out of the corner of her eye, Nyla saw Cedric mount the staircase. There wasn't enough space between her and them. The closer each of them came, the less Nyla felt that she could breathe.

"Stop!" Her grip on the magic bubbling over inside of her slipped.

The chandelier swayed and rattled. The entryway trembled. The room crowded her and shrank until it was a fraction of its true size in her mind. Magic sparked from her fingertips, but still they came closer. Nyla was blinded, her vision dark as they closed in on her. Fear overcame every sense she had until she couldn't see or hear or do anything. The room began to crumble and, with it, the world. Nyla found that she still had a voice—a voice that shook but was forceful all the same.

Her body trembled as she put her hands up to keep them from reaching her. "Stay away from me!"

Her heartbeat slowed until it barely beat, just as every movement, every flutter of the air's currents slowed until time seemed to stand still. The thick wood beams overhead snapped. The windows burst, and glass rained down on the foyer. Nyla threw her arms up and covered her head. The magic she had tried so hard to keep down boiled over.

She peeked open one eye as she tried to keep her footing. For once, it wasn't dizziness that made the room around her move but rather an earthquake she didn't know she was capable of conjuring.

Nyla glanced up at the ceiling. A faint lilac glow clung to the plaster. She focused her energy there, all the while her legs tensed, ready to flee. Slowly, her body became her own again, and her mind took back control as she pushed against the fear that had tried to enslave her.

Rubble and bits of plaster fluttered down from the ceiling like snowflakes. If Dinora or Cedric had noticed, neither said a word, even as their advance had halted. Nyla kept working with her magic. She exhaled a long, slow breath. Before her very eyes, deep, wide fissures opened up and cracked along the once-smooth surface above her. Nyla braced herself as a chunk of ceiling came down between her and Cedric. Pieces of it shattered off in all directions. Dust and powder flurried all around them as the vaulted ceiling groaned.

Everything was suspended, frozen in slow-motion. Nyla blinked. The ceiling cracked like a giant was able to snap a tree in half, simply a twig underfoot. Another blink. The world began to spin at its real pace again. Someone was shouting, but Nyla didn't hear them, not really. With time and the world caught up to speed, she didn't waste another second as her heart pounded against her chest once more.

In a flurry of adrenaline, Nyla darted up the short set of stairs she had only moments ago descended in search of food. The cacophony of the ceiling coming down was left behind her as she urged herself onward. Her mind raced, but every thought was half completed at best before her mind was off again, reeling to find some purchase on what to do.

There was nothing.

She had no plan, only a corridor that flew by as she raced back to Shamira.

Some way behind her, a different rumbling and distorted symphony took up. Stone grated against stone and sent shivers down her spine as someone worked to rebuild the foyer and clear their path, but she didn't dare look.

"Shamira!" Nyla shouted desperately over the tumult and Dinora's faint cursing.

Sick, scarlet magic flew past her. Nyla barely registered the blur as she hissed and clamped a hand over her grazed arm. Her skin burned, but not nearly as badly as her lungs craved and begged for oxygen. She risked a glance over her shoulder.

Dinora came into view, surprisingly spry for a woman that had far exceeded the natural lifespan of a human. She didn't seem to care that Nyla was sprinting and instead kept an even, though brisk, pace.

Nyla gathered her magic and forced the hallway behind her to cave in just as she had caved the foyer in. She ducked down the hall where she'd last seen Shamira. Where was she anyway? Of all the times for the cat to disappear, this was neither a good, nor convenient, time.

She flinched. Her eyes went wide as a door up ahead imploded in a brilliant sage light. Its splintered pieces slammed into the opposite wall with a thunderous *bang*. Shamira burst from the room a heartbeat later and immediately started toward Nyla. The cat's sharp teeth were bared, and Shamira looked every bit like the killer Xander had warned Nyla about in the days that followed the pumpkie's forced companionship.

Where are they?! Shamira spat.

Nyla stopped short. Her whole body lurched forward before she regained her balance.

"I don't know…right behind me, I think," she panted.

Nyla forced breath after breath into her lungs. She hadn't missed running for her life. And yet here she was again: running from a monster, from some danger that she wished with all her heart didn't exist.

She splayed her hands out in front of her and forced Shamira to stop. "I need you to find Xander; take this to him. They can't get ahold of it, and *I'm not fast enough!*"

She hastily shrugged off her backpack and thrust it toward Shamira. Nyla cast a frantic glance over her shoulder. Still no Dinora. No sign of Cedric either. Maybe that was a blessing.

But what about you? I promised—

"Someone has to get help, alert someone with more power than me! I can't stop them, and I'll only slow you down." Nyla's eyes were wide with panic and desperation, both of which bled into her trembling voice as the adrenaline started to ebb away. "*Please.*"

Shamira relented and took the straps of Nyla's bag in her mouth. Her sharp eyes held a steely determination that stoked the flames of Nyla's strength. The Woodlane Manor shook and rattled as another burst of magic forced Nyla to adjust her balance. Red dashed by her.

"GO!" Nyla urged Shamira, shooing her with her hands.

I'll be back for you! With that last promise, Shamira bounded off down the hall toward the window. Nyla barely formed the words for her to be careful when the glass shattered. Shamira dove through without another word or glance. She watched in fear as gravity took hold of her friend.

Nyla cried out in agony. Her knees screamed from the harsh impact against the thin carpet laid over the hard floor. Pain spread from her back and out into every extremity. Her body jerked against the carpet.

Unable to get to the window to see if Shamira had made it to safety, Nyla cursed. She wished the window was an escape option she could've considered too, but there was nothing she could do about it now.

No matter how badly Nyla wanted to throw herself out that window and follow after Shamira, she had a mission of her own now. She scrambled to her feet and squared her shoulders as Dinora stalked closer.

Nyla would *not* let her get that bag. She would *not* let her leave the Woodlane Manor.

"There you are!" Dinora sang. Nyla swallowed hard and held Dinora's gaze. The woman strode down the hall, regal and composed despite the grit and debris that covered her skin and clothes.

Magic sparked from Nyla's fingertips. She refused to be afraid again. Nyla *refused* to let Dinora do as she pleased, to escape, to instill that much terror in anyone ever again. With Cedric nowhere in sight, Nyla swallowed the heartbeat in her throat. She could handle this. Dinora herself had admitted that her magic was limited. How much could she possibly have left to wield? What did she still have left to fight for?

Certainly, Nyla had more to live for than Dinora did to avenge.

"You lack discipline and control. It seems every bit of magic you've used has been an emotional reaction to something, just like that little stunt with the ceilings just now." Dinora stopped just before Nyla. She sneered, and Nyla knew exactly what sort of look that was.

Dinora saw herself as some supreme being, well above Nyla and all powerful. Nyla's eyes shifted to the cautious movement behind the woman. Cedric slunk down the hallway, idly, slowly, as if he hadn't a care in the world. Or maybe he was injured. Nyla hated the little voice in her head that cheered at the thought. Even if Cedric was a horrible person, wouldn't hurting him or Dinora make her just as bad? Nyla shoved the thought away. This wasn't the time for her mind to have an internal debate on morality. She needed to focus, buy herself some time, some leverage.

"So, what are you going to do then? If I'm not a threat, you should just let me be on my way." Nyla knew she didn't stand a chance, but at this rate, she didn't have much to lose.

In fact, she had everything to gain. It's why she dug deep within herself. It was something to fight for, and even if Shamira came back for her, she'd never make it in time. Nyla was alone, and that was okay. She'd been alone for so long that she'd had to save herself so many times before. Through grief and anger and loneliness, she was her own savior through it all. Maybe Nyla hadn't been able to save herself completely, but Helpet had she tried. And she would continue to try, to fight, to save herself.

Right now, that meant she had to trust herself, her magic, her strength. Astrid's things were safe, and hopefully, that was enough. Hopefully, someone with more authority, more knowledge, would know what to do with them, with all that she and Xander had discovered. For now, the anger, grief, and sadness that had fueled her back in the ballroom when she fought Cedric washed over Nyla again. Her blood boiled with it.

The pain Dinora and Cedric had caused her somehow gave her the strength to stand there and fight them. More than that, the pain they'd caused Astrid, the things they unleashed unto the world, washed over her. Somehow, that grief, that anger, that pain, morphed into resilience and a light that shone bright inside her soul and cast out the darkness.

Nyla armed herself with the magic that brimmed inside her until it was a fierce embrace.

Dinora's laugh was like two rocks scraping against each other. It was equal parts bark and bite. "You think it's that easy?"

Nyla laughed, a sound so foreign to her own ears it was like madness personified. "No, it isn't, *but this is.*"

She thrust her hands out. Static filled the air as the wave of magic she pictured slammed into Dinora and Cedric. Both of them tumbled, thrown back against the force, and Nyla had to admit that it was satisfying to see those two *monsters* thrown to the floor.

Especially Cedric.

Glass shattered. Nyla didn't care enough to figure out what had broken as she darted past Dinora and started past Cedric, toward freedom. A hand wrapped around her ankle. Nyla pitched forward, allowing another hand to wrap around her arm as she tried to steady herself and break free of Cedric's surprisingly firm grasp.

"Let go!" Nyla clawed at Cedric's face as he managed to push himself up long enough to grab hold of her, his lips moving wordlessly. His grip on her arm barely faltered. "I said let go of me!"

Her hand glowed as she slammed it into his chest, shoving him into the wall with another burst of magic. Cedric's hand slipped from her arm as he slid to the floor with a groan and a cough. Nyla hesitated at the sight of blood on his lips, but Dinora's screech urged her forward.

If Cedric could recover from the ceiling collapse and their fight in the ballroom, one magically enforced shove to the chest couldn't hurt him.

Probably.

Another smaller, quieter voice in her head pointed out that if Cedric *was* hurt, or even killed, that was one less person she had to worry about. Nyla sent a tentative glance over her shoulder. Dinora crouched next to an unnervingly still Cedric. His head bowed forward. All Nyla could see was the crimson stain that slid down the wall behind him.

Dinora's head whipped up to meet Nyla's brief gaze. As if Helpet's hand urged her, Nyla surged forward. Every ounce of physical strength she had left was put toward her escape. Her stomach churned.

Was he actually *dead?* Severely injured? Unconscious? Nyla forced her concern aside. She'd deal with those nagging questions later.

Dinora screamed at her, but Nyla couldn't hear a word she said. It was completely indistinguishable above the beat of her heart and the strange tingling in her arm.

Nyla glanced down. Her arm was coated in a shimmery black liquid with a red sheen that slowly sank into her skin. Roughly the shape of a handprint, Nyla's skin continued to absorb the weird sap. Nyla's steps faltered.

"No time," she muttered under her rapid breaths.

And she was right: she didn't have any time at all. Nyla darted down the hall and onto the servant's stairs. Something shifted inside her and boiled. Her body flashed between bursts of icy chills and sweltering heat. Nyla stumbled and staggered down the rest of the stairs into the kitchen.

She lurched and grabbed onto the edge of the kitchen island where she and Xander had sat only the night before. Fireworks exploded in her head.

There wasn't any time for any of this. Nyla knew that, but her body didn't care. She eyed the thick liquid Cedric had left on her arm. It was the only way she could think it had gotten on her. He'd grabbed her so he could get this on her, whatever this was. It was blatantly obvious that whatever this potion was doing to her, her body didn't agree with it.

Nyla's heart spasmed and skipped a beat. Cramps nearly crippled her as she doubled over and took as many deep breaths as she could manage. She looked up at the kitchen door. Just a few more steps. If she could just make it to a point where Dinora couldn't follow her because of Astrid's curse, then she would be safe. She could wait for Shamira, for Xander, to come and get her.

Then they could leave this all behind.

Especially whatever she had done to Cedric.

Nyla staggered over to the door.

The stairs creaked in a low groan. Nyla's heart beat faster and faster until she feared that it would give out. With another glance at her arm, her heart stopped. The potion was almost gone, almost done sinking into her skin.

"Maybe I was wrong about you. You're resourceful and quite… dangerous." Dinora's voice wrapped around Nyla like a vise.

Her breath hitched. Nyla hadn't made it to the back door, and there was no way she could make it anywhere now. She was drained. Pain flared up and ebbed away with every inhale and exhale. Nyla was infected by something because of that stuff Cedric had put on her, and there wasn't anything she could do about it.

Slowly, hesitantly, she turned to face Dinora.

"What do you want from me?" Nyla croaked.

"What I've always wanted," Dinora purred. The woman thrust her hand out. A bolt of red lightning sprang from the hard gesture, and Nyla could only bring her arms up to protect herself, to hope that her own magic would shield her. "For you to suffer like I have!"

Nyla's back slammed into the wall behind her with a sick thud. She gasped for air. Magic sparked and crackled at her fingertips before it fizzled out. Whatever healing her body had achieved from not only the black liquid, but also from the ballroom fight a few weeks ago, was gone. Nyla didn't know if anything was broken, but she did know that her head spun, and her stability was nowhere to be found.

When her vision cleared from the stars and abysmal cloud that blinded her, Nyla whimpered. Dinora was gone. Worse yet, her surroundings were bright and hyper-focused to the point that her eyes couldn't stand the sight of them. The Woodlane Manor had a heartbeat, and somehow, Nyla could feel it. Every creak, every little move the manor's joints made as they settled, each and every footstep of unseen crawlers or the whisper of wind against the windows sounded in Nyla's ears or brushed against her skin.

She scratched at her skin. It didn't stop the things from crawling over her. Somewhere within her consciousness, Nyla was vaguely aware of Dinora and where she was and where she was headed.

Nyla rubbed the back of her head and blinked away the rest of her pain. At least that's what she tried to do as she got to her feet with a lot of protest from her body and more whimpers than she'd like to admit. She braced herself and shuffled after Dinora. Each step jarred her stiff and aching body, but Nyla couldn't let her get away. She just couldn't.

The farther she pushed herself, and the faster Nyla tried to move, the worse it got. She had to catch up to her.

She had to.

***

She had to make it. Shamira owed Nyla that much. That's what pushed her forward. The *thud-thud-thud* and *pallop* of her heart and galloping paws were lost to Shamira's ears as she sprinted in the direction she could feel Xander lingering. All the while, she was all too aware of the magics at work back inside the manor. It wasn't just energies that she sensed anymore, but the actual ripple of magic being expelled that traveled through the disrupted air currents like a storm.

Speaking of storms, she shivered. The one above the manor had all but disappeared, as if whoever had summoned it couldn't—or didn't want to—keep it up. That begged the questions *why?* and *what for?*

Shamira's drenched fur bristled. None of the possible answers she provided herself with were pleasant to think about.

The Godberd Woods passed her by until she soared through the farming fields. None of Shamira's surroundings concerned her. The only thing that did was reaching Xander and then going back for Nyla.

The magic being thrown around the manor paused. The tremor of the air stopped.

Shamira swallowed as best as she could with the straps to Nyla's backpack in her mouth. Her eyes watered more than they usually did, but no tears came.

It was only a small comfort that Nyla's signature continued to pulse with life in the distance between them. For once in her comparatively short life, Shamira was grateful for her ability to sense things.

An uncommon gift in her clan, she'd hated it. Feeling things that weren't her own emotions, always being in tune with the magics around her, it could drive any pumpkie—any creature, really—mad.

Shamira growled. This couldn't be right. One of the signatures she'd left behind—Nyla's signature—was in front of her, or at least a faint trace of it was. Two figures stood before six stacks of stone. They were chatting, and of course the boy could find someone to talk to all the way out here. Shamira wondered what it was that they were talking about, especially as the scarred fireplace and crumbling foundation came into view between the tall grasses and weeds.

Xander's eyes fell on her. She knew it the moment his demeanor had changed, invaded by unbridled panic.

Xander! It's them. They have Nyla!

The man that Xander was with turned to look at her next. Fear struck his heart faster than a blink. A small, distant part of Shamira was almost bothered by it. It was the same reaction she had gotten from Xander when they'd first met. Granted, it wasn't as wild, and the man's fear was untouched by hatred, but it still stung. Her kind was nothing for these humans to fear, but that was a point to prove on another day.

Xander put a hand on the man's arm and pulled another note from his pocket. As she came closer, Shamira heard Xander begging the assenting man to bring the note to Gossamer, to some trading company, before he broke out into a sprint to meet her.

"Where are they?" he called out to her.

The manor, Shamira panted. She'd never felt so much tense fear and desperation from a creature before. All of it, what Xander felt, stemmed from concern and a sort of connection Shamira didn't understand. Either way, it was powerful and sent Xander reeling in a way that would be dangerous if he couldn't control himself. Xander couldn't rush in and save Nyla, not against Dinora and Cedric.

***

Faster, faster, faster. Xander urged himself to go faster. He just needed to go *faster*. If he could somehow sprout wings and fly like lightning, he would, without hesitation. Out of his own selfishness, he'd left her all alone, and now?

Now Nyla was in trouble, and all he could see was raven-colored hair and blood.

But that wouldn't happen—it couldn't happen. Nyla had silver hair, and she had magic and—and what?

Take this! Shamira dropped Nyla's bag in the path ahead of him and took off at a rate Xander wished he could match. Before he'd even reached the bag four or five yards ahead of him, the pumpkie was out of his sight, swallowed up by the Godberd Woods.

Xander scooped the bag up as he sprinted and tried to maneuver the twisted strap onto his shoulder. It was the best he could do while his mind raced faster than his body could travel. One horror after another flitted across his mind.

What would he find when he reached the Woodlane Manor?

Xander prayed that the grim situations his mind conjured up for him were just that: the imaginings of someone petrified beyond their wits. Consumed by the overwhelming grip of frantic terror, he didn't even register crossing through the first gate or when the forest path gave way to the manor's paver-stone driveway once he ran through the second gate.

The moment he burst out into the manor's front courtyard, his world collapsed.

Xander's eyes immediately fell on the silver-haired figure doubled over against the pillar of the manor's stone steps. The magic that passed between Dinora and Shamira went unnoticed as Xander rushed toward Nyla.

Something wrapped around Xander's ankle and tugged. He groaned and crashed to the stone pathway. Another vine wrapped around his other ankle. Xander scrambled and struggled to find purchase on the slick stones of the courtyard. A third vine wrapped around his thighs and yanked him back across the stone pavers. He twisted onto his back, the position even more awkward with his bulky rucksack and Nyla's bag on his shoulder, in a panic and sat up. The vines refused to budge. No matter how hard Xander tugged and pulled at them, the plant only strengthened its hold on him. His rapid pulse thundered between his ears.

He glanced over his shoulder. Nyla hadn't moved at all. He looked over at Shamira and Dinora with wild eyes.

The cat had conjured up a shield of sage-colored magic. Dinora battered her with blast after blast of unadulterated power. Sick bolts of scarlet magic collided and splintered off in all directions against Shamira's shield until the electricity fizzled out.

Neither one of them could get to Nyla, and thankfully, Dinora was too busy to care about her. Xander shifted around until he could reach the shaft of an arrow with his hands. He pulled it free from his quiver. The tip of an arrow was the best he could do without a knife.

It fractured the moment he pressed the tip into the vine's skin. Despite Xander's utter disbelief, the vine split itself into two and extended one half out until it trapped his hand. He stabbed at it with the broken arrow, but to no avail. The plant's only response was to bind his other hand and then stitch the two sections back together. Defeated, Xander struggled against its hold.

Xander, watch out! He glanced in Shamira's direction and promptly ducked.

A bolt of lightning whizzed over his head. Someone howled in pain, and Xander forced himself to look in their direction.

Shamira was stock-still. Outlined by a pulsing red aura, Dinora had frozen her. Once the haggard woman recovered from Shamira's last attack, she straightened up, and the hand she had over her abdomen fell away. Now her eyes landed on Xander.

Again, Xander put all his efforts into pulling and pushing at the plant holding him captive. The vines loosened somewhat, just enough for him to slip his hands free, and frankly, that was all the time he could afford. Xander grabbed his bow and another arrow.

Dinora split the arrow right down the center of the shaft in midair. Xander's heart stopped. He nocked another arrow and shot it anyway. There was nothing left to lose after all.

The woman sneered and shot down that arrow too.

"You think you and your pesky arrows can stop me? Poor, misguided boy."

Xander shot a glance over at Nyla from the corner of his eye. As if it took everything out of her, Nyla got to her feet. Her body sagged at the apparent effort of standing. Xander focused back on Dinora and shot yet another arrow. Without so much as a blink, she obliterated it. The arrow's ashes fluttered to the ground.

Xander just kept firing; it was the only thing he could think to do. Maybe it would keep him alive, and maybe it wouldn't, but it was the only way he could distract Dinora now. It didn't even matter to him if Nyla only had the strength to flee. All that mattered to Xander right now was the fact that she had gotten up and Dinora hadn't noticed.

His fingers stumbled over empty air. Every arrow he'd had was now either split in half and useless or somewhere in the bushes where Dinora had redirected it or, worse yet, reduced it to ash on the pavers.

"I'll enjoy killing you," Dinora growled.

Xander gulped. Somehow, he knew that his fate would be like his arrows. Dinora wouldn't leave a body to mourn, not if the stories about the Caster who stole magic from the land were true. If she was that same woman, and if the Great Tenebris War was the same war as the legends about the Shadow Forest, then Xander knew he was staring down the worst possible death someone could face.

From the corner of his eye, something glittered through the air. And it was headed straight for Dinora.

A knife, encased by lilac magic, one he had seen many times, sank itself into Dinora's back. The woman howled a chillingly inhuman cry of pain and reached around. She plucked the bloody thing from her back and let it fall with a *clatter* to the ground, just as she did to her knees.

Her head snapped in Nyla's direction. Xander, too, found his gaze on the silver-haired girl. He tugged at his bindings again, but they only tightened their grip on him. His eyes never left Nyla. She had a hand pressed to her stomach and the other planted as firmly as she could manage on the stairs' pillar. Xander had never seen anyone so rundown manage to look so powerful, fierce even.

Magic crackled and fizzled in the air around her like an avenging angel.

Dinora got to her feet, but Nyla didn't give the woman a chance. A bolt of magic crashed into Dinora, forcing her into the air.

Xander could see Nyla's chest heaving as she gingerly made her way down the stone stairs. Her body shook, and he honestly didn't know how she hadn't collapsed yet. The magic around her weakened and wavered, and Xander wasn't so sure if any of them were going to make it out of this alive. The gravity of the situation, of the nightmare he found himself to be living, twisted like a knife in his gut when Dinora, bleeding and disheveled, forced herself to her feet.

Two images fought for control of Xander's vision. One was the scene of his nightmares, the other, a nightmarish reality. Like a prophecy, the recurring nightmare he'd had for a couple of seasons seemingly unfolded before him.

Dinora blocked the second attack Nyla sent her way. Back and forth the two went. Lilac, scarlet, lilac, scarlet. The color of the two different magics blurred together until Xander was blind to it. His head swam.

Wind whipped the world into a frenzy of wailing leaves. Xander tried to tell himself that none of this was real. He was asleep again, in some inn, and this was all just another nightmare. A voice in his head cackled hysterically. This was a nightmare, only a nightmare.

The moment when the two magics collided and pushed against each other, a pit opened up inside of him, and Xander knew.

This was real.

His eyes squeezed shut against the tumult, ears ringing, deaf to the scream that pierced the air. Light exploded and blinded him, his vision white, even behind closed eyelids. Xander was blind to the way Nyla had thrown her arms up just as the aftershock of the magic slammed into her body, sending her crashing into the stone stairs as her faint shield shattered. All Xander knew and felt was a force that shoved into him, knocking him onto his side, jarring his bound body.

The world beyond Xander's closed eyes stilled. The hiss of electric magic no longer rumbled over the air. The flashes of light were no more. Xander opened his eyes at last, squinting as the fine debris settled. He blinked and blinked several times more to regain his vision.

When the dust and wind finally cleared, Xander's eyes fell on Nyla, sprawled across the stairs. The spell over Shamira had broken, and she rushed forward.

Xander's heart dropped to his stomach.

It was too late. There was no way Nyla was still alive, not from what he could see where the vines still held him. Xander couldn't even move. There was nothing he could do. Absolutely nothing.

The vines receded, relinquishing their hold on Xander, and still, he couldn't find it in himself to move.

Dazed and slightly disjointed, Xander got to his feet after he'd sat for what could've been years. Nyla's knife lay on the ground some ways in front of him. Blood dripped from the blade, staining the cobblestone below.

At least Nyla had gotten that lick in. Maybe that was enough. Maybe Dinora was done for.

Xander hurriedly looked around. Where was that old hag?

It was with a mixture of apprehension and relief that he realized Dinora was gone. Xander's mouth went dry, and he smacked his lips together. What was he supposed to do now?

XANDER!

"Damn it, Shamira, what do you want?" He rubbed his temples. The earsplitting—or, rather, mind-splitting—shout did nothing to clear his head and everything to irritate him further.

I need you to hold Nyla down. She's alive!

"What?" Xander surged forward, shedding the bags from his shoulders as he raced toward Nyla on the stairs.

Alive?

Xander panted as he crouched down beside Nyla and Shamira on the stairs. Nyla's breathing was shallow and inconsistent. Blood trickled down from the corners of her lips. It started to bubble up with a wheeze, and she convulsed, her eyes not even open.

Hold her down! I have to heal her, or she won't make it!

Xander did as Shamira gruffly ordered him to do. The aches and the abandoned bags faded away. As Shamira healed Nyla—at least that's what he hoped the cat was actually doing—Nyla struggled against him. Her back arched off of the stone steps, and an agonized screech left her now-clear throat.

The only thing that stopped Xander from snapping at Shamira or tackling her was that the blood *had* stopped. Nyla's color *had* somewhat returned. The whimpers and cries faded away, leaving Nyla eerily silent. The scrunch of her nose and twist of her lips relaxed. Xander was almost certain that she was dead, that they were too late.

I've done what I can do. She still has some bruising, but I can take care of that later. I need to rest. We all do.

Xander leaned down over Nyla to hear whether or not she was still breathing. He sat up, eyeing Shamira wearily.

"She's okay, though?"

As far as I can tell, yes. But like I said, she still has some pretty bad bruising, but she's going to be okay, Shamira stated quietly. Xander sat back on his heels. *Xander?*

"What now?" he murmured, all too dumbfounded as shock wholly seized him.

We need to get inside and heal. I'll contact my clan. She paused. A dark look passed across her face. Her whiskers twitched. *There's a war coming. I don't think Dinora is dead, just severely wounded. And Cedric, I can't find him at all. Wherever they are, it's somewhere heavily guarded against outside magic.*

Xander gulped and looked down at Nyla. What were they going to do? He could only hope that her old neighbor got his letter to Gossamer.

After a moment's pause, he looked up at Shamira. "It's safe to move her, right?"

The pumpkie blinked. Any sign of whatever she'd been thinking fled from her murky eyes. *Yes.*

***

Nyla's eyes fluttered open and shut again. Everything was heavy. She couldn't even begin to think about what the weight over her body was, only that it was soft and apparently did very little against the icy kiss on her skin. She forced her heavy eyes open and turned her head to the side, away from the glowing embers of the fireplace.

Xander sat beside her in a chair, asleep and in no way comfortable if Nyla had to guess. She wondered why she was so high up. Then she realized that she was laying on a cushy cloud. A bed, a *real* bed.

Slowly but surely, feeling came back to her limbs. Nyla wiggled her toes and tried to stretch out her legs, but something tugged at her, and she whimpered. Beside her, Xander flinched and sprang forward. Nyla turned her head and looked up at him. Upon meeting his eyes, Xander broke out into a crooked, tired grin of relief.

"Hey," Nyla croaked. She made to sit up, but between the fatigue and the pain that flashed through her body, Nyla found that she couldn't. It didn't help that Xander had pressed a firm hand to her shoulder to keep her down too.

"Shamira said you can't move until she's finished healing you. Apparently, she can do that," Xander informed her soothingly.

"I killed him," Nyla swallowed thickly.

The smile faltered for a millisecond. "What?"

She closed her eyes. Nyla couldn't bear to see what Xander would think after she'd explained. "Cedric. I killed him."

Xander touched her shoulder again, gently this time, but Nyla didn't open her eyes. She downright refused to.

"Hey, look at me."

Nyla scrunched her nose and shook her head stiffly. Her temples pounded. Every inch of skin itched and thrummed with a pulse that wasn't her own.

Xander sighed. "Then I guess you won't know that I don't blame you." Nyla peeked her eyes open, and Xander smiled at her again, this time softly, solemnly reassuring. "It's all right, okay? Whatever happened, whatever you did or didn't do, it's okay. No one, and I mean *no one*, would ever damn you for killing him. Now get some rest, or Shamira is going to give us both an earful."

"She's okay?"

"Yeah. She's 'talking to the Elders.'" Xander rolled his eyes and shook his head. "Get some more rest and we'll talk later, alright?"

"There's a war coming," she started dryly, searching Xander's eyes. "Isn't there?"

He hesitated briefly, opening his mouth a fraction, and then stopping before he finally answered her. "I don't know. Shamira seems to think so."

"What about Dinora?" Dread twisted in Nyla's stomach. A part of her didn't want Xander to answer her. It wanted him to tell her not to worry about it and just to get some rest, but with the flash of guilt in Xander's eyes, she knew that wasn't happening.

"We can't find her. Cedric either, but that doesn't mean..." He paused, licking his lips. Roughly dragging a hand through his disheveled hair, Xander closed his eyes for a second as if he needed a moment to convince himself of the words he obviously didn't believe. "Just because they're missing doesn't mean they're alive. All it means is that they aren't here, and given what Shamira's sensed...it isn't likely that Cedric...would be in good shape if he did manage to flee the manor." For a heartbeat, his words hung in the crackling silence between them. Xander's eyes swept over her in assessment. "You should really get some rest."

Nyla nodded weakly, but even as her eyes fell shut again, everything came crashing back to her.

Xander. Cedric. Dinora. Shamira. Her necklace. Black liquid. Fight. Magic. Astrid. War.

ACKNOWLEDGEMENTS

After years and years of writing, editing, and daydreaming, I finally get to hold *Fire & Flight* in my hands, and I could not have done this without the team of people cheering me on throughout this whole adventure.

First, from the bottom of my heart, I would like to thank you, the reader, for joining Nyla, Xander, and Shamira on their adventures. I hope you enjoyed this world of mine as much as I have enjoyed bringing it to life for you!

There is not enough gratitude in this world to show or tell my family, my parents especially, how much their support and excitement has meant to me as I chased after my dreams. Without you awesome nerds, this book might very well be sitting on my desk still, just waiting for "the right time." Thank you, truly, for pushing me to pursue my dreams no matter how much I may have pushed back because of my own fears and doubts.

Credit and a mountain of gratitude for this amazing cover design goes to Marcella. From a disorganized pile of notes to a concept to bringing that concept to life and stoking it until it hit the next level, I have loved working with you, not only on the covers for the Heirs of Tenebris trilogy, but for all of the artwork you've supplied throughout this journey. Thank you, thank you, thank you! I cannot wait to work with you again, whenever that may be!

For helping me through the self-publishing process, I'd like to extend a huge thank you to my team at Paper Raven Books. From your guidance to editing feedback to helping me with the final touches, I could not have navigated all the finer details of self-publishing without all of you and your encouragement. Your help and contributions to bringing *Fire & Flight* to life has made my debut experience so much better, so thank you again for all of your wonderful input and guidance.

Lastly, but certainly not least, I'd like to thank all of my mentors and friends. You've each impacted my life in a different way, and while I'm not naming names, *Fire & Flight* wouldn't exist, and I certainly wouldn't have pursued this dream if it hadn't been for all of the different ways you all have encouraged me. Thank you, not only for the lessons learned along the way and your support when I needed it most, but also for your friendship. I hope you're all doing well and chasing after your dreams, no matter how out of your comfort zone that journey may be.

By the time I reach this point in my acknowledgements, I'm either bawling my eyes out or worrying that I forgot someone. While I'm not saying either of those things are happening now, I am truly overwhelmed by the amount of people who have supported me not only through this journey with *Fire & Flight*, but also in my life. Even if you feel I forgot to mention you, please know that I am deeply grateful for your part in this journey, however big or small, too.

CPSIA information can be obtained
at www.ICGtesting.com
Printed in the USA
LVHW040838120623
749431LV00020B/4

9 798986 173214